In the distance, Dion could sense his presence. It was a roiling cloud on the edge of the gray, hot and full of fury. It c___ ___ ___read, and it struck out in rage and ve___ ___ ___ ___ ___ and fierce det___ ___ ___ ___ was hunting h___ could not rid ___ way up and ___ ___ sober look. "The man who hunts me . . . he is driven—either by the wolves or by his own wishes. And he is a man of fury. A man of grief and violence."

"You can tell this through the wolves?"

She laughed without humor. "Always."

"An___

"He___

answe___

give u___

By Tara K. Harper
Published by the Ballantine Publishing Group

SILVER MOONS, BLACK STEEL

Tara K. Harper

A Del Rey® Book
THE BALLANTINE PUBLISHING GROUP • NEW YORK

A Del Rey® Book
Published by The Ballantine Publishing Group
Copyright © 2001 by Tara K. Harper
This book contains an excerpt from *Wolfwalker* by Tara K. Harper, published by Del Rey® Books. Copyright © 1990 by Tara K. Harper

All rights reserved under International and Pan-American Copyright Conventions. Published in the United States by The Ballantine Publishing Group, a division of Random House, Inc., New York, and simultaneously in Canada by Random House of Canada Limited, Toronto.

Del Rey is a registered trademark and the Del Rey colophon is a trademark of Random House, Inc.

www.delreydigital.com

ISBN-13: 978-0-345-40635-4

ISBN-10: 0-345-40635-4

Manufactured in the United States of America

First Edition: November 2001

10 9 8 7 6 5 4 3 2 1

With many thanks to

Richard Jarvis, Stephanie Castro, Alex Medler,
Ernest V. Curto, Ph. D., Bob Jarvis, Lieutenant Joe Grisham,
Detective Amber Lewis, and DK and Sandra Keen

The dedication for this book is private.

O never say that I was false of heart
Though absence seemed my flame to qualify
As easy might I from myself depart
As from my soul, which in thy breast doth lie
That is my home of love . . .
  For nothing this wide universe I call,
  Save thou, my rose, in it thou art my all.
—THE POET SHAKESPEARE, *oldEarth*, A.D., *1642*

I

Ember Dione maMarin

Wolves call; men answer.
It is the way of the world.

— *Randonnen saying*

He struck like a viper, fast, biting. His fist whipped toward her head. Dion was already ducking, parrying the blow aside. The heel of her lean, scarred left hand hit his ribs like a small shovel, lifting him on his toes. She twisted to stomp the back of his knees, but in the instant in which her hip aligned with his, his arm snaked around her ribs and he jerked. Her leverage disappeared. The wolf in her snarled. Her violet eyes glinted. As he started the flip, she snapped a vicious kick to the back of his head that had Batayon's narrow jaw clicking shut and his ears ringing to wake the seventh moon. She grabbed his thigh and arm and wrenched out. He recountered. Both slammed down.

He missed her wrist; she missed his temple with her ridge-hand as he scrambled away to face her. They came back together in a blur of hands and knees, elbows and feet. He took an impossibly close side kick like a hammer, grunted, dropped his elbow on her ankle, saw the bones of her face tighten for an instant, grabbed the slender joint, and twisted. Dion whipped like a top, midair. Her rotating kick caught him on the shoulder as he ducked. She broke free, went to one knee, back-kicked instinctively to force distance, and whirled to face him again. Batayon slowly grinned. When they came together this time, it was his spinning ax kick that clubbed down across her shoulder, even as she rode the blow. She ducked; he twisted;

1

they broke apart and danced in broken rhythm, setting and discarding patterns of movement to tease each other into attack. A feint, a side kick, a glancing blow . . . Neither one spoke; they simply fought with silent intensity. Batayon was breathing hard, and there was something increasingly feral in Dion's expression. He saw an opening, shot a kick, and it brushed her side, touching cloth, not ribs. She dropped under and swept, but he felt it coming and threw himself forward. She could not avoid the tackle. She had time to grasp one of his sweat-hot wrists and, with the speed of a dozen wolves, partially redirect his momentum, but she was still flipped in the tangle.

When they broke free again, she was down on one knee, right hand pressed to her belly, her face twisted in pain.

Batayon saw it just before he threw his spinning crescent kick. He halted abruptly midstrike. "Dion—"

She exploded up, caught him off-balance, threw him with her left arm under his leg, the other at his neck, and followed him down. Her knee dropped like a rock on the joint of his pelvis. *Strike!* It was the voice of a wolf in her head. Her left hand was an eagle's claw digging for his brachial artery, her right fingers curled on his throat.

Batayon froze. Dion's teeth were bared. Her breath was quick—too quick for a woman who thought only in human terms. Batayon's pulse pounded in his temple. Sweat trickled down his neck. He didn't move. Didn't flinch. Didn't try to shift away. If he moved at all, Dion's wolf-honed instincts would close those half-curled fingers and tear his throat like fangs.

The prey is down. Make the kill. The blood lust of the gray mental voices tightened Dion's muscles like wire. The trickle of moisture that slid around Batayon's ear toward his pulsing carotid artery was a fascination for her dilated gaze.

Batayon's world narrowed to that pair of wolf-blinded eyes. There was a hint of yellow around her violet pupils, as if the eyes were no longer completely hers, but partly belonged to the wolves.

Tear. Slash. Taste the blood in your teeth.

He started to suck in a breath, but her hands became steel

on his neck. Slowly, carefully, like hauling in a ketch with a thread, he took air into starved lungs. For months, Dion had been running with the wild wolves, not with the partner wolf who knew humans. She was too close, too full of the Gray Ones. They gnawed the inside of her skull as she poised, they licked her lips with her tongue, tensed with her muscles, snarled in her throat. It was not Dion who hung above him; it was the wolf pack in the distance. Batayon knew all this— was slammed with the realization in that fractional time before her hand tightened, before her nails dug fatally into his flesh, before the wolf in her was loosed. With that flash of knowledge, he recentered himself with the same lightning speed.

His brown eyes projected the calm he forced himself to feel. He let the tension leech from his muscles so that the change from resistance to no threat was fast, silent, soothing.

Dion felt the challenge in his body fade. Felt the intensity of the moment shift. Felt the hammer of his pulse steady beneath her fingers where her left hand had clawed for his artery. She sucked in a breath. The wolves in her head—ten, twelve of the wild ones—blurred her vision between the man on the training mat and the indigenous eerin that had been downed by the wolves barely two kilometers away. The two kays of distance were not a barrier to Dion. Even across that space, the gray mental voices frayed the edge of her thoughts as one of the wolves latched onto a haunch of the dying animal.

Speed. Tear. Yank back.

Dion's hand tightened around Batayon's throat.

Batayon did not move. He forced himself to watch her with that smooth, calm expression.

She dragged in another breath. She could partly see him now, his brown-gray hair damp and curled, his brown eyes steady as he waited for her to regain control. Control. Woman. Not wolf. But she could feel the bodies, the iron-hard muscles, as the wolves leaped and dodged the eerin's desperately tossing horn. Fur ruffed on broken branches, icy mud squidged up between toes, musk and blood odors clogged her nose. Lupine hunger-lust leaked through her mental shield like a sieve, and her chest knotted as a Gray

One slashed the distant eerin's flank. Batayon did not move. Dion forced herself to focus, to see the man, not the prey. Forced herself to strengthen the mental wall until she closed off the taste of dirty hair and raw muscle that came to her with the packsong. She licked her teeth and reaffirmed the tiny serrations of human enamel, not the curved fangs of the wolves. She flexed her hand and felt thumbs, not dewclaws, let her legs feel the weight of her knee on Batayon's pelvis. *Withdraw.* She formed the word mentally. Wolves growled in her mind. She shuddered, but pulled back. *Control,* she snarled to herself.

The ten adult students who ringed the wide mat watched the two teachers silently, and she knew that most did not understand what they saw. Batayon said nothing as she gave up the depth of her grip on his throat and artery. She did not quite let him go. Instead, she turned her head to look at the students on one side, then the other. Their attention was riveted as they tried to grasp the intensity that even now was evaporating. Her voice was more of a growl than a human tone, but her words were clear. "If you are weak, become strong. If you are strong, seem weak. Either one will get you the kill."

No one mistook the predator that glinted in her eyes.

She released Batayon suddenly, as if she could not continue touching him without also completing the strike. Calmly, he rolled to his feet. Dion rose fluidly with him, and they saluted each other to complete the ritual. Batayon gestured for the students to resume their exercises, guided by the other teacher. As they walked from the main training room, a few students watched Dion surreptitiously, and Batayon hid his amusement as one man was caught unawares by a partner's ridgehand to the neck.

The brown-haired teacher turned and snagged a towel to wipe some of the sweat from his brow as he walked with her. "I enjoyed that, Dione," he said. He used her formal name deliberately, as if that would give her another human structure to cling to.

Dion gave him a crooked grin. "As did I, Batayon—a bit too much."

He pitched his voice so that only she would hear. "You're close to the wolves, Dione—closer than I'd heard. It makes for interesting sparring."

Her lips tightened, as aware as he was of what neither one said. She dipped a towel in the water basin and pressed the cold cloth to her neck, while Batayon slung his over his shoulder and wondered absently why women—especially scouts like Dione—never dripped with sweat like men. Dion chuckled suddenly, and he followed her gaze to a young man trying to throw another student. The victim student used the wrench-out that Dion had shown with Batayon, but the attacker was more successful. He managed an uppercut to his partner's gut as the other man missed the reverse. The victim student suddenly found himself on the floor, whoofing for his air.

"It seems we taught them something," Batayon commented.

"You'll have to show them the counter now, or you'll have cracked ribs by the dozen."

He grinned. "They already know the counter. If they've forgotten it, they deserve every bruise they acquire. Pain is an excellent teacher."

Dion's eyes went carefully blank. "You can learn too many lessons that way."

"And learn some not at all," he said meaningfully.

She looked up sharply. Batayon met her gaze, and the silent message passed. Feel pain, face pain, beat pain. The words of one of her old Randonnen teachers echoed in Batayon's brown eyes. She smiled crookedly. "I hear you," she said without rancor.

He studied her as she gazed out at the class. Her complexion was slightly flushed with the exertion. Her braided black hair was fuzzy where the shorter strands had come loose, and she tightened its length almost absently with hands that still wanted to tremble. Her body was not wiry, but slender and lithe from a dozen years of riding and running trail, and the fading claw marks on the left side of her face were a coarse reminder of the other savage scars that had cut more deeply, giving her a limp she could not hide. She might have the speed of the wolves in her arms, but she had lost much of her own physical strength, and half her sparring movements had been to redirect, not oppose or attack Batayon. Had she been whole, the strength of the wolves would have added to, not replaced, her own, and he suspected she would have thrown him much sooner, much harder, and with much more damage. She had lived in danger too long to fully pull back the intent of her strikes when the wolves entered her head. As it was, considering the rumors about her, he was lucky to have gotten her to spar at all.

There were always rumors about the wolfwalkers. They could hear with the ears of the wolves, see in the dark, smell danger before it struck. They fought like wilderness rearing up against order, not like a human who touched the wild. It was said that, with each passing decade, wolfwalkers lost more of their humanity. Batayon nodded to himself as he studied Dion's stance. Sometimes myth was true.

Ember Dione maMarin—or Dion to her friends—had moved beyond rumor into living legend. She had been trained since early childhood as a healer, and she had achieved her master rating a year before she bonded with the wolf Gray Hishn. Since then, her reputation as a healer and wolfwalker had somehow achieved its own life. Now she was a tracker who could follow a tree sprit through the very air, a scout who could ghost through any forest, a wolfwalker who could Call any wolf to her side, a healer whose patients were not touched by death. She was a woman who had fought a dozen raiders to try to save her mate, and a mother who had fought a thousand lepa with her bare hands to try to save her son. She was the Gray Wolf of Ramaj Randonnen, the Heart of Ramaj Ariye. And if he believed the songsters, she could dance steel with the best of the swordsmen, shoot rapids like a war bolt, and climb even the sheer north face of Dountuell by herself, on a windy day, over the ice—barefoot. Batayon snorted to himself. Aye, she was a rock climber, a fighter, a kayaker, a scout, but so were almost all Randonnens who had grown up in that county's northern peaks. With white-rough water in every glass-steep canyon and the lure of some of the best climbing in all nine of the human counties, every Randonnen with half a heart became a mountaineer. And one couldn't get to the climbing peaks without learning to fend for oneself in the forest, which meant swimming and kayaking, tracking and foraging, archery and knifework. Although in Dion's case, her father and her twin brother were as much to blame for her scouting skills as was her home county. She had followed her twin, Rhom, like a puppy, using his bow for hunting and his sword for fighting, until her father had brought her a bow of her own and smithed her her own steel blades. By the time she bonded with the wolf cub Gray Hishn, Dion had already had the scouting experience of a two-decade wolfwalker. Since then, she had run trail for the Ariyens for almost fifteen years, honing her skills until she was a veritable ghost among the trees.

It was too long, Batayon thought. Too long for anyone to face danger without relief. Raiders, worlags, badgerbears . . . Moons alone knew how many friends she had buried along the Ariyen trails. Those graves had left their own kind of mark. He had seen it too often even here in Ramaj Kiaskari: the overwary stances, the hard eyes, the near-blank expressions of those who had fought too long and were held now only by threads of humanity. Dion was close to that. Her violet gaze no longer held the calm concentration of the veteran scout, the quiet compassion of the healer. She was too much the predator: the wolf, alone, torn from old wounds, and blind to anything but threat and attack. The ghosts that haunted those violet eyes were drowning the woman within.

It had been six days since she and her two companions had arrived on the edge of the alpine fields with two wounded dnu, a broken sword, and a saddle half slashed by a poolah. By the end of the ninan, she would likely be gone, disappearing back into alpine forests and shadowed peaks. If he could just keep her in town for two more ninans, the passes would begin to clog with snow, and she would be forced to stand still in this county. Forced to face herself, not run from the demons that clung to the edge of her cloak. Eighteen days, he thought. It would be eternity to her.

He nodded toward the class as she hung her towel on a

hook. "Shall we go at it again tomorrow?" Dion frowned absently as she watched the students, and he knew she was already seeing the trail. "Stay, Dione," he said quietly. "We have much to learn from each other."

The wolfwalker cocked her head and considered the words. "For tomorrow," she agreed obliquely.

But he caught the self-blame that glinted in her eyes. "It was I who asked you to share ring."

Dion regarded him for a long moment. It was a telling statement, she thought, to share ring. With a potential life span of three hundred years—although few reached that age on this world—one could study a dozen different martial styles and become well-versed in each. Sharing ring had become a sharing of skills, an opening of one's essential knowledge to the other—friend or enemy—as much as one opened to one's self.

Dion studied Batayon's calm expression and realized that he had deliberately drawn her into the sparring ring. It was his bid to save her from herself, she realized, and she felt a spurt of anger. But she had certainly given them no other image to deal with, she admitted, just the "wounded wolfwalker," the "legend" in need of mending. She rolled the phrases in her head as if the wolves that gnawed at her mind would shred the words and make them more palatable. She shook her head. "With my skills, to let the wolves that far into my head . . ." Her violet eyes were sober. "I could have hurt you badly."

He cut his gaze meaningfully at her lower torso. "As I could have hurt someone else."

She glanced down in spite of herself, even though her belly had barely begun to swell. "A womb is a comfy, padded place. Even at the worst, you'd have hurt me, not my daughter." She gave him a wry smile. "Others spar until the fifth month, the cozar ride until the seventh, and it's said that the Yorundans will work the fields till they feel the labor pains set in. I'm not even four months along. Besides, I'm Randonnen. We—" She touched her abdomen gently. "—have a reputation to maintain." She looked back up, and her gaze sharpened speculatively. "You wouldn't have hesitated if it had been real."

"No," he agreed. "But it wasn't."

But to her, for those interminable, infinite seconds, it had been real, and his blood had pulsed at her fingertips, waiting to be torn and tasted. She pursed her lips and bit back her recrimination.

He shrugged as if he heard the words she didn't say. "I have no intention of being cursed for a thousand years in the memory of the wolves by harming a pack leader—" He nodded at her. "—or her cub." He tossed his towel toward a hook. "I'd rather lose the match. Besides," he added, gesturing with his chin at the students, "it was a good lesson for them."

She cocked her head. "To watch me lose control?"

"Aye," he said calmly.

She raised her eyebrows at his bluntness.

He nodded at her expression. "They need to see that kind of intensity, to feel that edge of danger. They won't get that here in the village, safe within these walls. They'll get that only from facing something real. You brought that sense of peril inside the ring, gave them a hint of what waits. It will serve them well, teach them to attack without holding back. It will also teach them the value of centering as I did, to control a situation as much by what they don't do as by what they do."

"But?"

He smiled faintly at her expression. She had never been one to shirk truth—no Randonnen was. She knew there were things he wanted to say, things to which she must listen, regardless of her reluctance. "You've been on the trail too long, Dione. You've run too much with the wild wolves, too far from your home. You're beginning to forget how to step away from their reality and back into your own world."

Dion was silent for a long moment, watching the students as they struck and blocked in two ragged lines while the drill forced them back and forth. As Batayon had said, their use of energy was obvious, external, and flat. They knew they didn't face a real threat. None of their partners clawed at them with desperate worlag jaws or starving badgerbear fangs. None of them faced a raider whose only goal was to skewer their entrails on steel. Dion felt herself clench when one student missed a block, even though his partner's kill-strike fell short.

She cursed herself as Batayon noted her instinctive tensing. Now even strangers saw through her like a window. Batayon was right. She had been drinking danger for too many years. It had become all she knew until she breathed it like an animal, waiting always for the talon to strike, instantly ready to dodge or hit back, knowing that the moons—and the Ariyens—could take what was left of her life at any time they focused on her again.

If she was honest with herself, she would admit that she had been riding to avoid the Ariyen elders as much as to avoid admitting to her own inner wounds. Those elders would not wait much longer to bring her back to Ariye. The skills they wanted were in her hands, linked to Ariye through the wolves and to the other wolfwalkers that she could hear in the gray, mental packsong. For a moment, she indulged the sense of the Gray Ones so that it washed through her brain like a murmur. Then, quietly, she drew back. For months, there had been others in that howling, hunters who did not belong to the wolves but who had somehow pierced the packsong. They were seeking something—possibly Dion herself—and had flavored the gray with urgency. She had faced enough predators that she could not mistake the intent. But before, she had faced those hunters willingly; now she had someone else to protect.

He followed her gaze to her belly. His voice was quiet. "What will you teach her, if you know only danger yourself?"

She stared at him for a long moment as he echoed her thoughts. Then she nodded, a curiously courteous gesture that acknowledged the question, yet left the answer hanging.

She turned away and quietly gathered her things: the overtunic, the belt and knives, the silver healer's circlet, the herb pouches she was never without. She slipped her feet into worn trail boots and gathered up the gray cloak with its blue-trimmed edge. Then she buckled on the sword belt and long knife as if she no longer noticed the dichotomy of the healer's circlet against the steel. She breathed life and death through both, and when she left, it was as if the studio exhaled power, leaving the merely human behind.

Dion didn't look back. She made her way along the stone

walk toward the boardinghouse as her workout-warmed body chilled hard. Overhead, two of the nine moons seemed spitted on the jagged, snow-draped mountains that made up the horizon, while three more crossed the cold sky. She pulled her cloak more tightly to her. To the west, a wolf howled thinly at the moons. It was a sharp call, even at that distance, and Dion's head whipped around at the sound. The wolf howled again, and she changed direction without thinking.

Moving quickly, she wove between broad alleys and homes toward the western fields. She returned a woman's nod absently, the greeting of a few men with irritation as if their words were somehow in her way. Two wolves howled now, and her feet quickened on the cold stone. Her nostrils flared as if she could smell the musk in her own nostrils, not theirs.

She passed the outer ring of homes and common corrals where the six-legged dnu grazed the last enclosed pasture. With their engineered, slightly segmented bellies, the dnu looked like double bubbles perched on spindly legs with comically overlarge feet. They were a distortion of aesthetics that had never been meant as riding beasts, but as beasts of burden and breeders for the original colonists' livestock. If the Ariyens had their way, the dnu would also carry soldiers and swords, not just elders and farmers and scouts. Her lips thinned at the thought. There were already enough graves on this world; they had no need of more. She had fled her own ghosts and graves to Randonnen, then to Kiren and Kiaskari, riding north until she was stopped at the base of the impassable alien mountains. And yet she had not run far enough. It had served no purpose to curse the Ariyen elders. In the end, it hadn't been they, but her own sense of duty that was bringing her back to the counties.

Oaths, the gray whispered.

She stared at the rounded fields of untrampled snow that surrounded the alpine village. While Ariye had used her, the wolves had waited patiently for her to fulfill a promise she'd made to them long ago. They too had tried to save her, filling her mind with ghosts as if those lost voices would make her whole. Now they pushed her back toward Ariye, toward the single wolf she had left behind. She smiled grimly. The Gray

Ones or the Ariyens . . . If, or rather when, the Ariyens caught up with her, they might be surprised at the choice that she would make.

A snarling deep in her skull answered the unspoken thought, and her smile widened to a feral grin. They unnerved her, these wild ones, but they were strong as a band of worlags. They made her growl at humans who drew too close, made her howl at night with the pack. It had been useful, she admitted. No one pushed questions on a wolfwalker who bared her teeth too often. Too close to the wolves, he had said . . .

She ducked quickly through the split rail fence into the near field. No one was working the sweetrye. The fields had been cut to red stubble and were now dusted with the first light snow of summer's end. The ground was hard and slick along the smooth ruts, and halfway across the outer field, she paused, closed her eyes, and listened. The late-summer clouds filtered the sky between the ragged peaks. The wind was bitter, and behind her, the gray expanse swallowed the thin village smoke trails like barren thoughts. She could hear the wolves clearly now. They curled around her mind, tasting her thoughts, drawn to her even though she did not Call. She waited. The wickedly barbed barrier hedge was thick, but it would not stop the Gray Ones. They would come through the S-curved channels like sly men, undaunted by the odors that repelled other predators like worlags and poolah and broo. To her left, the chunko birds called sharply, and she knew the Gray Ones were just on the other side. Then two of the wolves trotted silently out from the hedge, and slunk through the rails to the field.

Wolfwalker! The mental call of the wild ones was almost abrasive. Three other wolves threaded in, and Dion felt herself smiling. There was no danger to the corralled livestock near the town. Unlike badgerbears and worlags, wolves rarely bothered a healthy herd, and never did so when the herd was fenced. That, and the fact that the wolves ate the field rats and mice made them friends, not enemies of farmers. Yet even with easy field pickings, the wolves rarely penetrated the barbed hedges. The packs preferred the less-cultured, more isolated forests. They were engineered to bond to humans, but they were still wild animals, and most humanity unsettled them. The presence of a wolf near the village could mean only one of three things: a sick animal in the herd, a wolf-walker nearby, or a Calling that men must Answer.

Dion's smile grew at the invitation to hunt, and the sense of her expression transmitted automatically to the wolves who listened to her mind. The Gray Ones did not hear her specific words, but rather received an impression of what she sent. Over time, they had learned to interpret her human thoughts in lupine terms. In turn, she had learned to focus her own thoughts so that they were more easily read, and to translate the gray senses to human images and concepts. It had been fifteen years since she bonded with the wolves. She heard them now like family.

A gray-and-white female gulped a mouse and prowled for another scent. A young male snuffed at a mole hole. The old male with the darker haunches lifted his head and stared across the field. *Come,* he sent. *Run with us.*

Too close to the wolves, Batayon had said. But she felt her legs tense to answer.

Wolfwalkerwolfwalker . . . The voice of the dead echoed softly. It was an offering from the Gray Ones, an answering of the need she unconsciously projected.

Dion shivered and stared blindly back. They would take her into their memories if she wanted, back to the deaths, the graves, the blood on her hands. Any wolfwalker could follow those threads, could see what went on in the past, could hear again the voices of those long gone. That was a journey Dion did not want. She carried her reminders with her. Her sword was rough where steel had chipped steel. The edge on her long knife was thin from years of sharpening, and the handles on her weapons were black and shiny with use. She no longer felt comfortable without them, no longer slept deeply when she lay down. The wolves offered the past as if it were yesterday, as if those ghosts would assuage her overwariness, her sense of loss, and although she desperately wanted to reach for those lost images, she closed herself to that curse. If she ever hoped to release the dead, she must turn away from the ghosts. She would give her child to the future, not the past with its grief and graves.

Another wolf lifted his head as they waited for her answer. *Do you run with us?* There was eagerness, but also a hint of impatience in the words. Dion's expression softened. The wild wolves seemed brutally simple. Without the intimacy of a true bond, the impressions she received were crude and rough, lacking the smooth, complex weavings she had with her own partner wolf.

Three of the wild ones stared at her. *Wolfwalker,* they howled. *Do you run?* The rest of the pack poised at the white-fringed forest as they waited for her answer.

They were restless. She grinned suddenly: So was she. The urge to cut her cloak free and sprint through the trees was in her blood, not just in theirs. There was a call to baptise her unborn child with the wolves, to set in that fetal blood the need for wilderness. She had lost much in the past few years. Now she held tight—too tightly perhaps—to the child that grew in her womb. She could simply stop, she realized, and let the hunters catch up, for winter would come early to this town, earlier than in Randonnen. It would trap her in the peaks for the Ariyens to retrieve at their leisure. Or she could run with the wolves and let the hunters live as she did, with frigid mornings and sweating trails, blistered heels and aches. She smiled grimly to herself. She made the decision even as she thought the choice. She saw no reason to make it easy for the Ariyens to take her back. Besides, they were not the only ones to whom she owed a duty.

One of the Gray Ones raised his head and howled into the wind. Back near the corral, a boy and three men climbed up on the fence to watch. A shiver of unease crept into the pack as they became aware of the villagers. The baying rose and fell, fell, and others began to howl with him. It was the pack call, the call to gather and reaffirm each one's place in the group. From the field, the five wolves loped away through the twisted hedge and joined the rest of the pack. They howled again, reminding her of her promise to them. Her throat tightened as she fought the urge to answer.

To whom do you bind your life-debt? It was not a question

from the wolves. It was a layered voice, an icy inhuman voice that spoke deep in her mind. The wind bit tauntingly at her cheeks, whipping the forest birds up and over the trees. There was nothing menacing in the flight, but Dion was suddenly afraid. She was too far north, too close to the alien breeding grounds. If humans had originally thought to share the planet with the aliens, the birdmen had had other ideas. Promises bound the wolves to Dion, so the mental link between them was strong. If the telepathic birdmen could hear the wolves, they could also hear the wolfwalker. Dion shivered. No matter how many others were bound into the packsong, the oaths had been made with her voice in the gray, and it was she who held the internal power the Ancients had once wielded. Now, just as men hid their science underground, Dion must hide her mind in distance from those alien peaks, even if it turned her south into the hands of the Ariyens. She stared north. Nightmare images rose from deep in her mind, and talons seemed to slice her body . . . Her lack of motion suddenly seemed like fetters. She made her decision abruptly: some promises were best kept at a distance.

The gray song seemed to read her determination, for it became sharp and focused. Automatically, Dion reached for the wolf she had left behind. She stretched toward Ariye, seeking the voice she knew as well as her own. *Hishn,* she breathed into the gray. The wolf pack seethed with the name.

Hishn, Hishn. A female wolf echoed the name into the mental packsong. The image of Dion's partner wolf howled back like ripples across the hundreds of kays, across mountains, through forests, and into the racial memories where threads of other wolves had carried that lupine name. The call diluted, wavered, and passed on until it was lost. The distance was deafening.

Dion closed her eyes. She had been gone too long from her gray half, and her need for the wolf had been growing like an addiction. If she was ever to meet her promises, she must be whole again. She threw back her head and let her human throat mimic the lupine call. "Hishn," she howled.

Wolfwalker! the wolves bayed back.

As if bidden, they flowed back toward Dion from the

forest. Like a gray wave, fourteen wolves loped through the wicked barrier hedge, across the stubbled field. Dion stretched out her hands to pull in those threads of gray. Gray-white, gray, gray-black. It was a flow of power that swept her with almost frightening intent. The wolfwalker did not flinch. Yellow eyes gleamed. Fanged teeth bared to the cold. They struck her position like a solid wall of gray, then melted against her. Like a dustdevil, they swirled at her thighs, not quite brushing her trousers. Musk, hot breath, grinning jaws, golden eyes . . . Then they streamed away.

Dion's cloak hit the ground before she was aware that she had shed it. Then she was sprinting after the wolves, unbuckling her sword on the run and slinging it diagonally across her back. Her boots crushed stubble, slicked ruts, crunched snow. Her breath left clouds in the air. She vaulted the rail fence at the end of the field, then dodged through the barrier channel. Iron-hard thorns reached out for her sleeves when she cut the S-channel too short, but she laughed and snarled in return. On the other side of the barrier hedge, the trees swallowed her like a gnat.

Ahead, a young male paused on the edge of the pack, and his voice spiked the clouded sky. Rising, falling, falling. Dion grinned at the trail between them. She dodged an overhanging branch and felt twigs snap off in her braid. She didn't care. The cold air was huge in her lungs, and the ground like a lover, demanding her pace, her pulse, her sweat. She jumped a short boulder, then balanced for an instant on a larger one beside it.

Wolfwalker!

Her throat answered the wolves, her human tone rising, falling, falling. Four of the Gray Ones answered.

Her legs stretched and she jumped, staggered slightly, and leapt after the pack. Ahead, the lead wolf caught the scent of a mountain cat, and as far behind as she was, Dion's hand went to the hilt of her knife with the leader's mental stiffening. But the tawny cat merely watched the pack flow past its perch, its nostrils filled with their musk. As she passed, Dion looked up and met the mountain cat's gaze. *Oaths,* the voices whispered. The wolfwalker snarled and ran faster.

* * *

On the corral fence, the boy and three men watched her disappear into the forest. The youngest man sent the boy to retrieve Dion's cloak. "I wonder if she'll come back," he murmured.

The oldest man picked a splinter from the fence to chew on. "Might not, I'm thinking," Muraus said. "She's close to the wild, not us."

They were comfortably silent for a moment.

"There was that wolfwalker down about a hundred years ago," Muraus commented.

Pratton picked his own splinter to poke at his aged teeth and frowned around it at white-haired Muraus. "Old Marl? Hundred and seven years ago, if I recall rightly."

"Hundred seven," the other man agreed amiably. "Ran trail with his wolf for forty-two years. Wolf got old, but wouldn't come in to the village, and old Marl had to live in the forest. Took off one day and didn't come back. Left his cloak and sword, even his boots on the trail."

Pratton tugged absently on his trimmed, gray beard and nodded consideringly. "Some say worlags got 'em."

Muraus chewed his toothpick. "Some say it was poolah. Jemeni's grandfather saw footprints near a kill 'bout two months after Marl disappeared."

Pratton grunted his agreement. "They say he still haunts the trails over Backaround Ridge. You can hear him in the howling."

The white-haired man nodded toward the forest. "We'll hear her, too, more than likely."

" 'Less the Ariyens take her back."

" 'Less that," he agreed.

"Sometimes she acts more hunted than hunter," Ire said softly.

Muraus gave the young man a sharp look. "Aye, that she does."

Ire gazed toward the mountains. "I wonder if she really went all the way north, really saw the birdmen."

Pratton gave Ire a sly look. "You could ask her when she

comes back. You brag enough about your handsome face and how women do anything for it."

The younger man grinned. "It's not my face they love. Besides, it's you who should ask her when she returns. You got along fine at the shooting games yesterday."

Pratton shrugged uncomfortably. "She's a good shot and a master healer, and my hip ached like a wounded worlag. Besides, she doesn't need some gray-haired old man prying about in her head."

"That's not where you'd be prying if you had your way."

"And what way would that be?" Pratton retorted.

Ire merely said obliquely, "The old women in this town don't hold their tongues any more than you do, and their bedtime stories are better."

Muraus hid his grin in his white beard.

Ire's eyes got a distant look. "Would be something, wouldn't it, to see the breeding grounds, get a glimpse of one of the beasts?"

"A wise man doesn't bother the wolf," the oldest man murmured.

They were silent for a moment. Then Pratton offered, "She wouldn't be sticking her knife in you for asking a simple question."

Ire grinned slowly, unaware of how much his manner was already like that of the two older men. He added his own persuasion. "Even if she did, she could sew you back up like a split pillowcase as long as she found all your stuffing."

Pratton chuckled at the reference to Muraus' thickening belt line, but Muraus gazed toward the forest. "Have you looked in her eyes?" His voice was soft, almost breathed into the wind as if he was afraid of its being heard.

Something in the old man's voice struck a chill along Ire's spine. "Have you?"

"Aye."

"What did you see?"

"I saw . . ." Muraus's voice trailed off, and the old man shook his head. "Energy. Power. Something cold." He ground his toothpick absently into shards against the rail. "I saw secrets," he said softly.

All three glanced involuntarily north to the distant peaks, then surreptitiously made the sign of the moons' blessing. The birdmen, those creatures who lived in the north, who watched what humans did, who killed those who approached—they held plague in their talons and hung that threat over the world like an ax hung by four spider threads. Disturb them, and the blade would fall again over human cities. Eyes in the sky, the younger man thought. He knew, when the wolfwalker returned, that none of them would ask.

II

Talon Drovic neVolen

Life is fire;
Fire, ambition;
Ambition, tragedy;
Tragedy, life.

   —from "Circles," by Wile neRaya, Kiren songster

It was near dawn, and the shreds of fog that clung to the low hills waited with Talon in silence. Four of the nine moons floated overhead, but their fading light no longer bleached the ground between the shadows. Instead, pale dawn rinsed the moonlight to a dull gray and threw the small valley into harsher darkness.

Talon stared at the faint, gray ribbons of road. Long ago, they had been half built from new rock and half from the slag-stone of the Ancients. Now they echoed with the quiet, and the echoes settled like night spiders along Talon's broad and bony shoulders. It was late summer, but he had been cold for over a month. Now even the streets gave him chills. It was as though he stared at headstones, not hundred-year-old sections of paving.

He glanced around, making sure that no gear glinted. With Drovic's men and women, it was an automatic, not a necessary check. These riders were experienced, skilled, hardened. Most had three or more years of scouting or fighting; some had more than six; and two had more than a hundred. Two-thirds had joined Drovic after the fight that had left Drovic's band decimated and Talon more dead than alive, but some, like Sojourn and Darity, had been with Talon's father long enough that they seemed to execute the man's thoughts more than his orders. Those people were the lethal heart of the group. Now they rode for Talon.

"Anything?" Sojourn asked in a low voice.

Talon let himself open to the echo of gray. Long ago, that faint sense of wolves in his skull had been a thicker fog. Now there was too much blood on his hands. The pack could take no comfort in the killer he had become: Lone wolf. Lobo. Worlag wolf. Still, three, four months ago something had changed in them—or in him, perhaps as a result of his wounds. He was susceptible now, weakened and open to the gray. They gnawed at the edge of his thoughts even in the daytime, worrying him like a marrowed bone, urging him north to the cold. They were too much like him, trapped by the will of another, and they snapped at his thoughts as they fought to find their release from men. He would have freed them if he could, but it was not he who had trapped their minds in his skull.

He stared into the dull darkness as if he could see their yellow-black eyes. They had to suspect what he would do that day, and with their engineered abilities, had to know that it was wrong, but they sent nothing to him but their own urgency, a growing need, and the blind frustration that accompanied both. "Not yet," he finally answered.

In the dark, the slender man's murmur was dry. "We trust your eyes, son of Drovic."

Talon kept his expression calm. Some time ago, a swath of beetles had passed through the woods and left the shredded bark clinging to the trunks like shrouds. With the wolves heightening his senses, he could smell the torn bark better than Sojourn, but it had been they, not he, who had found the hill in the dark. With his father's hatred of wolves and wolfwalkers, Talon's use of the Gray Ones was not a wise confession.

He tuned out the slight sighing sound of the trees and listened instead to the dark. Beetles, birdbeasts, gelbugs, worms—in swarm years like this one, the world itself seemed to gather and strike at humankind. Raiders such as Drovic swarmed with it. They gathered in the shadows like worlags and struck out with anger and vengeance. That same urgency for blood filled Talon. He had once clenched at dreams; now he struck out almost blindly at others. Rage, entrapment, frustration, rage—not even the dark could obscure that circle. He felt his jaw tighten as he watched the road below. That valley road was a snake of gray-white legend made by the Ancients. The colonists had sworn to return to the sky and had died instead of the plague they brought down on themselves. Like the tension that coiled Talon's hands, the stone-road snake that was their legacy tried to writhe up as he did, from the dirt toward the taunting stars.

Beside him, Sojourn glanced at the sky, then murmured softly, "Soon."

Talon fought the urge to turn on the other man, and he gripped his sword hilt with long, lean fingers that wanted to clench and draw and strike. Worlag piss, but of course it was soon. It was nearly dawn. Did the man think his weakness made him blind as a summer stokal?

He knew that the other man watched him closely for any signs of weakness. They had ridden together for how many years? And still, Sojourn watched him. The other man had a right, Talon admitted bitterly. The past few months had left Talon so lean as to be almost gaunt. His black, close-cropped hair framed a hard, sculpted face; his high, harsh cheekbones only emphasized the hollow lines that had changed his looks so severely. He had a square jaw, a nose that had been broken at least twice, and dark eyebrows that sat heavily above icy gray eyes. He was not handsome. He had his father's looks instead: too much power, strength, and will; and little to soften the lines.

The sun shifted closer to full dawn, and Talon forced himself to relax. Eight hundred years ago, he would not have played such games as those he would today. Hands like his would have gripped the controls of a skyhook or guided a spacecar up from the mountains and into the starry void. He would have flown starships and explored a dozen different worlds, not bathed in blood each ninan. His father claimed that blood and steel would give him that dream again, but Drovic's vision had twisted in like a shark that savages itself. Now, Drovic strove more for revenge than for any sort of future. Talon wondered when he, himself, had turned from the world to follow his father instead.

He shifted irritably. His saddle creaked in the dark. Five, six more minutes, and the watch down below would change. The village guards would relax, and those who slept would rise to break their fast while others began their chores. Talon could feel it like a voice in his head—the routine that screamed to be broken. He heard the hard speed of his heart and welcomed the iciness that gripped his mind. His thoughts ticked off the seconds. The tension, the cold steel, the creak of saddle-warm leather—yes, those things felt right and natural. It was the town below that felt wrong.

From behind him, some of the riders shifted. Jervid, a large-framed but oddly ropy man, muttered just loud enough for Talon to hear his words: ". . . still think we ought to go in on the south side."

Talon's lips tightened at Jervid's gall, but he kept his mouth shut.

"It's a fool's ride to go through an exposed field when you can approach beneath the trees," Jervid added, a touch louder as Talon did not respond. "And more fool to take our flight through a cluttered woods when you could have the speed of the open fields. Backwards, that's what it is. Bass-ackwards like a fool."

Talon's eyes narrowed, but in the gloom, the others could not see it. Someone chuckled, and a woman—Oroan perhaps, or Roc—said something that silenced the laughter abruptly, except for a dry comment too low to hear. Talon had listened closely, but it could have been Fit or Morley or Mal who had laughed at Jervid's complaint.

But Jervid wasn't finished, and the man's voice grew louder as he found he was not challenged. "Every father thinks his son can lead," he scoffed softly. " 'Put him back in the saddle,' he said. 'Get the blood back on his blade.' It's too soon, if you ask me—just look at this approach. I'm the one who knows these trails, but did they listen to me? Not by the hair of a stickbeast." The stocky man did not bother to keep his voice low any longer. "Fools we are, to sit up here. Addled like winter poolah."

For a long moment, Talon held his breath. It did not calm his growing rage, and he thought he might crack apart in the ice of his own fury if he tried to breathe again. Slowly, he twisted to regard the other man. There was something so menacing in Talon's posture that even in the gloom, Jervid, who had opened his mouth to speak again, broke off and became very still.

Talon turned back to the village.

At his side, Sojourn nodded almost imperceptibly in approval, and Talon felt some of his tension ease. The muttering behind him was quiet.

Four minutes, and the sun shifted up to hug the jagged skyline. Far below the mountain ridge, the town was swallowed in darker relief. Talon found himself closing his eyes. He felt oddly frozen, caught between dark and light. A year ago, he would not have thought twice before trying to save one of his rider's lives. Even a month ago, things had been different. There was that bollusk stampede, when Sojourn had been knocked from his dnu. Talon had barely hesitated before racing in and catching the man up. He had nearly gone down himself—the effort had torn his shoulder again where the muscles were weak as paper. But a ninan ago, Wakje had been trapped by fire in a barn, and Talon had stared through the flames at the other man as if weighing his life before charging through to reach him. It was as though Talon no longer had the conviction that these riders—his riders, his own men and women—were worth the trouble, and that was a guilt that ate at his guts like acid.

The dull pound in his temple wore on, and the din of the Gray Ones cut at his ears. It took him a moment to realize that he was fingering the pouch at his belt. Deliberately, he withdrew his hand. It had become a challenge to hold off taking the medicine as long as he could. That, and the pain would come harder later, and he would need the herbs more then.

He glanced over his shoulder at the two dozen riders who squatted like a curse on the hills. He resisted the desire to look at the outvillage guard who was now silent at his post. The warning bell—too heavy to saw down—had been wedged still, its clapper carefully wrapped with moss, and it hung silently while the guard's corpse sprawled close. The man's death had been clean—Harare was nothing if not efficient— and the body now lay half obscenely against the bole of a nearby tree, its legs spread and its face as slack as an empty waterbag. The skin around the guard's lips and eyes had already whitened; the blood that had not spilled out to soil the ground had begun to settle and swell out the lower half of the body. The thought persisted that the man had died carelessly, and Talon's anger at the sloppy guard disturbed him. Rage, every day—it was now a regular meal. Or had he simply been sick so long that he was now sick of others' blood?

He signaled curtly to the riders around him. "Gear check."

Around him, the riders rustled. Weapons first, then torch bags, then the padded bags for the science they hoped to steal. In over eight hundred years, humans had achieved little since they had landed on this planet. What technology they did create, they hid underground like rats hiding their young. Now it was chemistry, bioform science, and mining worms that were sought, traded, stolen. Those bits of knowledge and technology were gems that would pay for a year's worth of leisure. To Talon, that knowlege was power and the reason to push toward the stars; to his father, it was a weapon to aim at a county's head. Someday, Talon would take what they stole and build instead of destroy. But, he thought, his lips thinning with a bitter grin, today was not that day.

He checked the torch strapped to his saddle. The contents of the two bags fitted over its end would not mix until the torch was withdrawn. Then there would be heat, flame, and light. That, at least, they had not lost—the crude chemistry of the Ancients.

Talon raised his open hand in the gloom and signaled the riders again. "Ready." His voice was sharp. The air seemed to tense with the sound. He hid his wince as he held the signal— he must not let pain blind him or allow himself to look weak. So he held the gesture and reveled in the growing agony in his shoulder, then in the sharpening pain in his side where the muscles strained as he breathed. Something changed in the town—the light, perhaps, or a sense of clumsy movement. His forearm tensed. The riders hung on his breath. He clenched his fist and pumped it.

There was no cry or shout from his men, just a sudden, silent releasing as the riders spurred their dnu with him. Their surge was a flood of darkness. Talon held his fist up to continue their charge, but he could not have stopped them now. They were away and down the hill, and the thunder of hooves was a growing cascade of sound.

Something flickered in Talon's side vision, and he realized that Jervid was splitting off. He whistled the short command to stay in formation. The other man ignored him. Talon cursed viciously. If Jervid's charge roused the south end of the village, Talon's escape route would vanish. But the other man raced away, and Talon shouted sharply, "Roc, Morley, Eilryn—break off! Back Jervid!"

The three riders turned their dnu in a wide curve to race away after the other man. Talon swore again under his breath as his force was split. If Jervid thought Talon would follow with the entire group, the man was mistaken. The stables and target accesses were at this end of town. "Damned, bollusk-brained idiot," he cursed. With Jervid gone, he would lose one of his attack angles. It would be a shorter attack—more a rush than a search—and less to gain because of it. The center riders would have no left flank to protect them and draw the return fire. He raged at Jervid silently.

They swept through the first field, trampling the brittle grains. His ears were full of dirt-dulled thunder and the whistling of a gallop wind. His hand tightened on the steel.

No oldEarth horse had been born on this world to carry men like the wind. These engineered dnu, with their spindly legs and six-legged gait, covered the ground like a dry-grass fire, a fire that Talon now guided, a blaze as heady as wine.

The thick hedges between the fields muffled the full force of the charge. There was only a single pair of startled shouts as they broke across a low separator hedge and swept onto the road of the Ancients. Then the thunder drowned the voices, and the dawn farmers were left behind.

Two riders split off and fell back. They would wait and draw fire from the village to suggest that the escape route was on their side of town. And if that didn't work, they would simply fire to confuse and divide the townsmen and make Talon's escape easier. It was a trick that Talon had proposed two months ago, and that Drovic now used almost every time in one pattern or another. Talon did not look back to see the two riders slow, but he knew when they pulled to a stop: the lupine eyes that followed his charge also watched that false rear guard.

He passed an empty outer corral and reached the stone fence that led into the village. Shadows held no color in the gloom, but Talon saw these things clearly. When the first of his riders reached the outermost circle of buildings, he ripped his torch from its breakaway straps. The chemicals mixed with the quiescent spores, and the dried material sparked. Flame spouted. The fungi flashed. The sharp chemicals bit at his nose. He thrust the torch up to be seen.

In the midst of the thundering hooves, light flared up from the hands of the other riders. Four men veered away: two right, two left. Talon felt them go. He saw the looming wall of a workshop, smelled fresh-cut wood, and threw his torch with a vengeance. His aim was good—it hit with a thunk in the scrap pile. The flames would be quick, add fear, and distract the villagers' eyes from the riders who raced through the shadows.

Four more sets of riders broke away toward the four target homes. Wakje flanked Talon as he made for one of the common stables. Sojourn and Ki were behind him, and he whistled a short burst of orders: Grab only the dnu. With his men split like peas, they would be lucky to get more than six extra mounts.

He cornered sharply, and his dnu grunted at the speed. It was dry, he noted—the dew had been light, and the homes in the town would burn quickly. Living wood would bleed, then shriek as fibers crisped and snapped. Living flesh . . . There were already screams in the houses they had passed. But the fires would draw the villagers away from the target homes. The small warning bells on the outermost homes began ringing to beat the dawn.

Something whapped past Talon's shoulder, and a half-dressed man rushed toward them from a doorway. Wolf-song tightened in Talon's mind. With lupine instinct, he saw everything—angles, shadows, movement. His human mind judged trajectories and training. Instantly he turned his dnu to half collide with Sojourn's beast. Sojourn cursed, half-unseated, but the villager's second arrow missed, and Ki, coming up behind the man, cut the townsman down.

Cries were going up, and one street over, a woman screamed. Talon stiffened at the tone. His dnu sensed the change and faltered. Sojourn glanced back, and Ki shouted a question. But a Gray One howled in Talon's head. *On,* they urged him. *Find her.*

He kicked his dnu hard in the flanks. The segmented belly heaved, and the six-legged beast jumped a short gate with a grunt. Its middle legs were not drawn up in time, and it knocked the slats out like straws. Wakje shouted after Talon, but he ignored the other man. Instead, he veered toward an alley. The night was already split with the clarity of the bells. Two stables, four homes . . . With fewer riders, Sojourn and Wakje would have to give up one of the stables. He whistled this at the other men before the alley ate him.

The darkness was narrow and closed-in. *Find her.* The gray voice rang inside his head.

He broke out of the alley, burst across an open street, and disappeared again into another narrow passage between two craft buildings. Two men were running down the street, one holding up his pants with one hand, a short sword in the right, and the other young enough that he kept looking back at the other as he drew ahead, slowed, and drew ahead again. Others began to appear in the distance. "Fire in the woodshop," Talon shouted, hunching in the saddle and deliberately making his voice rough as if with fear. He gestured wildly toward the outer homes, and the older man veered off, taking the younger man with him. It would be precious seconds—if ever—before they realized that Talon was a raider.

Hurry, the wolves sent, feeding his urgency.

He jumped his dnu over a hedge that still offered withered blooms to the sky. Like a hammer pounding chaff, he shattered their faded dryness. The Gray Ones were close—he could feel them just as he had on the ridge. The hot scent of blood rushed in his nostrils along with that of the dead summer buds, and he knew it was the wolves' hunt, not just his own urgency, that swamped his guts with eagerness. Like an eel, he slid from the saddle before the beast had halted.

Two riders staggered away from the lamp-lit house as he jumped the flowerbed. "Biekin?" he shouted.

"Inside," Liatuad shouted back as he thrust Mal up on his dnu.

Talon vaulted the porch railing and automatically cut down the house bell as he passed it. It fell with a muffled clang. There was a shout inside the home; something hit the floor. Talon burst through the open doorway only to jerk back as Biekin staggered backward into his arms. The rider was saturated with blood—not his own; Biekin's blade was half buried in the villager's gut. Biekin pulled out and jabbed forward again, unnecessarily. The two men went down with the villager's weight. Biekin cursed and yanked himself and his sword free, then stooped to wipe his blade on the villager's shirt above the opened torso. He glanced up at Talon coldly. "Townsman surprised us, gashed Mal on the head when he blocked for me. I sent him out with Liatuad."

Talon nodded, his jaw tight. "We have three minutes. Maybe four."

Biekin did not bother to nod. "I'll take the side rooms. You take the back."

Talon did not move. He stared down at the dead villager. His body was tense as if he needed to lash out, to fight, to feel the blood hot on his hands, but his feet were rooted in place. In the kitchen, Biekin ripped at the cupboards and kicked at the shelves, shoved a worktable aside as he looked for hidden doors. Talon could hear the dull thuds of cured meats and goods as they were automatically thrown into his sack. They would be dumped out in an instant if Biekin found access to the underground lab they suspected. He heard the screams from outside, heard the fire take hold in the roof overhead, heard the cry of the living wood.

The shuddering took him suddenly, and he bent, then dropped to his knees. Wolves howled. His guts rebelled. Vile acids splatted on the floor and mixed with the blood of the dead. He stared at the spew, then at the clean steel of his unused sword. The blade dropped with a clang. His fists—they were pressed against his head. The pain was blinding. Wolves snarled. He staggered up, fell against the table, then stumbled over a chair, breaking its back legs as he hit the floor on top of it.

Panicked, he groped for his sword. Only when his hand closed over the hilt did his heartbeat calm. Biekin's sounds were muffled, and it took Talon a second to realize that it was not his hearing that had also dulled. Biekin was in the drying room, thrusting aside the well-stuffed shelves in his hasty search of the floor.

Talon forced himself up and stumbled toward the rear doorway, but when he put his hands on the latch, the cold metal brought some clarity to his vision. The howling in his head pulsed with the pain that swept in as red-black waves.

Find her, the Gray Ones snarled. *Protect.*

He shook his head and pressed a fist against his temple. "Not now," he forced out at the pain through clenched teeth. "I refuse, you moonwormed, piss-soaked—" His fingers crushed his own fist. The hammer in his head deafened his voice. "—dag-chewing, spit-trimmed, lepa-spawned son of a worlag—"

Protect, the wolves howled beneath the pain.

Leave me! The words he sent back were more of a cry than an answer.

But the wolves snapped in return. They gathered, then

leaped at his consciousness, sweeping in like a flood of gray. This time, it was dull and merciful. The lancing agony faded.

Talon blinked. There were tears on his cheeks. His lip was bleeding where he had bitten it to stifle his cry. A thunder of hooves faded past the window, but it was a herd of riderless dnu on a lead line behind a raider. Individual shouts and screams made a sporadic din.

Someone—a woman—was in the room beyond. He could almost feel her fear with his pulse. Outside, three more riders crashed by. Fire flickered down one of the window frames and began to eat at the wall. Smoke sharpened his nostrils. The gray voices snarled. *Hurry.*

He rattled the door latch, cursed it silently, stepped back, and kicked, then kicked again. The soft hinges tore. The door smashed into the narrow room beyond, breaking the canning jars on the shelves before crashing down on the floor. For a moment, Talon simply hung in the doorway, his mind clouded with the howling that held his pain at bay. Automatically, he noted the almost dusty taste of the room, the faint, sanitized odors of a workspace, the scent of a woman and child. His lips tightened. His hard face was all angles, and the light cast his high cheekbones into harsh, demonic relief.

"Please . . ." The woman had scrambled back into a corner. She cringed now, her face shadowed by the hood of the cloak she had hurriedly cast around her, and her arms encircled a child whom she half hid within the cloth. Her voice was barely a breath. "Please . . ."

Something gray flickered at the edge of his sight. It was strong, and he welcomed it like a mate. For a moment, he was whole, and the wolves were thick in his skull. Balance and strength flowed into his limbs. His hand tightened on his hilt.

He kicked aside the shattered timbers and like a cat, stepped through the debris. The floor felt strangely hollow. Sloppy . . . The thought brought a tightness to his anger. And there were others below—he could sense them breathing. Quick breaths. Children and one, maybe two young adults. His icy eyes gleamed with an almost yellow light, and the woman who had hidden her family whimpered. With a fury born of pain and blood, he kicked the remains of the broken door so that it jammed into the shelves as he stomped it, wedging the trap-door down. He didn't look at the wolf-deafened corner of his mind that had hidden the trapdoor seams.

Biekin cursed in the outer room as he discovered the fire, and Talon raised his sword. The woman bit down on her own forearm to stifle her half scream. She shrank back. Talon hesi-tated. Almost without volition, he stretched out his other, weakened hand. The boy's dark eyes followed the movement as if hypnotized, but the woman sucked in a ragged breath. Time seemed to stiffen. Then he gripped and ripped back her hood. The woman clutched the child; her brown eyes stared—

Brown eyes. A pale face ugly with terror and lined with years of indoor work. Brown eyes, light brown hair . . . He clenched her cloak and did not realize that she writhed within his grip. Nor did he truly hear the steps that approached be-hind him.

It was a lupine instinct that made him thrust the woman away; yellow-tinged eyes that sensed the man from behind. He whipped around, sword up. For a moment, Biekin was framed by the doorway. Then the other man caught sight of the woman, gestured with his blade hand. "Bring her along if you want her."

Talon stared at him.

Biekin grinned. "I'll take her, then. You carry the goods." He started to thrust the doubled cloth at Talon, but the tall man jerked back with the wariness of a wolf.

"What about the boy?" Talon forced himself to speak.

Biekin stepped forward, the crude bag of food tossed aside. "We'll give him vertal and sell him in Helten."

Talon leaned some of his weight on the hilt and took a ragged breath. Vertal burned out the voice, and it wasn't a pleasant burning, but a mute slave couldn't contest his sale, and once the sale papers were signed and filed, no protest would save the boy's future. Wolves howled, and Talon clenched his fist. Slaves—they were all slaves to the gray.

Biekin's eyes narrowed. "The fires are barely spreading, Talon. The townsmen will be pushing back past Oroan's line before we can finish the job. If you want the woman, bring her along. If you don't, leave her to me."

"No," he managed.

Biekin misunderstood and stepped forward.

Talon's grip tightened on his sword. "No," he said more sharply.

"Like hell." Biekin gestured with his own blade. "They have eyes. They have seen us. It's vertal or the sword. Even you know that." In the growing light, the steel glinted. The woman stared at Biekin's face as the raider stepped toward her, then screamed with such terror that she made no sound except that of a harsher breathing. The sound slashed through Talon's skull. He could not help his response. Like light on glass, his own blade flashed up.

And bit deeply into the door frame.

Biekin jerked back. The shaped plank splintered; the sharp thunk of steel froze them both. Biekin stared. The living frame bled whitely. Biekin, blocked by the blade, sucked in his breath. Then he spoke, his voice soft as dusk. "Your wounds have sapped your judgment, Talon, not just your strength and speed."

Talon found his strength in the wolves and stared into the other man's eyes. His own gaze was like chips of slate. "There is no one here."

A muscle in Biekin's jaw jumped. "They have eyes. Take them or kill them—it's your choice." His lips twisted. "Do it yourself, or stand aside, and I'll do the job that your own father suspected you might not have the guts to complete."

Talon's fingers seemed to be blackened lupine claws, not human fingers, and he flexed his grip almost imperceptibly to rid himself of that feeling. His voice was hard. "We found no one here." He yanked the point of his sword out of the wall. "No one," he repeated. The point of his sword rested against the other man's gut for an instant before being withdrawn.

The sound of riding beasts racing outside cluttered the air. Thin smoke began to fill the outer room. Talon's gaze flickered as the fire finally caught on a sofa and flared up like a summer sun. In the flash, Biekin moved like a snake. The man's thick forearm snapped up and struck Talon's weak right wrist, shoving the taller man back. Talon staggered, and Biekin slammed a fist into his gut, propelling him back into the shelves. His spine hit an edge with a blast of pain. His knees started to buckle.

And a blizzard of fury engulfed him. He blocked a blow to his weakened ribs. He feinted left. Biekin parried, but Talon stepped in and slammed up with his hilt so that it jammed into the other man's gut. The man grunted harshly, caught for a moment without air. Talon kicked out and caught Biekin in the inner thigh, then stomped down onto the other man's foot, but Biekin rolled with the kick and Talon missed the man's boot, hitting door debris instead. Biekin staggered back to get distance. Like a wolf, Talon followed. *Speed. The flash of paw . . .* He struck the man's shoulder, and the force of it slammed Biekin against the wall. The other man put his weight behind the uppercut he threw in return as Talon's arm extended, but Talon half dropped, got under it, jerked up, and the other man's left guard was open. Instinctively, Biekin twisted as Talon drove his own right punch home. His fist was clenched around the hilt of his sword—he was too close for stabbing, and the blade caught in the shelves, robbing the blow of its full force. He missed the solar plexus, cracked two ribs instead. *Floor dust and fangs. The sharpness of snapping bone.* Biekin staggered back a half step, coming up short as he hit the door frame. But he snapped up a brutally fast kick that hit Talon square in the guts. Talon felt it coming in and rode the kick back. He almost tripped over the woman, who scrambled frantically out of his way. The other man's sword flashed up. *Faster,* the gray surged. *Catch flesh in the teeth and tear.* Talon beat-attacked, then dropped point and lunged. Biekin turned the blow but barely, and Talon didn't bother to stop his momentum. He hit Biekin full-body on. They went through the doorway like tacklers, slammed into the floor, tangled, lost their swords, scrambled up, broke apart, and lunged back toward each other like worlags. Smoke blinded them, and they fought viciously by feel. Biekin's meaty fist caught Talon on the side of his head and half threw him to the floor. For an instant, he was dazed, but gray instinct put his long knife in his hand, and it met Biekin like a wicked thought as the other man stomped down. Like a fork through veal, the blade stabbed deep into the other man's thigh bone. Biekin's scream was harsh. *Blood. Hot tang and sweet scent. Tear down, snap.* Talon lunged to his feet, wrenching out the blade as Biekin's furious backhand caught him on the side of his head. Fire licked at the inner walls. The wolves in Talon stiffened as Biekin's knife flicked up for the kill. Talon parried and shifted aside to reattack, but stepped on the dead townsman instead. Felt the shift and, falling, kicked up while he struck a side block with both hands. Biekin's knife went flying. Talon staggered up, choked on smoke, and felt Biekin grab his jerkin. Smoke or wolves—he could not see. He struck out by instinct. The knife hit bone and cracked another rib like an egg, slip-slashing through the muscle. Biekin grunted hoarsely. His boot caught Talon's thigh. Talon buckled, but, falling, stabbed again. He shattered smoke and what was left of the broken chair. Heat washed his face. He could not see for the burning and tearing of his eyes. But suddenly there were only the burbling breaths of the other man and the scuffling of his own hands and feet as he tried to regain his balance.

Run! the wolves cried out in his head. *Flee the hunters.*

There were men out front, in the streets. His men. Talon slipped in a mass of guts, staggered up, doubled over from the smoke, and then, blindly and automatically, wiped his knife on the other man's jerkin. He groped around for his sword, found it, and wiped that as quickly. Then he crouch-ran, not for the door, but for the back room.

The woman cried out as he burst back through. He braced himself against the door frame. The nausea was beginning to build as smoke and pain mixed. His blade drooped to the floor, and he bit back a moan. "Get out," he managed.

The woman stared at him, her fear deafening her to his words.

Thin smoke crawled into the tiny room. He half straightened. In the fire's glow, his face was a mask of rage. "Run," he snarled. "Now. Get out!"

She cringed at his gesture, and he staggered toward her. She screamed and screamed again as he brought up his bloody sword, but he struck the wood beside her. Stabbed the thin wall again as the wolves howled in his head. *Hurry. Steps on the wood, steps on the stairs.* Hunters. The woman, they howled. *Hurry!*

"This house will come down around your ears," he snapped. "There is another way out of the lab?" She stared at him like a rabbit. He didn't think. He slapped her.

Her head snapped back, and the boy ripped himself from her arms to fling himself at Talon's chest, beating the man with his fists. "Leave her alone—"

Talon struck him almost absently. The boy flew back, stunned. Talon's voice was icy. "The lab under the floor. Your children. There is another way out for them?"

She gasped. "Yes."

He hewed at the wood with a violence he did not question, then kicked it with the remains of his strength. The fibers cracked, then splintered, and a black nose poked in through the ragged hole. Like snakes, smoke lines rushed toward the fresh air and the wolf that blocked it. Talon snarled at the Gray One. It withdrew, and he kicked at the hole until he broke out two planks, and it was large enough for the woman. For a moment, he crouched against the wall, coughing and catching his breath.

"Go," he managed raggedly. "Follow the wolves."

But she stared at him without moving, and he realized she and the boy would stay and burn in their terror.

"Move, damn you—the outer rooms are on fire; the raiders are out front." My raiders? Me and my lepa and worlags? He grabbed the woman by the shoulder, cursed her as she clutched the child. "Damn you to the second hell, will you burn here in your fear?" He shoved her toward the hole. "Stay in the shadows. The Gray Ones will lead you—" His voice broke off in a spasm of coughing. Dnu raced away from the front of the house, and someone shouted at the stragglers. He raised his fist to strike her.

She panicked and shoved the boy ahead of her. The cloak she tried to keep over her mouth tore on the splintered wood. She cried out at the screams that sounded from the end of the street, and Talon's stomach twisted. She was an animal, not a human, soaked in mindless terror. There was no fight in her—no courage, no gray. He bit at his fathomless anger. For an instant, he stared out the hole into shadows where yellow eyes gleamed. Then he crouched to follow after.

"Talon—" It was a man's voice, outside the home, distorted by the crackling fire.

Talon straightened abruptly, felt his lungs contract as he breathed in the thicker smoke. His eyes burned with tears. Gagging, he dropped back to his knees. He cursed with a fury that was only half pretended and dragged down the shelves beside him. They fell with a crash and hid most of the hole. In the gloom, it should go unnoticed. He stumbled back over shattered glass toward the fire and Sojourn's voice.

"Talon!" the other man called more urgently.

"Inside," he shouted roughly. In the other room, his eyes smarted. The flames had caught along the floor near the backroom doorway. The smoke was thickening. He held his breath, whipped his cloak up around his head and arms, and threw himself through the small fire line. There was an instant of furnacelike heat; then the slam of the floor as he landed badly. The smoke burned, but he could still breathe—the Ancients had engineered the living wood for safety, and Talon threw his thanks to them as he blindly searched for Biekin's food bag.

He found the raider by stumbling over his body. Talon went to his knees in the blood beside the townsman and grabbed the food bag just as Sojourn charged into the room. The other man automatically dropped to a crouch as soon as he jumped through the flaming doorway. He crawled over to Talon. "All right?"

Talon nodded, coughing. He swung the sack to his shoulder.

Sojourn noted the blood smudges where swords had been cleaned on the shirts of both Biekin and the townsman. "We have the dnu," Sojourn said quickly. He kept his face muffled to breathe. "Kilaltian got to the message tower in time. We'll have an hour—maybe three if we're lucky—of clear riding before they can get the word out." Sojourn's eyes began to run with tears. It didn't stop him from hastily stripping the pouches off Biekin's belt and stuffing them into his own.

They crawled to the door, keeping under the smoke, and stumbled out onto the porch. Sojourn wiped at his tears and glanced back at the orange-lit windows. It was a futile gesture. He was tearing so badly that he saw only a blurred ball of light. He cursed without anger and grabbed the reins of his dnu as Talon swung up beside him. Then they raced through the smoke-filled streets.

Dawn left the town as Talon had: fired and smoldering, but even with the heat from the fire still on his skin, Talon's bones were cold. Perhaps it was the chill of death, and the fingers of cold were a warning. He cursed his father under his breath and led his riders at breakneck speed through the gloomy forest trails.

Long after the thunder of fleeing hooves had paled, thin pillars of smoke wisped into the sky to mark the burning homes. Talon did not stop to watch. He paused only three times to check their back trail, then left the rear guard to Harare.

Sojourn nodded as he came abreast. "Did you find the lab doors in the target?"

"No," Talon said shortly. He clenched his teeth against the pain that throbbed in his shoulder and leg, and tried to ignore the ax that kept splitting the side of his skull.

"No access? Drovic was fairly sure."

"None," he answered even more tersely.

"And Biekin and Morley and Eilryn dead. Your father will not be pleased."

Talon's gray-tinged voice was surprisingly dry. "I imagine not," he agreed.

III

Rhom Kintar neKheldour

Never trust a Randonnen map;
Only the Randonnen.

   —Ariyen saying

Gamon rode into the mountain town at a tired canter. He was hot and hungry, and his graying hair was as full of dust as the road. After four solid hours of riding since before dawn, his legs were numb as a well-stuffed poolah. Yet if the Randonnens had their way, he'd be back in the saddle by noon and heading on up the trail.

He lifted his war cap, ran his hand through his short-cropped hair, then settled the leather-and-metal mesh cap again while he waited for a fresh mount at the stables. Like most of the towns he'd seen in the last several ninans, this one was deceptively quiet. It had its main streets and workshops, its craft houses and inns, but the faces that gave him friendly nods now would shutter as soon as they heard his voice and placed him as Ariyen.

The stableboy returned, and Gamon accepted the reins of yet another dnu. He didn't mount immediately. Instead, he stumped over to the message wall to loosen the blood in his legs.

The wall was a slightly curved expanse of wood, steeply hooded against rain and snow. It boasted over two dozen carved or woven rings and sticks, along with ten or twelve sheets of weather-treated, text-oriented papers. Gamon studied the paper messages, then read the carved and painted lines on the sticks and braided rope. He nodded grimly to himself. "Moons-damned Randonnens," he muttered. The one he had sent was missing. But he realized that this time, it might have meant that it had been received, since he found the answer he looked for hidden behind a wide double-stick that was thick with feathers and lengths of knotted line.

Gamon's gray eyes narrowed as he took in the simple, bluntly carved stick of wood that hung behind the other, fancier stick. He would have recognized that concise style of carving anywhere. He had run trail for months with the man who had slashed in those symbols, and the brief, accurate cuts were as much a signature as if Rhom had signed in ink. "Worlag-pissing mountain men," he cursed softly, knowing that other Randonnens had hoped he would not see the answer stick, just as they had hoped Rhom would miss the question. But Gamon had seen the answer, and now he knew the smith was here. There were few places a man like that would be staying in a town this size. Gamon should find him within the hour, if not sooner. "About damn time," he growled. He studied the town map without pleasure, then swung painfully into the saddle and made his way down the streets to the smithy.

A woman nodded pleasantly as he passed, then noted his boots and the way he sat the dnu, as if he was used to double-horned saddles. She turned abruptly into one of the shops, but not before Gamon had seen her expression shutter. He kept his gaze steady. He understood the woman's feelings, and if he was honest with himself, there was a touch of shame in him that justified her expression. Ever since the wolf-walker had left Ariye, the Randonnens had reclaimed her for their own, blaming Ariye—not unrightly—for the grief she had carried with her. Gamon grimaced as he realized that even he referred to the wolfwalker as if Ember Dione were the only one who ran with the wolves. But she wasn't just one among many, he reminded himself. She had learned to reach beyond the wolves to manipulate the mental energy of the bond. Gamon was one of the few who knew just how powerful she was and just how vital she could be to any cause—if he could win her back over.

He heard the smithy before he saw it. The rush of the mechanical bellows was clear, as was the ring of metal on metal. An apprentice nodded at the older man as Gamon walked in, but continued monitoring the fire. Everything was mechanical, run by water or steam. The Ancients may have used electricity, but like Ariye and the other counties, Randonnen was limited to other systems aboveground. Gamon's lips tightened. It was another reason for the Randonnens to distrust him. The agreement between Ariye and the other counties to develop biotechnology was stretching thinner every year. It didn't help that there were now rumors of Ariyen advances that were not shared with the other counties. Losing both the wolfwalker's son and mate had strained things even more.

At the moment, the smithy was well lit. High ceilings of hewn stone and heavy wood made walls and arching windows. Tempered and insulated skylights brought in light from above, and the center of the building was also open as a working courtyard, although each forge area was shadowed. There were four medium forges and two smaller ones, along with six spot-pits for applying more specific heat. Only two of the forges were hot. Three of the larger duck nests were obviously designed for swords and long implements, while two more were small enough for hand tools and knives. One duck nest was square enough for wider implements. The last furnace was massive, cold and quiet, used for the rare, large job that required greater amounts of the metals that were so precious on this world. There was an anvil and slack tub, quench tank and grinder by every forge, and a short shelf on a central pillar that held burn cream and bandages as if to remind the smiths that metal did not have to look red to be hot. There were racks of tongs and crowned hammers, heavy gloves, leather aprons, leather overboots. Gamon catalogued all this at a glance—a quick-see skill that most weapons masters developed for recalling almost perfectly what they passed. It had been more than useful when he had ridden with Rhom before.

The man Gamon sought was standing with a small knot of other smiths around a long worktable. Behind them, the heavy wooden doors of the stock shelves were open, exposing the wall of steel bars of different sizes, lengths, and alloys. Killed steel, semikilled steel, capped steel, rimmed steel—Gamon's eyes widened in spite of himself, for the value of those alloys was greater than any four towns this size should have. He grinned sourly. The Randonnens had a saying: "The smith banks the wealth of the town." Randonnens hid their riches well. It was something Ariye should remember.

". . . nicely cased," Rhom was saying as he ran his hand over the flat part of the steel and eyed it carefully in the light. "Good finish. Took the edge well too."

One of the other men nodded. "Added more vanadium and used a one-one of tungsten."

Rhom nodded. One-one meant one-point-one percent. It was a lower percentage than in some of the other alloys, but that kept it from being too brittle. "Small crystals, tough blade," he murmured. He'd like a knife made out of this alloy himself.

One of the apprentices cleared his throat. "Crystals?"

Rhom glanced at the boy to his right, then returned his attention to the blade. "Forging isn't just about pounding out the right shape," he said absently. "It's about making the smallest, toughest, most durable crystalline structure you can. That means balancing your technique against the composition of the alloy. You can't see the crystals, even under a microscope, but the oldEarthers had better ways of seeing, and they refined this technique for over two thousand years. You'll see after using it a few years, just how well it was made." He spring-tested the blade and nodded to himself. "Air-hardened?"

One of the older smiths nodded. "Aye."

The apprentice said hesitantly, "I thought you couldn't tell by looking."

"No one could," Rhom answered patiently. "But what else would you do with this alloy? You made some other samples." It was a question, not a statement.

The other man picked up a slightly longer sword. "Used D-two on this one. Now that's a mean steel," the man said, tapping his finger along the blade. "You could throw rocks at this all ninan and nothing would happen. Not a dent, not a ding once it's hard."

Rhom hefted the blade. It was heavy but well balanced, made for a strong forearm and wrist. Probably took ten hours to sharpen, he thought as he put it down.

"That's a damn ugly steel, all right," the other man continued. "Could snick a worlag's head off without half trying, then cut up rocks all day. Now take this blade here. This is like an S-seven with a hair more manganese—" His voice broke off as he caught sight of Gamon.

Rhom glanced up at the suddenly uncomfortable silence. For a moment, he felt his lips stretch toward a smile as he saw his mate's uncle. Then, as with the woman on the street, his expression shuttered. There was only one reason that Gamon had followed him here.

Gamon nodded at the burly smith and said simply, "At your convenience."

Rhom regarded him for a long moment, then put down the blade. He ignored the open curiosity in the others' expressions. Instead, he merely nodded at them to continue and gestured for Gamon to lead the way from the smithy.

Rhom had changed little since Gamon had last seen him. Fairly tall, fairly burly, violet eyes, black hair. His skin had that same light tone that Dion's had, but hers was a creamy complexion, whereas Rhom had the rougher texture of too much exposure to hot and cold extremes. The smith's hands were a bit thicker than before, and Gamon wondered how much Rhom had been working the smithy versus working with the blade. Rhom used to be an effective swordsman, a better archer, and deceptively quick on his feet in a fight. He also used to smile when he saw Gamon, the uncle of the woman he had Promised.

Gamon ignored the smith until they reached the benches near one of the common squares. He had no intention of talking in a tavern, no matter how thirsty he was, not with a dozen ears to overhear. Until Gamon knew which way the wind blew with Rhom, they would be better off outside.

Gamon gave Rhom a searching look. "You got my message ring about Aranur's death." It was not quite a statement.

"Aye," the smith returned shortly. His violet eyes, so like those of his twin, were not friendly. "Over three months ago."

"And Shilia?" He asked after his niece.

"I sent her on to Ariye with the children. I stayed to wait for Dion."

Gamon snorted. "You didn't stay anywhere. I've been almost two ninans tracking you down in this part of the county alone."

Rhom raised one of his black eyebrows. "I wasn't exactly hiding."

"And I am not Randonnen."

In spite of his cold expression, the smith looked startled at the non sequitor.

"Ever since . . ." Gamon's voice broke off, and he shrugged. "Ever since Dion lost her son—"

"And her mate, and her wolf," Rhom interrupted flatly.

Gamon was silent for a moment. "She didn't lose her wolf. She made Hishn stay in Ariye so the wolf could rebond with Gray Yoshi. They wanted another litter come spring." His avoidance of the other point underscored his silent agreement. "If she wanted Hishn, the wolf would come back."

Rhom nodded, but it was to himself, as if to say that Gamon had just proven how much the Ariyen didn't understand. "Dion's too far north. Hishn would have to cross the desert or the mountains, and no wolf can do that, not on her own, no matter how strong their bond. So my sister is alone, and you left her to the trail with ghosts for company. She'll accept no one with her now. We can only wait for her to come home on her own once she faces down what's hurting."

There was accusation in Rhom's voice, and Gamon held his breath for a moment before answering. So this was the point of anger. Not the wolf, not that Dione was alone, but that Gamon had abandoned the wolfwalker when Rhom trusted him to stay with her. His voice was quiet. "She wanted to be alone, Rhom. Aye, she's like a wounded wolf, all anger and grief, wanting no one around her. But whether or not she knows it, she needs you, and I came to take you to her."

"Then you took your moonwormed time about it."

"I left my message with your neighbors," Gamon said more sharply than he intended. "I figured you'd be close behind me when I returned to Dion's trail but—" He shrugged, unable to hide his anger. "—there's a lot of blame attached to Ariyens these days. I don't think you ever got my message."

"I got it—day before yesterday, and in Siegen, ten kays down the road. I started north yesterday to meet you. I'm only here for a few hours."

Gamon nodded sourly. "And in the meantime, I've been running around in circles trying to track you down. It started the moment I sent off that message. I should have known that every ring-runner between here and oldEarth would read it and pass the word, and they sure didn't waste any time starting in on their moons-damned games. Right off the bat, I was stonewalled in Legge for two days when they told me she hadn't ridden on, but was making the outer rounds as a healer. She had passed Press Point by a ninan by the time I figured out her trail. The elders in Graft were no better."

Rhom raised his dark eyebrows.

"You didn't know? They sent me to the other end of the county. Then I was directed to Bone Trail out of Chester, and was halfway up Banshee Ridge before I realized that I'd missed the turnoff to Sheets."

Rhom's lips twitched. From the date of the message stick he had received, and from the way the worn stick had been passed on to him, he had suspected something like this. "And in Sheets?" he asked mildly.

"They don't call it Three Sheets to the Wind for nothing. I picked up a map from a ring-runner—another Randonnen rast who gave me some rag with just enough accuracy that, with all those ridge folds, I was off by seventeen kays by the end of the second day. Finally found myself on Walkin' River with two more nights wasted before I could backtrack to town. I had some hard words for the elders when I finally caught up to them."

"I'm sure they apologized."

Gamon didn't miss the Randonnen's amusement. "Oh, they apologized, all right—and sent me out on another road where the clove bushes were so thick I cried for a day and a half before the acid from the thrice-damned warning puffs washed fully out of my eyes. By that time, Dion's trail was cold as a lepa's heart, and I could have died of old age before I found her. I figured my best bet was to find you so you could do the directing." Gamon shot him a hard look. "That was no easier, Rhom. They sent me up Three Minute River, then halfway across Flatnose Trail where it's so steep you could sleep comfortably standing up. Twice they put me onto Concentric Road before I figured it out. Moonworms, but they even tried to get me to ride the Oracle—claimed it was the fastest route to the sea."

The skin around Rhom's eyes crinkled. That was a Randonnen way of saying the route was the fastest way to your goal. The Oracle River was indeed the fastest route to the sea, but it was also deadly with steep waterfalls and rocks that would tear the bottom out of any kayak that hit the standing waves wrong. Gamon might have made it downriver—about half those who dared it did, after all—but it would have been a long, white-water route without climb-out banks, and it would have taken the Ariyen weapons master two ninans to return from its endpoint. "And did you ride the Oracle?" Rhom asked, curious in spite of himself.

"Worlag piss, of course not. I took one look at that water and backed away with my knife in my hands. Damn good thing I did. I practically had to draw sword when they tried to force me near the kayaks on the way to Tiltin' Tavern."

Rhom barked a laugh, then slowly sobered. "They were just trying to protect Dion."

"Like you?"

Rhom regarded the older man for a long, silent moment. When he spoke, his voice was quiet. "I knew you before, Gamon, but that was many years ago. What are you now?"

Gamon's voice was tight with irony. "Ariyen, Rhom, as I've always been."

"And now?"

"And now, I ride to find her again."

"To make it right, or to take her back to Ariye?"

Gamon hesitated.

Rhom forced his hands to remain unclenched. He was not the round-bellied, good-humored blacksmith of town tales. He was a woodsman and mountain climber, a fighter who had followed his father into smithing because he loved the feel of steel in his hands, a man who had seen his share of violence, who had seen his twin weather the same. His sister was as much a part of him as his arms were part of his body. His instinct to protect her, even at a distance, was as strong as a pack of wolves.

"And if I said it was to bring her back to Ariye?"

"Then I would say, you'll need the luck of all nine moons."

Gamon's jaw tightened as he withheld his anger. "I'd have that luck if you'd ride with me."

"Why should I?"

"Because danger lurks around your twin like a badgerbear. It calls, and she answers eagerly, like a dying wolf trying for one more bite at the world that savaged her."

Rhom's eyes flickered, but his voice was steady. "She's a wolfwalker. The wilderness is her home. She cannot avoid its dangers."

"Then ride with me because we need her."

"Ariye has other wolfwalkers."

"Not as many as are here in Randonnen, and none that are Ember Dione." Gamon tried a different tack. "She's lost, Rhom. She needs saving."

"And you didn't leave much of her to save."

The edge in Gamon's voice sharpened. "We're not the enemy, Rhom. And if we don't find your sister soon, we could lose her. Not to herself, but to the wolves." He nodded at Rhom's frown. "She's running with the wild ones like a pack leader, not like the human scout she should be. She's ignoring the message rings, moving from town to town like a cozar, staying out of reach of the elders."

Rhom opened his mouth to retort, but Gamon cut him off with a small gesture. It was a simple movement, but it had all the years of Gamon's calm command behind it, and Rhom subsided warily.

"And I'm not the only one tracking her, Rhom. There will be others on her trail, others who need or want her skills, others who won't be so gentle. At least I'll give her a choice."

At that, Rhom's own anger flared. "She had no choice the moment she mated with Aranur."

"And Aranur is dead."

"Aye." The word held a wealth of meaning.

Gamon looked at the younger man with a steady gray gaze. His voice was quiet. "When we find her, look at her eyes, Rhom. She's too far into the gray. She'll not return to you or me, not to her home, not to the sons she left behind. Bring her back now, or give her up to the wolves. She will run no other trail."

Gamon waited, and Rhom scuffed absently at the dust under his boot. Years ago, he had led his twin out of Randonnen and into Ariyen danger. Now it was she who pulled him from their home. He could almost feel the hard hands of the world gathering in the shadows, feel steel stretching down from the peaks. Those blades reached for Ember Dione, and the wolfwalker was his sister. If the threat he sensed was only an echo of what Dion felt through the wolves, what did it portend for her?

He stood and gazed at the older man. His voice was flat. "I will ride."

IV

Talon Drovic neVolen

To hell and farther into the fires
Toward truth and all its pain

—from The Lost Ring,
  by Aranur Bentar neDannon

Talon's bones were cold. He clenched the reins more tightly as he led his riders at a distance-eating canter. Even beneath the pintrees where the morning heat grew quickly oppressive, he couldn't ignore his shivers. He leaned low under a branch as his dnu scrambled across a dry ditch, and winced at the lurch and jar. Char was caught under his nails, and dried blood crusted in his knuckles. The pain in his head was now a hammer that struck with every hoofbeat. Behind him someone cursed, and a woman—Oroan, he thought— laughed harshly. None of the villagers had charged in pursuit. In the gloom, he did not blame them.

They left a trail that a blind man could have followed at a dead run. It didn't matter. By the time the fires back in the village were fully controlled and the townsmen could form a venge to hunt the raiders down, Talon's men would be out on the eastern road. By that time, the initial fury would have passed. Reality and fear would rule, and the townsmen would have to consider what they could lose if they followed the raiders too closely.

Kilaltian's dozen had joined Talon's riders an hour out of the raid. Neither group spoke or slowed as they merged. Talon simply motioned for Kilaltian to fall in behind them. Harare's riders moved up and left the rear guard to the fresher men. Now they rode as one group, one long arm of violence.

Talon's father had stayed with Darity's group, keeping the escape route clear ahead and holding the gear they would need as they ran. With Darity's group, the band would be over forty strong, and few villages harbored enough fighting skill to challenge them as a whole. That was no boast. Talon, Kilaltian, Rakdi, Sojourn, and Drovic were graded at various weapons master levels—although Talon was still healing and had yet to regain his full strength. As for the others, they were an effectively motley lot. Some had actually been soldiers in the rare Bilocctar army; most were more like oldEarth mercenaries. About half were young and fairly new to raiding. Others, like Mal and Rakdi, were older. For a competition archer, Mal couldn't shoot worth beans under pressure, but the dour man was remarkable with a sword or staff. Wakje was coldly skilled with any weapon. Ilandin was mousy and unobtrusive until a fight, where she turned nasty as a five-clawed lepa. All were competent except Weed, who didn't seem proficient enough with any weapon to have survived as long as he had; and Dangyon, who often relied more on size than skill. Most of these riders didn't have the finesse of decades in the fighting rings, but Talon had decided long ago that that wasn't a disadvantage. Wooden swords and rubber knives were no substitute for steel, and these raiders had spent enough time killing with brutal efficiency that finesse would have been silk on a worlag. He ducked a branch and guided his dnu around a clump of stinkweed. By the time the message towers started tracking his riders, they would be past the nearest settlements. Unless they ran straight into a venge, they should be clear by the end of the day and could start working north again. He looked left, then back, then called sharply to Dangyon, "Where's Jervid?"

"Holdin' shoulder on Mal." The barrel-chested man had a heavy accent, marking him as yet another man from the northwestern counties. With few exceptions, almost all of Drovic's current band were from the western lands. Two were even from the rare territories that had opened outside the counties. Only Talon and Drovic were from Ariye, Jervid from Eilif, and Harare, with that distinctive blond hair, from one of the eastern counties on the other side of the desert.

Talon looked again and made out Mal and Jervid. Mal was stuffing a bloody cloth up under his warcap as he rode, and Talon's lips tightened. Holding shoulder should not have been necessary. Mal's wound and those of the others should have been minor, except that they had gone in from the south where the martial ring was located. If Jervid had not roused the fighters at that end, the raid could have been a cakewalk. A dash in through the fields, the shock to the north end, the fires to distract, a quick, directed search and grab for the rumored bioforms, and then the retreat back into the gloom, circling the village fighters who would run directly toward the attack. But it had turned into a battle, and now three of his men were dead as the moons, while Mal and six others were wounded.

Through the brush, he glimpsed the shadowed eastern road and didn't bother to slow. Kilaltian shouted at him to wait to check the expanse, but he burst out on the rootroad without pause. There was no danger. He felt that with a certainty that would have unnerved him before. It was the Gray Ones who gave him that confidence, and in spite of his wariness, he threw a shaft of mental gratitude toward the gray beasts who had watched the rootroad for him. They would help him, aye, as long as he headed north or east. The wolves howled at the edge of his mind, then raced away. Talon led his group on.

And threw up his fist to halt his riders abruptly. From their full canter, they came to a ragged stop. "What is it?" Kilaltian called sharply.

Talon was already off his dnu. "Wait," he ordered over his shoulder.

Kilaltian's eyes narrowed, but he gestured for his group to obey.

Talon's nostrils flared with the hint of a sweetness the wolves had smelled barely a moment before. The gray ones might be trying to force him north for their own goals, but at least their nearness was useful. He pushed his way through the bushes, closed his eyes, and tested the air. The grass was still springing up from the back-kick of gray paws. Left— they had smelled the scent to the left.

He shoved through the light brush till he saw the woody shrubs. The chopper pods were still tightly closed—with the shadows from the hills and the thick tree trunks, the sun had not yet touched them. Years ago, one of his uncles had hung a strand of young pods on Talon's saddle. In the dim barn light, among the pea strings he had carried for food, he had not noticed the pods. But when he had ridden out into the sun, they had exploded like tiny darts. That had been followed by two hells of a long ninan spent picking them out of his skin. It had been a sharp lesson, as it had been intended, to be aware of everything, especially what he would take for granted.

But that had been early spring, and those chopper pods had been young. This was the end of summer. These cream-colored pods—he snapped them off carefully and placed each one gently in his war cap—were neither young nor soft. Tightly closed by night, they loosened their wings at the touch of direct sunlight, and when loosened, a simple vibration would launch them. These pods would cut through a man like starving knives to bury their seeds in flesh.

Talon hurried back to the road. The raiders waited impatiently.

"Chopper pods," he answered Kilaltian's unspoken question. "Take my dnu," he ordered Sojourn. "Move ahead."

Fit grinned as he saw the seeds, but Kilaltian gave Talon a sharp look. "How did you know they were there?" the man asked.

"They've been growing along this stretch of road for years," Talon said truthfully. He knew they would think he had regained more of his memory than expected, but better that lie than explaining the wolves. "Move on," he repeated. He opened his warcap to expose the pods, knowing that even Kilaltian wouldn't argue with the ripe pods in his hands.

The other man shot him a dark look, but rode ahead. Sojourn stayed behind as Talon set the pods out across the road. Talon ignored the bead of sweat that slipped down his temple as he placed the sensitive pods in the shafts of shade. Against the pale root planks, the dusty pods could go unnoticed by anyone traveling at a canter until they were practically on top of the seeds. A moment later, and Talon mounted his dnu, spurring it to a gallop to catch up to the other riders. Sojourn was no less eager than he to leave. A few beams from that sun, and the pods would have flown at them like wasps.

They met up with Darity's dozen near noon. Drovic gave Talon a sharp look as the overall count came up short. Neither man said anything over the thunder of the hooves. They circled a small settlement without worrying about noise, and ignored the calls that first were greetings, and then alarms. Finally, they reached the caravan meadow. It was a wide space, cleared for over a hundred wagons and used for county fairs. The short, sturdy grass that covered it was one of oldEarth's toughest strains, and it grew thickly in spite of the beating it took from the dnu and men and wagons.

"How much time?" Talon asked shortly.

"We'll take ten minutes." Drovic gestured sharply as the rest of the raiders came to a halt. They hardly needed the direction. As usual, they began unlashing their bundles and dropping them to the ground. "Sort there," Kilaltian directed curtly. "Pack there."

Talon slid from his saddle with forced smoothness. He had been prepared for the weakness in his leg where Biekin had struck him, but a spasm also caught his shoulder where the muscles were still healing. He had to hide his irritation as his father's eyes glinted. As usual, Drovic had noted the flinch before Talon could suppress it.

Four raiders quickly sorted the goods into piles. Another foursome packed the loot into saddlebags and panniers. Nortun moved quietly among the wounded, producing bandages and salves, and like a packrat, tucking objects into others' packs. Talon joined the group at the well basin. A quick scrub took most of the soot from his face and rinsed the blood from his flesh, if not from under his fingernails. The smells that clung to his jerkin were rancid. Quickly he shrugged into cleaner, more deceptively stylish clothes. The others did the same. The pattern was well rehearsed. By the time they left the clearing, they would look more like a venge on its way to action, not like raiders riding away.

Talon pursed his lips as he gave a quick once-over to his own riders: Cheyko, Harare, Oroan, Weed ... Ki had a bloody cloth around his upper arm as he sorted the last of the goods, but that bandage would be hidden under his tunic when he finished dressing. Mal, his long face tight, was no longer bleeding from his forehead, but the saturnine man rubbed at his temples often enough that Talon thought their headaches matched. Roc sported an impressive welt along one pale cheekbone. Her honey-brown braid was spattered with mud, her usual calm was absent, and she was jittery as a watercat. Her hands shook as she slicked down and rebraided her hair. Dangyon, unmistakable with his barrel chest, was resetting his saddle after treating a slash on his dnu's flank. Sojourn, who had come out without a scratch, smelled of smoke and fire. Biekin, of course, was dead.

Drovic barely nodded as his son joined him again. "Report."

Talon felt his lips tighten before he spoke. He tried to ignore the wolves near his mind. Their call to hunt that shadow woman had become distracting, blurring his vision with images of violet eyes. He could almost feel the gentle hands that had roamed his fevered body in his dreams and made him hard with desire. His urge to find and protect that woman was becoming as pointed as a starving man's hunger—a gray geas strong enough that Talon had begun to make mistakes. Four ninans ago, he had actually mentioned the wolves to his fa-

ther, and Drovic had struck him with a fist like a club and left
him lying in the dust. Enraged, Talon had leaped to his feet,
then had almost fainted from the blinding pain that had
lanced back through his head. Drovic had merely watched,
waiting like a badgerbear should Talon stagger back to his
feet. Now the wolves snarled in his head as if he should challenge his father's arrogance. But he had to heal, had to give
himself time. Had to regain his strength before he could
strike out again on his own to follow his goals or theirs. His
fist clenched on his blade, and his edge of anger grew icy as
he felt the hilt of that sword. He hated that blade for its light-
ness, but his wrist was still not strong enough for the length
of steel he craved. Before the fever, he had healed quickly,
sometimes with lightning speed. He was not used to being
weak or slow—*crippled,* he thought the word harshly—and it
grated on his nerves as much as on his father's. He was crippled now as Ki could have been because of Jervid's error.
"Three dead, six wounded," he returned tersely. "Two targets
were searched, but only cursorily. No access found."

Drovic's blue-gray gaze was sharp. "Yourself?"

"Scraped. Bruised. A little smoked from the fire."

Drovic turned to the other raiders. "Merek, Slu—start the
fire for the discards in the waste pit. Ebi, take care of the
spoor." He didn't bother to address the second command to
Strapel too; the two men always worked together. Drovic
gave the rest of the orders to everyone. "We'll follow East
Road to Welin Fork, then cross to the Cades River." Drovic
caught Talon's frown as he chose one of the contingency
routes, rather than the main one. Drovic lowered his voice.
"Jervid knows the roads between here and the Cades. If you
have doubts, now is the time to speak."

Talon shook his head shortly. "The route should be sound.
I studied the maps as you have. And by nightfall, we'll be on
ground more familiar to me, at least as much as I remember.
It is Jervid, not the route, whom I doubt."

"Jervid grew up in this county."

"Aye." Talon's gray eyes grew icy. "And he may lead the
way with Kilaltian or you or by himself if he wishes. He will
no longer ride with me."

Drovic's gaze sharpened. "He is assigned to you."

"Not anymore."

"We ride in teams, Talon, and those teams are our lives. We don't make changes on whims."

"This is no whim."

"No? We're riding from a raid, with at least one venge on our tail. We have wounded to carry and an unfamiliar county where we have few contacts to help if we screw up. But you want to change the teams now. Why?"

Talon did not mistake the mildness of Drovic's tone, and his own gray eyes narrowed. "My reasons are my own, and they stand," he said curtly.

"Not unless I know them," Drovic returned. And I will take no rebellion from you, he seemed to snarl silently.

For all that they were unspoken, Drovic's words could have been snapped through the air. Talon felt a muscle jump in his jaw. Drovic's expression was hard, almost untrusting, and Talon felt it like a blade. All these years, and all the blood and death they had shared, and it still came down to this: the differences between them. He had oathed to Drovic years ago—the day he had turned eleven—yet he could not seem to keep from challenging the older man. He had not acted as a leader for months, not since his injuries, but it felt right, he acknowledged, right to stand firm, to assert his own judgment, and he knew he had done this so often before that it was as expected as the drawing of steel, regardless of his oath. A few ninans to get out from under this constant medicine, a few more to get enough of his memory back to know where he wanted to go, and then they would settle this leadership. A son could not follow his father forever, no matter how much he owed the man. There were other things to hunt. Talon had made his own promises to the moons, and weakness and wounds aside, he would be no man's shadow.

His words were soft. "If you do not trust my judgment, Father, then do not let me lead."

Drovic's gaze did not waver. "Are you challenging me?"

"If you like."

They were words Talon had spoken long before, when he was just a boy. Back then, Drovic had laughed at his son's angry face, then had thrown him to the ground. Every year, it had been the same: a contest for Talon to earn the sword that his father held in trust. He had taken up that sword almost three decades ago, but he did not carry it now. Instead, he wore a thinner, lighter, bloodier blade, and the words of challenge leaped to his lips almost instinctively.

Drovic regarded his son in silence while the other raiders worked quickly around them. Talon's weight was balanced perfectly, with the grace of decades of fighting. His muscles appeared relaxed, but that was deception. It was a perfect calm, the poise of action that waited for breath. It was a balance that Drovic had begun to teach him when he was just a child, but that Talon had developed on his own, and that he now wielded as a weapon. Something bleak flickered in the older man's eyes, and Talon felt a stab that might have been his injuries, or that might have been his guilt, but he did not back down. Instead, his own steel-gray gaze remained steady, and it was Drovic who finally gave in.

"Your judgment is my own." The older man's lips twisted. "I could have hoped for nothing more."

Something changed between the two men. It was like taking a step, Talon recognized. Like the day his father gave him his first fighting stick, or the first time he faced a worlag. Each event was a shift toward becoming the man his father had raised him to be—or a step toward becoming his father. Other faces—uncles, aunts, siblings, his mate—had softened Drovic's pattern, but Talon was the mirror cast in the mercury of time.

Talon's voice was soft. "You see yourself in me."

"I always have."

"And Jervid?"

"He will no longer ride with you."

Talon nodded, satisfied. Only then did he explain. "Jervid split from us, rousing the town at one end as we came in on the other. I had to divide the attack so that the southern route was kept open for our retreat. We lost most of the element of surprise. Morley and Eilryn and Biekin died, and our escape was jeopardized. We were unable to get to two target buildings, and our search of the other two was cut short." He lifted his war cap absently and ran his hand through his hair. He did not mention the trapdoor he had felt in the villager's storeroom. "We lost men and opportunity, and neither can be replaced."

Drovic regarded him for a moment. Absently, Drovic noted the movements of the other raiders around them. The last of the panniers were being lashed onto the dnu. Ebi and Strapel had already swept most of the hardened ground with small brooms. The brooms wouldn't hide the fact that riders had been there, but they would do much to hide the number of riders who had passed, and that was valuable. Drovic's gaze flickered as a flock of tree sprits flittered from one side of the caravan space to the other, but they flew without urgency. His voice was deceptively mild. "Was your plan flawed? Did Jervid see a better way in?"

Talon's voice was hard. "The man, not the plan, was flawed."

"A leader does not accuse his men."

"Nor does he accept such stupidity."

"Stupidity?"

"You prefer 'arrogance'? He disobeyed an order, thought his own judgment better than mine. He broke the plan, roused the martial end of town early, and gave them minutes to prepare to meet us. When will he do it again? And are you willing to pay with your own life for the next mistake he makes? I cannot trust him to follow me."

Drovic barked a laugh that drew the eyes of Kilaltian. Drovic lowered his voice. "He's a raider, Son. You cannot trust him at all."

"Aye," Talon agreed softly, and knew he included himself in that statement, and hated himself all the more. "But still, I will not lead him."

"You are not strong enough to hold the command I gave you?"

It was not quite a question, and Talon regarded his father steadily, but the subtle flicker in his cold, gray eyes did not deceive the older man. There was anger behind that icy gaze, and Drovic filed that note away as Talon answered softly.

"You cannot give me their loyalty as you gave me the authority to lead them. You know that as well as I. Leadership is not merely a matter of presence. One earns obedience and respect. One doesn't just expect it."

Drovic's expression hardened. "I can expect it."

"Then you have blinded yourself, and that blindness sits poorly upon you." Talon's tone was sharp.

Drovic stared at his son for a hundred years as the mirror flexed and cracked. The same wind lifted both Drovic's hair and Talon's, brushed their chapped skin, left a sense of chill. Silver or steel, Talon thought. Either one could buy the blood that would eventually be spilled. Someone made a joke behind them as the men and women began remounting, and someone else chuckled. Drovic's voice was hard when he finally spoke again. "You fail your attack, you challenge me, then accuse me of being blind?"

"In this, yes."

"And still, you choose to lead?"

"All but Jervid."

Drovic's glance flickered to the slim man. "Consider carefully, Talon. Most of our men are new, and they're still coming up to speed on our goals even as they learn these roads. Jervid has been with me for years, and he knows these trails, even if it was as a child. Fit knows only the northern part of Eilif, and I've traveled these Eilian roads myself only three times in the last forty years. Your knowledge starts at the border routes, not the backtrails of the main county." He stopped Talon's interruption. "Oh, you've ridden through, right enough, but that was years ago and mostly on the borders. The land changes over time. And you've been weak in more than your wrist."

Talon's eyes narrowed at the reminder that his memory had also failed his father after his injuries. It was no salve to his pride that it was common with so much blood loss. Instead, it was a thorn in his boot, pricking him constantly with the realization that he didn't even know what sort of things he had forgotten. The physical memories were still in his hands—the way to work a knife, soap a saddle, weave a screen of camo.

But he couldn't even tell if he knew how to do those things until he tried and his body took over. "I'll remember enough," he said finally. "You can hire some other man till then."

Drovic snorted. "And trust a stranger on the spur? Not unless you want to end up with your head on an Ariyen chopping block."

Talon's voice was flat and uncompromising. "Then let this one go. He is killing us in the raids."

Drovic studied him for a long moment. When he spoke, his face was expressionless, and his eyes distant. "So be it."

His father turned away, and Talon breathed but did not feel his gut relax. There was a violence in Drovic that turned his blood cold, colder than the chill that seemed part of his very bones. Talon's own violence echoed his father's. It was a drive they shared, a drive so focused it could negate any others who rode with them, and he knew he had used his own family the same way that Drovic had used him in the past.

Drovic strode toward Jervid. The other raider was finishing with his saddlebag, and he half turned as Drovic approached. Drovic gestured with his left hand. Jervid's gaze followed the motion instinctively, and Drovic's right hand slid his long knife neatly out of its sheath and up under Jervid's ribs. Jervid, with clothes in one hand and straps in the other, was trapped between Drovic and the dnu. He caught only a glimpse of steel before the point slipped up through his gut. He stared at Drovic in disbelief as he hung on the end of Drovic's blade. His mouth worked soundlessly.

Talon felt his breath choke off. Felt the violence freeze in his blood. Felt a hand grip his arm and realized only then that Sojourn was beside him. As if that contact called the wolves to his mind, a howling rose in a din. In the sudden, dead calm of the caravan clearing, Sojourn's words were like slate. "Do not interfere."

Jervid, like Talon—like the others—did not move. The raider simply hung, sagging against the dnu, his hands instinctively grasping Drovic's, so that it looked as though he had helped stab himself. Then Drovic's knife twisted, and Jervid gasped and made a choked and wretched sound. The dnu stamped their feet and shifted uneasily. Then the raider folded over and followed his blood to the ground. Summer dust soaked up both the drumming and the blood, and the rest of the riders watched.

Talon barely noticed Sojourn's hand still gripping his arm. In his own mind, he saw again and again Drovic's blade sliding out and in. Some part of him noted the casual strike that spoke as much of instinct as it did of martial-learned patterns. Drovic's movements were smooth, with more decades of skill than Talon had lived, and he noted the steady hand of his father, the flat expression in Drovic's eyes, the curious streaks of blood on steel, and knew in his gut that he could not yet take his father.

The howling gathered. Cold steel seemed to slide into his own side, and even though he knew it was memory, not real, it shocked him. He heard Drovic shouting, heard himself cry out in those echoes. He did not know that he tried to leap forward as Drovic stepped back, until Sojourn's voice cut through the images. "Stay out of it," the other man hissed. Sojourn's hand was a vise.

Wolfwalker! The voice was in his head. *Wolfwalker- wolfwalkerwolfwalker* . . . But it was he who cried out, as if he could draw strength from the wolves. His nostrils flared with the scent of blood and bile.

Drovic knelt and wiped his steel on Jervid's clothes. When he rose, the others went about their tasks, readying for the ride.

Drovic walked back to Talon. For a moment, the older man studied his son. His voice was calm as he said, "You will not lead him; he will not be led. He has no place in our goals."

Talon did not trust himself to speak.

Drovic's voice was almost gentle. "This, too, was your decision."

V

Ember Dione maMarin

Are there ghosts in your head?
If there are, then they are part of you.

   —*From* Wrestling the Moons

In the snow, Dion gasped.

Wolfwalkerwolfwalkerwolfwalker . . .

The gray echo was a lance into her mind. Blindly, she half raised her hand toward her temple. It was a mistake. The glacier worm swayed toward the movement. Dion froze, perched on her showshoes like lunch on display. Around her, the snow glittered brilliantly, and the sun glistened on the back of the worm. It should have been beautiful. It had been, until she had moved. She had been safe until she had shifted; the worm would have snaked on. Now it knew she was close, and all it had to do was stretch a little to the left . . .

Dion's knuckles were white on the alpine vellace. The fresh sap was already hardening on the cuts, and the yellow liquid glinted dully. Her belt knife was in her other hand— sharp, lethal, and useless. Silently, she cursed the echo that had broken her stance, and she tried to breathe without moving.

Six meters hung between her and the glacier worm. That distance now seemed like a hand's width. Back, forth, with wickedly sharp teeth, the glacier worm sought her breath. Its round maw opened in an iris pattern and sphinctered shut again as it worked its sensory organs. Inside, exposed by the movement, the curved, opalescent teeth were seated in neat, concentric rows like soldiers surrounding a tomb.

It wasn't a large worm, she told herself. It was only a few

years old, only a few meters long—four, maybe five. Only a baby worm. But the shortest teeth were as long as her little finger, and all of the teeth were like razors.

The wind cut her face, and she let her breath out in its wake and sucked in air for her starved lungs. The worm stiffened, undulated, and edged a little closer. Baby worm, Dion repeated, forcing her arms to remain where they were instead of protecting her belly.

Wolfwalker! This time, the lance of gray was pure wolf, without the taint of that distant human voice.

Unconsciously she sucked at their strength. Her hand clenched her knife more tightly, her legs tensed to leap away. The wolves were kays behind her group, hunting snowhare, but as they read her sudden fear, they broke off and sprinted toward her. Kiyun was five worms' lengths to the right. Tehena had been setting their noon camp a hundred meters away. The shallow snow that covered the rocks and the long-stalked vellace had been a dangerous lie. There was a deep cut in the mountainside, and the worm had been waiting within it.

The worm writhed, and its body seemed to suck back into the snowbank. Then it surged out again and hung in the air, its head shifting back and forth. Fear settled in Dion's belly, snugged down with her unborn child. Adrenaline took the place of her blood. Left, and its tiny eyes pinholed with the light. Right, and it hesitated. Close, closer . . .

Some hint of breath caught its attention, and Dion, frozen, stiffened more. The snow almost creaked beneath her woven shoes. Her knife became her claw. Her mind filled with a chaotic burst of gray as she reached for the speed she would need. Abruptly, hooves smashed through snow to the right.

"Here!" Tehena shouted.

The worm whipped its head around.

Dion forced the wolves out of her mind and tensed to throw herself back.

"Here!" Tehena screamed at the worm.

Graysong howled.

The skinny woman charged bareback across the drift. The dnu's hooves flung back powdered divits till it plunged into deeper drifts. Its sudden halt left it floundering in fear. Tehena kicked its barrel belly viciously and almost unseated herself, but the dnu bucked out of the drift. The worm instantly sucked its length back into its hole with palpable eagerness.

Dion poised on the snowshoes. She couldn't move fast, she was still too close, and her baby—

Tehena forced the dnu closer. Kiyun grabbed the hilt of his sword as she closed, and the worm snapped its head back around. The dnu hit a deeper pocket in the snow and reared up, knee-deep in the drifts. The worm tensed like a spring. Its tiny, piggy eyes flicked to the dnu, but returned to the closer meal of the man. Kiyun braced himself to leap sideways, as if that would somehow save him. Then Tehena passed like a tornado as the dnu scrambled onto shallow snow. Too close—the woman was too close to the worm. But Dion was still in the glacier worm's range. The worm's eyes sharpened. It shot out like light. Teeth closed. Tehena screamed and flung herself from the dnu as teeth bit down on flesh where her leg had been.

The dnu shrieked. Its gut burst in the mouth of the worm like an overripe melon. Dion cried out as a foreleg caught her shoulder. She dodged back desperately in a wide-legged scramble. Without snowshoes, Tehena floundered in the drifts. The worm shook the dnu until it gurgled and went limp with one hind leg sticking up like a flagpole. It began dragging the creature back. The dnu was too large for the baby worm, and the worm writhed as it wrenched the weight along. Kiyun stepped carefully back, but light flashed from his blade, and the worm paused.

Dion and Tehena and Kiyun froze again. The worm undulated in place, uncertain. Then it clamped down harder on the slipping dnu. It finally withdrew into its now overlarge hole with a long writhing motion, leaving a red-stained ditch in the snow.

For a long moment, the three held their breath. Then Dion raised one foot and stepped carefully away from the hunting hole. Tehena's pale eyes were hard and dangerous, but her skinny body shook with adrenaline and fear. Kiyun's pulse beat in his neck like a sledge. Dion took another step, saw no movement, and motioned with her knife hand. She cleared the way for Tehena, who forced her way through the slightly packed tracks. Carefully, they eased back. Kiyun brought up the rear.

When they reached the road, they stood for a long moment to catch their breath. Dion bent to release her snowshoes, and Kiyun broke the silence. "Moons. That was . . ." He shook his head.

"Enlivening," Dion said wryly.

They stared at her.

She grinned ferally. The Gray Ones still vibrated in her mind, and she knew they were still running toward her. The sense of a man behind them, of his need to protect her, was strong, and she realized that the wolves' desire to keep her alive was tainting other links. Deliberately, she projected the kill. The satisfaction in the wolves was clear.

Tehena cleared her throat. "I thought you always knew where the danger was." She wiped the half-freezing sweat from her hands on her trousers.

Dion fitted and lashed the shoes together, then slung them over her shoulder. "The worm wouldn't have been a danger if I hadn't moved, and I don't know what the wolves don't send, unless my own eyes see it first."

Tehena and Kiyun exchanged a glance. They were one day out of the last town, and two days from the next. It was discomfiting to remember that, heightened as the wolfwalker's senses had become, Dion had no better way to see the unseen dangers near the road than their own ears and eyes. "Would have been nice to know that before you wandered off in the hunting ground of the worms," Tehena muttered.

Dion's voice was quiet. "Vellace only grows at this altitude, only in the snow, and can only be harvested this time of year. A couple grams of this will pay for our next night's lodging."

"We have a tent," Tehena retorted as they reached their gear.

Dion shrugged. "Even I like a few nights in a real bed."

The skinny woman snorted.

"We'll have to move now to cook." Kiyun picked up the small packstove to stow it. "There's rockier ground down the road."

Dion tossed her snowshoes beside her pack and worked quickly to resaddle the dnu. She was as uneasy as the others, but it was not the thought of other glacier worms that made her pause and glance often at the jagged horizon. It was the echo that had wracked her concentration, the voice of the dead in her mind. The Gray Ones had passed memories to her before, but usually only when a wolfwalker asked. For them to push other voices . . .

The wolves continued to prowl at the edges of her mind as they closed the distance more slowly. They loped now, instead of sprinting, but their need for reassurance was clear. Their awareness of her was a separate harmony beneath the mental chorus. In the packsong, the sense of herself was a doubled image: hers and theirs. As they came close, they echoed her scent, the sound of her breathing, the timbre of her voice, the cloud of her steaming breath, her lean strength, her will, her hopes and fears . . . Their sense of the wolf-walker was a picture of their perceptions, not simply an image of her physical body. It was a sense that sometimes caused confusion among the wolfwalkers who read those images. The image of a small man with great inner strength could be clear and bright, larger in the wolves' packsong than in their vision. At the same time, the image of a muscular man could be weak and withered as the will that had died within him. Dion cocked her head with a sudden thought. With all the hunters who were using the wolves as one more way to find her, it would be a useful skill to learn to project a false self-image. Something to think about in the coming winter, when almost everyone was home-bound. She had been hunted too long, had seen the determination in too many raider faces to toss off the thought once it occurred. She pictured the face of the man who had killed her mate—heavy brows, squared jaw, peppered hair. His will to capture and mold her to his use had been as inexorable as the tide, and just as deadly. And the tone of the hunter she had just heard in the packsong was as fierce as any raider. She shook her head as she hooked the last pannier on the dnu. Whoever that hunter had been, he'd had no true bond with the wolves. The contact between them had been made by the Gray Ones, not by him, and what she'd heard had been barely human-colored by her memories.

She set her gloves beside the short stone wall that lined the road and let herself gaze south with the wolves. The walls had been shaped by stoneworms or hand-hewn and fitted into a mosaic of glittering beauty. It was an icy painting that pulled as much as the wolves, and she judged the curves she saw against her mental map of the county. She smiled grimly. The Ariyens would have a difficult time getting her to stand still after so much time on the road.

Tehena, about to mount her dnu, caught Dion's slightly unfocused gaze. The lanky woman said nothing, allowing Dion to listen. Tehena's own mind became blank, simply waiting. For years, she had followed Dion like a shadow, snarling at those who would threaten the wolfwalker, stepping between Dion and those who might attack. She owed Dion her life a dozen times over, though Dion would never admit it. At this point, Tehena's life had wrapped so far around the wolfwalker that she didn't know where she herself began. It was not disconcerting. It gave the woman comfort to know that her purpose was clear, and that Dion was that purpose. So Dion waited, and Tehena waited with her. Dion was silent, so Tehena also listened.

Dion looked south again, toward Ariye and Eilif, but aside from the wind, the cliff was still as a headstone. She could see nothing, hear nothing out of place, but the sense of that hunter was clear. Finally, she shrugged, tightened her dnu's cinch, put on her gloves again, and mounted her dnu.

Tehena and Kiyun followed suit. As usual, Tehena muttered so that Kiyun would think she was irritated by the wait. "Another five minutes, and you'd have had to chip me free from the ice." She kicked her dnu into a trot.

Kiyun grunted and urged his own riding beast after Tehena. The thin woman didn't fool him. He had followed the wolfwalker as long as Tehena had. The skinny woman might nag up one side and down the other, but she would never leave Dion's side.

As they rode, Kiyun watched Dion protectively. She had moved well when the worm attacked, faster than he had hoped. He should have expected it; after all, wolfwalkers healed quickly, but he could swear that the old scars had softened more than they should. By the time they reached Ariye, the marks would look more like decade-old scratches, not six-month lepa-clawed gouges. He wondered how much energy she was using to heal herself, and how much she kept back for the babe. It had to be substantial, for her recent history was now written less in the lepa claw marks, than in the old, ridged flesh on her left hand—a hand that Dion flexed and stretched too often, as if it hurt worse now than when it had first been injured years ago. He had wondered if that motion was more reminder than actual pain, as though the discomfort kept her from thinking of what else that hand had lost.

He nodded to Tehena. "She's riding better now."

Tehena adjusted her thick scarf to cover her chin from the cold. Her reply was noncommittal. "She should; she was born in the saddle."

"Born to the wolves, you mean." He guided his dnu around a slick spot where shadow preserved the ice, and back into the faint rut that paid tribute to countless wagons.

The woman's voice was bitter as they kicked their dnu into a slow trot to follow the healer. "Born to the mountains into which we ride," she corrected. "The wolves are just shadows of Randonnen peaks."

"You blame her for them?" Kiyun asked mildly. "They are her strength, not her curse."

"Like a pack of moonworms," Tehena retorted. "They hound her like a nightmare. Her mate was her strength; Gray Hishn was her focus. With the first one dead, and the wolf long distant in Ariye, she wanders like a ghost in the howling."

"It is a woman's way," he said slowly, "to explore the hurt, to find its boundaries, to see if she can live beyond it."

"And you would let her do that alone."

"She was kum-tai with her mate, Tehena. They had the forever bond. With him dead, she will always be alone, regardless of what we do." He shrugged. "Besides, the wolves gather around her like thieves. They're company enough."

"Like ghouls," she muttered.

"I don't think they're the real problem." Kiyun pulled

briefly ahead between ice patches and matched paces again with Tehena. He had never been good with animals, and his dnu was more calm when he rode beside another. "The Ariyens don't have to be here with us to be the greater threat," he reminded her. "They've been sending out message rings like fleas. And Dion may be avoiding the message walls, but she can't have missed the talk, not with half the elders and healers wanting her for this meeting and that favor and this healing and that advice."

"Well, she's running right toward them, now."

"But she has something to fight for: her child, the wolves. Even pushing as hard as the Ariyens are, I don't think they will keep her this time."

"Unless they find something else to bind her to them."

"Something that can get through both you and me?" He snorted. "Hells, but half of Randonnen would go to war to keep her out of Ariye if that was what she wanted. She may go back to face the Ariyen elders, but they won't be able to hold her. It's the wolves driving her now."

Tehena said nothing.

He knew she agreed, and he shot her a slanted look. "Well?" he prompted.

She scowled at him. "Perhaps."

He merely waited.

"You may be right," she said finally.

"In a pig's eye," he returned mildly, not hiding the touch of smugness that he had made her say the actual words.

She shot him a fulminating look. "I'm not going to say it again."

"I wouldn't want you to strain yourself," he added dryly. "The day you admit I'm right and mean it is the day I give up art."

She cast a disparaging look toward one of his saddlebags where there was a conspicuous bulge. The twisted carving wasn't even clearly human or alien, just a jumble of shapes and colors. "Considering your taste in art, that might be a favor for the whole county." She chewed her thin, chapped lip, glanced ahead toward the wolfwalker, and didn't bother to hide her shiver.

Kiyun followed her glance. "I think I froze my eyebrows this morning."

"Get used to it," Tehena returned without sympathy. "It's a long road to reach the main heights, and we're on our way up, not down. Besides, there are advantages here." The lanky woman gestured at the lupine prints in the snow. "If we take the pass routes instead of the valleys, we'll eventually be high enough that the Gray Ones won't be able to follow, and that will give Dion some peace."

"For a few days, maybe." The man glanced toward the white line of mountains that still rose ahead like a wall. "You know as well as I that some other wolf pack will pick her up on the other side of the mountains."

The lanky woman's voice was sour. "You could leave me my fantasy for at least a few minutes."

"That the wolves will leave Dion alone?" Kiyun snorted. "That's not much of a fantasy."

Tehena shrugged. "It's as much as I can manage. You know what they say: the greater the dream, the greater the risk to make it come true."

"And you don't take those kinds of risks."

"Not me," the woman agreed.

"You long-faced liar."

"Wart-nosed bollusk," she retorted.

His eyes narrowed. "You're a worm-tempered stickbeast, if ever I saw one."

"And you're a clod-brain, if ever one was born," she snapped back.

"Puce-veined cave-bleeder," he threw back at her.

"Piss-patter," she snapped.

He sucked in a breath. "You fat-hipped, lepa-lipped, puff-haired piece of refuse from the worlag-bit end of a poolah."

For a moment, Tehena glared at him. Then a strange, almost haunted look crossed her face. She started to choke. Obediently, her dnu stopped in the middle of the road as she lost control of the reins.

"Moonworms!" Kiyun halted abruptly and reached across to steady her. "Are you all right?"

But the woman continued to choke. She gargled something and hit his thick arm with her fist.

He opened his mouth to call out for the wolfwalker, then stopped. He frowned. Tehena's skinny fist still beat helplessly against his rock-hard arm, but now she was doubled over her saddle horns. She gasped, gargled her words, and choked again, and he simply stared.

She was laughing.

"Damn all nine moons to all nine hells," he murmured to himself. "Thirteen years I've known you, and I've never heard you laugh. Gamon said he figured it would happen someday, but I didn't believe him. Guess it's fitting that you choke to death on a sound you don't know how to make."

"Fa-fat-hipped," she choked.

He raised his eyebrows. She was so lean as to be almost bony.

She pounded his arm. "Pu-puff-ha-ha-haired—"

What hair of hers that could be seen was—as usual—thin, grayed, and stringy. He shrugged.

She gave up beating on his arm, straightened up only to double over again, and finally regained control of her reins. She rode off after Dion, still gasp-laughing as the humor forced its way up and out of her throat.

Kiyun gazed after her, then spurred his dnu to follow. He could not help taking stock: a ghost of a healer who heard the dead like demons tearing at her mind; a scrawny woman who would rather choke on dung than laugh out loud; and a man who rode blindly after both because, long ago, he had left his home to follow the gray of a legend. He wondered if he had misjudged the two women, and it was he who was not sane.

VI

Talon Drovic neVolen

Who is the hunter?
You, who seek your destiny,
Or those who drive you to it?

—Question of the elders at the Test of Abis

Clouds of gnats hovered over Talon's face in the dull gray of dawn. His skin was slick with sweat. The eyes of the wolves pulled him abruptly from the nightmare, but the images left fingers on his skin. It had been Jervid's body sprawled at his feet, but it was Talon's knife, not Drovic's, that had sunk into the other man's gut. Talons hands had grown warm, as if he clenched them too tight. But when he had looked down, the knife was in his own gut, and it was his blood that burned his left hand and gushed out from his fingers like night. Drovic had smiled and withdrawn the blade, patted his arm as if to comfort, and said, "This, too, was your decision . . ."

Talon rose with a mutter to do his morning duty. He should be grateful, he thought as he rubbed his aching, half-crippled left hand and then his aching right wrist. At least it was a variation on the dreams of the dark-eyed woman. If he could just touch her, feel her skin under his hands, scrape his teeth over her throat—get her out of his system along with the wolves—then other bedmates would look better.

He roll-stuffed his sleeping bag almost brutally. In spite of the weighted bag, he had not been warm, and as he mixed the hot morning rou with his bitter tincture, the shivers wracked him again. "Cold," he muttered as he downed the drink. "Cold as a grave's ambition." Moons, but how long would Drovic hunt the underground labs? They'd already dropped off three packs' worth of bioforms in the town of Verge for transport to Bilocctar. What they carried now was for Drovic's contact in the north, and after that, they'd begin again: hunting, finding, stealing. Killing. He rubbed his temple without relief. He wished he remembered as little of that as he did the rest of his life. Instead, the images of fights and battles seemed engraved on his mind. Raiders, worlags, slavers, venges—the dead were everywhere.

Behind him, a riding beast snorted, and he made his way to the crest of the ridge so that he could study the roads down below. There was still a faint glow to the root planks, and they made a web in the dark, a web that caught the world. It occurred to him that it was not time—the centuries since the Ancients—that held the world in place without progress. No, it was the heavy slabs of this nine-mooned world. The roads that men themselves had set down now locked progress in place like a leech-chain on a wolf.

Dust, trails, freedom . . . The gray impression broke in as he stalked down toward the stream, and he knew that at least one wolf was close. The pressure from the Gray Ones was as much a vise as the pounding ache in his head. He waded shin-deep into the cold and splashed it on his face as the sun lightened the tiny ravine. When he looked up, his gaze met that of the old male.

Leader.

The shock of that intimate contact made Talon's jaw tighten. The word-image was confused with lupine patterns he could not quite interpret in his human mind, but the message was clear enough. "I hear you," he muttered. "But I am no leader here."

You let a lesser wolf command you.

Talon thought of the way Drovic had laid him in the dust two ninans back. The unconscious skill of the older man. The power in those arms, and the rage. Lesser?

Gray Ursh seemed to nod, and the sense of splitting from Drovic was clear. *Hunt with us,* he urged. *The trails are close. We know where you must go. We know what you need.*

The image of bonding, of the closeness of the pack family, was unmistakable, and Talon's own rage erupted. His mate, his children, his family—gone. His strength, his sense of self—destroyed. He remembered the village woman cringing in her cloak, crawling at his feet. Knew that the cloak should have been different, that the woman was wrong. And realized that killing Biekin to save that woman had crystallized something inside him. Even without the wolves, he could not go back now to following his father like a bollusk in the herd. They had brought him to this, had hounded him until he could not even stay with his father. "Do you realize what you've done?" he demanded.

Home, the den, the mate, the cub.

His low voice was cold with fury. "You think you can replace my family with some ghost woman? That I want someone else in my heart? That I want to be someone else in your eyes? I want what I was, not this. I want what I had," he snarled.

The wolf's yellow eyes gleamed.

Abruptly, he turned away, breaking the link between them. He knew the wolf was still close. "If I hunt," he muttered, splashing back to the bank, "I'll do it because I want what *I* will find, not because you force it on me."

His words seemed to fade into the gray, met by a sense of lupine satisfaction as if Talon had somehow agreed with the wolf's urging.

He cursed again to the water. "I'll be no pawn of wolves or men," he muttered. In his skull, the wolves disagreed, and they gnawed at the inside of his thoughts as he stalked back to find his breakfast.

In camp, Ki was cursing to start the day. Beetles had gotten into his bow bag, and the bowstring was half shredded. "Moons-damned, pickled crap of a constipated cow." Ki snarled quietly as he unwound the fragments of the string.

Talon snorted as he passed the brown-haired man. "You don't even know what a cow is."

"Not all of us live only by the sword, Talon. Some of us went to school." Ki pushed the curly, silky hair from his eyes. It was the man's one vanity, and he never wore it braided. Someday, thought Talon, it would get him killed. He studied Ki for a moment. In some ways, Ki was the opposite of everything Talon had learned from his father and the other weapons masters: Never take the first blow, for any damage is disadvantage. Test your enemy with opportunity, but don't actually let him hit you. Strike first from strength; don't wait for false weakness. Keep your hair trimmed and your eyes clear.

Ki was what Drovic called a secondhand fighter. The brown-haired man let his opponent strike first, so that he could see his attacker's style of fighting; then he hit back fast and hard. When he created openings, he gave too much advantage to his enemy to draw that first feint out into a committed blow. After sixteen years on first venges and then raids, Ki was collecting scars the way a deer collected ticks.

Talon had begun to think that Ki's icy demeanor while fighting was a mask, not a true picture. Whereas Talon's mind seemed to crystallize in action, Ki seemed to be blinded by the ice. Talon's awareness was a heightened state in which he saw every movement with an instinctively accurate realization of risk. Ki seemed to be coldly dangerous, not with heightened awareness, but as a desperate mask that covered chaotic sensation. The man was a secondhand fighter because he reacted to what he felt, not what he saw. Ki had to feel the threat first as movement, and he might not ever actually see it. Only the man's reflexes had so far kept him from getting killed, and age and the cumulation of scores of injuries would slow those down before long. Talon shook his head at his own thoughts. Ki was as much an enigma as any man who rode with Drovic for any length of time, and he answered the other man dryly. "School for six years barely gets you to the study of dnu, let alone the cows of the Ancients."

Ki searched for another bowstring. "So you think you know about cows?"

"Do you?"

"It's a bollusk with split hooves."

"That's a goat," Talon corrected absently, tugging on the pack straps to check their strength.

"What?"

"Goats have split hooves."

"That's the only difference?"

He shrugged. "Cows have four stomachs. Bollusks have

one. You'd be better off checking teeth if you want to tell the difference between the animals of oldEarth."

Ki gave him a suspicious look as he wound the new string on his bow. "What do you mean, teeth?"

"Those things in your mouth that help you chew." Talon finished checking his own gear.

"You mean they have or haven't any?"

Talon grunted something noncommittally.

Ki scowled as he bent the bow to test it. "Well, nine hells on your backside, Talon, Drovic has bragged often enough about your education that if you know about stomachs and hooves, you must know about that." Satisfied with the repair, he unstrung the bow and packed it. "So are there any or not?"

"What?"

"Front teeth."

"In a goat?"

"No, in a cow."

"Moonworms." Talon rolled his eyes and led his dnu away.

"No one ever talks about cow teeth," Ki muttered.

Talon watched him toss the ends of the old bowstring into the refuse pit. By now, insect scavengers like those in that pit would have left Jervid's bones and moved on to fresher meals. Gelbugs, largons, chameleons, worms ... Within hours of death, Jervid's body would have been a stiff and half-hollowed carcass; within days, it would have been clean as a ten-year ham bone. The Ancients had a saying: "Three flies eat as much as a lion." If oldEarth flies were anything like this world's largons and worms, Talon could well believe it. The only things they would have left would be the metals on Jervid's gear. No raider had taken those coins or weapons. It was one of Drovic's rules. One could take another raider's life, but not his wealth, his home, or his mate. That would be a breaking of brotherhood, a breaking of the pack. It was one more thing that set Drovic's band apart from other raiders.

Talon glanced left at Sojourn. Sojourn had not known that Talon had killed Biekin back in that town. Talon knew that his silence had probably led Sojourn to assume that the townsman had killed Biekin, and that Talon had in turn killed the townsman. No doubt Sojourn had thought Biekin's copper had been free for the taking. Talon rubbed his jaw and eyed Sojourn speculatively. The brotherhood was already broken, but the other man did not yet know it.

The slender man glanced at him and caught something in his expression. "All right?"

Talon shrugged deliberately. "Sore as a one-legged dog," he returned tersely. He slung his saddle bags onto his dnu.

Sojourn grinned at the oldEarth saying. "Dogs have teeth."

"Dogs are polite bihwadi. They bark first, bite later. You hear a dog, at least you've had a warning."

Sojourn's voice became soft. "As it is with the wolves?"

Talon stilled for an almost imperceptible moment, then shrugged casually. "Wolves aren't half as mean as dogs. It's why the oldEarthers found it so easy to kill them near to extinction."

The other man installed his bow on his saddle. "You've a mean, cold streak yourself, Talon."

"Thought that was part of a leader's job," he muttered, lashing his sleeping bag behind his packs.

Sojourn paused. He kept his voice low. "You're not going to keep leading anyone if someone pikes you for it."

Talon gave the other man a long look. "That someone will find that my bite is worse than my bark."

Sojourn raised his eyebrow. "That would be a fight to see."

"Which fight?"

"Drovic and you."

"Drovic? You think he would challenge me over a little dissatisfaction?" Talon yanked the cinch strap tight. "Even if he was of a mind to do so, I wouldn't fight him over that."

Sojourn raised one slender eyebrow. "Now that raises the question: Over what, then?"

Talon checked his botas. "Over nothing—as long as he keeps to his goals and leaves me to keep to mine. I won't challenge him while I ride with him. We share blood, not just bread, he and I."

"Honor among family or honor among thieves," Sojourn murmured.

Talon swung up in the saddle. "It is a flexible concept," he agreed.

The other man looked at him sharply.

But Talon shrugged, and there was nothing in his expression that could have been taken as insult.

As they rode out, Talon knew that Sojourn watched him closely. It was as if the other raider knew that Talon's mind was clouded, not just with the wolves, but with rage and grief and hatred. Like his father before him, Talon had been betrayed, left for dead, his family gone. It was history repeating itself, and in blood, always in blood. Talon had regained part of his memory since that aborted raid, but even the parts he did remember were patchy and starting to fade again like grass in summer sun. If it kept on like this, by the end of the year he'd be lucky to know his own name.

A wolf growled faintly in his mind, breaking his thoughts. Instantly, Talon stiffened. He pulled up short, a warning on his breath, and Morley and Ebi almost ran him down as he slowed. The oaths as the other riders piled up were thick as lice.

"Talon?" Sojourn asked sharply.

He smoothed his expression from the blankness of listening to the wolves. "Danger," he said shortly.

"A venge?"

He shook his head, but it wasn't an answer. A stinger bit the back of his neck, and he slapped it, squishing it against his skin. He took a breath and whistled a sharp blast to call his father, followed by a trill and a rising one. Ahead, the other riders came to a straggling halt. "Back to the last trailhead," he shouted.

In the lead, Drovic gestured for the rest of the raiders to remain where they were, and instead cantered to his son. "Report," he snapped. "And don't use that whistle again for anyone but me. That's a family tone, not for others. Use the standard call-back trill."

Talon met his flinty gaze with one of his own. "Two flocks of pelan flew up to the right. I caught a glimpse as we hit an opening." It was truth, but not the answer; he had read the threat from the wolves. "There's something in the forest."

Nearby, Ebi slapped at his neck, then his cheek. "Pissing moons," Strapel cursed beside him. The tiny stingers were irritating. A dnu jerked, and Drovic's gaze sharpened. "Talon?"

Another stinger bit Talon's neck, and his dnu shifted uneasily. He slapped at the insect. But when he took the reins again, the color of the dead insect on his palm caught his eye. The small splotch was solid red, not yellow-red as it should have been. And in the back of his skull, through that faint gray fog, he saw a red shadow hum over the brush. The wolves were high up looking down on the forest, safe above the swarm. Their unease was for Talon, not the pack.

"Moons, it's a swarm," he said sharply. "Cover your eyes." He didn't wait for Drovic. He kicked his dnu to a gallop. The riding beast needed no urging; the growing cloud of stingers had it prancing in place.

Drovic spurred his dnu after Talon. The milling riders turned and charged after them. Behind them, the air buzzed as more stingers flew out of the heavy brush. Talon didn't waste time with orders. Those insects were scouts, not even the leading edge, but they were already thick in the air. The following swarm wouldn't kill the raiders intentionally; the stingers were going for the dnu. Either way, falling or stopping was death.

"The trailhead," he shouted to Drovic.

Drovic slapped at his ear. "That trail turns east."

Near the rear of the group, neVoan's dnu reared up, unseating him. Piven's dnu, next in line, panicked and bolted sideways into the brush. Piven's scream as the swarm caught up was lost in neVoan's shrieking.

"Moons," Talon cursed. He could do nothing, nothing. This wasn't a foe to fight, but to flee.

Drovic did not look back. "They'll hold the swarm for a while."

Talon cursed at the callousness.

"Rye Road is ahead," Drovic continued sharply.

"That will put us ahead of the leading edge like rabbits before the wolves," Talon returned in a hard voice. "The east trail will take us up the ridge, above the swarm till it passes."

Drovic cast him a dark glance at his choice of words, but nodded his agreement. Behind them, a thick arm of stingers swirled around the downed riders and dnu who now lay still on the rootroad.

They pulled up hard at the trailhead. Talon jumped down. First in, first duty—the rule of the road. He sprinted into the brush. Wajke, Roc, and Weed joined him quickly, hastily holding or tying back the worst of the branches. Drovic barely waited for them to clear the trail before leading the raiders through. "We'll wait at the summit," Drovic told him. He spurred his dnu to a gallop.

The others blasted past. Talon kept his arm over his eyes to protect it from the dust. One whipping bough caught Weed on his cauliflower ear, leaving a line of blood. It automatically attracted a stray stinger. Weed didn't bother to curse. He just waited for the dnu to pass, then slapped futilely at the swelling bite and let the branches gently back over the trail.

Roc and Wakje grabbed the reins of the four dnu to lead them out of scent range of the swarm, but the dnu fought the reins, chittering their fear. Wakje dodged a foreleg, and Roc swore as one of her beasts nipped at her hands. She forced herself to croon. The dulcet tones were at odds with the violence in the woman's eyes. Talon grinned as he noted that the words she sang were all curses.

A few more stinger scouts found Talon. "Four, five minutes," he told Weed. The other man nodded. They twisted some brush into crude sweepers, moving quickly to brush the trail. Even a swarm would not make them forget the threat of a curious venge. Any riders who stopped would see the brush marks as distinctly as tracks, but Talon was hiding their turn-off only from a casual eye that would pass at a fair clip.

Weed and Talon broke their crude brooms apart, slapped at the growing cloud of stingers, and ran for the chittering dnu. Weed quickly checked the brush for the loose threads that he always seemed to shed, found one, and jerked it free as he vaulted into the saddle.

Talon felt his tension grow as he looked back quickly to judge any telltale signs, then kicked his dnu into a gallop with the others. Behind them, the stingers hummed on the road, then spread out loosely over the forest. A thin arm followed the trail for a moment, then curled smoothly back into the main wash of insects that drowned the brush. Talon felt the adrenaline surge leave his body as they climbed above the swarm. The road below would not be safe for hours, possibly not till morning, but that was no longer his worry. They could slow now to let their dnu catch their breath.

A flash of gray caught the corner of his eye as he approached a fork in the trail. *East and north.* The wolves were eager.

Talon nodded. He could turn off, keep riding east, stay behind the swarm. He could— His thoughts broke off abruptly. "Damn worm-spawned mutts," he muttered. He forced himself to take the left fork, not the one that ran east.

"Talon?" Wakje murmured.

"It's nothing," he snarled back.

But he felt trapped as if driven before a storm, not of stingers but of gray. He couldn't truly blame the wolves. They were caught in his wake like waves rolling after a ship. They couldn't break free any more than Talon could; they could only echo his needs back at him, howling them into the gray. Wolves, the gray, a woman, a bond . . . He ground his teeth and savored the splintering pain that shot up his skull with the pressure. They would come back, he knew, to remind him of what they wanted, in his dreams if not in the day. It was only a matter of time.

VII

Talon Drovic neVolen

The sword
  makes a better handshake.
The knife
  makes a smoother speech.
An enemy
  makes a wilder lover.
A foe
  creates a stronger goal.

The mother
  uses the sharpest pin.
The win
  offers a hard descent.
The friend
  accepts both envy and rage.
The asp
  at your bosom is hardest to see.

  —Ariyen proverbs

Talon and the others caught up to Drovic's group at the base of a cracked granite ridge. They had lost two riders and dnu to the stingers, along with two of the pack beasts, almost all in Darity's group. Drovic wasn't pleased, but in a swarm year, losses were expected, and at least the pack dnu had been carrying standard gear, not the bioforms they had stolen. Drovic nodded and motioned for his son to climb with him to a vantage point.

Talon knew he shouldn't take offense as Drovic automatically assumed the lead. His right wrist was not yet strong, and his left hand was still half curled in a claw where the tendons were healing short. The sword thrust he'd taken to his upper arm had damaged nerves, not just muscle, and his right shoulder ached with what would become a chronic pain. But he looked up at his father climbing smoothly above him, and resented being second. Drovic was strong as a bollusk, but too heavy and fast to be graceful. He brute-forced his way up the rocks, just as he slashed his way through the counties. Push, ride, fight, drive forward—that was the sum of their lives. Talon cursed the stone that broke away under his hands and tried not to wish it was Drovic.

He topped out with a wince and squatted beside his father. For long moments, neither one spoke. "There," Talon said softly. "About six hundred meters due west of that patch of dead pintrees, half a kay north of the swarm line."

"A camp," Drovic said softly, a moment later.

"Two dozen men. Maybe more."

"Good eye, Son."

Talon hid his unexpected pleasure at his father's words. It was a small thing, a vain thing, and it would be a thorn in his gut in the future, when he tried to break away. He caught his breath inaudibly at the sudden surge of gray that came with the thought of leaving Drovic. Blinded, he held his tongue until it cleared, then took a careful breath. He could still see the edge of gray in his mind, hear the howling that crept along his skull, but the rightness of the thought remained, and his hands twitched with the strength of conviction. "There are more dnu than riders. The extras might be pack beasts, but I can't see traders taking this route."

"It's a venge," Drovic said flatly. "I can smell it. If they ride this way, they'll run right up our nostrils." He cursed under his breath. "What were they doing there? Just waiting for the swarm to box us in? If they bother to keep even a simple watch, they'll see us like white warts on a worlag."

"There was smoke this morning to the south, near Siphel."

"I saw it," Drovic said sourly. "Was pissed enough to consider joining a venge myself."

Talon hid his humor.

"What worm-spawned idiots would raid that place?" Drovic continued softly. "They have nothing. No steel, no trade, no science. All they did was stir up trouble for the rest of us."

Talon bit back his comment. Had that town harbored even a single lab, it would have been Drovic who opened their graves to steal what they created. "It won't matter once they get our scent." He hesitated, then said deliberately, "We should backtrack and swing east to put at least one ridge between us before nightfall."

"The eastern route circles the whole damn ridge. It would add three more days to the ride. I want to reach the Bilocctar border by the end of the ninan."

"Then it's south where we've already burned our bridge, west into the swarm, or north into the arms of the venge." Talon's cold gaze swept the forest again, judging the size of the camp. "If they're two dozen strong, they'll put up a hard fight."

"Pah," Drovic spat. "I doubt we'd lose even one man. Those riders are green as spring grass, worse than the youngest among us. Look at them. I can see metal flashing like a woman's eyes for half the saddles down there. No experienced rider would carry such a giveaway."

Talon felt his lips twist. "Weak, arrogant, and inexperienced? Then we should attack them for the gear alone, for the practice, for the joy of killing."

Drovic did not miss the self-mocking bitterness that crept into his son's voice. "If you needed more practice killing, you should have told me," he said mildy. "I could have arranged something more convenient. As it is, they're too far away. We'll ease back and wait a few hours. If they haven't moved on by then, we'll double back and take another route west."

They moved quietly back down the trail to a lower set of clearings. There they set a guard and watered the dnu more thoroughly at the small pond beneath the trees. Talon let his dnu drink deeply and tried to ignore the game trails that he knew twisted east.

Roc moved up beside him. "Talon," she murmured. The gash she had received on her cheekbone had healed to a ragged mark, and with her hair in its finicky braid, she looked oddly well-coifed against the jagged scab. She glanced at the forest. "Are you communing with the trees or—" her voice dropped low with meaning—"daydreaming of a better bed than your empty one last night?"

"Right now, I prefer to think of the trees," he said. His voice was sharp from the Gray Ones, and he took a breath to lower it.

Roc put her hand on his sleeve, and like a wild wolf, he flinched away. Her face tightened. Her voice grew hard. "Talon—" she started.

"Leave me be," he returned curtly. He didn't realize that, like a male Gray One to his mate, he automatically turned the back of his shoulder to her to protect his face and neck from her snapping.

Roc's eyes flashed. She was a slender, shapely woman with high cheekbones and hungry, soulful brown eyes. She moved with grace and speed and fire, and yet had a startling strength. It was a strength born of hate, not of muscle. Her two vanities—her honey-toned hair and her voice, a lovely voice that could charm a badgerbear—made her seem a thing of beauty, but Talon knew better. That beauty, like a blade, was merely a weapon. She used it as others used knives. Now, she leaned against the rock cairn with studied elegance, and her gaze was that of a worlag. "You avoid me now, after all we've shared?"

Talon's slow smile was at odds with the litheness of his movements. "And how much have we shared?" he asked lazily. "Was it of so much value?" He felt the wolves within him growl at the woman as if she grated on the gray. Then he moved aside so that others could take their turn at the water. He indicated the spring with a nod of his chin that somehow took in her figure. "I'm done here," he said softly.

Roc's gaze shuttered. She stepped so close to him that her breasts almost brushed his chest. Her glittering eyes stared up. "You dream of someone who's not even here? I healed you, Talon—not that Ariyen bitch who left you. You're changing," she breathed. "Beginning to think you're better than me and the rest of those who ride with you. That is a dangerous game, son of Drovic."

He merely smiled. Roc almost trembled with rage as he turned away, and he knew that his careless expression would eat at her like fleas. He didn't look back as he led his dnu away to make room for Morley and Ki.

From the shadows, the wolves watched the raiders. They did not follow Talon back to the camp. Instead, they took the high, thin game trail to the top of the ridge, where they could watch what went on below. Had they been any other creatures, he would have been lost to them among the other raiders, but the wolves saw with more than their eyes. His taste was in their mouths, his scent was in their noses; and an image of a stronger man was bound into their minds.

They raised their heads and sniffed the air. The packsong echoed with longing. The eight Gray Ones felt the weight of other packs join them, and the determination that rang through the packsong goaded them to go after Talon. It was becoming a naked need.

Gray Paksh nudged the yearling, Chenl, and looked at Ursh and Thoi. Chenl was the only pup born last year to their pack, and after hundreds of kays, he was leaned down to the hardness of his elders. Gray Ursh whuffed softly as the yearling licked his mother's torn ear. *We are far from home,* the male sent.

Paksh shrugged mentally and nipped at Chenl. *We agreed,* she returned. *We Answered. We are bound.*

Gray Thoi felt the tight barrenness of her own womb. She had not forgotten the burning convulsions Paksh had endured as the other pups died in her womb, or the fact that the memory of that birthing, which had echoed in the pack, had not been alone. *The Wolfwalker promised. Life for life. It is for all the packs, all the pups,* she reminded him.

There was a sense of agreement.

Thoi raised her muzzle and sought the taste of Talon on the wind. *He still hears us,* she reassured herself and the others.

Ursh's yellow eyes gleamed. The male stretched in that indefinable, mental way, the dimension that was the gift of the Ancients. He tasted the edge of Talon's thoughts. He felt the recognition of his presence in the man's mind and the man's rejection of his pressure—the frustration of the man—and was satisfied. He turned his gaze to his mate. *He listens. Like us, he has no choice. Our voice grows stronger in him, and he*

*is beginning to feel her, to see his need. When his need is
strong enough, he will find her.*

He rose and padded after the raiders. The other wolves
went with him.

VIII

Ember Dione maMarin

*Necessity teaches;
The moons judge.*

   —*Randonnen proverb*

The mountain valley was a rift of green among the
whitened peaks, but Dion couldn't seem to relax. Tirek, a tall,
hazel-eyed man, lifted a few leaves from the stubby green-
house plants as he continued, ". . . didn't do well this year, but
the meigia bloomed twice." His assistant scurried down the
aisle to shift a set of half-planted pots out of their way.

Dion listened with only half an ear as they walked the green-
house. *South,* the Gray Ones urged her. *South and west . . .*
She glanced out the half-steamed windows, but the wolves
were kays away, waiting restlessly in the dry grass beneath
the cold-stunted trees.

Dion shook them back in her mind. The sense that the inn
was not her proper den was partly her own, not just that of the
wolf pack. It was the road, she thought. She had become too
intimate with it. The white stone may have branched off to the
village, but its main body coiled among the peaks, and that
snaking route called her as much as the wolves did.

"Of course, that means it will only have half its usual
strength," Tirek added. He squatted to show her the row of re-
ducing jars that sat beneath one of the benches. Dion's nostrils flared with the sweet copper scent.

He smiled at her expression. "The foxfire oil was more potent than usual. I'd be happy to trade some for that vellace you brought in." He kept his gaze on hers, but his appreciation of her was obvious. For all that she was scarred, there was beauty in her bones and a remarkable grace of movement. Too, there was a sense of power in those violet eyes, and it made him curious. It was said that wolfwalkers were as wild in bed as they were running with the wolves. He wouldn't mind touching that wildness for himself. He let his smile grow wider.

In her mind, the Gray Ones bristled. Dion ignored them. Tirek was no threat. He was a handsome man with a good face and a well-kept, muscular body. His hair glinted with a dozen shades of brown, and his dirt-stained hands had been gentle as he separated the bluewing ferns to show her the spores. He was also an excellent archer, but whatever death he had dealt had not left him dark or bitter. Dion envied him that calm, and wondered. A moment ago, he had put his hand on her arm to guide her around a pile of freshly dug tubers, and the warmth of his hard-calloused fingers had been deliberate, almost shocking. It had been months since a man had touched her like that.

The wolves bristled again, and Dion raised startled eyes to Tirek. Wolves tended to start bonding near the end of summer in preparation for spring mating. This pressure from the wild ones to ride south and west—it was not simply a need for Gray Hishn or the pressure of her promise to heal the wolves. The urgency was flavored with desire for a mate.

Tirek regarded her with growing intensity as he misinterpreted her expression. "Healer maBrist mentioned that if you'd consider staying a few days, she could dry whatever herbs you needed." Up the aisle, his assistant watched them curiously.

Graysong tightened.

Even though her pregnancy barely showed, Tirek knew of her child—his sister had guessed it immediately when they had been introduced—women could never hide that sort of thing from each other. Still, he looked at her with desire. Dion studied his face with almost blank curiosity.

In the back of her mind, the Gray Ones growled low.

But it had been so long since she had been able to forget her duties, her reputation, her supposed skills and simply lean on a strong man; so long since she had been simply a human being, not a legend. She fingered a fuzzy-leaved plant. "I could use some angelica," she said softly.

The wolves tensed as they read her thoughts, and their unease became lupine anger. *Not him,* they sent in her mind.

Tirek couldn't hear the wolves. "We've got some drying over here. Wait, hold still," he said quietly. He brushed at her cheek where a feathered wisp of fern had caught. His touch lingered a moment too long.

The wolves seemed to erupt in her head, blinding her with sudden aggression. *Not him,* they snapped. Dion's mind swirled with gray. *Only Leader. The hunter to the moons and back.* They snarled at Tirek through her eyes. The sense of another man was indistinct, but the voice was clear, the voice of her mate, the voice of the dead. *Wolfwalker . . .* The Gray Ones threw it at her like a vow. Mentally, Dion staggered.

Tirek yanked his hand back. Dion stared at him as her vision cleared. Her lips had curled back to bare her teeth, and her hands were tensed into claws. Tirek's weight shifted as he read the threat in her body. "I meant no offense, Healer Dione," he said quickly.

For a moment, with the wolves snapping in her hands, she thought she would strike him. She had to steady her voice before saying by way of apology, "I've been too long on the road." But there was a glint in her eyes that spoke of anger in spite of her words, and Tirek carefully shifted away. He did not touch her again.

Dion was seething as she made her way to the local healer's clinic. Threads of gray still snapped in her mind, and she snarled back at the wolves. *Why?* she demanded. The gray-song shivered under her anger.

The den, the bond, the mating . . .

She stared at the hills where the wolves waited. Her voice was harsh. "My mate is dead, for all the good you did him." *Let the wolves in,* he had said. *Use their strength.* Her hands had been claws in his arms, but his weight had been an anchor, pulling down, down. The wolves had surged, blinding her. Steel had flashed, raiders had cursed, blood had splattered the seawall. *Call the wolves,* he had told her. But it had not been enough, never enough to keep the dead from the moons. She had torn his jerkin, his sleeve, then his flesh with her nails, digging into his weight. But she hadn't held on, not long enough. And he'd fallen, fallen onto the rocks and then drowned in the hungry sea.

The Gray Ones howled deep in her mind, and she bit back at the sworling gray. She didn't need their engineered memories to constantly revive her own, but she couldn't keep them out of her mind. Their strength was like a prisoner, and they were bound by those last desperate moments in which she had fought for Aranur's life, locking the wolves to her with her Call. Time had passed, but they had not let go. Instead, they had taken her need and turned it into their own, trapping and hounding her toward what they wanted instead. South and east, into Ariye, to face what—or who—the wolves demanded? She clenched her fists until the growl was audible in her throat.

"Healer Dione?"

She whipped around with almost lethal intent.

The other healer stumbled back.

Dion held up her hand, palm out, to stop the tall, willowy woman. She was still blinded by the sense of gray. She controlled herself with difficulty until she could make out the silhouette. "Yes," she said finally.

But her voice was still too much the growl, and the other woman steadied herself before speaking. "I'm Healer maBrist. We had arranged for a tour of the clinic."

Dion took a breath and forced herself to smile. "I'm sorry, Healer. I was just woolgathering."

"I would have said wolf-gathering." MaBrist gathered her calm back around her like a cloak. "And it's Siana, please." She was an older woman who had made master healer late in life because of the isolation of her town, but her maturity stood her in good stead. She had a serene manner about her, one that said, "I am calm, and my hands are gentle but strong; you can trust your life to me." Now, her light blue eyes studied Dion with quiet intensity. Dion kept her face expressionless as the taller woman noted the shallowness of the scars that the message rings reported had laid her open to her cheekbones. "You heal well," was all Siana said, though, before motioning Dion to the clinic.

Dion swallowed the gray in her throat and forced herself to chat as they walked to the small stone building. Inside, the clinic was surprisingly large, but only two beds were occupied. "We use the other half for meetings when it's clear," Siana explained. "Alpine accidents tend to involve more than one person, and our fever seasons are heavy." Dion nodded at the intern who sat near the opposite wall. The young man had been studying a book and watching the patients closely, but he got eagerly to his feet as they entered.

Siana checked the latest notes the intern had made. "They are trappers," she explained, motioning at the patients. "They were caught in Subtle Valley by a series of storms and avalanches, and they ran out of extractor roots before they could make it out by the backtrails."

Dion nodded. The slack expressions and drooping eyelids were a giveaway of the accumulation of toxins. The Ancients had not had time to fully adapt to the world before the alien plague stole their technology. Delion and other extractor plants had been seeded throughout the continents as a short-term solution. That had allowed the original colonists to filter out the toxins of this world's flora and fauna until mutations could be developed that would give humans the tolerance they needed. But with their technology gone barely a decade after landing, humans now lived on the dregs of the seeded species the Ancients had had time to provide. Extractors, pee-trees, rootroads—they were the visible basis of human science. It was the species that had been developed since then—the fungi, the plankton, the bacteria—on which humans now pinned their hopes.

"How long were they off the extractors?" she asked.

"Fourteen days. They were picked up a few days ago by a caravan and dropped off here."

"Cozar or merchant?"

"Cozar."

Dion nodded. That meant they would likely have had their

own healer and would have started treatment immediately. Dion laid her hand lightly on one man's neck to feel for the pulse. The trapper's brown eyes flickered dully, but he made no sound, and Siana watched as Dion's gaze became unfocused. She realized that the wolfwalker was drawing on her bond with the wolves, and felt a twinge of envy that surprised her. "They're responding well," the willowy healer murmured. "I expect them to recover within the next ninan."

The pulse was a low, sluggish hammer beneath Dion's fingers, but her perception went deeper than that. With the wolves heightening her senses, she had learned to touch the patterns of other bodies. Blood, vessels, tissues, bone—she could almost see the molecules that had attached to the trapper's blood and organs, could feel the chemical sponge of the massive, concentrated doses of extractors that Siana was giving him. Power shivered inside her. Wolves seemed suddenly dim, and lightning seared her nerves with the pattern of the trapper's body. The lance of energy startled her like a deer. Abruptly, she clamped down hard. For a moment, it was all she could do to breathe. Then the sense of power subsided. She let out her breath carefully and glanced at Siana, but the healer was taking the other man's pulse.

That energy had not been the wolves sharpening her senses. It had been something else, something cold and eerie, something deep in the back of her mind. The wolf-human bond was not natural, but what Dion had just felt was purely alien—something she had felt only in the north. Moonworms, but as long as she was in these mountains, she was still too close to the aliens. Those cold, slitted yellow eyes seemed to hang at the edge of her consciousness. They were as unlike the warm golden gaze of the wolves as cold crystal was from honey. That, and the link between the aliens and her mind was a purer, harder form of energy. It was like a sheath of ice along the inside of her skull, one that would reflect internal energy like a mirror or lens should she let her mind focus in any one direction. She wondered suddenly if the wolves were driving her toward the distant hunter to protect her from herself, or to distract her from the alien cold they could not help but sense in her mind.

Dion took another deep breath. She could have released the power she had just felt, could have manipulated the patterns of the trapper's body to accelerate his treatment. For a healer, such a skill was priceless—and forbidden. This Ovousibas, the internal healing art of Ancients and aliens, was deadly as a worlag. Wolves who helped a healer do Ovousibas died with the plague burning their nerves. Healers could be sucked mentally so far into the patient's body that they could not escape, or they died with their brains seared from within. Dion touched the edge of power within her and shivered. An instant more, and it would have been her brain that burned.

In eight hundred years, hundreds of healers had tried to recapture the art that Dion and her wolf had practiced. All had eventually died from the very fevers they tried to prevent. Now even the attempt at internal healing was forbidden. But there had been no board of healers to forbid Dion from learning the art the day that she had tried. There had been no one but the mountains, the wolves, and the dying all around her. Necessity teaches; the moons judge, she reminded herself harshly. Perhaps her turn would still come. She removed her hand from the trapper's neck, but she could still feel the pulse that would have guided her in.

Wolfwalker. The gray crept back in. They were as unnerved by the spike of power as she had been, and their voices were uncertain.

I am here, she reassured.

But the packsong shivered. They needed to see her, to smell her musky sweat and rub against her, to reaffirm her with the pack.

With that need tensing her own shoulders, Dion made her excuses and left the clinic, striding to the inn. She barely stopped to exchange her cloak for her running boots and weapons. Then she rode out of town toward the hills. She didn't need her eyes to see the wolves waiting beneath the trees. She could hear them, pulling at her like taffy. She dismounted, staked the dnu in a patch of grass, and sprinted into the trees.

Gray wolves scattered through the scrubby fir trees like thoughts. Her thighs numbed quickly from exertion. The trail was dry and smooth, and her feet pounded with simple rhythm as the Gray Ones loped around her. They moved close, then farther away, wanting contact but being unwilling to sustain it for more than a moment. If she reached out, they would melt away like silk. But their soft mental symphony drove the yellow edge of alien power back from her conscious mind so that she simply clung to the gray and ran.

The air was almost cold beneath the trees, thinly hot in the sun. Old pain twinged in her left leg, but she ignored it. It felt good, she acknowledged. Good to push herself, to feel the burn in her legs, to feel exhaustion push out what was left of her emotions. Aches ran across her back as scars stretched with the swing of her arms. She had healed herself using the wild wolves in place of her partner wolf, but even she could not replace all the flesh that had been torn away. Now, her unborn child was a telling weight on her endurance, and she considered slowing. But she was also stubborn and needed to run, to pound out the fear that was beginning to drive her as much as she drove herself. She could not afford to give in to that persistent edge in her mind just because she was with child. At this distance, the aliens would clearly sense that lessening of will and rip her mentally as they had torn her physically before. As long as she felt that alien cold, she must be strong enough to reject its chill, or lose both herself and her child.

The wolves could not help her with that fear. They were bound up in their own desires. For months, they had been passing her from pack to pack. She hadn't noticed it at first, had been too wrapped up in her own grief to recognize what was happening. But the Gray Ones had gone after her like a worlag after a hare. Their teeth had latched into her mind with a vengeance, and now her dormant promise to help them was a steel cord in the packsong, pulling her toward Ramaj Ariye and the man who haunted the packsong. Or rather, toward the man who was herded toward her as she was hounded toward him. These wolves ran with her now to keep that lupine link tightly braided with gray, to blind her to the aliens so that nothing would pull her away again. That distant man was part of the link between them. Human enough to meet human needs, hunter enough for the wolves. What she would be to him or he to her was already hinting through the gray.

She shook out her hands and forced herself to run faster. On this cliff, she was merely a wolfwalker, not a healer, a scout, a mate, or a mother. There was no duty here to wolves or Ariyen elders, no fear of alien eyes, only the savage pleasure of running till she had no more strength in her legs, till exhaustion burned out her mind.

Higher, the gray ones howled. *The hunt is on the heights.*

Gnats, gathering over the warming grass, whirled and boiled in the heat. Downwind, faint wisps of steam rose from cracks in the rocky ground. Dion had seen it in winter once, and the rings of ice that had formed around the vents had made fantasy towers that glowed blue and green at night. Now, the cracks were half hidden by yellow-red grass, and the wind blew the gasses away from the trail so that the air seemed thicker with pollens.

She scrambled above the valley while the wolves took the long trail around, and the wind cut across the ridge and dropped, drying her sweat and leaving her skin salt-tight. The dirt trail was fairly straight, dodging only an occasional outcropping or twisting around a boulder. Dion didn't notice the almost feral grin that stretched across her features. She didn't realize that her violet eyes held an almost yellow glint. Her braid, slapping her quiver on one side, then the other, kept rhythm with her feet as she sprinted along the rise.

Ahead, a tiny chasm opened up. Dion skidded to a halt and bent, hands on her thighs to steady her legs while she tried to catch her breath. The wolves flowed up along the trail behind her, then across the ravine like gray water. Dion watched them enviously. Then she laughed at the old fear of heights that stamped her gut as she watched them. It wasn't even a wide jump; a child of ten could have made it. No, it was simply the height that made Dion pause. She felt the tremble in her fingers and knew that the fear was so much a part of her that she no longer questioned its presence. Instead, she accepted the thrill like a known flaw in an old friend. She raised her face, felt her pulse pound in her throat, and then flung out her arms and twirled madly on the edge of the cliff. "Ariyens be damned," she shouted. Her child would know this—all of it. The freedom, the fear, the thrill. Let the Ariyens try to claim this child as they had herself, and she would throw them all off a cliff. Whatever the wolves wanted, they would get it in time, but here, now, she was only a woman running to break her demons. She let her momentum turn into a run back from the edge. Then she spun and sprinted toward it. Her moccasins hit the edge, and she felt the rough points beneath her feet. She began to launch herself—

The rock cracked beneath her weight.

Midstep, her stomach froze.

The rock split, three meters back, and her weight drove down against . . . nothing. The edge of the cliff broke away. Momentum carried her out into the air, over the black jaw of the narrow ravine, but the cliff was even now sliding down. Her arms went up in a desperate bid for lift. For a moment, she hung between the cliffs. Then she dropped like a stone. Her body slammed into the other edge instead of landing on top. Her knees smashed flatly against dark rock; her outstretched arms just managed to reach over the cliff. Her breath was gone like a boot kicking a ruptured ball. Then her own weight began to drag her back, down toward the rocky teeth. Far below, the broken cliff hit bottom with a series of shocking cracks and a cascade of rattling stones.

Wolfwalker! Gray Ones howled. Power seemed to surge up and out from the depths of her mind.

Rocks spattered into the darkness. Her elbows and hands ground into the trail. She was pinned against the cliff with her armpits, her legs hanging like sticks as she ate the dust in the wind. Her child . . . She was slipping. Her elbows dragged, leaving flesh behind. Her nails tore in the ground. Her daughter . . .

The wolves had turned; they were bolting back in her direction. *Wolfwalker, take our strength.*

She reacted instinctively to the power they thrust toward her. In her mind, the icy glare brightened. She froze. She hung on the edge with blood on her legs and the ravine far below, and knew with a sudden flash of both clarity and dread that the wolves were as eager to bind her infant to their needs as they had bound herself. Take their energy because they willed it, not because she asked, and her use would feed her debt to them like a greedy child. Dion's daughter would be locked into Dion's duties and promises before she was even born. And Dion had already bound this child to one of the aliens by claiming the birdwoman as mother. The horror of that link still writhed in both human and alien minds. Aware, always watching, the icy edge of power behind the wolves would thicken with strong use of Ovousibas. Like the needs of the wolves, it would creep into the mind of her unborn child like mudsuckers worming toward prey. It sharpened as she hesitated, its cold glare tightening with the wolves in her mind. Fury filled the mother's arms. She would not lose this child, she snarled to herself. Her daughter would choose her own path, her own duties in life. Her voice was hoarse. "Back . . . off."

Gray Zair scuffed to a half just beyond her reach and panted as she met Dion's eyes. The female wolf didn't understand. The creature tried to send her strength into the wolfwalker, but Dion refused to take it. *You need us,* Zair snapped. *Use our strength.*

"I'm not falling yet," the wolfwalker snarled. She drew up her right leg until her foot found a ledge in the rock. She could feel the blood welling out of her knees through the dust and grit.

The Gray One growled in her face. *The cub . . .*

Dion bared her teeth and growled back. "I've climbed two dozen mountains on my own, and a piss-poor cliff like . . . this piece of rotten . . . rock isn't about to finish . . . us off now." Her foot slipped, and she jerked a fraction. Her fingers dug into summer-dry soil.

Wolfwalker, for the cub, Gray Lash sent urgently.

"This is . . . for my cub—my daughter, dammit. If you get your mind in her through . . . me, you'll never let her go. And if I can't make it over one rough edge, then I never . . . deserved to be called a Randonnen climber in . . . the first place." Carefully she eased weight toward her right elbow. Now the left foot searched for a nub. Small, loose rock cracked away and fell, fell into the blackened distance. Dion pushed down on her elbows, but her clothes caught on the rock. "Moonwormed piece of a mudsucker." Had she been in actual danger of falling, she would have taken the offer of the wolves and to hell with her resolution. Better alive and bound to the wolves, linked to the aliens, and drowned in the elders' duties, than dead in a blackened ravine. She rotated her body to the right and eased her hip up a handspan. Her arms began to tremble. She pressed out with her feet, but with only the pressure downwards on her forearms, the friction was barely enough to hold her in place.

Gray Zair's teeth bared, and three other wolves paced with her, stirring up the dust. Dion lost another inch. *Wolfwalker,* Zair snapped. The wolf grabbed Dion's forearm in its teeth, and the contact made Dion flinch. She jerked, slipped wildly, and almost screamed in fear as she lost the tenuous friction of her forearm in the dust. Her child . . .

Wolves howled in her head, and strength flowed toward her. Dion sucked it in. She shoved hard on both elbows. Her tunic caught for a moment, then tore free; her stomach scraped stone. She found a finger-wide spur with one moccasin. Automatically, she twisted to get the ball of her foot on the spur, then slowly set her weight. It held. She could feel blood from her knees soaking the tops of her moccasins. She swung her left leg up just under the cliff. She rested a few breaths, then raised the leg to the overhang. A moment later, she had her heel over the edge. A shift, and her calf was resting on the ledge, and Gray Zair had her teeth in the leather. Dion cursed while the wolf hauled on her like a distressed rabbit. She finally wormed the rest of her way over and sprawled in the dust, her limbs trembling and her scrapes clogging with dirt.

Gray Zair sniffed the blood and dodged back as Dion pushed herself to her knees, then her feet. On legs that still trembled, she leaned over the jagged edge to examine the rock face beneath her. Only then did she step back. Her hand remained on her abdomen. Fear may have been an old friend of hers, but not one she wanted to challenge when she carried Aranur's child. In that moment, she would have given almost anything to feel his strong hands on her waist, his calloused palm against her belly, the heat of his body coiled next to hers, surrounding and filling her. He had been a weapons master and leader in his county, a man called hero too often for his people to understand what was in him. To her, he had been a climber, a fighter, a white-water kayaker, the man she had kissed on a wind-swept cliff, the father of her children, the other half of her heart. She had given him death when she let go on that seawall. He had given her life. Her sons— moons watch over them, wherever they were—and now this second heartbeat which filled her womb and echoed her adrenaline. "Taste that fear, that rush, that adrenaline," she murmured. "Know it well, because the Ariyens would have you drink that, not my milk, in time."

Gray Zair growled low, and Dion gave a shaky laugh. "Your first climb," she told the child in her womb. "And may you use better judgment in picking your routes than I do. Otherwise, you'll end up like your father, as fodder for every songster in Randonnen and Ariye, and dead as the dreams of the Ancients."

Gray Lash whuffed and turned away to sniff at the trail, and although her hands still trembled, Dion grinned wryly. The moment was gone; the wolves were ready to move on, to follow the ridge to the south. Dion traveled the route with her eyes. The bare, weathered stone was interspersed with dying patches of summer grass. The overhead sky was blue-gray with high, thin clouds, and the early sun was harsh across the mountains that marked the edge of the county. That, she thought, was Ramaj Ariye, that balance of height and shadow, the rugged rock and plunging streams, the hunger in the same moment for both the den and the stars. Her mate had been like that, always driven, always wanting more than the world around them. Where she had been content to run with the wolves, he had kept his face to the stars. He should have lived long ago when he still had a chance to reach them. She looked back at the now-widened chasm. It was a painful truth to realize that it had been her lifestyle, not his, that had put them in greater danger. The world had torn her life apart, but she had offered it up for the tearing.

A wet nose nudged her hand, and one of the young males panted against her skin. *We are here. You live forever in us.*

She felt the edge of power in the gray mind. Behind it was still that faint, icy taste that seemed to scrape at the packsong. It was something the Gray Ones shied from as much as she did. She bit her lip, her breath still uneven as she glanced north. How many times had a wolfwalker realized that the tinge of ice in the back of the packsong was the voice of the aliens? And how many of those wolfwalkers had then died? The alien birdmen protected their breeding grounds like fanatics, and wolfwalkers weren't known for long lives. Dion's lips thinned as she brushed dust gingerly from her bloody knees. By her own hand or theirs, it was still the path to the moons.

Dion raised her fingers to her lips and tasted her own blood. She had met the aliens and challenged them, and they had nearly killed her. They suited this world, she realized. Thrived on its danger and violence. Dion had succumbed to the thrill of that danger, just as she had succumbed to the wolves. She laughed softly as she stared at the mountains around her. "You're bound to me now," she told them. "As bound as I am to you. On this world, there was no other path, not with the strength of your needs in me, or of my needs in the packsong." She raised her hands and howled. The sense of power in her hands was addictive. The Gray Ones backed away, snarling. "Run," she told them. "Run!" Her voice had them sprinting away. "You can hound me back to Ramaj Ariye, but I'll forge my own life from there." She followed them at a dead run.

IX

Rhom Kintar neKheldour

Cliffs so dry that rocks are ash;
Sunburned sand like pitted glass;
Shimmering roads like moons submerged;
Wavering heat like tidal surge;
Dust that scours the skin exposed;
Grime that cakes in eyes and nose;
Air that sears the flesh it touches—,
  This road is thirsty, long, and brushes
  The path to the drying moons.

Rocks so cold their shadows freeze,
Moonlight gives no rider ease;
Firewood is scarce and thin;
Sands leech evening's warmth from skin;
Night winds cut inside the lungs;
Dry air chaps both lips and tongue;
Icy botas split and leak—
  This road is daunting as the peaks
  Of Randonnen and Ariye.

  —Traveler's warning, carved in stone at the entrance to the high
  desert road between Ramaj Randonnen and Ramaj Ariye

Twelve hooves hit like hammers on the hardened summer soil. With the steady drumming of the six-legged dnu, Rhom and Gamon did not speak on the dusty, overhung shortcut. Not until they reached the white stone road did they pull up to rest the dnu. It was about time, Gamon told himself. Once the Randonnen committed himself, Rhom didn't waste any time. It had been one of the traits he had appreciated in Rhom when they had ridden together before. Now he wished he could get the man to slow down.

The two riders studied their choice of directions. Jealous

Fork split the road like a serpent's tongue, wagging in the heat. One road curved southwest through Fenn Forest, then snaked into a long valley before shooting due west toward the river. It was the route that linked the peaks and the ocean, the major caravan route. It was the smooth route, the safe route, the route that provided water. But both men looked the other way, at the dry dust leading north.

The northwestern fork aimed like a bone arrow into layered, yellow mesas. For a space, the white stone road was visible as a thin split across the cracks of rock and soil. Then it disappeared into waves of shadowed heat. Rhom absently wiped the sweat from his collar as he regarded the wavering road. He looked a silent question at Gamon.

Once again, the Ariyen weighed the choice. It was the end of summer, but it had been a dry year, with no rain touching the desert. Out there, the ground was hard as iron or powdered like wind-blown ash. It wasn't a desert of dunes, but of barren rock and soil that was thin with the remnants of wind-ground stones and pebbles and sand. There could be years in a row when no rain fell, others when winter laid down a layer of snow that fed the thirsty soil, and still others that suffered so much rain that the canyons were cut even deeper. At this time of year, because of the altitude, the night air would be close to freezing; by afternoon, it would boil their brains like stew.

Gamon ran his hand under the edge of his leather-and-metal-mesh war cap. Take that northern route, and by day, his skull would be a dutch oven of the Ancients, roasting his thoughts to death. And the dust . . . The grime that caked the sweat on their necks and discolored the legs of each dnu—that dust would become a cruel grit. Like hungry flies, it would scrape at their skin until their flesh was raw and open to worms. The wind would scour their eyes like a sandpad. Parched air would suck dry their mouths. Aye, they would make Ramaj Ariye, but they would be stalks of men.

Rhom followed his gaze. "It must be both our decisions."

"She might have turned back."

"No. She went on."

Gamon did not dispute him. Instead, he gazed again at the

desert. It was not that the distance was so great between Randonnen and Ariye—it was barely 110 kays as the crow flies. It was that they would have to ride a twisting path in and out of the canyons, climbing down and back up and out, and leaving the road for water. The actual distance was over 200 kays, and it would be more for he and Rhom.

Gamon had crossed those mesas many times with caravans and on dnu, but he had never crossed as late as this, and never in a swarm year. 'Seven years for the lepa; seven times seven for the lesser'—it was an old saying, and not really accurate, for the bird-creatures called lepa could swarm every four or five years instead of migrating in pairs and small groups. But every few decades, those small groupings would explode into mass migrations and extend to the lesser beasts. In those years, even the beetles and gelbugs would mass and move like scythes through forests and fields. This was one of those swarm years.

If they were lucky, they would somehow avoid the sweeps of hunger and violence that could reach even into the desert. Luck, however, would have nothing to do with how often they could find water. Five of the major wells would be dry, and at least two of the closer springs would be dust. They could have carried water on a wagon, but they would have had to hire six men to ride with them to help get the transport down into and back up out of the canyons. The steep roads begged for accidents. On the other hand, each riding dnu would suck water like a sponge, and the dnu might not even last half a ninan, not with the desert predators.

"We could still ride north," he murmured. "Follow their path up through Ramaj Kiren to Ramaj Kiaskari."

"That trail's cold as a stillborn poolah. We'd always be ninans behind her."

"There's the route Shilia took, the southern route to Ariye."

"It adds fourteen days to the trail. No, we ride straight, we ride fast, and we reach the passes before her, or we'll lose her among the ridges. Something is worrying at Dion's heels. I can feel it like a hound on a cougar. She'll not stay with the roads once she's into Ariye. She'll head straight into the forests."

"We can't ride right across that desert if the water wells are dry. Speed may be something we sacrifice to follow this road to Ariye."

"We can't afford to make that trade-off, Gamon. We'll jog or walk or crawl if we have to, but those days will make a difference. By the time you reached me . . ." He shrugged meaningfully.

"Is it my fault you Randonnens are stubborn and stupid as bollusk? It's not as if I wouldn't have found Dion eventually."

"Aye," he agreed mildly. "But we wanted it on our terms, not yours."

Gamon noted the use of the plural pronoun. "This road is risky, Rhom. We'd be certain of reaching Kiren if we took the caravan route."

"No." His voice was firm. "The southern route takes too long." He gestured with his chin at the mesas. "We cross this quickly, then ride north and meet her before she hits the hills, as she comes back down through the passes."

"Into Ariye," Gamon said deliberately.

Rhom gave the older man a steady look. "Into Ariye," he agreed. "Though she may not remain there long."

Gamon chewed his lip absently as, one more time, he went over the route in his head. This late, they would have to leave the road at least four times to reach the few tinaja and tenor trees that would help to keep them alive, and that would add days to the route. And Rhom was heavy with muscle; he would need more water than he thought. That, and Rhom knew only the mountains. The Randonnen did not know how to endure the heat—how to lower his body temperature, how to breathe carefully, how to drink enough to sate the body without giving away water to sweat . . . Gamon regarded the desert and waited in studied silence.

Rhom glanced again at the southern fork. It had been eight years since he had last traveled to Ariye. With his mate, his children, his father, and his forge, life had simply been too full to extend far toward his distant twin. Now, time mocked him with its shortness, and the urgency that had pushed him this far spurred him on like a thorn. Gamon was right. This world was a danger to Dion. And he had left his sister on her own too long. Now it was time, not the heat, that worried him.

Nine days here, nine days there . . . They were far enough north that it would take two ninans to ride down through Fenn Forest to the river road in the valley. It was another half ninan to reach Ariye, and four more days to the upper towns. The desert route took half that. That was fourteen days of difference. Fourteen days of life.

Rhom looked north at the faint line of white that crossed the dry desert. He urged his dnu toward the canyons.

The older man rode with him.

X

Talon Drovic neVolen

Whose trap is it,
If you go in willingly?

—Question of the Elders at the Test of Abis

Talon's vision gradually became fuzzy again as he rode, but he didn't bother to shake his head. It wouldn't help; it was the wolf pack that blurred his eyesight, while the edges of their packsong gnawed at his thoughts. He had been around wolf packs for years, though he had never bonded with them. He found his lips twisting in a mockery of a smile. Even as a child, Drovic had pushed him to take up the steel, rather than follow the path of the wolves. Now Talon's toys were swords and men, and Drovic was no different. Drovic played with lives like a chess game, not caring what was sacrificed to his cause. Steal technology, find a cure for the plague, fight the aliens, and regain the Ancients' stars . . . Talon's blind acceptance of those goals was slipping away with each contact with the wolves. It wasn't that the goals couldn't be reached, just that every day seemed to leach a little more focus from his mind, steal more of his memory just as Drovic stole bioforms.

His gray eyes narrowed as he studied the forest. How close were they now, those ghosts? They held some knowledge of the plague—he knew healers who had touched that. He stretched toward the foggy gray and hoped that it would somehow clear the other fog in his head.

Instantly, the mental howl strengthened. There was no meshing of consciousness, no perfect blend of thoughts, just a maelstrom of lupine need. The lure of that packsong made him nearly writhe until he wanted to throw back his head and snarl with emptiness. He clenched his jaw just in time and strangled the sound in his throat. It was a long moment before he regained control.

"Moons-damned idiot!" He cursed himself under his breath. He should have known better. A man who was linked with the wolves could be haunted by any gray voice, pushed to any goal the Gray Ones set in his mind. The wolves tried to touch his mind again, and he cursed audibly until Dangyon, riding ahead of him, began grinning at his oaths.

Talon had managed to turn them east twice, once to avoid a venge and once to take advantage of the heavy traffic for a fair. But although they were still in Ramaj Eilif, they were inexorably shifting west. It was a direction that was beginning to gnaw at Talon as much as did the wolves. Ariye was the key, he told himself. Center of the counties, home of the Ancients' science, base of the aliens' mountains ... Even without looking in the Gray Ones' eyes, Talon could feel their intensity as they seemed to follow his thoughts.

Drovic noticed his expression and dropped back to a canter beside him. "What is it?"

"We should have gone east," he said flatly, swatting at a grafbug. "Up into the mountains, out of the range of the venges."

Drovic's voice was equally short. "We don't have the gear for that."

"Then we'll sell the lighter gear and buy what we need."

The older man gave him a withering look.

Talon forced himself not to roll his eyes. "Steal it, kill for it, soak it in blood—does it matter? It's gear, not technology. Why risk our lives for something so mundane? If I were lea—" He broke off at Drovic's expression.

"But you aren't leading, are you?" The older man's gaze was as cold as his voice. "The day you can beat me with your own sword in hand is the day you will make decisions. Until then, it is I who makes the choices." Drovic snorted. "Have you forgotten everything? We don't buy what we need. We steal and kill so that we look like other raiders. If Ariye ever realized we were more mercenaries and soldiers than raiders, we'd be hunted down like carriers of the plague."

"So we hide what we take with fire."

"Or with slaughter or slaves."

Talon's lips thinned. How many men had Drovic killed, not to further his goal, but simply to protect his own group as he planned his long-term revenge? And when had his father ever actually struck a blow against the birdmen? He bit his lip to silence. Drovic took that as agreement.

They rode up the next ridge and back down into the cut on the other side, stopping well back from the next junction to wait for the caravan they had spotted. Automatically, each raider dropped from the saddle in silence, led his dnu into the brush beneath the trees, and forced his riding beast to its knees. Talon and Wakje left their dnu with the others and crept forward to keep a watch. Shafts of afternoon sun heated the air on the south side of the ridge, and the warming oils of the plants made a heady perfume when sensed through lupine nostrils. *Dry leaves, skibug dung, the soft brush of the ferns . . .*

Talon settled where skibugs had cut through the undergrowth. As with other swarms that year, the bugs had left their mark, and now the soil would hold their dung until the coming rains diluted it. Once wetted, the tiny eggs excreted in the protective dung would hatch, and the larvae would burrow, separating themselves by sex. The trail of the skibugs would be a double-track of male and female larvae, running nearly parallel to each other, spreading out as they grew, until they reached maturity and merged. That merging place should be noted for Nortun, and Talon automatically judged

how far away that point would be. Garvoset, an herb that
Nortun used in his wound lotion, grew well over skibug
mergings.

Wolves howled abruptly. Talon's eyes were instantly blinded.
The thought of the herbs had triggered the Gray Ones like an
eggbeater, scrambling his concentration. It was *her*, he realized. The image was almost clear. The woman: dark eyes,
black hair, soft skin. The woman with the wolves. His fists
clenched on grass. A woman who had trapped him, forced
him to need something he could not recognize. Brittle strands
shredded beneath his nails. A woman like Nortun, who worked
with herbs.

Dion froze. The scars on the side of her face went white.
She tried to blink, but her violet eyes were unfocused with the
weight of a hundred wolves' howling. *Dust, old dung
pounded into roots, the scent of rich forest soil* . . . For an instant, the stall gate under her hands disappeared and the distant images became sharp. Her hand clenched the herb
pouches at her belt. *Wolfwalker,* they sent. *The den, the mate,
the bonding.*

Kiyun put his hand on her arm to shake her gently, but she
twisted and snapped, and he snatched his hand back to save it
from her teeth.

"Don't touch her," Tehena said sharply.

Dion breathed with difficulty, but the sharp burst in the
pack was fading.

The thought in the gray was clear: *The hunt sharpens.*

Whose hunt? She forced out the thought.

Yellow eyes gleamed in her mind. *Yours.*

"Dion?" Kiyun asked.

She shook her head silently. She could not voice what she
had felt. Whoever was in the packsong was now strong
enough to force the sense of his own needs across the distance. They weren't simple like hunger pangs or thirst. No, it
had been desperation deep in the gray—a need to break out,
to break free of a bond that he rejected but could not avoid. A
need to strike at the world that had hurt him. Dion felt the
pain like burning blood, and that frightened her almost as

much as the icy fury behind that will. It was her own pain, her own needs, echoed in the pack. She shivered again, this time almost violently. The wolves in the distance were pushing that violence north and east, while those here drove her south. There was an invisible point at which their two packs would meet, and it was somewhere in these mountains.

She needed Ariye, she thought blindly. In spite of the elders, the duties, the graves, she needed home, her wolf, Ariye. The wild ones were too rough in her mind. She needed the smooth bond, the single wolf-bond that was intimate and calm, but Hishn was in Ariye. The need to protect the child in her womb colored the packsong's urgency to protect their own pups. *Protect,* they whispered in her mind. *Home, bonding, mating, life. Take away the burning. Promises, Healer. Ours. Yours.*

Talon felt the clarity of his realization sing out into the gray, and the urge to snarl was almost unbearable even as the first wagons came into view. He gritted his jaw till his teeth ground like glass over sand. He forced himself to breathe. Forced himself to remain still and not spring up to run as the caravan riders drew closer. He wanted that woman. He recognized it now, that need that was borne in gray. In the wolf pack, she was his. That was what he had lost when he lost his family: home, a bond, his other half. He didn't even know how much time had passed since he had been mated, but it had been long enough that the gem studs in his sternum had bound themselves to his bones. Long enough that his need had become a driving force that matched the will of the wolves.

Something whuffed beside him, and he started. *Find her. Protect,* the Gray Ones growled. *East and north to the cold.*

Talon cursed under his breath. If Wakje saw, or if his father caught the scent of wolf on him again . . .

The wolf crept forward a meter. Its black-rimmed eyes were intent on the road, and like Talon, its shoulders were tense. But the wagons rattled with smooth precision, and the soft voices of the drovers kept the dnu from starting as they caught the raiders' scents.

"You don't belong here," Talon whispered to Gray Ursh.

It turned its yellow gaze to him, and he felt the shock of that voice like ringing crystal. *Then follow,* it commanded.

"Not yet." He closed his eyes and broke the contact.

The wolf growled low but did not move away.

At the junction, two mid-caravan scouts pulled up to check the road. Both were older, with gray streaks in their hair and faces that showed the weathering of nine or ten decades. They were as much a mismatch as any pair: the woman was stocky and almost pudgy for her height; the man was lean as a bean-pole. But they were just as obviously so closely in tune that they had little need to speak. The woman simply raised her eyebrows slightly; the lean man nodded, and they moved on without looking again down the road, leading the wagons past. At some point, those wagons would meet up with the venges; someone would mention the other tracks . . .

Hunters, the Gray One agreed. Talon flicked his gaze at the wolf, but the Gray One did not blink.

It took twenty minutes for the last wagon to roll out of sight, and by that time, Talon was tight as a wire. As soon as the last wagon was fifty meters away, Wakje began to roll out of the ferns, but Talon hissed at the other man. The raider froze. A moment later, four trailing scouts rode into view, and Wakje's face became blank and hard.

The trailing riders passed, and Talon got carefully to all fours before remembering his feet. Wakje gave him an odd glance, but said nothing. The gray wolf crept away.

They crossed quickly onto Gain Trail and began the steep climb through five kays of towering spruce and pintrees. The relative calm beneath the trees wouldn't last. Like Roaring Ridge and Howling Hill, the wind was as unpredictable along the crest as a woman with child.

Talon rode point for his dozen, fifty meters behind Ki-laltian's group. They were last, not because he had been first before, but because he had most of the wounded. If anyone slowed down on the trail, it would be Talon's group, not the others. He watched Mal carefully as he turned up another switchback. The dour man had still not recovered from his head wound, and his face remained pale, his headaches as blinding as Talon's. "All right?" Talon asked quietly.

"How long to the top?" Mal muttered.

"Thirty minutes. Two more drop-offs."

The other man didn't bother to nod.

They rounded another switchback and brushed through a stand of high-altitude huckleberries. Each rider picked a handful of berries as he passed, but the lead riders did not strip the bushes. Every man could see how many berries there were; they took only the handful that would leave some for all the others. Talon noted it with satisfaction. Discipline was one of the reasons Drovic was successful.

A signal passed down the line for Talon to ride forward and join Drovic, and Talon had to admit that the older man had chosen this year's riders well. Young as some of them were, the months had welded the group into a single mind. They could read each other's body language, realize as a whole the threat that one of them felt, and automatically compensate for a weakness here by shifting their skills over there. Talon's group in particular seemed to be achieving cohesion. It was something Drovic watched closely.

He'd worked his way past most of Kilaltian's riders when behind him, there was a sudden flurry of motion. Thaul shouted a curse as his dnu half reared, and Tchouten's dnu backed wildly, jamming against Merek's beast behind him. Something small and dark—could have been a rabbit, might have been a whirren—flew down the trail beneath the hooves. The edge of the trail crumbled. Tchouten's dnu panicked. Tchouten felt his dnu's head go down for the buck and tried to kick out of the stirrups, but his left boot caught in the irons. He half unseated to the left and grabbed for the saddle horn. His dnu actually leaped off the cliff, and Tchouten screamed as the dnu started to tumble. He broke free—moons alone knew why he did so—he wasn't going to land any better without the dnu than with it—and they fell apart for an infinite, shrieking moment. Then they hit, far below, and the screaming ceased abruptly.

Thaul and Merek fought their dnu back under control. The sides of the other dnu heaved in the thinner air as the line jerked to a halt. Curses rippled through the riders until finally the beasts were quieted. "Well, shit," Ebi muttered softly. Strapel nodded silently.

"Trail's weak by the boulder." The warning was called back along the trail. The line began to move again, and Tchouten's body, far below, got barely a glance from the others. Talon shrugged off his anger and kicked his dnu up the trail. There was no sense of grief for the man, but only an icy rage at the waste. He wondered if he would have felt differently if it had been one of his men, not Kilaltian's, who fell so uselessly. He already knew the answer.

Near the top of the ridge, the wind grew to a buffeting series of slaps. They plodded into the thick layer of windfern, and the whipping motion made the steep trail disorienting. It was beautiful in its own way: a sea of vibrant green and gold with waves that threatened to push them off the cliff. There was no place to rest. Stopping meant losing momentum, and it would have taken a whipping to get the dnu going again.

The lead riders went over the thin crest, waist-deep in ferns and skylined in spite of their caution. Then the pack dnu started over. Like the others, Drovic's face was windwhipped red, and Talon tucked half his face into his elbow as he urged his dnu up those last meters. From up ahead, a faint shout reached him. For a moment, his eyes teared from the wind, then the violent gust brought the rest of the shocked sounds to his ears.

"Look out!"

"Get down!"

"It's an attack!"

Talon went off the saddle like a rabbit seeking a bolt-hole. A ragged hail of war bolts shot wildly through the front part of the line. NeHrewni fell heavily at the feet of his dnu, and maClea was dead before her head hit the rock that split her skull on the trail. Stobner was caught like an overstuffed target in the saddle, a war bolt buried in the V of his shirt, and his thick body only beginning to shudder. The others threw themselves into the ferns.

The fire became suddenly heavier, and Talon hugged his sword and bellied into the stalks, gagging on powdered spores as he scrambled away from the dnu. His father elbowed in fast beside him. He glanced at Drovic, noted that the man wasn't harmed, and felt some of his tension ease. "We surprised them," he said, his voice just sharp enough for Drovic to hear him over the wind. "They can't know."

Drovic signaled agreement. Drovic's lead riders and pack dnu looked like a merchant's train—it was what the man counted on to keep them safe from the venges. What they hadn't planned on was another group of raiders setting up an ambush for merchants on the shortcut.

Another hail of war bolts tore through the ferns. An attacker popped up like a prairie dog, shot in a tiny, useless lull in the wind, and disappeared back into the green before the arrow skittered over a saddle. It was almost impossible to hold sight on anything in the waving sea of ferns. Except—a pocket of fronds whipped with abbreviated movement, and Talon knew there was a man beneath it. He drew his knife and waited for the wind to gust. Then he lunged to his feet and duck-ran with the howling burst of air, leaving his startled father behind. Ferns snapped and crushed beneath his boots, spores puffed up like dust. He was nearly on the man before the other raider heard him. The man twisted and, startled, released the bolt too quickly. The arrow ripped through Talon's sleeve. He blocked the pain and the bow aside and stabbed down hard, slicing stalks and flesh. The other man thrashed wildly, clubbing Talon's arms, face. Then the blows weakened and the man went still. Talon rocked to his feet, crouching, listening to the sounds in the wind.

Kilaltian's men wormed over the ridge, leaving their dnu behind. Two went down immediately, but the ambushing raiders took one look at the amount of steel coming over the ridge, loosed their last shots, and fled. Talon followed, scramble-tackling a man who burst up almost beside him. A fist caught Talon on the cheekbone, and another on the ribs, but his knife was already moving. Blade met blade; steel skittered; Talon drove in. Ferns puffed. His fist caught the other man's arm, half turning him. The arc of his knife sliced clean. Spores released. The carotid spurted. The man jerked back and down. It was in his blue eyes, that knowledge of death.

The raider grabbed at his neck. Talon stabbed again, punching his knife through leather, ribs, lung. Blue eyes glazed. A weak arm blindly cut air. Golden spores floated down onto momentary pools of blood, speckling the rich red color. And the green-gold sea washed overhead in a lovely rippling pattern while blood soaked into the soil.

Talon crouched in the broken ferns, alone and breathing harshly while the other raiders fled. His heart was pounding, his gray eyes hard and searching for threat, for movement. He didn't notice the green or gold, only the sounds in the wind. Finally, he rubbed his arm, felt the warmth, and looked down. He cursed quietly, coldly. Blood soaked his sleeve. The jagged cut was shallow, but as his heartbeat slowed, it began to sting like a son of a worlag. His ribs ached where he had hit the ground hard, and one of his legs was weak. He heard Fit and Strapel killing someone they found hiding, and nearby, he heard the deliberate snap of ferns as his father searched for him hastily. Carefully, he wiped his knife on the other raider's jacket. The sense of the wolves kept him silent.

Drovic found him there, sprinkling wound powder in the gash. The glint of fear in Drovic's eyes vanished as he saw his son alive, and flashed to cold anger as he saw the blood. "What the hell were you doing?" Drovic demanded. He dragged his sleeve across his mouth where a knife had cut a tiny line across his lip. "Jumping an archer but moving as slow as a gods-damned Lloroi?"

Talon gave him a hard look and snapped, "I don't see you racing to Ariye to take the post."

"When I'm ready," Drovic snarled, "I'll take that post and everything that goes with it."

"You damn well ought to be ready now," Talon returned coldly. He one-handed the vial shut and stuffed it back in his belt pouch. His anger seemed to grow with every breath. "Thirty years you've been skulking toward that county. We're so close to Ariye I can taste the dust in their bakeries, but you keep turning away." He pressed on his arm to force the wound powder deeply into the gash. "Get me a bandage," he snapped. He ignored the glint in Drovic's eyes. "What the hell is stopping you, anyway?"

Drovic jerked a wad of gauze from his belt pouch and thrust it at his son with equal anger. "The people didn't want me. Moons!" he said explosively. Then, to Talon's surprise, Drovic dropped beside his son. Talon noted with petty satisfaction that someone must have loosened Drovic's teeth, not just cut his lip, because the older man dug out a pain stick to chew on desultorily.

"They didn't want me," Drovic repeated quietly. "They wanted soft words and soft plans, not my brutal"—he spoke the word with an almost dispassionate sarcasm—"honesty. They didn't want the hard path to a better future, but the comfortable life instead." He swatted at a grafbug attracted by the blood on his lip. "They knew as well as I did that the Ancients manipulated power like the Aiueven. We could have that power again, or even create something better if we would just stand up to the birdmen."

Talon wrapped the gauze smoothly around his arm. "Leading by steel is always dangerous. 'The warrior, unwanted after victory.' "

"Warriors and swords, elders and plague; black steel, blood steel. What does it matter? Any goal that requires a single death is equal to any other."

Talon could not help his words. "Some goals are more destructive."

Drovic's lips tightened. "Which is more destructive, boy? The languid, lingering death of the hairworms? Or—" He nodded at Talon's forearm. "—the sudden strike of steel? Would you rather die because you slept in the wrong place in the dirt, or risk great war once, and after victory, have the choice of turning your steel blade into towers and ships of the sky? We lived in domes built from marvels when we first landed on this world. Now we live in trees and huts and scrabble to stay alive. Steel is freedom, boy. It's the path to the stars and beyond."

Talon wrapped the ends of the gauze tight over the thick wad, then tied a one-handed tight knot over the bulge. "Steel destroys not only those it kills, but those it leaves behind."

"Pah." Drovic got to his feet. "Steel strikes swiftly, so the grief it brings is a single event—over like a bloody sunrise as soon as day begins. The soft death, the wasting death, is the one that drags you down, not only for the victims, but for all who must care for them. We use up our resources trying to treat the dead who still breathe, and there is nothing left for the future. But it is 'comforting' to the living, and it bolsters our righteousness, assuages our guilt and sorrow by serving the living grave." The older man paced the broken ferns. "Leave the bodies," he shouted as other men began to drag them free of the ferns. "They'll see no difference between ours and theirs." His blue-gray eyes glinted back at Talon. "I offered our people a harder path, one with privation and sacrifice and the reward of regaining the stars within a hundred years. Face and fight the twice-damned Aiueven, or acknowledge that they rule this world."

Talon picked up the sword and knife from the dead raider. His heartbeat was still high, and the adrenaline was only now beginning to soften in his body. "And the Lloroi?" he asked.

"He twisted the choice and offered the people a dream instead, as if life on this world should be our goal should our sciences fail to free us. So he wasted men and time and money on making the world livable in a limited way instead of treating it like a prison." Drovic squinted across the ridge. "The people chose. Aye, and they did not choose me. So we maintain our barbaric appearance aboveground and hide our science in cellars. People." His voice grew sharp. "Blind as glacier worms, soft as gelbugs, and ambitious as cats in the sun. In this world, with these Lloroi, the stars will never be close at hand, but always far away. But the people are comfortable with their businesses and tree-shaped homes, their careful limits on growth and goals. Comfort!" Drovic spat the word. "It is comfort that will kill us."

Talon glanced at his father's expression. Time had dried his father of softness and left him hard as bone, but it had made Talon dangerous with ambition. He wanted leadership of this group, and if he could not have that, he wanted a group of his own. He said deliberately, "It has been nearly thirty years. There are new elders, new guild heads. The Lloroi—"

Drovic cut him off with a sharp gesture. "The Lloroi took my job, my future, and my family. He stole my son and my daughter to raise as his own, without memory of me, and left me a shell of a father."

"And my sister?" He thought of a girl with light brown hair and laughing green eyes, and the wolves in his head started growling.

"My son was destroyed by the Lloroi, and my daughter fled the county as we did. The Lloroi has done his best to erase me from his history, just as he's done the same to you."

"You will hold that grudge till it turns to stone and paves your way to Ariye."

"And you of all people should understand that. You were abandoned as I was, left for dead, your children taken away."

Wolves howled with a blur of images, and Talon stifled a gasp as a lance of pain shafted through his head. "Why focus on Ariye when the whole world is ours for the taking?"

"Because it is my home, as it once was yours. And no matter how much I want the world, I want Ramaj Ariye more."

And I want my family back, Talon thought savagely. The Lloroi may have erased Talon from Ariye, but Drovic was doing the same by keeping him out of the county. Someday, he would find his mate again, and moons, he hoped she was strong, for his fury at being abandoned was more than a moonwarrior's rage, and it would need a long, long venting. Like the woman in the wolves, he swore his mate would find no peace, for he would send her to the seventh hell and back, just as she had cursed him when she stole his sons.

East, Talon thought. To the north and east. First the wolf-woman, then Ariye. "Let me go in your place," he bit the words out. "I will speak to the council for you. I will face the Lloroi."

"Not if all nine moons met on solstice." Drovic's voice was hard. "The last time you rode through that county, you rode carelessly and fast. You were seen. You were recognized. Your actions have not been forgotten."

Talon's lips tightened at the implied criticism, but he said calmly enough, "One rider leaves little backtrail and is as hard to see as a white mink in the snow."

Drovic regarded him for a long moment. "Talon, I tell you this utter truth: If you set foot in Ariye, you will die."

Talon stared at his father. It was not the conviction in Drovic's voice nor the steadiness of his gaze, but the bleakness in his father's eyes that convinced him of that truth. Slowly, Talon nodded.

Drovic turned away and stalked to his dnu, leaving his son to follow.

Talon did not immediately move out of the ferns. The wolves pulled him east toward the ramaj that would kill him; his father drove him west for blood. The venges were beginning to close like a noose. He was caught like a hare between worlags. He found his lips curled as if he would snarl, and he forced himself to relax. One of his goals was already shifting, growing stronger, closer with the wolves. That gray woman was no longer waiting for him in Ariye. She was riding like him, pounding the roads to dust with the same rage he ate with his stew. He rubbed his half-crippled left hand and smiled grimly as he realized that he looked forward to their battle. He had been raised to fight—that will was half his nature, and his weakness was growing less each day. He tested his legs, and although he limped, the muscles bunched and took the pain well. One more ninan, he promised himself; then he would tear through Ariye on the backs of the wolves, and hunt down the wolfwalker woman. He howled with the gray in his mind.

XI

Rhom Kheldour neKintar

What is the bond between brothers?
Is it love, hate, or blood that binds?
And does it even matter,
When to each other they cannot be blind?

   —From Questions, *the fourth text of Abis*

By late afternoon, the desert heat peaked, and Rhom and Gamon pulled up in a well-used camping circle on the edge of the desert proper. Gamon dismounted, stretched, and checked the stone-lined well. He didn't expect much. The well cover was coated with dust, and as he suspected, the brittle grass that clung to the wall rocks had not seen moisture in ninans. But he lifted the cover aside, looked below, and sent the bucket down. When he winched it back up, he ran his finger across the bottom of the bucket, then reset the container and recovered the well with care.

"Anything?" Rhom asked.

"Dry as a winter sow."

Rhom studied the older man. Like Rhom, Gamon's ears, face, neck, and hands were smeared with sun-grease. They wore Ariyen-made sunglasses that wrapped around their temples to protect their night sight; the desert light was bright enough to degrade their night vision for a day and a half after each harsh exposure. Both men had discarded their heaviest garments for lightweight, tight-weave, billowy clothes. Last night, when the temperature had dropped like a stone, they had layered everything and slept spooned to keep each other warm.

There had been almost no gradual change from the Randon-nen peaks to the high-desert drylands. Instead, the mountains had simply flattened into layers. For the past thirty-six hours, the sun-shrunk hills had been broken only by the beginnings of the mesas. Gamon glanced back at the black-haired smith. "Still sure?"

"Aye." Rhom did not hesitate.

"Even with that on your boot?"

The younger man looked down and jerked back from the edge of the well. The head of the thin worm that had been exploring the leather sank back into the sand. Rhom swallowed. He could have sworn he had seen teeth in that tiny mouth, sharp fangs like a mudsucker. Mudsuckers, sandworms, cave-bleeders, eels—they were all related. He had forgotten how calm his mountains were, where it seemed as if the only things that tried to kill him were the rocks and the run-off floods. He forced himself to shrug in answer to the other man's question. "It's just a sandworm," he said steadily. "And a small one at that."

"They aren't the only things with teeth."

"Glacier worms," Rhom said absently.

The heat that wavered up in sheets mocked the dusty, rain-split canyons, while overhead, the sun burned the sky away to a cloudless, thalo blue. "Dion?" Gamon asked obliquely.

Rhom stared across the mesas. "I can feel her, up in the cold, in the mountains." He gestured toward the ravine. "I look at this drop-off and see a different cliff. Or I look at that sandworm and see a glacier worm instead. It's like a flash of fear or a memory that isn't mine. She's traveling south, but it's into the mouth of danger." He rubbed his left hand unconsciously, and Gamon frowned as he noted the gesture. Dion's left hand was scarred, and she often rubbed her fingers along the old marks when she was thinking.

"You are close to the wolves." It was a question, not a statement.

"Aye," Rhom agreed. "As Dion's twin, I couldn't help but be close."

"Can you use the wolves to reach her?"

"I'm no wolfwalker. Even if I could find a wolf on the other side of the desert, Dion would be out of range when I did. She's heading higher into the mountains even now, and the wolves can't follow where there is no game. Eventually she'll leave them behind. By the time I reach Hishn, Dion will be deaf to the wolves, not just to me."

"So as the pack falls behind, the distance will also make their voices faint."

"And help to keep her human," he agreed.

"As much as she was before."

Rhom gave him a sharp look.

The older man shrugged. "She's your sister. You think of her as human first, and a wolfwalker only second. I don't have that blindness. She is a wolfwalker—one of the strongest I've ever met, and one who was caught only briefly in a human mating. Surely you can see that. Growing up with you, she ran wild in the Randonnen mountains, and when she came to Ariye, she ran wild in our peaks as a scout, and we encouraged that. We needed her skills."

"She paid too high a price to work for you."

Gamon did not disagree. His weathered hands tightened on the worn leather reins, and he looked down at his fingers. They were gnarled now from decades of riding and fighting. They would be aching knobs in fifty years, long before he could see himself quitting. But he could not let go of his sword any more than the wolves could release Rhom's twin. He looked back at the other man. "It's a hard road you are choosing, Rhom."

The burly rider gazed at Gamon. "No harder than the one she has taken." He followed Gamon's glance north past the sands. "If we go up through the Ariyen pass, we'll find word of her one way or another. There are only two ways into Ariye from the north, and even Dion must take one."

"She has always found her own routes, Rhom."

Rhom's voice was flat. "She won't be able to feel the wolves thickly at that altitude, and that will frighten her, remind her of her mortality, keep her from bushwhacking the snow. Without the wolves, she'll be stuck on the roads like us. And this is the first time she has been without her own wolf for so long. I don't think she can stand it much more." He frowned slowly. "But, we could help Gray Hishn call Dion more strongly to Ariye."

Gamon raised his gray eyebrows. "What do you mean?"

"We could take Hishn with us. Take her north."

"Into the mountains?" Gamon was already shaking his head. "You just pointed out that the Gray One would starve before we passed the first peak."

"Not if we carry food enough for her as well as us."

"You're talking about provisioning a wolf, Rhom."

The younger man grinned. "Yes." He made the word a so-what question.

Gamon cocked his head, then slowly grinned in return. "I won't share my dnu."

"You will if Hishn gets hungry."

Gamon chuckled, then grew serious. "If we take Hishn with us, Dion will know we are coming."

"Then she will know she has to face me." His voice was quiet. "We are twins, Gamon. I will not let her go."

The older man nodded slowly. He stared out at the alpine desert, and his memories of the sand and grit of previous crossings clung to his skin and made him want for water. Finally he said, "If we are to continue, you should know where the next two tinajas are." The younger man nodded, and he knew that Rhom would listen and remember just as accurately as his twin recalled wolfsong. "That red streak on the left ridge, that is the road we follow. Trace that line down to where it disappears in a dark vee. Two thumb-widths to the right you will see a speck of shadow that is shaped like a worlag's main claw-hand. That's the overhang under which we'll find our first tinaja if the next roadside spring is dry."

"How far?"

"About ten hours from the next well. One good night of riding."

"And the next well?"

"Twelve hours if we rode straight through. But we'll camp at dawn when we reach the first tinaja, and sit out the heat of the day."

Rhom nodded, then paused. "Why did we ride in the heat yesterday?"

The older man's voice was dry. "So that you could feel it firsthand, before we had gone too far to take a different route."

Rhom's violet eyes grew cold. "You hoped I would choose to circle to the north or take the southern road instead. You gambled that I would give in to comfort, rather than risk the sun."

The other man corrected, "I hoped that you would make the decision about this route while fully understanding the risk, not just what you imagined it to be."

Rhom nodded, but his eyes remained narrowed.

The gray-haired rider shrugged, wiped his brow, and reset the wide-brimmed hat that had replaced his war cap. "At least for today, it will be a flat, easy road."

"Except for the heat," Rhom returned shortly.

"Aye, except for that." Gamon pulled his bandana up over his mouth.

The younger man followed suit. He glanced down at the sand that had hidden the worm. It was smooth again like a liar.

XII

Talon Drovic neVolen

Violence and fear are our arrows,
Agony, our sword.

　—*Ariyen saying*

The raiders followed Drovic up through Eilif like a flock of lepa, swift and dark and dangerous. With their numbers down to just over thirty, they could no longer afford to work round-about up the county. They had lost four riders on the ridge, one to their own hands rather than leave him bleeding, and five others were wounded. With Mal and Ki still out of action, that meant they had barely twenty-five fighters. Drovic was pissed as a pregnant worlag.

They passed the blackened skeletons of a short caravan, then rode around a small village where the husks of two burned houses still wept sap. The once-living ribs of the homes were cracked and charred, and clouds of insects covered the pitch that streaked the black posts with a sickly, sticky yellow. Drovic muttered as he saw the ruins, "Goddamn raiders will bring every venge in the county down on us."

Another day, and they were still fifty kays from the border, and far enough from Drovic's contact for handling the bioforms that Drovic began snarling and snapping at everything like a rabid dog with broken teeth. The man's desire to cut through everyone, caravan or village alike, was becoming almost a living entity. Talon understood his father's sentiments, though not for the same reasons. He found himself flexing his weakened wrist more often, and noted that the sword he carried was becoming light for his hand. Soon, he told himself.

Drovic's face was set as they made a dark camp in another of the clearings he had marked on his maps. There were always dips and hollows between ridges, places where thirty men could hide without being seen or heard. Drovic collected such places, marking them on his maps, sending scouts to check them out, and caching wood in some. Talon had kept a similar set of notes once, but those notes were gone. Now he relied on his father, and that was one more irritation that worked at his aching mind. He rubbed his temples and cursed the ax of pain that kept cutting his skull as he pulled up beneath the trees.

This place was a dry pond about sixty meters long, nestled between two hills. The surrounding trees were broad-leaved and dense, and there were few exposed rocks to pass along the sounds of the camp. Still, the raiders made no fires and cooked only by stove. Bad enough that the food smells would waft along on the wind; fire would be worse. Light flickering up into the leaves would be as blatant a sign to their presence as if they hung a body on the trail, and the smell of a wood fire was so distinct that a hunter could scent it kays away.

Drovic squatted beside Talon as his son brewed his bitter tincture. "How bad is it?"

Talon shrugged. It was the old wound, not the new bruises, that pounded his skull. Without the herbs, that pain would have been blinding. "It's been over three months," he said sourly, watching the rou. "You'd think I'd be better by now."

Drovic raised his eyebrow. "You're stronger, you can ride longer, and the dizzy spells are mostly gone. Keep taking those herbs, and you'll be whole again by the end of the year."

Talon took advantage of the suggestion to test the mixture and avoid his father's eyes. The dizzy spells were completely gone; it was the tincture, not the wound, that fuzzied his mind, and the wolves that made him stagger. He sniffed the brew and drank it quickly down. It was bitter as usual, and he followed it with a long drink of water from the bota Drovic handed him.

Drovic took the bota back, swigged, and wiped his mouth with the back of his hand as he looked around the clearing. The sky had remained clear, and it would be chilly by early morning, but the trees would shelter them from the sun, and they had water in the stream. "We'll stay here a day," the older man decided. "There's too much traffic on the roads. I want to let some of it pass."

Talon nodded. He understood Drovic's concern. The venges had not let up, and this far north, the communities were more tightly knit. It was easy to note the strangers. "Too many hunters," he murmured. He caught his father's dry expression and grinned in spite of himself. "Pots and kettles," he agreed.

"Could be a general housecleaning," Drovic mused. "Either way," he said sourly, "You have your wish. We'll have to head east for fifteen more kays before we can turn back toward Bilocctar."

Talon shrugged deliberately. He had no choice in the urging of the wolves, but the wolves would not let him go. He no longer argued. The images from his dreams were becoming clearer each day. The woman, slim, dark-eyed, dark-haired . . . He watched his father walk away, and worked his wrist to strengthen it.

In the morning, clouds swept down from the mountains until they were enveloped in a constant drizzle. Drovic cursed the rain, cursed the daylight, cursed the dnu and raiders. He finally sent Talon, Wakje, and Ki up a ridge to scout a better route. They were thirty kays south of the Circle of Fifths, and Talon could actually see the pass that led into Ramaj Ariye. It drew his eyes like glue, and he had to bite down on the surge of gray in his head as he squatted by Ki and Wakje.

"Think that's Edinton over there," Wakje pointed.

Talon followed Wakje's gaze. Neither used binoculars. A flash of light on the glass would be worse than a torch for announcing their presence. "That's the roof of the message tower," he confirmed.

"Too bad we can't stop in," Ki murmured. "I hear they make a rabbit dish that would make a dead man salivate."

Wakje grinned sourly. "No difference between rabbit and rast if it's your last meal."

"I'd risk it," Ki returned. "No subcutaneous fat, just juicy, tasty meat in a sage-and-orange glaze . . ." He sighed. "The Ancients really knew what they were doing when they brought rabbits here."

Talon raised one dark eyebrow. "You know about rabbits but not about cows?"

"I've never seen a cow." Ki gave him a suspicious look. "You going to tell me that there's something odd about rabbit teeth?"

"No, not unless you mean that they grow right through its skull."

Ki looked startled. "Through its brain?"

"Brain, bone, jaw, and skull. Top and bottom, just like two french curves, one inside the other."

"Right," he sneered.

"Truly. They chew on rocks to wear their teeth down and keep from stabbing themselves."

"Sure, Talon."

He held up his hands. "I swear to the seventh moon."

Wakje sent Talon a sly look as Ki turned away. "You keep swearing on that moon, and it'll fall out of the sky and crush you."

Talon merely grinned. But when they made to climb down from the ridge, he didn't follow immediately. Instead, he stared to the east. *Find. Find her . . .* Wakje turned back and watched him for a long moment until Talon met his gaze, deliberately looked north, and moved to join him and Ki.

They regrouped, and Drovic kept them at a canter and

turned them west again. Talon nearly bit his lip as they passed another road east. The chill in his bones was getting worse, as if the farther north they rode, the more his limbs grew icy. "We should reconsider riding the old trails," Talon suggested to Drovic. "Or head farther north where the farms peter out, before turning west. It might even be better to go all the way up to the Circle of Fifths before cutting over to Bilocctar."

"That's a hell of a long ride."

"Yes, but at least we'd reach Bilocctar without losing half our men. We're too noticeable here." North, he thought. Or east. Either one relieved the pressure of the gray geas.

"Still sure about the trails?"

"Sure as a woman in love."

Drovic nodded his approval.

They turned onto a wide trail that Talon had no trouble identifying. Some things were apparently never forgotten, and he knew he had scouted here when he was a young man: he had a vague memory of running trail with his father's brother, of a clumsy pack with straps cutting into his thin shoulders, blisters on his heels from his boots, and a curse in every breath.

As the day wore on, he rode with that too-familiar tension. The skin around his eyes was tight, and he had to force himself to concentrate. Behind him, Mal listed slightly as his own riding beast stumbled, and Talon, hearing it, let his own dnu fall back. "All right?" he asked sharply.

Instinctively, Mal straightened up. "Fine as the fur on a stickbeast," the dour man retorted.

It was something the barrel-chested Dangyon would have said, and Mal had perfectly mimicked the other man's accent. Talon's lips quirked. He caught a flicker of wry appreciation in Mal's eyes. The man knew that Talon had seen his weakness, but the raider also knew that Talon, with his own stubborn pride in riding in spite of the pain, would not humiliate Mal by offering his support.

They made Long Road without incident except for leaving the dust of the shortcut hanging in the air like nooses. Talon brushed at his war cap to knock away the mites that might have clung to it. "Left shoulder," he told Sojourn as the other man trotted beside him. Sojourn slapped at a tiny knot.

"Damned parasites," the other man said sourly. "I wouldn't mind them so much if they wouldn't bite more than once. Know the difference between a mite and a mate?"

Talon shook his head.

"Neither do I, but I hear the mite bites less often."

"You've been alone too long if you've become that soured on women."

"As have you, if you're turning down Roc when she's offering that kind of body."

Talon's gaze narrowed. "Roc sees everyone as a toy to vent her hate on. Perhaps I want more than a body that holds only violence."

"Hate and rage have to be expressed as much as love and kindness." The other man grinned slyly. "And an enemy can make a better lover than a friend."

Talon didn't answer.

By late afternoon, when they reached the south branch of the Cades River, Talon's headache was pounding like the hooves of the dnu. Drovic glanced back at his son and gestured with his chin for the younger man to join him.

"Water's low, but swift," Talon said shortly as he reined in.

Drovic pointed. "We'll cross there."

Talon nodded and resisted the inclination to look back at Ki or Mal.

Drovic motioned the point riders across, their dnu stepping gingerly down into the flow. Strapel had his bow strung and an arrow in hand, though the bolt was not yet nocked. Ebi, in the lead, had his sword half drawn.

"They share everything, don't they," Talon commented, noting the way each man was completely aware of the other.

Drovic recognized the nonverbal question, the need for his son to know more about his own men. If Drovic was disappointed that Talon did not recall more, the older man hid it well. He said merely, "It started when they were the only ones to survive a raid they had been on together. They joined up with me after that. A month later, we were hit by bihwadi— it was a swarm year, just like this one, and we lost three-quarters of our men. Ebi pulled a beast off Strapel's back. Strapel returned the favor when Ebi stepped in a poolah's trap. For the last two years, they've believed that each survives only because of the other."

Strapel's dnu hit a deeper spot and was swept downstream a few meters before it regained its footing in the shallows. Ebi poised, ready to help, but the other man didn't need it. As Strapel splashed through then thinner water, Ebi moved into the main flow, keeping his sword chest-high.

"Neither will be effective until they reach the bank," Drovic noted sardonically.

Talon shrugged. "There is comfort in holding a weapon near-ready while crossing an open space."

Drovic glanced at him. "You begin to think as your men do, not just for yourself."

"Is that not my nature?"

"Always," Drovic said dryly.

"And that is a disappointment to you?"

Drovic shrugged, his eyes on the river. "I had hoped that, someday, you would follow me as Lloroi, but even by the time your mother died, I think I knew that you would never take my place on the council. You had the focus and strength you needed, but not that kind of will." His voice grew quiet, as if he spoke more to himself than to Talon. "There have always been two kinds of leaders: the ones who pass up victory because they might spill their own blood or lose men, and those who risk everything to do what must be done, regardless of the cost. I always feared you would be the first kind of leader."

Talon kept his mouth shut with difficulty. There was a slow burn in his gut from his father's words. A ninan, he reminded himself. He should be strong enough then. He had not gained back much memory, but he was slowly putting on weight, and the wolves, in spite of hounding him, were focusing on his strength. He flexed his hand on the leather reins and kept his eyes off his father.

Ebi and Strapel reached the far bank, surged onto the bluff, and gave the all-clear signal. Drovic was moving before they finished. He guided his dnu across the rocky river in a series of plunging leaps until it stretched out to swim the deep run. Near the other side, the older man's dnu lost its footing, but Drovic forced the beast's head perfectly toward smoother water so that it regained its footing within seconds. Talon watched without expression. The dnu was no living thing to Drovic, only a means to reach the shore. His father thought of the raiders the same way—as tools, not people who could be led to reach for a better goal. The thought ground against the insides of his skull like the packsong, and he was curt as he motioned his group into the water. No one spoke except to curse softly at the chill.

Oroan and Cheyko made it across without difficulty. Ilandin's dnu faltered but recovered. Talon let Weed reach the midstream before he eased his own dnu in. The shock of cold water hit him hard, and his shivers made him angry. "Soft as a broken beast," he snarled under his breath as the frigid water plunged down into his boots. "Swim, you moonwormed weakling."

He kicked hard, keeping himself afloat across the back of the dnu as the creature nearly submerged. Roc and Ki reached the shallows, but Mal was having trouble, and just as Talon spared the other man a glance, his own dnu lost its footing on the rocks. The roan's middle legs lost their weaker grip; its forelegs were lifted by a wave he did not see coming, and the beast went under. Talon was submerged to his neck before the dnu struggled back to the surface. The dnu grunted to clear its nose, and Talon gasped as he regained his seat. "You want a bath? I'll give you a bath—" His voice broke off as they were washed downstream and slammed into a rock. For a moment, the weight of the dnu crushed his leg against stone. Then he wrenched its head toward shore, and the beast grabbed its footing back from the river and fought its way over the rocks.

Talon was grinning when upstream, Mal's dnu stumbled into the hole where Drovic's beast had lost its footing. For a moment, Mal dragged in the current, one hand gripping the reins. Then the dnu shook free of the man and plunged ahead, leaving Mal to the water. Instantly, Mal went under.

Talon didn't think. He shoved himself from his saddle and, one hand clutching the reins of his dnu, plunged back into the river. The current pulled like a poolah. Mal dunked and was swept toward Talon. Talon kicked against the anchor of his dnu, and the beast grunted in fear as his grip on the reins forced its wedge-shaped head after him. He didn't hear the shouts. Didn't see his father plunging back down along the bank, cursing and clawing at the brush as Drovic fought to match the speed of the current that tried to kill his son.

Talon kicked hard and choked on a wave. Gray howls seemed to hit his brain with a burst of power, and he snarled wildly as he struck out. His weakened left hand was wrapped in the reins so tightly that the dnu chittered in growing fear as his weight dragged its head back toward the deeper water. He reached blindly, caught a glimpse of something dark. He caught fabric. Dunked, he sputtered as Mal's weight swung awkwardly in a half-circle, pulling Talon into the heavier current. He kicked with all his strength. The dnu was fighting him now. Its forelegs scrabbled to regain the shallows, while its other legs churned the river. One of its middle hooves caught Talon a wicked blow on his sore thigh. The leg went dead. He refused to let go of the other man. His knee scraped rock, then his shoulder struck, and then Drovic was pulling him out. Someone was shouting at him, but for a moment, all he could see was churning water and striking hooves in his face.

"Talon, let go."

"Grab him!"

"Watch his head!"

Talon was dumped unceremoniously to all fours. Water cascaded off him. Drovic's words made no sense in his ears as he stared up and saw, for the first time, a crack in his father's hardness. He reached up and gripped his father's forearm, caught his breath roughly, coughed, spat water, and managed, "Can't drown today. Got to make the border."

Drovic's eyes glittered. Then the older man shouted to the others, "Five minutes." He turned back to his son, took a breath to calm himself, and slapped Talon so hard that Talon fell back on his butt on the rocks.

"Son of a worlag," Talon cursed. He pushed himself to his knees. The water weight of his clothes made him stagger. "You moonwormed, dag-chewing poolah—"

"Of all the idiotic stunts." Drovic's voice was hard again, as if fear for Talon had never touched his expression. "You have the brains of a spotted beetle," the older man hurled back. "If you weren't my only son—" He broke off and dragged a hand through his hair. His words were low and so intense that each one was almost a curse by itself. "Don't ever do that again."

"Do what?" Talon got to his feet. "Save a life?" he shot back.

"Throw your life after one already gone."

Talon bit down hard on his fury. Mal sat on the bank some distance away, out of earshot for the noise of the river. The dour man was shivering, his head in his hands as if his fingers were all that held it on his neck. Talon thought he knew how the other man felt. His voice was flat. "So I should have let Mal drown?"

Drovic's eyes narrowed. "We're not riding to a county fair. We don't have time to coddle a wounded man."

Something bit deep inside Talon. He carefully reined in his temper. "He stays with me. You want loyalty, you can't go around abandoning men just because they're wounded."

Drovic's voice was uncompromising. "He rides or he dies."

The gray edge in Talon's icy rage startled him, and he struggled to hold in his anger. "I didn't save him from drowning just to lose him now. I'll be damned if I let him fall off his dnu or die by your blade because of a dizzy spell."

"You'll be damned if you let him slow us. And you're still weak, boy," the older man spat the word, and Talon flushed. "If he can't sit his saddle, you think to ride for two?"

A woman—his mate in his arms . . . A muscle jumped in his bony jaw. "I've done it before."

"Not with a venge behind us."

"Either way, I won't leave him for dead. He's a good man—"

Drovic stared at him. "Good? He's a raider, Son. He's not 'good' except with a sword. He's no more moral than you are, with your bloody blade and that violence burning in your guts. Don't narrow your eyes at me, boy. I've seen the rage in your soul—it's my own. I gave it to you the day you were born, and I've cultivated it like a bull. It's a skill, like any other, so don't waste it on a dead man. You'll need it more when we reach Ariye."

Talon glanced at Mal. The pale man was wringing out his tunic while Nortun brought Mal's dnu downstream. "We can't keep bathing our goals in blood."

Drovic cut him off again with a sharp gesture. "You think it matters to the moons how we reach our goals? The end and the means is a tired argument and not worthy of a soldier. We have a goal. We achieve it. It's that simple." Drovic watched his shoulders tense. "You want something to save?" he demanded. "Something worthwhile? Something historic and great? It had best not be a raider's life. I trained you better than that."

Talon regarded his father for a long moment. "Still. Mal's life is mine to take or leave. If I have to tie him to his dnu to keep him in the saddle, I'll do so, but it will be my decision, not yours. Mal rides with me."

Drovic nodded slowly. "And you ride for me. Never forget that, boy."

Talon watched him stalk away and stared down at his hands. They were long, lean hands—hands that had seen more of riding and fighting than farming or business work. Forty-year hands that were scarred with a dozen white lines where steel blades and claws had gotten through his guard. The dust was devouring decades as they rode, and forty more years from now, he and Drovic would look like brothers, not like father and son. He saw himself through his own eyes and through the eyes of the raiders, and he knew both portraits were true: He was his father, in habit and history and heart, and that, he realized with loathing, was what he hated most. He looked after Drovic, then over at Mal. He would take Mal with him when he left his father. Mal and maybe Weed.

He had not lost his sword, and that seemed a minor miracle. He no longer had his war cap, but his pockets still held his compass and striking bar. Only his herb pouch and cornlids had suffered. He rinsed out the soggy masses and crumbled cornbread flats out of the pouches, and shook the water out of his boots.

He was not surprised when he heard a low growl that caused his dnu to chitter. The gray wolf was almost hidden by the brush, but those yellowed eyes gleamed. Quickly, Talon turned his dnu and stepped forward so that its body hid him from the other raiders.

Gray Ursh snarled, and Talon could see his lean sides. Like the rest of the pack, the wolf had run hundreds of kays in months, and the male's hunger gnawed Talon's gut. The tall man fumbled at his belt until he found his soggy pouch of jerky. Without taking his eyes from the wolf, he opened the bag and threw some of the jerky to the Gray One.

As usual, the creature caught the jerky in his jaw, but did not fade back as the wolf had done before. Instead, the male worked and gulped the jerky, then snarled more loudly. The dnu, nervous at the closeness of the wolf, danced on the stones. The wolf met his gaze, and the shock of the contact made Talon stiffen. *Come,* the wolf snarled. *The hunger calls you. Den to den. Fire to fire. Blood to blood. It is for all our cubs, and for yours.*

Talon breathed. "My son is dead."

As are ours. But there are other cubs.

Talon shook his head, rejecting the images that seemed to claw directly into the grief and rage he could feel but not remember.

Gray Ursh, skittish for all that he had followed Talon for months, darted forward and nipped at Talon's leg. Talon jerked, and Ursh flinched back. Gray eyes again met yellow. Colors shifted. Memories merged. Fever blistered Talon's veins with fire, and his eyes went dark with remembered convulsions and pain. He knew that he had faced death before and that the wolves had been there to save him. It had been Talon, but not Talon. The memories were not his. And the woman was there, he realized. The woman whose hands were gentle, but who carried a lethal power. A woman who, like a witch, injected his mind with Gray Ones, and then bound them there so that none of them could escape. She wore a gray cloak like the pelt of a winter wolf, winter boots, a war cap like his. A woman with eyes as soft and dark as violet dusk. What kind of power did such a woman hold to call him across the mountains? Talon slowly stiffened. And what could he do with that strength? The wolves wanted him to find her, protect her; and what the Gray Ones wanted, they got. Talon knew suddenly that what Drovic sought would come to his own hands instead.

"The woman," he breathed harshly.

You need her.

"You drive me to that need."

She needs you.

And she held power in her hands. Power to fight himself, the wolves, the world. He grinned coldly. "Then she will be mine."

The wild wolf's yellow eyes gleamed as he tasted Talon's sudden determination. Then the gray beast broke their link and leaped up on the eroded bank. Ursh turned and looked at Talon for a long, silent moment. Then he faded into the brush.

Talon jammed his feet in his boots, jerking his socks as they caught in the soggy leather. For a moment, his feet had felt like paws, and his hair like fur. He shuddered, then shook it off and tested the strength of his left hand before carefully wiping his face of all expression. He'd take Mal and Weed, he told himself, and maybe Wakje with them.

He rejoined the other raiders.

XIII

Ember Dione maMarin

"I hear death in my mind," the wolfwalker said desperately.

The Eighth Moon answered, "That is only my brothers and sisters."

"But why is it so constant? Cannot they ever be silent?"

The moon shrugged. "They always speak in the dark, for there are many souls there to guide."

"Then blind me, so that I see only the light."

"That I can do, but I cannot deafen your ears, for what you hear is part of you, and until it dies, it will continue to fill your heart."

"Leave me then," she said sadly. "For if it is part of me, I cannot escape myself."

The Eighth Moon stepped back into the dark and watched the wolfwalker mount the wind. "You cannot escape," murmured the Moon as she watched the wind blow away. "But you can destroy yourself or ride till you find purpose, and there is always hope in that."

—From Night Mares and Wolfwalkers: Tales to Tell Children

Dion stared into the fire, deliberately letting the light blind her eyes to the night. She had been tense all day, as if she wanted to strike out at her companions, and only now, with the dnu bedded down and her thighs aching from hours in the saddle, did she seem to be relaxing. Her leg ached more than usual, and her left hand seemed weak from the ride.

Tehena poured broth into three mugs and set them on a log to cool, then turned back to cutting up tubers. Kiyun worked quietly, mending a stirrup that was beginning to crack. It was Dion who broke the silence. "Have you ever noticed how the wolves come to me, unlike other wolfwalkers?"

Tehena gave Dion a speculating look, but Kiyun shrugged. "Your mind is strong," he said simply. "You're a skilled scout. You were born in and love the mountains. Why wouldn't they come more to you?"

"There are other wolfwalker-scouts. Five in Ariye, three in Randonnen, half a dozen in the eastern counties. The other wolfwalkers are mostly village folk who stay in town, but there are plenty of other scouts like me. No, the wolves have been different in me for years—stronger than in the others. They come easily when I Call, they soften my sleep, they bring me what I need before I know it myself."

Tehena paused with the knife in her hand. "Dion." The woman cleared her throat. "Does this have anything to do with what happened up north?"

The wolfwalker's lips twisted in what might have been called a smile. "It all started there, I suppose."

Kiyun frowned. "What do you mean?"

She did not answer directly. Instead, she said, "Gray Hishn does things for me, as I do them for her, because she and I are bonded. The other wolves, they do them because I am their . . ." She searched for the word.

"Pack leader?" Kiyun suggested. Tehena remained silent. In the minds of the wolves, Dion was no pack leader. The healer was something more.

Dion smiled crookedly at the man. "When I was with the . . ." She hesitated again. With whom? The aliens who killed the Ancients? The birdmen who taunted her with an internal power she could not hope to match? The alien who was now her mother?

"Aiueven," Kiyun supplied quietly.

"Aiueven," she agreed finally. "They heard the wolves in me and thought I was one of their own—a young one who couldn't form my thoughts well. They thought I was lost, abandoned perhaps—they didn't know. But they took me in, and when they finally realized I was human and saw me with their eyes, not their minds, it shocked them. They tried to kill me."

Tehena hid her shiver. Her first glimpse of Dion back then, with the splash of frozen blood across her belly and the staggering run across the ice field—it had stopped her heart. Carefully, she continued cutting the tubers. Her voice was dry. "They almost did kill you."

"In some ways, I think they did." She shrugged at the other woman's suddenly sharp look. "I am no longer the woman I was before."

"And dnu fly with worlag wings." The woman dropped the tubers into the pot and threw in some extractor root so that the liquid hissed with sudden turmoil. "You're still a healer, a wolfwalker, a fighter, a scout. You change only as much as you allow it."

But Kiyun had felt an edge in the wolfwalker for ninans. Ever since she had contacted the alien birdmen, she had seemed different, as if she now held power in her breath, not just when she focused her hands. "What are you now, Healer Dione?"

Staring into the fire, she did not notice his expression. "A ghost with a shadow goal."

"And the goal?"

She didn't look up. The fire burned with tiny pops as moisture expanded in the wood. Wolves growled low in her head. *Warmth, the den, the bonding. South. Destroy the fire that burns us.*

She poked the blaze to stir the coals that had begun to glow. Her voice was soft. "I made a pact once, with the wolves."

Kiyun and Tehena exchanged glances. "In Changsong?" Kiyun asked.

"No. Before that. Before Still Meadow, before Ramaj Bilocctar. It was in the mountains off the coast, the first time I left my home. Years ago. We were on Journey, Rhom and I. We were so very young," she said softly.

Kiyun eyed her warily. "What kind of pact, Healer?"

"A simple one, born of the need to survive." She tapped the stick on one of the looser coals and watched it break apart. "We were trapped in the mountains. Namina had a broken leg, Tyrel had been bitten by rastin. My twin, my friends—all of us were dying. Bodies were burning up with fever, muscles convulsing, eyes going blind. Bones beginning to break."

"And the pact?" Kiyun repeated.

She poked the fire again, watching the sparks whirl up.

"Dion?"

The gray fog growled low in her mind, shifting her thoughts along the inside of her skull. She finally spoke, her voice flat as shale. "That the wolves would teach me Ovousibas so I could heal my friends, and I would find a cure for the plague that still lay dormant in their bodies."

Tehena sucked in a breath. Kiyun held his for a long moment. His voice was carefully neutral, when he said, "A cure? For the plague?"

South, south and west . . .

Dion pushed the stick into the blaze and watched it begin to blacken. When she raised her gaze, the firelight glittered in her eyes and flickered on her silver circlet. Her voice, when she spoke, was the voice of the master healer she still was, not the grief-etched woman she had been. "You think it was arrogance to make such a deal? No one has cured the plague in eight centuries, so who was I to claim I could in exchange for my brother's life? You forget, I was also bound to Hishn, and so I could feel the wolves' pain as clearly as that of my twin, as clearly as my own. The plague still affects the Gray Ones just as it does us when we go to the Ancients' domes. We don't carry the plague, but the wolves do. It settled in their wombs and has been killing their unborn pups ever since. Did you know that, on oldEarth, the wolves had litters of three and four pups? Our wolves are lucky to have one cub apiece. But with a cure, the Gray Ones would no longer burn from fever or lose their cubs to stillbirth. With a cure . . ." She shrugged and picked up another stick to poke irritably at the glowing fire. "They accepted the pact, and we lived."

Tehena said slowly, "Ever since then, the wolves have answered your needs."

Dion's hand tightened on the stick. "Aye. When I Call, they Answer. When I need them, they come. Wild wolves, bonded wolves—it doesn't matter. That pact is as permanent as a stone in the packsong. It's in the memory of all the wolves." Her voice hardened almost imperceptibly. "So when I needed my mate, they hounded him after me. When I need silence, they fill my mind so I cannot hear anything else. I needed to escape the graves, and so the Gray Ones led me north. After Sidisport, I gave up. Aranur—he had left me. He'd died, and left me with our kum-tai bond, our forever bond, and no one to share it with. I wanted to follow him to the moons, but the wolves refused to let me. They had to keep me alive for them, for the promise I had made." Her knuckles tightened on the stick. "They have haunted me with Aranur's voice, as if he were still there to give me strength, and then they came after me themselves to give me a goal to live. I told them I couldn't keep my word. That I needed him, his strength, his focus. That he was my heart. That I could not go on without him."

Kiyun and Tehena exchanged glances. The burly man cleared his throat. "Dion, what are you saying?"

She looked up, her violet eyes burning gold. "Don't you see?" The stick snapped in her hand. She didn't notice. "They answer my needs because I promised to save them. All these years, they have answered me easily, while other wolfwalkers had to strain. All the dreams and nightmares of Aranur's voice calling, crying out to me. All this time, they have kept his memory alive in the packsong because they knew I needed to hear him. They knew I needed the link with him even though he was gone. And now—" Her voice broke off.

There was a voice in the packsong, a man trapped by the wolves, a man who hunted a dark-eyed woman with fury in his hands. She stared at Kiyun, but he thought her eyes were blind. He couldn't tell if it was rage or grief or lupine hunger that glowed in those violet eyes.

"Dion?" Kiyun asked hesitantly.

"The wolves," she said. "They are bringing him here. A man like Aranur. A man who is strong and driven, violent and controlled, sharp and far-seeing, and yet who can hear the wolves if I need him." She threw the last half of the stick in the fire, where the blaze flared up to consume it.

Her voice tore.

"A man to replace my mate."

XIV

Talon Drovic neVolen

A man of courage and peace
Will preserve life in his striving—
But what evils does he allow to live on?
A man of courage and passion
Will take life in his striving—
What innocence has he also destroyed?

Balance courage and courage,
Or your path will descend, not rise;
Balance passion and peace,
Or your triumph will be stained with destruction.

—From the Book of Abis

Hours pounded by until Talon's head spiked hard with every hoofbeat. Since the evening before, after the loss of his herbs, his headache had been throbbing. Now it was banded with agony. Drawn and white, it was all he could do to slide out of the saddle when they stopped to refill their botas at a roadside well.

Weed twirled a loose thread on his jerkin as he watched Talon wince. "Herbs aren't helping?"

"No," he managed. He didn't admit that it was because he

had no herbs to take. But he was tired of the headaches, tired of the weakness, and tired of the tonics and herbs. He'd heal on his own if it killed him. Surely the wolves could help with that—they did so for the wolfwalkers. Even if Talon couldn't run with the wolves, the Gray Ones haunted him as thickly as any wolfwalker could wish. But he nearly passed out from the sledge that slammed inside his head as he tried to mount his dnu. His muscles trembled tightly, and his back almost convulsed. He dragged himself into the saddle and waited infinite blind moments until his vision cleared. By all nine moons, he cursed under his breath, it was the wolves or begging for drugs.

As if they had been waiting for that realization, the gray seemed to reach out for his mind. *Leader.*

To Talon, the voice was a battering ram. *Softly,* he snarled in return.

The wolves growled. There was a jumbled impression of a foggy blanket, a mental shield that he had felt before. The image was incomplete and coarse, but he grasped it like a drowning man grabs a branch. Instantly, the Gray Ones surrounded his mind. The fog thickened until it soaked up the pain like a sponge. There was a momentary adjustment, as if the wolves distributed the discomfort to a hundred gray minds. Talon shuddered in relief. His fists, clenched on the reins, relaxed; the muscles in his back released their cramp; the color returned to his face.

He shifted in the saddle. The faint flash of pain at the movement made him realize that the wolves had not truly relieved the agony, only separated him from it. His body continued to burn. His lips tightened as he realized what he was doing, for if there was no shame in his use of the gray, then he was a spotted worlag. He could not face the fires of his body and maintain any semblance of strength, so he had passed his pain to the wolves. He was hostage to his pain, and only that wolfwalker woman could free him. He owed them all now like brothers, and he knew they would collect.

When they stopped in a small meadow to gather the late-summer berries, Talon caught a glimpse of Mal's face. The other man was as pale as Talon had been that morning, and Mal gripped the dnu's mane more tightly than usual.

"All right?" Talon asked quietly.

Mal's voice was sharp as he returned without preamble, "You had no obligation to me."

"No," Talon agreed. He popped a handful of berries in his mouth around the obligatory plug of extractor root. He knew Mal referred to his actions the day before. Mal gave him a hard look, and Talon shrugged.

"Dizzy," the other man said finally, answering Talon's question.

"Can you ride?"

"Can always ride."

Talon nodded, dropped a few last handfuls of berries in a carrier pouch, and made his way to his dnu.

Sojourn waited for him on the road. The slim man's voice was low. "You'll do yourself no favors building loyalty with some."

Automatically, Talon glanced at Mal. Had Sojourn guessed?

But the other man kept his voice pitched for only Talon's ears. "It's all or nothing for Drovic here, Talon, not for you, and if you remember nothing else from your father, then plant that back in your brain."

Talon regarded the other raider for a long moment. "And where do your loyalties lie?"

The other man chuckled softly. "You ask that, after what I just said?"

Talon studied the slim man, wondering how well he knew him. Physically, they were not so mismatched: Sojourn was as well balanced and muscled as Talon had been before the wounds and fever. Like Talon, Sojourn moved like a hunter, and his eyes—an oddly piercing color that was dark as slate—constantly judged the wind and sky. Their differences lay more in the shape of their faces. Where Talon's features were harsh enough to seem sculpted; Sojourn's were straight and regular. Sojourn's cheekbones were not high enough to draw attention, nor were his brown eyebrows too heavy or light. His short, gray-brown mustache was trimmed to balance the rest of his regular features, and his medium-brown hair was just beginning to show a few strands of gray, along with a faintly receding hairline. In fact, everything about the man was gray-brown and regular—except the sharpness of his gaze. Oddly, though, there was little mobility in Sojourn's face. Instead, the man's expression was usually restricted to his dark-gray eyes, as though he considered everything else to be wasted motion.

Talon glanced at the leather wrap on the other man's sword hilt. It had once been as gray-brown as the man, but was now blackened from sweat and grime, tightly molded to Sojourn's hand. Talon looked back up into those dark, piercing eyes and thought that, had Sojourn wished it, the man could have challenged Drovic and won—as Talon could not yet do. The thought was a shock, and Talon swatted at an insect to hide his sudden knowledge. It was Sojourn, not Drovic's lieutenant, Kilaltian, who posed the greater danger.

"We all ride with Drovic," he said finally. "But I will leave no man behind. If a man eats steel for my cause or my goal, he deserves no less than that."

Sojourn casually stroked his dnu's neck. The riding beast was as gray-brown as the man, and Talon had a sudden vision of the two merging into a single, ten-limbed, drab-colored beast.

"Loyalty again, to your men," the man murmured. "You succumb to an Ariyen's ways."

"And you are so different? I don't see you eager to leave Mal or Ki behind."

"But I am not the leader. It's not my decision to make—not until it affects my survival." Sojourn kept his voice soft as the dnu's chirping. "Aligning yourself with the wounded will not make you a stronger man. You're still weak enough that the only reason you've taken the lead is because Drovic's been giving you the raids." Talon's jaw tightened, but Sojourn merely nodded at his expression. "Since the fever made you weak, Drovic has treated you softly."

Talon's words were hard. "I will not be so frail much longer."

"Aye," Sojourn agreed. "But you're not strong enough yet

to protect your wounded from Drovic or Kilaltian—or from me. A wise man chooses his battles, Talon. He doesn't step eagerly into them because of misplaced . . . loyalty. Your father drummed that into you again last month. Don't fight him on it now."

Talon's voice was sharp. "We ride like raiders, yes, but we're still men. We're not worlags who turn on our own to kill them when they become inconvenient."

"No?" The other man chuckled again, and the sound was oddly grim. "Look around you, Talon—really look. Drovic doesn't tolerate weakness—he never has, in friend, family, or foe. And this is Drovic's band, not yours. In this place, you have two choices: you can simply follow him and put the steel where he wants it, or you can be your father's son and help lead toward the stars. He doesn't care, as long as you don't slow him down. Mind that, Talon, when you next fight for Mal—or for any other among us—or you'll find yourself on the sharp end of Drovic's blade. Son or not, you'll not stand in his way." The slim man gestured with his chin at Talon's head. "He nearly killed you once before. Don't give him cause again."

Talon met the other man's gaze with narrowed eyes. But he noted as they moved out again that Sojourn placed himself near Mal in the riding line, and Talon felt no fear for Mal. It was as though, by speaking his threat, Sojourn had promised the opposite, and would now hold shoulder for the wounded man in case the other man faltered. Part of Talon's mind seemed oddly clear as he considered the other man. Mal, Wakje, Weed, and he would take Rakdi too—the ex-elder was too wise in his ways and too good with a blade to leave behind. Oroan? She had steadied plenty in the last few months. But now possibly Sojourn? A few more riders to stand with him, and he'd be able to challenge Drovic himself even against the other raiders.

XV

Rhom Kheldour neKintar

What motivates a man?
What determines a goal?
What defines your attack?
What binds the defeat?

   —Third Riddle of the Ages

Rhom thought of his sister and stared at the dent-pitted ground. "That's the trail?"

"Aye."

"How many did you say there were?"

"Two, three dozen. Maybe a few more. It's been a dry season."

Rhom looked at the steep cliffs that bound the trail. "And we can't go back or around?"

"Sure, if you want to lose two days and be damn thirsty by the time we find the next spring. We'll be fine, Rhom. Just keep talking. They're more like oldEarth bobcats than our badgerbears. They don't like being disturbed, but they'd rather run than fight. Our voices will warn them away."

"And if they decide they feel cornered instead?"

"Then I suggest you move your burly butt as fast as you can so they don't catch you out on the flat."

Rhom rubbed at his sternum, feeling for the gems that studded the bone. He was glad Shilia wasn't here to see what they were about to do. The badger pits were similar to those of the larger badgerbears, but where badgerbears hunted humans as prey, badgers preferred to avoid them. The problem was that these badgers had begun denning around this stretch of trail some time ago, and now the ground was riddled with sand wallows and tunnel entrances. This being late summer, the young would be good-sized but without the wisdom of their elders. They would be more easily startled into attack. They might be a sixth the size of a forest badgerbear, but the badger had as nasty a reputation as the oldEarth animals, and once they latched onto flesh, they didn't let go. The whole pack would swarm out and attack.

His skin crawled as Gamon stared confidently forward. "Talk, Rhom. Your voice is your protection."

Rhom cleared his throat. "Somehow I'm having trouble thinking of anything other than being silent as prey."

Gamon chuckled. "You'll be complaining of the lack of heat nonstop by the end of the hour."

"Maybe. That or the distance." He forced himself to hold up his end of the conversation. "We've gone barely thirty kays as the crow flies." Sweat had made permanent tracks down the sides of his face, and his clothes chafed his salt-rough skin. He shivered as the air temperature seemed to drop again, but made no move to put on his second shirt.

Gamon's voice was as dry as the sand. "That's seventy kays real trail. You think we should sprint in this heat? That would be a fast path to heat stroke or exhaustion. Dion would appreciate neither, especially from her twin, who ought to know better, having grown up with a healer. In this heat, you move slow, you move in the dark, and you follow water, not road."

"I know that, Gamon, but I also know that now we need to hurry."

Gamon squinted at the shadows near two of the pits and eased on. "Why?"

"Because I feel my hands clench, and I think it is her. My heart pounds suddenly, and I know it's her fear, not mine. There is a tension in her, and it makes me think that you were right, that there is danger moving toward her."

Gamon's voice was suddenly intent. "Can you tell what kind of danger?"

"No." Rhom shrugged irritably. His dnu stepped too close to one of the pits and the soil sank away, unbalancing the creature. Rhom steadied it but guided it too close to an outcropping. He jerked back at the tiny hiss that answered his careless movement. "Moonworms," he muttered before answering. "Raiders? Hunters?" He shook his head. "It's something closing in, not something that lunges out like a glacier worm and is over just as fast."

"I can't see raiders willing to do a long stalk."

"You said they've been growing aggressive. What would stop them from working their way into Kiren or even Ramaj Kiaskari just for the hunting?"

"Randonnen roads?" Gamon eased his dnu around the half-buried boulders that littered the ground near the pits.

Rhom snorted. "You complain about our roadwork? This is an Ariyen route."

"Only after the midpoint, and at least the Ariyen side of the desert is paved."

"With oven stones, perhaps," he retorted. He glanced at Gamon and hid his resentment; Gamon seemed to have pulled inside himself until he left nothing but a shell for the sun. Where Rhom perspired like a randy bollusk, the older man looked dry as a nut. Rhom's only consolation was that Gamon's graying hair was as dull with desert dust as his own, and Gamon's eyes as red-rimmed and demonic.

A desert bird bolted up from under Gamon's dnu, and the creature half reared in fright. Rhom's pulse leaped, but Gamon only cursed mildly and brought his dnu back under control.

"Watch the rocks," Gamon warned. "There's some that look like razors." He pursed his dry lips and pretended he didn't see the eyes that gleamed in the moonlight. "The raiders followed the usual pattern this year like any other: strike, burn, run," he answered finally. "They kept to the smaller towns, then disappeared into the cities or back over the Bilocctar border. There was nothing unusual in the pattern, except that they tried to take some of the wolfwalkers alive, just as they had some years ago."

"Except this time, it was Dion they took," Rhom said softly.

Gamon was silent for a moment. "She'd been called away to an accident at one of the glassworks. Aranur followed her as soon as he realized she was gone—he hadn't chased her all the way down Wyrenia Valley just to let her go riding off by herself again. He took the dnu of one of the maids who had just arrived. We were minutes behind him—we had to saddle up, get the tack. By the time we started to catch up, the raiders had Aranur and Dion up against the seawall. The raiders bolted, damned rasts that they are. Had a boat waiting and the tide going out like a racehorse. We got Dion safe, but Aranur . . ." Gamon's voice went flat. "They were wrestling him over the wall. Dion tried to hold him, but his grip was weak." More than one man had gone over that seawall unwillingly, and neither the waves nor the rocks had been gentle. The shards of bone and hair had been dark testimony to that. "He must have hit the rocks like an egg," the older man said softly. Rhom winced, but Gamon didn't notice. "Even if he had survived the fall, without Dion to do a healing, he would have been dead in two days from the parasites in the water. By the time I got there, he was already gone, and the raiders got clean away, like sailing off to a tea party."

They were nearing the end of the tunnel openings, but Rhom knew as well as Gamon that there could be more creatures watching from the nearby rocks. He eyed the older man carefully in the moonlight. "There is something about that that bothers you."

"Everything about that bothered me," Gamon said sharply. He took a breath to control the bite of his own temper. He indicated the next part of the trail with a curt gesture. To Rhom's bone-dry eyes, it was a barely flatter line on the ravine floor, but the Randonnen followed with relief as they left the pits behind. He looked over his shoulder and noted that there was more than one pair of eyes watching them from the tunnels.

"Something felt familiar," Gamon admitted quietly as they went on. "A move perhaps, seen at a distance, or a particular stance or voice. Not enough to identify. I keep going over it in my head, but I saw only one of the men who went over the wall, and that only briefly. Of the raiders who were left or who escaped through the streets, I recognized only one, and he was already dead."

"You've got a bad-luck family, Gamon. Just about everyone in direct line with the Lloroi has been kidnapped if they haven't been killed."

Gamon smiled without humor. "The luck of the Lloroi."

"And Dion?"

Gamon didn't pretend to misunderstand. "She chose to live with Aranur, to share those risks."

"And so, his enemies became hers." Rhom's voice was suddenly harsh. "You gave her a kum-tai path to the moons when you mated the two of them. She was never safe in Ariye. Even if she and Aranur never became leaders, they were targeted as such."

Gamon glanced over his shoulder. When he ran his hand through his hair, there was a sweat line where his hat had rested; seeing it, Rhom felt an obscure satisfaction. "There are many types of leaders, Rhom: those who are elected, those who are forced into it, those who worm their way into a position of power, and those who are popular. Which ones would you strike if you wanted to provoke the greatest response?"

Rhom started to answer automatically, then paused.

"Aye," Gamon turned back to the trail. "Those who are elected can be replaced. Those who worm their way in usually work at odds with the other leaders. And those who are forced into leadership make good martyrs but often step down as soon as the need for them is gone. Neither Dion nor Aranur wanted to lead; they were popular by their own actions. They were leaders not because they were elders, but because other people wanted to be like them."

"Aranur could have challenged the Lloroi for leadership any time he wanted," Rhom said slowly.

"Yes, but he would never have issued that challenge." On that, Gamon's voice was firm. "Oh, perhaps before he lost his parents, when he was young, like all boys, he wanted to rule the world. He was driven even then. He was fierce as his father in reaching for his goals, and sometimes blind to the path to get there. He needed someone to balance that, someone more unstructured, more willing to run for the simple joy of running, more willing to simply be. Aranur may have been Dion's strength, but she was his humanity. He would never have made a good Lloroi, and I think he recognized that. He was too focused, too violent in the pursuit, too strong by himself."

Rhom's voice was bitter. "And Dion wasn't part of that violence?"

Gamon kept his voice quiet. "Aranur understan—understood," he corrected, "violence as Dion never will. He looked at people and saw what they were. She looks at people and sees what they should be, what they should do. She acts to rebalance the world to the should-be, instead of simply accepting reality. Violence to her is the horror; to Aranur, it was a tool. It is Dion, not Aranur, who accepts the compromise. It's she who can be manipulated by the threat of violence. Aranur would simply have destroyed the threat and considered the job well done. Give Dion the right threat, and she'll go along to the seventh hell itself."

"You don't understand wolfwalkers, Gamon. The packsong they hear and call to is always real, either by memory or by the action of the moment. Dion must act willingly, or the wolves will pass along her reluctance as a Calling. A wolfwalker has to deliberately lie to hide truth from the wolves, and extreme emotions are still read and passed along to other wolfwalkers. Threaten Dion, and a dozen wolves will Answer."

"Dion has been able to lie to Gray Hishn before," the older man disagreed.

"That was when their bond was new, but even then, Hishn was able to read the emotions behind the lie. At this point, I don't think either can truly lie to the other."

"There are herbs that will play with a man's mind."

"It's a moot point, Gamon. If raiders wanted her alive, what would have been the goal? Ramaj Ariye?"

"Slow control of leadership?" Gamon countered. "She was influential, and a weakening here and there will break the strongest dam."

"I can't believe you wouldn't see something like that coming at you like a worlag. You'd be more likely to mate with a Yorundan than let blackmail, rumor, or threat taint the council."

"Yorunda is a haven for misfits," Gamon retorted mildly.

"They're not misfits," Rhom corrected. "They're just like Randonnens—too independent to control."

Gamon's voice was dry. "Aye, and if they weren't so justice-minded, they would make good raiders themselves." He shook his head. "Ariye is a central county. It's one of the reasons we remain responsible for directing the recovery of the Ancients' sciences. Whoever controls Ramaj Ariye could control most of the humanity on this god-forsaken planet because everyone has to pass through Ariye to go from east to west."

"Does Dion realize this?" Rhom asked quietly.

He pulled up to study the rough cliffs where they closed in again on the trail. "She is a wolfwalker," he answered simply.

Rhom reined to a stop beside him. "Yes, but does she understand the implications of what you're saying?"

Gamon looked at him then. "Aranur understood them."

Rhom's gaze did not waver.

The older man was silent for a long moment. "Your twin has never been involved in the politics of the county. She left that to Aranur and the elders. Yes, she knows Ariye is important, but that very fact is unimportant to her. She reacts to the moment, not to the vision of the future, and whether the county is controlled by one Lloroi or another won't change her bond with the wolves." The gray-haired man shrugged. "No one thinks it strange. Randonnens aren't known for their excessive politics."

Rhom's voice was carefully neutral. "And Dion less than most?"

Gamon looked at him steadily. "And perhaps we protected her from it to keep her burdens lighter."

Rhom heard the underlying grief in the older man's voice and felt ashamed. His sister was still alive; Gamon had lost a man who was like a son to him. "It was not her duty," he murmured to himself. "She had other obligations."

"Other obligations?"

Rhom missed the tone in the older man's voice. "She had her duties as a healer and scout, mother and mate. She didn't need to take on others."

"So it is their duty, not hers, regardless of her other obligations?" Gamon rounded on him so harshly that the smith's dnu took a step back. "Their duty, not yours or mine? Where do you draw that line, Rhom? At what point do you say that it is Aranur's duty, not Dion's, to have vision, to protect the county? Or that it is my burden, but not yours?"

Rhom stared at the older man.

Gamon closed his eyes. He took a deep breath. When he looked at Rhom again, his voice was low. "Forgive me," he said. "I take my anger out on you, when of all things, that is my burden to bear."

"No," Rhom said flatly. "Anger we can share. It is grief that must be private."

Slowly the older man nodded.

Gamon pointed with his chin at the trail ahead. Rhom followed his gesture. The air cooled further, and a chill crossed his heat-dried skin. Beneath the three moons, he could make out another stretch of pitted, tunneled ground.

Gamon's voice was quiet. "Shall we go again?"

They moved on into the shadows of stone.

XVI

Talon Drovic neVolan

The worm turns;
Man abides.

   —Ariyen saying

Another day, a dozen kays. Talon bore the ride in near silence. The wolves seemed to make his thoughts sharper, his memories more acute, but the gray fog that held back the pain was blinding in its own way. The shield they built between him and his own body was thick with foreign memories, faint visions of other people and times. Wolves howled constantly in his head, and half the time he answered mentally without thinking. Yet still he had no real bond with them, only the link of pain. Soothing hands, healing hands . . . The woman, he told himself almost blankly. In his mind, she was inexorably linked with his pain. Reach her, he thought, and the agony would fade, his strength return, his bloody sword find peace. Reach her, and he wouldn't need Drovic anymore, wouldn't keep craving the herbs.

Another day, and Darity's lead party killed a small band of beetlelike worlags that nosed too close to their noon camp. Kilaltian's party lamed two dnu on a stretch of trail riddled with sinkholes. To complete the circle of bad luck, Talon almost lost Wakje to a slow-moving river. Halfway across, Wakje had begun listing in the saddle. Then slowly, comically, cursing at the inevitability caused by a broken cinch strap, the man had slid, feet caught in suddenly loose stirrups, upside-down under the dnu and into the frigid water. Wakje's dnu bolted out of the loose straps for the shore, leaving the saddle and man behind; Wakje was caught on submerged debris till he tore free and came up spitting. With a muttered curse, Drovic moved the other two groups on ahead. It took Talon's men half an hour to find the saddle on the bottom of the stream and another half hour to clean it of mud and repair it. In the meantime, Talon, Rakdi, and Oroan climbed a tiny outcropping to check their backtrail while they waited. It was a good thing they did. They caught three glimpses of riders along a stretch where the road curved out from under the trees.

"I count twelve," Oroan murmured to Talon. She used her thumb to judge the distance. "They're about two hours behind us."

Rakdi nodded his agreement. "I don't see any pack dnu," he added.

Talon squinted, but his vision was alternately blurred with gray fog or pain. Next to Wakje and Talon, Oroan and Rakdi had the best eyesight, and he didn't question their statements, just motioned for them to return with him to the others. It took all his will to make it down the steep, rock-strewn slope. He stumbled twice, and the second time Oroan caught his arm, letting go as fast as he regained his balance. She moved on without a word. It was Rakdi who met his furious gaze, but the ex-elder merely nodded back at the trail. Gods, Talon thought angrily. They all thought he was an invalid. It took him moments to realize that Oroan had not ridiculed his weakness as she usually taunted the others. He scuff-slid down a patch of embankment and eyed her back below. It suddenly occurred to him that she and Roc had hung out with Jervid, Fit, and Biekin when Talon had first taken over his group. Since then, Oroan had gravitated toward the older Rakdi and Dangyon. She was a chameleon fighter, he realized. She reflected those around her. When Drovic had raged and stomped around, she had done the same. With Talon, she had become more calm, more centered. He watched the woman and wondered, if she did have a choice, if she would choose to follow Drovic's revenge or Talon's goals instead.

The late-summer heat was dry, and the riders bore their sweat in relative silence as they cantered fast. Tracks of sweat ran down from Talon's armpits; his tunic was sticky, his eyes squinting as they rode between shadow and light. By noon, he figured that they were only twenty minutes behind Drovic. With the threat of the small venge on their backtrail, they pushed the dnu hard.

Talon's tension also remained high. The wolfsong had continued growing stronger as if more Gray Ones joined it. That was not abnormal. There were more wolves in the north and east than in the south and west. Years ago, there had been a Calling in Ariye, and the wolves had gathered like lepa, streaming across borders and mountains to Answer. Now, there were few wolves in Bilocctar, only a few more in Eilif, and many in Ariye and Randonnen. The valley—the Circle of Fifths—the meeting place of five counties, had been a place of the Ancients and their original wolves. With the more recent migration from west to east, the valley held even more gray creatures. The closer Talon got to that meeting point, the stronger grew the graysong, and the more he needed the north and east. That wolf-sent urgency was like mold, insidious and touching every thought. He flexed his wrist, then his left hand, then the muscles across his shoulders. In the past two days, he'd swear that his strength had grown greater, even if his muscles were so tight they threatened to blind him and break his own bones at the same time. The only thing holding him together was the wolves, and behind them, the need for the woman.

Protect, the wolves seemed to echo.

He smiled grimly. That was not what he intended to do once he found the wolfwalker woman. She had power in her hands, and she had used it to trap him in gray. Whatever danger she fled from, it would be nothing compared to him.

They had just topped out on the forested rise that dropped down into the valley when the wolves tightened Talon's skull. Instantly, he threw up his hand. Dangyon and Sojourn snapped awake as the group came to a milling halt, and Talon closed his eyes to listen. Dnu shifted, but no one spoke.

Ahead, blood scent. Fear.

"Who?" Talon asked softly.

Hunters. Prey. Blood in the grass.

He felt a chill. Drovic. "Where?"

He received a rough image of man-scent along the flanks of the small valley, with the heavy scent of a knot of men in the center. The contact faded, and he knew the wolf was gone. Talon blinked several times before he turned to the others. "They have Drovic."

Sojourn eyed him warily. "A venge?"

He nodded. "There aren't many in the venge," he said shortly. "They're probably the other half of the group we saw on the road, but they've got flank guards watching the approaches to the valley. Dangyon, Sojourn, Oroan, Mal—you take the west flank. Cheyko, Roc, Fit, Harare—you take the east. Rakdi, Ki—find the venge dnu and secure them or drive them off. They're on the west side of the valley. Wakje, Weed—you're with me. Get me descriptions and locations of every man whose firing on my father. And no killing," he added sharply. "Tie the guards, knock them out, let them run if you have to. But leave the venge men alive."

"Aye." Harare returned crisply among the murmur of assent. Harare resisted the impulse to add "sir." With the conviction returning to his voice and the confidence to his body, Talon was sounding more like Drovic every day.

But Fit and Roc didn't move. Roc's voice was wary as she

objected to Talon, "It's a hell of a lot harder to take a man alive than to kill him or let him bleed out."

"Why alive?" Sojourn put in.

"Think battle chess," he said shortly. "Take out the flanks, position yourself for a crossfire killing zone, then show your foe your strength. There's no need to go for blood if the enemy backs down."

"This venge has enough men to trap Drovic without letting a single man out to warn us—"

"And there are no parallel trails around here. They think we're all riding together, and that they have all of us trapped in that valley. That's why we leave the flank guards alive." Talon's slate-gray gaze was cold, but his blood began to tighten with anticipation. "Once the flanks are secure—use the finch calls, they're obvious enough—the venge will realize that they're now between Drovic and us. It would be a bloodbath for them to continue then."

"County men know that they're better off fighting than being taken by raiders."

"Not if I offer them their lives. We'll have the flank guards to prove our intentions."

"Drovic will never allow it."

"Drovic's is one of the lives I'll save."

Sojourn's lips quirked. "It will be interesting," he commented, "to see how he repays you."

"Aye," Talon said simply.

He led Wakje and Weed at a hard gallop into a thick stand of black spruce. There they kicked out of the stirrups and dodged into the trees. Wakje and Weed were right behind him as he hit the valley meadow and went full-length into the grass. Something flickered a meter away, but he was rolling, belly-crawling before he consciously realized that the flicker had been a war arrow. He could hear Drovic's men, but he wasn't sure if the cry was in his ears or the wolves'.

Heat, pollens, crushed grass, hot wind. Protect. Protect.

He dragged his sword hilt-first beside him and ignored the howlings. Classic, he thought. A perfect X-ambush with overlapping fire lines. The venge men must have been waiting for hours, long enough for the wildlife to settle back down and consider the motionless men part of the terrain. Even the chunko birds wouldn't give Drovic a warning.

Another arrow cut grass near Talon. "They're in the grass," a venge man called out. "Watch yourselves."

There was no answer from the other ambushers, but Talon did not expect one. There was safety in silence. In the bowl of the meadow, a voice was as good as a target.

Another war bolt missed Talon by an arm's length. Near the center of the field, someone screamed. Drovic's voice rapped out a set of quick, harsh commands and fell silent. Long grass blinded Talon as he elbow-crawled to circle the direction from which the arrow came. He left a snake trail of crushed grains, but it didn't matter; the ground had dipped, and he was lower than the archers thought—the bolts missed by over a handspan. He breathed as quietly as he could, but the smell of the wild grains was overpowering. He choked and found that it was his snarl that cut off his breath, not the scent he smelled through his nose.

Blood scent, hot and sweet. Taste the wind. The human wounds were like a tang to the wild wolves.

An arrow slashed through the grass a finger's width away. He flattened and lay still. To the left and behind, he heard Wakje and Weed. Somewhere to his right, he recognized Thaul's hoarse cry from the center of the meadow. The raider began to curse. "Moonwormed villagers. Couldn't find the sharp end of a sword if it stuck in your lily-white guts!"

Trembling, eager. Find. Protect.

A four-toed finch call came shrilly from the left, and Talon smiled grimly. One of the flank guards was down. He squirmed farther into the grass, seeking the broken trail of one of the venge shooters. The county folk here wouldn't try to kill everyone, although they wouldn't pass up a good shot, either. Their job had to be to pin the raiders in place until the other group could join them. That meant that they were using message birds or ring-runners, or—he stiffened—that they had themselves a wolfwalker.

"Nose-spotted, bug-eyed townsmen," Thaul shouted. "Your babes will suckle worlag piss before you can hit a barn."

Heat, rising dust, the scent of bile. Watching, panting.

A wolfwalker. Such a man or woman could reach into the wolf pack and read the lupine senses like a map, could pinpoint a raider band like a beacon. Such a person would be like the woman he saw through the wolves: a slender figure whose clothes were so muted with wilderness that she could have stood next to him and still faded back into the world. Wolf teeth clamped down on his mind. The woman in the gray seemed to snarl more with the voice of a wolf than with words. He could feel the power in that image, feel it seep into his muscles and feed his strength as he elbowed quickly forward.

A wild wolf howled, deep in the trees, echoed by another, and even at that distance, Talon could feel the triumph in the county men. The venge men thought the wolves were there for them, to locate the raiders and help guide their arrows. Talon's lips curled back in a snarl. The wolves might dull the pain in his body, but they would not protect him from a wolfwalker, and especially not from another wolf. They could not be pitted against each other—that was a breaking of the bond engineered into both wolves and humans. With the racial memories of the wolves, such a betrayal would linger forever in the packsong and could turn all Gray Ones against all humans on this world. No human would ever again sing the gray.

The hot wind gusted, and he dug in his elbows and toes and eased forward. Another finch call came from the left, and Talon nodded to himself. A few more calls, and the flank guards would be down. He reached a dusty trace and rolled into it without hesitation. In spring, it would have been gurgling with water; now it was dry as a bone and wide enough that he could traverse it without disturbing the grass. Wakje, then Weed, broke off to circle the meadow, and Talon followed the dry run on his own.

He crawled rapidly six meters before he heard the rustling. He went flat and controlled his breathing. A whistle trilled out from up ahead, and a flurry of arrows shot toward the knot of Drovic's raiders. The bolts went through the grass with a rapid, stalk-tearing *pht-pht-pht*; at least six struck saddles and packs. But two dnu screamed, and to Talon's left, Drovic's men struggled to keep the animals down as they grunted and thrashed.

Talon heard the sounds grow closer and lay still even though it was almost unbearable not to look up. There was the scent of woodfire and dnu. The rustling grew louder, seemed to be right on top of him, then passed and faded away. He waited for the breeze to rise again before moving forward. A few moments later he saw the fork in the tiny water run. The venge man had bellied up the right fork, while Talon elbow-crawled down the left. He grinned wolfishly and crawled on.

Once he found the venge man in his area, Talon wormed back and into the thick brush that grew at the edge of the forest. Few arrows now flew out in the meadow: the venge was waiting for its other men.

Wakje slithered up, keeping his head at ground level and using hand signals to indicate what they had found around the meadow. How long before the rest of the venge shows up? he asked silently.

Forty minutes, Talon answered with his hands. Maybe a bit more.

The thick-shouldered man shifted to allow Weed to belly up beside them. Like the others, Weed used hand signals to pass along the descriptions of the two townsmen he'd found. A moment later, Rakdi joined them, while in the meadow, Thaul continued to taunt the venge. "Dag-chewing poolah," the man shouted from behind the body of his dnu. "You've more blood on your hands than a host of worlags, you spit-hypocrites."

Rakdi grinned at the oaths and rubbed his beak nose to keep from sneezing at the pollens. He silently answered Talon's gesture. The dnu and two young guards had been in a dip behind that crest. The dnu hadn't even twitched as he had approached. They were thick-necked farm animals, not skittish at all, and Rakdi had resorted to slapping them and whipping them with arrows to make the beasts take flight. As docile as they were, they wouldn't go far, but at least the county men would feel cut off. They were no real venge, he told Talon with hand signals, but a group from a village that had volunteered for this duty.

Did you kill? Talon asked silently.

The ex-elder signaled the negative. The young guards were trussed and alive, he answered. There were at least three other raiders in the grass, but they were pinned down by two of the county men. That would not last long. One of the raiders would break for the trees, drawing fire, and others would start to break out.

Talon signaled for him to return to the rise and find a good field of fire. Rakdi was gone a moment later, and Talon motioned Weed to another spot. Although the view from that hillock would be limited, Weed would be able to target the two venge men on the western side of the meadow.

Talon let the urgency of the wolves feed his limbs as he and Wakje wriggled back and to the side. With instinctive grace, Talon eased his long weight over the old twigs so that none of them snapped beneath him. He would be back in the grass in a minute. The smell of the ground, the drying brush, the musty scent of ferns—these filled his nostrils along with the musk of the wolves. *Sweat, fear, eagerness. Find,* they sent. *Protect.*

Behind him, he could sense the wolves tracking Rakdi. The distant venge-wolfwalker would be able to read those Gray Ones and know where the raiders were, but since Talon did not have a similar bond, a wolfwalker would hear Talon only as another hunter. Talon tried to discern more from the gray, but that fog was too dim, too distant, too *right.* In the sunlight, it made the field seem dirty.

Talon began to belly toward the two venge men on his side of the meadow, down by the edge of the forest. A thin, trailing blackrope vine caught his ankle and began to drag with him, but he stilled as he felt its clutch. Behind him, Wakje lifted the vine from his boot before it pulled dangerously at the brush. He started forward again, but his arms suddenly felt foreshortened. Gray Faren, he noted, startled. The young female was creeping with them, some meters away in the brush. *Human, sweat scent. Find.*

His eyes narrowed. "Stay back," he said sharply, his voice scarcely a whisper. "This is not for you."

You hunt with the pack, the female returned, catching his meaning even without their eyes meeting.

"Not against men," he snarled back. And not with a wolfwalker in the following venge to read Gray Faren's images of him.

Gray Faren's eyes seemed to gleam in his mind, but the young wolf obeyed and did not creep forward when Talon toed his way on.

Together, he and Wakje skulked to the edge of the meadow. Talon smelled it before he saw it—the brush-track of the man he hunted. He signaled Wakje to continue around the meadow to the other nearby track. Swiftly, Talon followed his trail into the grass. Thirty meters in, he caught a glimpse of boots. He shifted, crawled forward, let the wind help cover the grass sounds. He was within three meters of the other man when the county man realized he was there.

The venge rider glanced back, then twisted violently, but that hesitation was enough. Talon lunged straight from his knees. He used his hand to parry away the other man's bow and hooked a vicious punch to the younger man's gut, cutting off his cry. The man was well muscled, and Talon punched him hard, even from his lunging position. The county man fell back flat, his breath lost. Talon lifted his sword, and the young man froze.

"NeWald? NeWald!" Someone shouted urgently.

From the meadow center, Thaul taunted, "Lost a babe in the woods? You'll lose the rest of your bladehands next. Go ahead; hide in the grass like poolah. Cower like dogs. It won't save you."

Talon found himself staring into the face of the young venge rider. The man's jaw was slack with gasping; his face was suddenly slick with sweat. "Please," the man choked out. He didn't even try for his own knife.

Talon's sword hesitated. *Please,* the woman in the village had said, the boy clutched to her side. *Find, protect,* the wolves had howled, blinding him in his mind. Steel caught sunlight and distorted the light like a flash of memory. The edge of the sword looked black.

Please. The man mouthed the word, unable to make a sound.

"NeWald? Pizi, say something!" The venge voice hid a tight panic, and Talon recognized the fear of a father in the words.

"Damn you," Talon whispered. "Damn you to the seventh hell. Give me your weapons belt," he snapped, his voice still low.

The young man stared.

"Hand it over—now! And stay down."

The venge rider scrambled awkwardly to unfasten his belt. The young man's sword and long knife were still sheathed. They were used weapons, well crafted; but the man's movements were not confident. Talon pushed the belt over his arm, shoving the sword weight around to his back. "Now the quiver." The young man shucked it off with trembling hands. Talon slung that over his shoulder. "Call back to them: You are fine."

Humiliation flooded his expression, but he choked out, "I—I'm all right." The shame was nothing compared to the sudden terror in his eyes as Talon's sword flashed toward him. The last thing the young venge rider knew was the glint of dark steel in the sun.

The hilt caught the man on the temple. Pizi went limp. Talon grabbed the man's bow and began to crawl back through the grass. The father had given away his position with his shout. Time . . . Forty minutes? The other riders would be coming fast as their wolfwalker read the nearness of Talon's raiders to the venge.

He worked faster and reached the edge of the meadow in a few minutes. The venge men seemed to think he was Pizi retreating and so didn't shoot at him. The raiders, however . . . Someone shot at the waving grass and missed his back by a finger's width. Someone else came close enough that the feathers of the bolt rasped across his shoulder. A minute later, he began to circle the meadow.

Dusty grass, dusty paws. The hunt, the wolves howled softly.

He found Wakje at a second grass trail, thirty meters from the first. The dark-haired raider was braced in the brush, his bow ready. Talon followed Wakje's gesture with his eyes, but it took movement to give this venge man away. The man had used grasses to disguise his shape, and until he shifted and exposed his bow, Talon did not see him. Talon nodded at the other raider's signal: Wakje had targeted his man, and was ready to shoot.

Talon caught a glimpse of yellow eyes and snarled in his mind. Gray Ursh faded back with a growl. He hurried, crouch-running behind a rise until he circled another forty meters. He was careful as a jeweler: the careless could always be found together—in a cemetery.

Finches began to call from all around the meadow, and Talon heard an answering call from several townsmen as they realized they were surrounded. He chose one grass trail and followed it with his eyes until he located the county man. He found himself smiling coldly. "Stay your fire, or die," he shouted. "You are clearly targeted."

From the center of the meadow, Thaul and Liatuad hooted. No raider was idiotic enough to stand up. Instead, Drovic whistled a signal, and Talon returned it automatically with a tiny trill. It was the signal for "follow my lead," and Drovic acknowledged with a double tone.

There was silence for a moment. The county riders did not respond.

Talon nodded to himself. He would have done the same. "Stand and give up your weapons, and we will let you live. Otherwise . . ." He let his voice trail off. "The man with the walnut-and-black stained bow, twelve meters south from the silverheart tree—he will be the first to die. The man ten meters northwest of the beetle hump, with the red sash at his belt—he will be second. The man on his left side, nocking an arrow—"

"Stop."

The shout came from the right.

"Stand and throw down your weapons," Talon repeated.

Slowly, a heavy-shouldered man stood up. No arrows flew.

"Resist and die," Talon warned.

"We'll die anyway. Rast spawn," the man cursed softly.

"I give you my word you will not be killed."

The heavy man laughed bitterly. But he gestured, and others slowly stood up. There were twelve, as Talon had guessed. The youngest, Pizi, was the last to stand; he staggered to his knees, to his feet, and then listed, one hand to his bloody skull. No one moved to help him.

The townsmen dropped their bows, loosened their weapons belts and let them fall to the ground. The raiders swarmed out like rasts. Wakje grabbed his man and cuffed him hard enough that he went to his knees. Merek and Liatuad grabbed another. Ebi and Strapel struck their man hard in the back of the legs so that he fell; then they slugged him in the gut and dragged him forward with the others.

Talon moved out from the trees, saying nothing as the raiders gathered their prey and forced them together. Drovic nodded at his son as Talon joined them, then ordered calmly, "Kill them."

"Wai—" One of the men panicked.

"Merciful moons—" the youngest gasped.

Ebi's sword was already moving, when Talon snapped, "As you were."

As if bitten, Ebi froze, his blade a handspan from the neck. The short, swarthy man stared at Talon with dark, unreadable eyes, while Strapel, holding the venge rider, cocked his blond head to watch Drovic's reaction.

Drovic studied the tableau. Then, casually, "A word, Son."

Talon stepped to the side. Drovic's fist caught him on the side of the head and rocked him back. He saw it coming, but did not duck. He staggered, but did not fall.

Drovic's eyes glinted as he acknowledged his son's growing strength. "You countermanded my order."

"You would make me break my word."

Drovic's face hardened. "Since when does your word bind me?"

"Since you gave me leadership," he shot back coldly. Drovic stared at him, but Talon did not budge. "I gave my word," he repeated softly. "We have little time, Father. There is another venge on the way—twelve more men, and they will by now have seen our signs on the road. They will know we are ahead."

"And what would you do with them then?" Drovic pointed with his chin.

"Strip them and leave them for their fellows to find." He forced himself to grin. "Stripped, they will be in danger, and will require weapons and dnu, the loss of which will weaken the other groups. And, stripped, they must face their friends in full humiliation. It will be more difficult for them to ride with the other venge while they burn with the shame of knowing the others would not have surrendered."

Drovic regarded him for a long moment. Then he nodded curtly. He turned to the raiders. "Strip them," he ordered.

Sojourn gave Talon a speculative look, but Kilaltian and the others took to their new job with glee. Roc cut one man's clothes away with her knife, leaving thin red lines down his torso. Mousy Ilandin stripped another man as Merek cuffed the fighter again to remind him not to struggle. Weed and Nortun gathered the weapons, broke the bows and took the arrows, strung the weapons belts on a line and lashed the line to a dnu. Three minutes, no more, and the venge was stripped, the men standing awkwardly, their heads up as if they could ignore their nakedness and the taunting of the raiders.

Wolves howled in Talon's head. "Father," he said urgently.

Drovic nodded. "Go," he ordered his raiders. They mounted as they caught up what was left of their dnu, leaving four dead beasts and three more raiders behind. Then they sped from the meadow in a ragged line, spurring the dnu to a panic.

The howl that trailed Talon's beast lost itself in sunlight.

XVII

Ember Dione maMarin

Face the fire—
   That is the test of courage;
Work through the fire—
   That is the test of will;
Finish the fire—
   That is the test of self-restraint;
Start the fire—
   That is the test of passion.

   —From the Book of Abis

It was a single snowtit that did it. The tiny bird had nested on the edge of the cliff, and as Dion passed, it shot out of its hidey-hole and under the nose of Tehena's dnu.

The dnu spooked. Tehena cried out. Dion shouted sharply. But the dnu tried to rear, and its middle legs slid out sideways. It scrabbled clumsily for purchase. For an instant, its rear hooves caught on a rougher spot. Then it hump-bucked like a bollusk, and Tehena lost her seat. The woman saw the cliff flash by, twisted midair, and slammed down on the ice on her hands and knees, collapsing into a roll. She wasn't smooth enough. Her wrist snapped, and she screamed as two jagged bones speared through her thin flesh.

Kiyun had kicked his dnu forward, and he lunged out for the other riding beast, but missed his grip on the saddle. The dnu hung for a misbalanced instant. Then it scrabbled off the icy mound. The pitch of its thin scream matched Tehena's, and it slid in a flailing mass of limbs and snow clods down the mountainside. It hit a tree trunk midspine and went limp, to slide motionlessly another fifteen meters. A moment later, it was buried in the wash of snow that followed it into the trees.

Kiyun struggled with the reins of the other dnu, shouting and yanking them by brute force away from the cliff. Dion skidded to Tehena over the ice, ignoring the jagged bumps of ice that bruised her knees through her trousers. For all her speed, she grabbed the woman's wrist in a surprisingly gentle grip.

The wild wolves were thirty meters away, but as she automatically reached for the gray, she heard them clear as bells. They howled mentally, surged, and seemed to leap to the left. Dion was sucked in after them. It was not a physical plunge. It was in her mind: a spinning, twisting sensation that stretched her consciousness out past her own self and into the other body. This was not the melding of minds that Dion had felt before. This was a fury of energy and awareness, like riding a hurricane. The wild wolf pack supported and thrust her at Tehena; and something else behind them focused Dion's mind like a lance, something that flickered yellow in the back of the gray. Something cold and eerily distant. Something . . . alien.

She felt the bones, the raw flesh, the heat of Tehena's blood. With her own healing knowledge and with the instinctive wrongness of the break, she saw the bones knitted and whole. In that instant of awareness, the power in her nerves and veins coalesced. She reached for it, but reached too far. Her wolf-bond snapped tight. Gray Hishn, far away in Ariye, felt her lupine mind yanked into patterns so Ancient that they were a frigid path of fire. Light—coarse light—flashed across their minds. It was fractured with energy, jagged like the splinters of a hundred types of wood. It pierced toward Tehena, and it burned, instead of healed.

Dion cried out as she tried to pull back, and the energy had nowhere to go. The surge backlashed her mind. Wolves panicked. The pack broke violently apart. Flames concentrated on Dion's flesh and fingers. Tehena screamed as fire seemed to lick her body. It was only the edge of that energy, but the woman jerked away, skidding farther as she fell awkwardly, clutching her wrist close.

Talon stiffened. His hands—they burned. He *burned* with fire. The pain lanced through him as hard as the days of his fever. He cursed almost silently through clenched teeth. "I won't give in, you piss-soaked piece of pain. . . ."

Wolves plunged through Dion's mind, snarling and snapping, deafening her to the distant howl of her own wolf. Near-blinded, she barely found her voice. She cried out a sharp, unintelligible command. The pack, startled, went silent. Then they swept back in, urgent and gray, seeking her thoughts in spite of the pain.

I'm here, she returned sharply.

The heat—

I know.

The fire—

It's all right, she snarled.

The wolves read the pain that roughened her mental voice. Slowly, they slunk back in her skull. They milled up the road, snarling when they looked back at Tehena, while they snapped at each other with fear. Overhead, the snowsprit flitted to an ice-stiff branch and cried piercingly at their presence.

Kiyun stared at the two women. Tehena's breath was ragged. The lanky woman gripped her wrist hard to slow the bleeding, but the bones no longer poked through her skin. Only the raw mass where the wound had been was still exposed to the cold.

Dion rocked lightly on her knees. She breathed roughly, her eyes squeezed shut and her neck rigid with effort as she hunched over her hands. Deep in her mind, one voice still howled with her pain. "Hishn," she breathed.

Far away in Ramaj Ariye, the female wolf plunged through the forest. Gray Yoshi was beside her, and the two wolves sprinted north through the trees as if they could somehow reach across the kays by speed alone. Dion could feel their legs like stretched pistons, feel the twiggy leaves slap their coats. Heavy dust and dried soil kicked up into her nostrils. Hishn strained until her gray voice stretched around the peaks, repeated by other threads until a tenuous, wasp-thin link touched the mind of her wolfwalker.

Hishn, Dion reached back almost desperately. Her human

voice wove instinctively into Hishn's patter with the smoothness of years, but the contact was faint with the distance. She blinked, sucked in a breath, and power faded into simple fire.

Wolfwalker, the Gray One sent. At that distance, the thinness of Hishn's voice could not hide the image of her muzzle pressed against Dion's neck, and her broad chest seemed to pant against Dion's.

I need you, Dion whispered hoarsely.

I am here.

The ghost images held for less than a moment. Then they began to shred. Not even the number of bonded and wild wolves in Ariye could sustain the link with that distance. But Hishn *knew.* In that instant of blending, the massive wolf had read Dion as clearly as Dion had heard the wolf.

Deep in the forest, Hishn suddenly stopped running. Gray Yoshi felt her absence beside him and halted, his forelegs on a log as if to leap over. He looked back at his mate.

We cannot reach her, Hishn sent, panting strongly.

We must wait?

For her pack brother. He will take us to her.

Yoshi dropped down from the log. *She is on the heights. We cannot run there. I could taste the thin air and ice.*

Her pack brother will keep us with him. We will not hunger.

Yoshi turned back toward his mate to nuzzle her, but she nipped at his thickly muscled shoulder. It was a love bite, not a snap, and he nuzzled her deliberately, as if to remind her that he too was part of their bond. *Then we wait,* he agreed.

Hishn nipped him more gently, and they turned back toward their territory, but Hishn stopped again and again to stare at the peaks in the north.

Dion felt the echo disappear. The wild wolves who had created the distant link separated from each other, back into individual packs. There was a brief howling up the road—more an acknowledgment of the strength of that moment of wholeness than of what had just been lost. In the mountains, it seemed almost hollow.

Dion raised her head. Agony burned in her hands. Her eyes

were bright-blinded as if she had stared at the sun, but she could see the silhouette of the others, and she *knew* where the Gray Ones were. She could taste the sweat-fear of Kiyun and Tehena, but as the link faded, she began to lose that too.

Finally, Kiyun cleared his throat. "That was . . . different."

His words broke the tableau, and Dion found her voice, though it was low and somewhat unsteady. "It was only Ovousibas." Her vision was clearing, though things were still in contrast.

Tehena shook her head violently. "If that was Ovousibas, then I'm a garden beauty."

Dion flexed her hands slowly and shuddered as the burned skin stretched and cracked in her gloves. Her flesh was on fire, and through that pain she could barely feel the wetness of her own blood welling through the cracks and soaking into the glove liners. She drew a ragged breath. Power, she thought. It had never been so intense. There had been a touch of her mother in that. Not the mother she had never known— not the human woman who had died soon after childbirth— but the alien mother Dion had adopted. The alien that could take itself to the stars or suck the life out of a worlag without thinking. The power that had first healed, then had brought plague to the Ancients. She shuddered again and controlled her breathing with almost visible effort. With only the tendrils of the wild wolves in her mind, she focused on herself. Spin left and in, left and down . . . Power still beat at the boundaries of her mind, but she was prepared now, and it was more controlled and almost faint, as if the patterns that had created it were too old to be strong or too new to be developed. The answering sweep of gray, lighter and thinner than before, softened the continuing burn until she could feel her flesh start knitting.

Then she forced herself to lean across the ice and look at Tehena's wrist. As Tehena tried not to flinch, Dion merely waited. The thin woman continued to stare at the wolfwalker, then finally extended her wrist.

Dion pretended to ignore Tehena's reaction as she examined the punctured wrist. Some part of her brain noted that, even after all these years, it was still becoming easier to open to the wolves. Their response to her was direct, and they almost automatically guided her now in that mental spiral to the left. She sat back on her heels again and forced herself to speak calmly. "It's not completely healed. The bones are set, but they're barely reattached; there is almost no healing of the other tissues. I wasn't in long enough." She looked up at Tehena's carefully blank face. "I scared you," she said flatly.

The woman's voice was tight and hard. "If you want to call that 'scared,' be my guest. You've touched me as a healer more than once, but you've never done *that* before." The gray-haired woman took a shaky breath. "By all the moons that ride the sky, that wasn't the wolves in there with you."

Dion started to remove her gloves and winced. Even though she had begun to control the pain, it took all her will to peel back the leather and liners on one hand.

"Moonworms!" Kiyun squatted beside them and took her blistered hand. The wounds ran the gamut from raised red welts to deep pocks with white-blistered edges. They covered her entire palm. Even the back of one hand was reddened. His own voice was hard. "You've never done this before, either."

The cold was already biting deeply into the wounds, and Dion began to feel weak. She gritted her teeth. "I have, but you weren't there the first time."

Tehena got awkwardly to her knees, then to her feet. The pain was less—more of a raw throbbing than the shock of the broken bones. Her voice was still tight as she moved to the wolfwalker's side. "This happened the first time? You burned your own skin? And you still tried the healing again?"

Dion smiled crookedly. "There were few choices—my brother's life, Gamon's, Aranur's." She forced herself to shrug. "Wolfwalkers heal quickly, you know. It didn't seem a high price to pay."

Carefully, Kiyun stripped off Dion's other glove to expose the rest of the wounds. Her right palm was like the left.

"If you'll wrap my hands," she forced herself to say clearly, "I'll splint Tehena's arm."

He shook his head as he got to his feet. "I can splint her arm as well as you."

She shrugged, but her violet eyes shuttered as Tehena looked almost relieved.

"It's not you, Wolfwalker," Tehena said quickly. "I trust you with my life. It's just . . . I mean . . ." The woman stood helplessly.

"It's all right, Tehena."

The thin woman regarded Dion for a long moment. Even after all that Dion had done for her, she could not stand up for the wolfwalker. She turned away, glad in spite of herself that the cold disguised her flush of shame as wind-chapped cheeks instead.

Kiyun herded the four remaining dnu into a cold-huddle, then got Dion's medical kit out of her pack. Dion watched him almost blankly. His image blurred, and it took her several seconds to realize that she had started to tremble.

"Dion?" Tehena said sharply. "Kiyun—"

"Hungry," Dion managed. She had gone pale.

Kiyun squatted beside her, removed his gloves, and put his hand inside her neck gaiter against her flesh. "Moonworms, you're like ice."

"Shock?" Tehena managed. Stationary as she was, the cold was beginning to reach her own bones, especially where the saddle had warmed her inner thighs.

"N-n-no." Dion shivered. "Jus-st n-need food."

Kiyun quickly wrapped Dion's hands, then jerked her gloves clumsily over the bandages. He got out some smoked meat, cut off a chunk, and fed Dion the first bite like a child before turning to bind Tehena's arm. His voice was low. "The next passhouse is three more kays. Can you make it?"

Tehena's voice was still a little high as she answered. "Can always make a few more kays. We ride with the wolves, remember?"

Kiyun exchanged a glance with Dion. The wolfwalker was sucking on the jerky, but she shook her head at his silent question. Tehena wasn't in shock. The woman was just upset at herself, at Dion, at the world. Tehena had put her faith in Dion, and Dion had nearly killed her. And now Tehena couldn't face herself. It was hard sometimes to remember that the gray-haired woman was almost ten years younger than Dion. The drugs that had aged that thin body so quickly and the steadiness that Tehena had shown in serving Dion so long made it easy to think that Tehena was more mature. Dion swallowed her hurt. This was no betrayal, she reminded herself. Tehena had stood by her for over a dozen years. The woman was only afraid.

Dion forced herself to bite off another smaller piece of the jerky, rather than swallow it whole as she wanted. She felt starved. Most of the energy that had burned out on her hands had been stripped out of her own body. Before, the drain on herself had been light, but she had never focused such power either. Except once. She pressed her forearm to her belly. She could still feel the claw that had split her open like a grape. There had been just such power in the creature that had put her back together—power beyond human ability. The power to reach the stars . . . She shook herself. Her mind was wandering with hunger and pain. She had to focus or go into shock.

She forced herself to tear another bite from the strip of jerky. It was an awkward agony, since the burning in her hands did not abate, and even her fingertips were blistered. At least with something in her stomach, she no longer shivered so much.

Kiyun finished with Tehena's arm, then studied Dion closely. "Healer?" he asked. "Can you make the passhouse?"

She glanced at Tehena and saw the edge of fear still sharpening those pale eyes. "I'm Randonnen," she returned mock-haughtily. "We need only the wind and the mountains, and we're strong as the world."

Kiyun smiled grimly. Dion had still been Randonnen when he met her years ago, but she had changed over time, let herself drift to the Ariyens' tune, forgotten her roots, set aside her own goals. In the past year, she had begun to remember who and what she was on her own. It was what she needed, he thought. If the moons had not pushed her so hard, she might have taken longer, but she would still have remembered: she was Randonnen, a wolfwalker, a healer, a woodswoman. She was tied to the world, not the stars; bound to the wolves, not the Ariyen goals. And when she was whole again, she'd have peace. "Good," he said. "Because wind and mountains are the two things we have."

As if to prove his words, it gusted like an elder. Tehena shivered, but it wasn't the cold. Dion acknowledged it expressionlessly. She understood Tehena's fear—she was feeling fear herself. Neither Tehena nor Kiyun had noticed, but Dion had felt and seen the water under her boots, and she had understood at once. She had made that water out of the ice. Had stripped the structure and tiny nutrients from the ice just as she had stripped energy from her own body. And she had fired the ice like pottery just as she had seared her own flesh. Too much, she told herself with hard-quelled fear. Too much power in her hands. She hid her fear in the pain, but it was there, eating at her as she chewed at the jerky, and churning around in her guts.

She let Kiyun help her into the saddle and smiled to reassure him, unaware of how haunted she looked. Kiyun turned to one of the pack dnu and rearranged the panniers to make a mock saddle for Tehena. It would not be comfortable, but it would do until they reached the passhouse. He stepped back and waited for Tehena to mount. He didn't offer help. The scrawny woman would refuse the help of a god if she had the chance, he thought sourly. Then he gathered the reins of the one remaining pack animal and started them all up the road. There was nothing to do about the lost dnu. With both Dion and Tehena wounded, they could not risk staying in place long enough to try recovering any gear. They needed warmth and food, and the passhouse would give them both.

Wolfwalker, one of the Gray Ones sent to Dion. They closed around her mentally, nuzzling her, comforting her with their own images of body warmth and strength. It was the same way they had dealt with her grief. They had smothered her, deafened her to everything but the packsong, and shared their own grief for their cubs. Gamon had not understood the depth of that grief, and his words echoed harshly: *You think you are the only one who has ever lost someone you loved?*

"Yes," she had torn back. "At this moment, in this place, I

am the only one. It is my grief, not your sympathy, that exists to me. It is my heart here, not yours."

The wolves had understood. Had lost enough of their own pups and packmates to give her the solace of solitude for her shattered self. They had also, she admitted, latched onto that understanding to forge a stronger link between them. They had bitten at her to get her up out of the dark place in her mind, had snarled in her ears when she tried to turn away. They had stayed with her until she tried to use the internal healing again, but in her grief, she had not been strong enough. That time, the healing had threatened to deplete her into her own death, but she had refused to stop. She had reached out for anything, and her hand had hit a wooden post. She had sucked the leftover life from that wood like a leech, leaving it powdered like old ash. Here, it had been ice that she left melted and distilled like a filter. That lance of power she had thrust toward Tehena—that was an Aiueven pattern, the energy lines that the aliens used to feed or fight. And Dion had tried to use it to heal.

The fear of what she had done and of herself was growing with every moment of realization. She had broken the ice with her mind. Dry fingers stretched into her mouth, pressed down on her gut, and pinched at her breath. She felt her control start to slip. Pain radiated back into her hands as she lost her grip on it.

Wolfwalker, the wild wolves howled. *The flames on your paws. The fire in your claws—*

"Breathe," she told herself harshly.

She hugged her arms to herself, guiding her dnu only absently with her knees.

Fear, her old friend, was harsh. She had used Ovousibas so lightly, so carefully through the years, never taking too much from herself or her friends. Never pushing too far, never risking her life too deeply. The wolves had been patient throughout, helping her focus the healing, shielding her from the energy, waiting as she learned. But she had never found the cure she had promised them. Never put aside everything else to focus on that promise.

There had been power in that flash. Power enough to spare,

and the wolves had known it all along. Dion chewed at her thoughts as if they would keep her from feeling the fire that still burned in her hands. The wolves had leaped with the sense of that power. But they had been too eager; their shield had been too thin. It was about control, she acknowledged. Control over herself to handle the energy, control over the wolves, control over herself when she next faced the elders, to keep that power safe.

"Breathe," she told herself under her breath. Breathe, and then control.

XVIII

Talon Drovic neVolen

Where do you find conviction
  When you follow another man?

  —Question of the elders at the Test of Abis

Talon's odd clarity continued as Drovic's band dodged east for a day, skirted a marshy lake, and made it another eight kays before Drovic called a halt on the ridge overlooking Welldeath. It was an old village and small—perhaps fifty homes—and it looked as if most of the field workers were in the northern field on the other side of the town.

Drovic handed the message stick he'd prepared to neBoka and watched the other man trot away. "He should be able to leave it at the ring-runner cairn without trouble. While he's doing that, I want to slip in and out for some supplies before they realize the rest of us are here."

Talon frowned. "You won't go alone."

"I'm taking Slu, Cheyko, and Pen. They'll watch my back."

Talon nodded. But Drovic had barely turned onto the village fork a hundred meters when a hill alarm started ringing. Drovic stiffened. "What the hell?" Almost instantly, one of the village alarms began sounding, and then others began chiming in from around the village valley. "Moonwormed rasts. Did they get a description of every goddamn dnu in the line?"

The field workers grabbed their tools and sprinted back toward the village, and Drovic cursed. He whistled a sharp command back toward Talon and, making the decision instantly, spurred his dnu to a gallop. The three riders with him were shadows of his speed. Talon opened his mouth, but the raiders around him didn't wait. Al and Sojourn, caught half out of the saddle, bounced once and swung up smoothly as their dnu charged with the others, and the whole line surged into motion and swept down the road toward the fields.

There was no time to argue, no time to stop the charge. Follow or let Drovic fall alone. Memories stirred. *A cliff rumbled; rocks fell; his mother's scream, and his father's . . .* Talon's mind tightened. His fingers shoved the securing strap from his sword. He yanked his bow from its sheath. He strung the recurve on the fly, using one stirrup for a brace. It was a maneuver more easily done at a gallop than a canter—the speed of the dnu smoothed its gait so that, as long as a man kept his seat, he could string bow and draw bolt in less than ten seconds.

In the lead, Drovic's group did not waste arrows on the slower villagers who had gone flat among the grains. Most of those townsmen did not have weapons, and it was Kilaltian's job to terrorize them to keep them down, as the man brought up the rear. The village was small—probably why they raised the alarm so quickly, and Talon saw immediately where Drovic was headed. There were only two streets of workshops, and even now, Drovic would take the chance to check for bioforms.

His dnu leaped a ditch on the side of the road and half reared over a woman in the grass. Talon dodged her and cornered hard, his dnu's legs angled like braces. He brought up sharp in a workshop courtyard and slid from his dnu. Harare and Ki lunged for another door to the side. Talon heard the bolts slide home inside as the doors were barred. He didn't bother to curse.

The window was flung up, and an archer leaned half out. Eager shooter, eager miss—the bolt bit into the post beside him. Some part of Talon noted the angle, the overreach, the lack of sighting pins. The other part simply reached over and grabbed the man's compound bow, jerking the shooter forward. He'd have to deal with them now or risk a bolt in the back as he fled. For an instant, he was face-to-face with a lined visage. He noted automatically the shock of shame and sudden fear as the other man let go. Then another set of arms—massive arms, gnarled hair standing out like wires, burn marks like purple pox—reached around the older man and locked on Talon's left wrist. Talon didn't jerk back, but his face went pale as a winter eel, and his mind screamed as the damaged nerves were crushed. He didn't think. He dropped the bow and launched himself over the windowsill, his knife like a claw. There was a wild tangle of limbs as others scrambled away. He heard pounding and shouts as Harare and Ki distracted other workers. But a hammer of a fist hit his ribs, and he forgot the other raiders. He slammed a side kick into a man as the glassman jerked his wrist. Then his knife was against the glassman's throat, and the knot of workers froze.

The glassman's hands crushed together. The man's strength was phenomenal—Talon could actually feel his veins squishing inside his pulped muscles. Some part of his brain noted the racks of vials and flat dishes, beakers and tubes and forms. If this wasn't a supply house for a biolab, then he was a balding badgerbear. He ignored the scream of his own mind, ignored the urge to warn the craftsmen to hide their wares next time. Instead, he let the edge of gray in his mind seep into his eyes until they near-blinded him. "Release me," he breathed.

Cold fingers moved along the glassman's spine. The glassman found himself unable to close his hand farther. Talon could have drawn the blade a hundred times across the glassman's throat in the time the man stood there staring.

That slate gray gaze reached inside the villager like fear. The glassman let go slowly. There was a gasp around him.

Talon backed away to the window. By the time the glass-man half stepped forward, Talon had already vaulted the railing and hit the saddle smoothly. "By the moons," the glassman breathed. Even with his bulk, he had to fight for a place at the window.

Talon ducked a hasty arrow that overflew his position from a workshop across the street. Drovic had already whistled the command to retreat, and Talon kicked his dnu to a hard gallop to follow. An arrow struck the dnu's neck at an angle, cutting one of the reins and sticking in the saddle horn. He jerked the bolt free and stuffed it automatically in his quiver. The loss of the rein didn't bother him yet. He rode more by his knees, and the dnu was too well trained to slow. Talon passed on the command to retreat. "They're bolted in," he shouted to Sojourn and Mal as they whipped around the corner of another building. Oroan and Wakje sprinted out from a house one street over; Roc and Weed from another. A war bolt hung out of Weed's lower back, but the lanky man pulled it free and vaulted into the saddle. It had hit his belt, cutting skin only shallowly. NeRuras was not so lucky. The three arrows buried in that man's chest felled him heavily on the stones.

Drovic and two others were already past the end of the street. The older man was cursing. The villagers had been too prepared. The workshop doors had been bolted as soon as the last workers ran in, and the craft buildings had been cleverly placed to overlook each other. Only the homes had been easy targets. Talon glanced back. NeRuras wasn't the only one down; NeFirth was missing, and Slu's sleeve was torn and bloody. Another few moments, and those in the main street would have been running a gauntlet of archers. There were other ways, he thought in fury. They could have ridden away or gone in more slowly, more deceptively, even bribed someone for the information about lab supplies. But no, Drovic had to charge in, had to draw his blade to kill to get what he wanted. The older man couldn't see county folk as anything other than targets.

Talon burst out with three others into the half-weeded

fields. Ahead of them, villagers popped up like rabbits trying to evade the wolves. Most of them were far enough to the side that they were out of reach. One boy was not so lucky. He was in their path, and his short legs would never get him free of their hooves.

"I'll take him!" Fit shouted.

But the knifeman's voice had a thread of excitement that made Talon's jaw tighten. "He's mine," he snarled back.

Fit shot him a challenging look and spurred his dnu viciously, but Talon had the angle, and his own dnu seemed to sense his urgency, for it put on a burst of speed. He leaned down, caught the sprinting boy by the scruff, and jerked him up. The boy screamed and flailed with wild, untrained blows. "Play dead," Talon snarled in his ear. He brought the knife down in a vicious blow that never touched flesh, then threw the boy into the stinkweed. The youth cartwheeled limply and hit with a flop of limbs. He didn't move as they thundered past. Talon hoped he wasn't broken.

Fit cursed behind him as they ducked back into the forest. "I could have used a tack boy," he snapped.

"We don't have time for hostages."

The other man didn't answer.

They slowed to let the others catch up, and Talon caught Drovic's nod of approval. He nodded back, his gray eyes hard, and Drovic never saw Talon's flare of ambition that judged the father's weakness instead of taking pride in himself. Never saw the steady gaze that had a hint of wolf. Instead, Drovic whistled his commands to re-form, and Talon fell back to lead his own group, seething with the gray.

XIX

Ember Dione maMarin

Power corrupts;
  Absolute power corrupts absolutely.
Power burns;
  Absolute fire is absolute strife.
Power heals;
  Absolute healing is absolute death.

  —Randonnen proverb

Outside in the twilight where the wolves could see them, Kiyun tried not to flinch from the suppurating wounds on Dion's hands. Dion tried not to flinch from the pain. Tehena just tried not to flinch. They stood in a rough circle in front of the passhouse, and the wild wolves watched them from underneath the trees. Dion's jaw was white with pain, but her violet eyes were sharp and focused.

In spite of herself, Tehena asked, "You sure you want to try this?"

Dion gave the woman a wry smile that was strained around the edges. "Would you go even one more hour like this if you had another option?"

The scrawny woman shrugged eloquently.

Dion glanced at Kiyun. He gave her a wry nod, then placed his hands on her shoulders to give her some of the strength in his body. Dion felt the warm weight of his palms and took a breath. She reached toward the wild wolves.

In her skull, a male wolf snarled softly. She held out mental hands toward the trees, and Gray Lash lowered his head and growled more audibly. The three humans didn't move. After a moment, Lash eased out and warily circled Kiyun. Tehena stiffened as the wolf sniffed at her legs, but the creature continued to circle until he was facing Dion. Violet gaze met yellow. There was a shock of intimacy beyond the mental gray, and Dion felt the male wolf's thoughts. She smelled the overpowering odors of humanity over the crisp cold of the snow, caught the odor of jerked meat and the stew that Tehena had put on the passhouse stove. And she felt the pain through a second set of nerves. The wolves could feel her just as she felt them, and the burning in her hands, which she barely held at bay, ate into their concentration.

There is fire in your paws.

She nodded mentally. *Help me heal it.*

Gray Lash's voice took on a hint of puzzlement as he felt her intention. *You walk with us, but you seek a different pattern.*

With the power, her use of the internal healing had changed, and they didn't understand. She kept her voice soft, knowing they could read her words as she thought them. "It's something you will remember if you look back far enough."

Gray Lash was joined by Gray Murah and Hrev. *Then walk with us, Wolfwalker.*

Their trust was almost palpable, and Dion felt her chest clench. "You honor me," she said softly.

You hold our lives, they returned. *You hold our future. We need that.*

Lash was the first voice along the inside of her skull. Gray Murah followed, and behind them, the rest of the pack joined in. The invisible bonds between them tightened. Her mind, her thoughts, spun dizzyingly to the left, then plunged down into darkness, into her body and pulse. The pain was suddenly a fire in her mind, not just in her hands—a blast of wild sensation that inundated the pack. She felt the wrongness of the burns, the blistered flesh, the rightness of the channels that would seal the flesh again. She saw the power in all the heartbeats. It was fast, too fast. She was already past the edge of control. She tried to pull back, but the power began to break free.

Then her heart jerked, and her breath rushed into her lungs twice as fast. It was the wolves, shifting and howling into a stronger wall. They became a whirling shield of lupine senses, as if those physical strengths would anchor her to her world. She gasped, yanking back against the gray cords. They surged forward, forcing the gray more thickly around her, but she shoved the wall sharply away. The power inherent in their bodies and minds was not for her. Moons, but it would trigger the plague that lay dormant in them and burn them out like shells. She cut off the depth of that wild merging and stepped back from that gray energy shield. It was her barrier now, not theirs. It protected her from her own pain, but also from their power. It was her mental pattern that stamped it now and forced it into place.

Quickly, she separated her mind from the pain. From her own heart, along her shoulders, down her arms, her consciousness swept through her own bloodstream down to her burned hands. She reached, touched the nerves, and felt them scream with overstimulation. She soothed them so that she could start to work, then went on to the charred skin and muscles. She felt the heat that still chewed at her tissues and used the temperature of the cold grass beneath her feet to cool it. Then she let her mind center in the muscles until their threads began to reach out to each other, past the burn-tingling tissues and over the cracked wounds. She touched the torn flaps of blisters and sealed them back together. Cauterized blood vessels broke past the blocks and grew again; cracked skin became solid with scabs before growing a new transparent layer. She could feel the nerves strain to push out the new muscle that began to form. But the beat of her heart tugged at her consciousness. She wavered. The edges of the gray shield started shredding as her focus frayed. A wolf dropped out of the link, then another, and Dion felt her mind spin up and dizzyingly out until her eyes opened.

She stared blankly at the twilight. Power still vibrated in her body.

Gray Lash stood beside her. He looked up and met her violet eyes. *Wolfwalker.*

"You honor me," she whispered.

You are ours, the Gray One returned.

The wild wolf suffered her touch for an instant, then

shifted away, but the bond was still open, and lupine memories rushed past her mind's eye, sucking her into a vortex of pain and grief, joy and protectiveness, challenge and lust, bond and loss and emptiness. The overriding howl tightened her own throat until she threw her head back and let loose the beast in herself.

Lash howled with her in the twilight, and the other wolves joined in, fractionally late, their voices rising, falling, falling in the cold sky. She held them at bay with difficulty. *Hishn,* she sent instead, reaching out for one voice across the distance. She was answered by a din of snarls. *Wolfwalker-wolfwalker,* the gray voices howled. Gray Hishn's voice, if it was there at all, was buried under the packsong.

Kiyun closed his eyes and lifted his face as if letting the sound wash over him, but Tehena remained motionless, carefully not tensed as the wolf scars on her arms and legs seemed to tingle. She had challenged the wolves once, and she bore the marks to prove it. What Dion did now still gave her a shiver of fear.

The second howling didn't echo in the air, only in Dion's mind, and she let her throat relax. Gray Lash trotted a few steps away, turned his head, and eyed her hungrily. She met his gaze without flinching. They owned her, yes, but she owned them, too. It was the give and take of the bond. She felt the Gray Ones fading, and as if that sapped the last of her energy, she sagged.

Kiyun caught her before she hit the ground, and held her arms till she could hold her own weight. He stared at her hands.

"How do they look?" she asked.

He released her arms. "I'll be pinched to death by a pack of three-headed worlags," he said quietly. "The burns—they're completely healed."

Dion bent her fingers carefully, then straightened them out again. "Not really. There are only two layers of skin over the blisters, and there's still damage deep in the tissue. I can feel a bit of burning."

He shook his head. "But I've never seen you do so much.

Even with Ovousibas, you usually take half a ninan to reach this stage."

"Aye," she said softly. "I learned something from the birdmen." She had seen their use of energy, and it had been like sustained lightning that sparked and fused wounded edges together, that spurred other tissues to heal. When those aliens fed, it had been like a blaze that stripped everything from the ice and the life around it. Dion's own use of the internal healing had been crude, weak, juvenile. She used her own body's patterns to channel her energy, but the aliens saw all patterns of life, not just their own. They simply followed those patterns down through each substance until they found the lowest energies where they could control the bonds between matter. Dion had been shocked by that control. She glanced down at her hands and tentatively tried to stretch back into that power, but it snapped and sparked on her mind. She was beginning to understand now. The patterns the aliens saw were the same as the Ancients' technologies: the power inherent in matter. It was a sort of clarity, as if she were seeing into the essence of an object and finding at its heart the physics of the Ancients. She wriggled her toes against the bare ground that she could now feel just as clearly. She could not go back to the simple healing from before. With her link to the alien mother, she would always be too close to the power. She had to control it now, for herself, for the wolves, for the world. Rightly done or not, it was the path that she had chosen, for herself and her unborn child.

Kiyun frowned as he watched her. "You've never done the healing like this before," he repeated. "Even I could feel the power. If you're pulling that out of yourself, or if you took it from one of us . . ." He shook his head.

"I'm not and I wouldn't," she said firmly. "I couldn't ask for that much energy from either of you without killing you. The Aiueven could, but they're built for that kind of power." She laughed shakily. "Moons, but this world isn't just a breeding ground to them, it's a massive power cell."

His brown eyes sharpened. "You mean they eat power?"

"Perhaps. I know that they use the energy in each creature or thing the same way we use firewood. It's how they hollow out the ice and keep the rock caves from collapsing. It's how they communicate, how they fly, how they reach the stars. They shift energy, channel it here and there." She started to pace, shaking her hands to keep herself from scratching the new skin. "The young ones couldn't control their own body temperature—that's why they were in the deeper, warmer caves. When they learn how to channel enough power to ignore the cold, they move out closer to the adults." She frowned to herself. "That's why they mistook me for an infant. I channeled so little power." She paused and seemed to look closely at herself from within. "But I won't be able to handle much more than I did today . . ."

Tehena watched the wolfwalker with pale, sharp eyes. "Dion, the legends, the Aiueven sucking the life out of intruders and leaving only husks . . ."

Dion cocked her head as if considering the point. "They're probably true," she admitted. "The aliens simply channel the energy right out of the human until he dies. It's effective. Clean. Good for intimidation." Her voice grew faint. "Aranur would have liked it."

Tehena and Kiyun exchanged looks. Kiyun frowned. "Dion, if you didn't take the power from yourself or us or the wolves, where did you take it from?"

She hesitated. "I did take some from myself," she admitted.

"And the rest?"

She looked down.

They followed her gaze. In the twilight, they almost missed it. There was no grass where she had been standing, and her boots no longer had soles. There was a shadow of powdered leather where she had stood, but no more than that.

Tehena cleared her throat. "Going to go through a lot of shoes."

"Better boots than bodies," she returned.

"Dion," Kiyun started.

"I won't experiment," she said softly. "Not here. Not right now. It took me years to learn the limits before, and that healing was only a shadow of this power. I won't risk you or the wolves." Or my child.

The unspoken words were clear, and Kiyun nodded, satisfied. But Tehena eyed the wolfwalker thoughtfully. The lanky woman had felt the edge of that power as she lent her own strength to Dion, and it had been seductive. She wondered how Dion resisted the urge to cut it loose and let it burn away all the pain she carried inside. Perhaps it was the wolves. The wolves might have been Called to help the wolfwalker, but the creatures had also made their own Answer. It was a circle, she thought. The Call and Answer—the need that drove them and the solution that saved—they were the same thing: Ember Dione.

XX

Talon Drovic neVolen

Temper rage with empathy.
Temper eagerness with wisdom.
Temper the self with the world.
Temper the world with hope.

   —from the Book of Abis

Dusk found Drovic's group on the outskirts of a remote farm, where only half the fields had been harvested. It was the last farm along the road, and Talon, Drovic, and Kilaltian studied it for almost half an hour before acknowledging that there seemed to be only three people inhabiting it. The three farm folk knew a threat was close; the two dogs in the yard circled and watched the hills with unease.

Talon resisted the urge to rub at his wrist. It was purpled and swollen, making the pain in the hand even worse, and he desperately wanted the ice he knew would be stored in the coldroom below the farmhouse. Drovic's men and women had cleaned up after the village raid, but had not yet updated the maps, and several of them—including Talon—needed to change the bandages over their wounds. "We won't kill them," he said flatly to Drovic.

Drovic answered absently as he studied the farm. "The dogs or the people?"

"Both," he returned shortly. "We're far north," he added. "We can use this place again, add it to your list of caches. We go in, we stay the night, we don't molest the woman, and we give her a few pieces of silver when we leave. She'll say nothing to anyone else."

Drovic turned from his study and regarded his son like a particularly unpleasant grafbug. "Why?"

Talon gestured at the run-down courtyard, answering the obvious, rather than the unspoken question. "Look at her. The barn is missing planks at one end; the fences are barely mended. One of those pumps looks like the handle is barely bolted on, and at least half her fields are fallow. She's poor. Her family isn't large enough to keep this farm running. What woman wouldn't take in a few boarders to help feed her children through winter?"

"We're raiders, boy, not boarders."

"And she will know it the moment we ride in. But she will pretend—and we can pretend—that we are a venge instead. She will shelter us tonight and cook stew and open the grog larder, and if we come back, she will shelter us again."

Drovic turned his flat, blue-gray gaze back to the farm. "The shelter will be here, whether or not she remains alive. Alive, she can change her mind after we leave, and point a venge straight after us."

"Alive, she will be convenient."

Drovic's voice was dry. "Aye, that's the way the men will see it."

"She is not to be harmed," Talon said sharply. "Not the woman. Not the girl. Not the boy."

His father gave him a hard look. "Brentak likes them female. Fit just likes them young."

"A mother makes a vicious protector. Harm the girl or boy, and she will fight us knife and stone, tooth and nail."

"All the more reason to take what we want and kill them before we leave."

"No." Talon struggled to suppress his anger. "Not this time. This time, we do it my way."

"Why?"

"Because—" Talon's voice broke off in frustration. "Because I see . . ." He shook his head. "We must not. Not this time. Not here."

Drovic studied his son for a long moment. He turned away in silence, and Talon's gut clenched. But Drovic merely motioned for the raiders to ride in after them. The man's voice was wry as he ordered loudly, "We are not a pack of raiders; we are a venge. Behave as one."

Sojourn raised an eyebrow, and Weed and Ki exchanged looks. But other than that, the hard-faced men simply nodded as the word was passed along.

As they approached the farmhouse, the two dogs rushed out. One massive mutt paced back and forth, its coat ruffled and its teeth bared, while the shepherd-cross dog barked viciously. The dnu, used to noise and danger, took their cue from the raiders and ignored the half-breed dogs.

At the house, the girl, then the woman and boy peered out the window. When the door opened, the woman held a sword in a half-ready position. Talon noted her stance: frightened, determined. She was obviously a novice with the blade, but she would fight. If she panicked, she might even wound one of them before she died. Talon hoped she would choose to live.

Drovic did not dismount. Instead, he held up his hand to halt the rest behind him and walked his dnu forward a few more steps. The dogs snarled and circled, but quieted at a command from the woman, and leaped to the porch to stand ready beside her.

"We are riding through to Kiren," Drovic said formally. "We request the use of your home."

The woman's hand tightened on the hilt. But she replied, "Our home is yours as it is ours." There was the slightest tremor in her voice, but she stepped aside to allow Drovic to dismount and enter. The dogs growled, and she hushed them, commanding one to stay on the porch, while the shepherd-mutt backed obediently inside. Drovic smiled as if to reassure her, but he dwarfed the woman, and his expression was more like that of a hunting lepa. She stepped involuntarily back. He glanced meaningfully at the growling dog inside, and she commanded it over to the children.

Drovic moved inside without glancing at her sword. It took only a moment to judge the rooms; then he returned to the porch, ignoring the farm woman who still held the blade, although now somewhat helplessly.

"Set up the barn," he told his riders. He gestured to the porch. "Unload here. With your permission," he added belatedly to the woman.

It was with difficulty that she kept her voice steady. "Of course."

He nodded. "We will want stew and grog tonight; hay in the barn for the dnu. Breakfast at dawn." He caught Talon's warning expression. "Other than that," he said dryly, "I suggest you keep out of our way."

The woman nodded without speaking. Her knuckles were white on the hilt of her sword, but when she turned to go inside, her back was straight and her head was held high. Drovic almost admired her.

The farm woman took the two dogs out back and chained them to the porch while Kilaltian's group took over barn duty. Drovic took advantage of the large dining table to set up his maps and notes. By the time Talon was done with his dnu, the great room was lined with packs.

Two hams stolen from the village were being cut up, and dried fruits had been dumped in a large bowl, from which the raiders grabbed up handfuls. The farmhouse had been painfully clean before they arrived, but the floor was now scuffed with boot prints and trail dirt. The walls, once starkly white, were now littered with smudges from dirty hands, while obscene smears already obscured the lower windows. Even as Talon took in the room, Liatuad stepped back from his latest window tongue-pattern and grinned at the man beside him. Al tugged on his red hair in admiration and nodded in return. "Not bad," he admitted. "But watch this." Talon turned away in disgust as Al spread his nostrils on the glass and began panting like a dog to build up enough steam on the window.

The woman and her two children were in the kitchen, cutting up tubers and mincing herbs. The three worked tensely while Fit leaned casually against the wall and watched the girl and boy. Talon barely glanced at the farm folk, except to note that, judging by the expression in Fit's eyes, the girl was not young enough to stay untouched in this crowd. She'd have been safer in a Sidisport harem, he thought, where at least the laws would protect her till she came of age and was willing. He found the coldroom and chipped off a piece of ice, wrapped it in a bandana, and pressed it against his wrist before rejoining the other raiders.

Drovic was at the plank table, listening to the reports and marking the information on his map. It was an exquisitely detailed map, originally drawn by a Yorundan master, and Talon envied that detail. Harare had supposedly studied under such a master. The blond man updated their maps often, but even he didn't approach the beautiful detail of the original. After giving his own, edited impressions of the village, Talon leaned on a chair while the rest of the raiders reported.

". . . a trap door, but it led to a standard coldroom. The basement was flooded about half a foot deep from some sort of leak in the pipes." Harare kept his voice as low as Drovic's. In the kitchen, the farm folk would hear nothing other than the noise of the other raiders.

Drovic nodded and gestured with his chin for Weed to report. Weed always looked like an awkward scarecrow to Talon, unbalanced by the bony breadth of his shoulders, unkempt with the loose threads that always seemed to pull from his jerkin no matter how tight the weave. His cauliflower ear was a legacy of Weed's own father, and one Talon didn't envy. Drovic may have been a hard man, but he had never hit Talon with more force than to bruise. It was different now, Talon admitted, but he had become a danger to his father, not just another raider. As Dangyon began his report, it occurred to Talon that, like Weed, Dangyon didn't belong with Drovic. The barrel-chested man had no desire to kill, though he had learned to do it with dispatch. Talon nodded at Dangyon as the older man finished his report and moved back to settle his gear. He realized that, as he had decided about Wakje and Weed, he would take Dangyon with him also. Then he grinned derisively to himself. He wondered if they knew he would be changing the course of their lives.

Ilandin spoke timidly and quickly, and Drovic nodded curtly to dismiss her. Wakje merely handed over a fast tally stick of his notes and takings, which Drovic set aside. Oroan and Fit had found one of the lab accesses for which Drovic searched, but it looked to be old, possibly as old as the village. The roof had collapsed less than three meters in, and the tunnel was long abandoned. Drovic carefully marked the information on the map, but Talon could see he was angry.

"Did you look for another door?" he asked tersely. "They wouldn't just abandon an entire lab because one part of the roof caved in."

The slender woman shrugged. Her wide-boned face was carefully expressionless, and her voice was flat as glass. "There wasn't time. I kicked the pile, but we were in a hurry."

"You kicked the pile," Drovic repeated. "What else did you pick up?"

"A few coppers and a kilo of cinnamon-laced rou."

Drovic's voice was hard. "And?"

Oroan regarded him for a moment. "A pearl barrette."

"You stopped and searched a woman's armoire, but spared less time to look for the access that you were sent in to find."

Oroan raised her eyebrows. Her crystal-green eyes fairly challenged the man, and Drovic stared at the woman for a long moment. The woman's voice was steady, but Talon watched the set of Oroan's oddly wide shoulders as they tensed the barest amount. "The dirt was hard-packed, Drovic. It was futile to do more."

"And that was your choice to make?"

"As long as I'm the one down in the hole," she agreed calmly. But her hands were too casual as they set on her hips, close to the hilts of her knives. "You owe me five silvers for the find."

Drovic leaned almost negligently forward. Oroan didn't flinch when his hard-calloused hand struck her brutally on the cheek. The woman's head rocked back, and her eyes went still for a moment. Then she smiled—stiffly, because her wide lips had been smashed back against her perfectly straight teeth. She ignored the trickle of blood. "You owe me five silvers," she said calmly.

"Get out of my sight," the man snarled.

The flat-boned woman merely waited.

Talon put his hand on Drovic's arm, and the older man shook him viciously off. Drovic fairly ripped the pouch from his belt. He cast the silvers down on the table so hard that all but one bounced to the floor. Oroan did not take her eyes from the man. Talon watched the silvers roll, noted the woman's square chin—defiantly high, the flared nostrils of that broken, aquiline nose, and the empty, jewel eyes above it.

Talon said softly, "Oroan."

Something flickered in those green-glass eyes. The woman finally stirred. She nodded once at Talon, wiped her chin of blood and, with an oddly delicate gesture, stooped and picked up the silvers.

Drovic watched without speaking. The woman rose and walked away without a backward glance. Kilaltian called out, "A drink, my wench," and Oroan grinned in return.

"A slitted throat, my fancy fop," she replied. The raiders laughed rudely, though none of them looked at Drovic. Wakje tossed the woman a flask of whiskey, and Oroan caught it one-handed. She upended the flask and took a double hit. Her glass-green eyes were brilliant when she tossed the flask back to Wakje. "I once was a loader in Breinigton—" She sang as she jigged a few steps on the floor. "—down by the lonely sea—"

The others grinned and chimed loudly in: "I mistook my pone for a piece of white bone, and shipped it to Portsindee."

Oroan jerked a flask from Dangyon's hand as she jigged past the barrel-chested man, then slapped the raider only half playfully as he tried to retrieve his liquor. She chugged the fluid and choked like a cat with a hairball as Dangyon whacked her hard in the gut. The massive man plucked the flask from her hand, and she grinned at him even as she coughed to clear her throat, then cast a deliberate look at

Drovic. "I once was an elder in Mandalay, over in high Ariye—"

The others roared, "I mistook my pete for some dried-up mesquite and burned it along with the tree!"

Drovic watched without expression, then turned back to his map. He studied it for a long moment, blindly seeing the notes and marks in his mind, not through his eyes. When he finally spoke, his voice was low beneath the guffaws. "Someday, I'll kill that worlag bitch."

Talon's voice was as quiet. "Someday, she'll thank you for it."

Drovic stared at his son. Then he barked a laugh. "Spoken like a true neVolen. I've missed you, boy." Talon grinned, and Drovic slapped his good shoulder so hard that his teeth rattled. "Look here, now. We've confirmed another lab, and old or not, it should be investigated next year. This western area here—this is where I want to strike in spring. The lab here has to be large—the glass and resin shops have too much activity for standard exports—and two of the smaller greenhouses are growing agar."

"Gels?"

"Could be, for that kind of quantity."

Talon nodded. The gelatin was used for growing the bioforms like the rootroad trees that now included a luminescent bacteria. Although most labs were simple workhouses for improving the Ancients' plants, some labs were geared more specifically. Those were the ones Drovic wanted. The chemistry and science could easily be turned into weapons, wielded like a sword in the right hands. Talon rubbed absently at the aching burn in his stiffened left hand, but stopped when Drovic noted it. "Tonic hasn't kicked in," he said shortly in explanation, though his hand itched to crush the pouch that the river had emptied of herbs.

His father nodded and turned back to his maps. "Still have eleven possibles in the northeast. This one's close. We should hit it as we go north. Then we can spend some time mapping this area through winter, then hit the first six targets by midsummer next year." The gray-haired man chewed his lip thoughtfully.

Drovic would be riding alone by midsummer, Talon thought, because he'd be taking his men away and heading east within ninans. Casually, he studied the line that marked the Ariyen boundary. Except for a few recent forays, Drovic had not crossed that line in over thirty years. "There are a dozen targets within striking distance of the main Ariyen pass," he commented. "You've let them accumulate like gel-bugs on a wound."

"Don't spur the stickbeast, boy," his father returned almost absently. "I want those Ariyens to feel safe up there with their nice, smooth roads and their winter-warm homes. When we're ready, we'll be like lepa on a hare. They won't see us coming, and they won't feel our steel till it sprouts out their backsides like grass. I won't jeopardize our future with the haste of a worlag just because you're feeling antsy."

And if they waited much longer, Talon wouldn't remember why they were attacking Ariye at all. He could not help the sharpness of his voice as he said. "So we stay south and west of this line."

A shadow flickered in Drovic's eyes. "I drew that line almost three decades ago, after your mother died. I haven't crossed it three times since that day—the day I was left for dead, just as your mate left you."

A flash of memories blinded Talon. He saw his mate laughing, slipping silently through the forest, dancing on the edge of a cliff, teasing him with stinkweed. He had held her in his arms, watched her life slip away. He had sworn to the moons that he would follow her, but he rode with Drovic in-stead. And now he heard only the voice of the wolf-woman, gnawing at his skull. He stared at the map without seeing it. His took a shallow breath. "I never knew how you survived," he said. His voice was almost steady.

Drovic didn't notice. "Neither did I at first. Your mother died a meter away from me when the raiders hit. I was hit in the chest by two bolts—enough to stagger me, but not pene-trate bone. I must have looked like a pincushion when the rockfall trap was released. My brother died trying to run, and I was knocked around like a gnat in a hurricane before the dust cleared. They cornered me, the raiders, but I challenged them. Killed three and wounded another before they brought me down. They were about to skewer me like a whirren for supper when their leader saw the rage in my eyes. He made me an offer instead." Drovic ran his hand through his peppered hair. "And here I am: ninety-eight and so soaked in blood that my skin reeks with its odor." He pointed to the line that had been drawn across the counties. "I drew that line north to mark my path back home. It's a good line, Son. Deceptive. Raiders never came in from the north before—the terrain is too rugged, too cold. When I first led my own band, I followed that pattern with care."

"And now?"

The older man looked back down at the map and fingered the sword at his side. "And now, my men find their goals in me, and I do not cross that line because when I do, it will be the releasing of the hate in their swords and the bloody lance of my rage."

Talon's voice was soft. "And the fall of Ramaj Ariye."

Drovic smiled without humor. "The fall of all nine counties," he corrected. The older man pointed to the southern area. "The Ariyen Lloroi knows that I won't cross that line and challenge those alien beasts—not until I have enough resources to win. Think of it, Son. Think of the other worlds we could explore once we make use of our rotting technology and leave this world behind."

"And there is no other way to achieve this goal."

Drovic shrugged. "When I first went back to Ariye, they gave me only two options: give up the stars and return as a good, obedient, quiet citizen under Lloroi Tyronnen, or give up my home and pursue Ariye like a worlag, worrying at its flanks, hunted by every venge in the county if I ever crossed that line." The gray-haired man smiled suddenly, and the expression was dangerously grim. "Without my mate, without my children, I found my home less appealing. My anger began the day you were born, but it has only grown since then."

"You could control it," Talon retorted.

"As you control yours—too much?" The older man gestured sharply at the map. "Anger, like steel, is a weapon. Let it out, let it be directed, and it could change the world."

"Then use it now, while it rages inside me. Let us strike here—" Talon stabbed his finger down on the map. "—instead of there. I know this land. I know the roads, the trails, the passes."

Drovic's gaze narrowed.

Talon's words were curt as he answered his father's unspoken doubts. "It is events, not land, that I do not remember." He pointed to a twisted line on the map. "I know that I've hiked this trail in autumn, with a biting wind so cold that I could hear nothing but its whistling in my burning ears. I know that I've seen this river dry as a hungover tongue, and that although it's not marked, there is a spring forty meters off this trail. This meadow is one of the major mating places of the badgerbear in summer. That valley is almost completely swamp except in the driest of summers—I was caught in the mud once for hours. And this height is actually two ridges, with a tiny fold in the middle where you could hide for a decade without anyone the wiser." Talon met his father's gaze steadily. "I know this land, Father. I could take us through here as silently as a dozen stickbeasts, and we could make enough trouble in less than ten raids to split this band between us and halve the time to the goal."

Drovic let out his breath. Talon had the sudden certainty that his father had been waiting for some other shoe to drop. But Drovic merely studied Talon thoughtfully. "You're still weak."

"Aye," he agreed flatly. "But I can still sit a dnu, still use a sword, and still find a lab with my eyes."

A gleam grew in Drovic's flinty-blue eyes, and Talon knew he had hooked the older man. "I could work you through winter like I used to do. By spring, you'd be mean as a worlag, ready to be a predator, not one of the weak and ravaged."

Drovic was almost eager. Talon's hands clenched, and he realized that he could not tell if it was because he had finally pleased his father, or because he would break the older man when he took his raiders away.

Drovic mistook his son's hooded expression. "We ravage, son, to re-create."

"Re-create?" Talon snorted.

"A win is not in the battle itself, but in the aftermath. It is in changing what you have won to be what you want. You cannot rebuild on the old foundation till you break the existing structure. And so, we must be destroyers before we can turn to building. Destruction itself is not our goal. It never was."

Talon's voice was soft. "And so fear is our weapon."

"Fear, blood, violence, death." Drovic shrugged. "A weapon is a weapon. You can't become squeamish about the means by which you reach your goal. Partial warfare—that was one of the things that got the Ancients into half the messes that destroyed their world." Drovic's finger traced the line along the northern border of Ariye. "An ideal has no value when it cannot be achieved. Set your goal and reach it. There is no other way."

Slowly, Talon nodded. "No other way," he echoed, almost to himself. His eyes sought out the men he had selected: Wakje, Weed, Dangyon, Mal, Oroan, Rakdi, Sojourn. He thought he could sway Harare and Cheyko, possibly even Ki. There were a few others in Darity's and Kilaltian's groups: Pen, the woman who had once been a baker; Nortun, who worked with the herbs—he'd be useful. A gray wolf howled deep inside his mind, and the image of the dark-eyed woman blinded him. Set your goal . . . His fists clenched. Ariye with or without his father, but he could not wait for spring. She was heading that way, south and west, and there were only two roads she could take to Ariye. The wolves howled again in his head. He welcomed the sound in the silence.

XXI

Rhom Kheldour neKintar

Danger comes in many guises:
Some are obvious, some more hidden;
Some creep up; some are sudden;
Some deceive with more than steel;
Some show threats that seem surreal;
Some will hide behind denial;
Some will offer pleasant smiles;
Smile back, but keep your knife
Sharp if you enjoy your life.

   —Kiren children's training chant

Sand. Dry sand. Hot sand. Burning sand. Choose your adjective, Rhom thought, and as long as it had something to do with fire, it would be accurate. It was twilight, and they had been on the trail for only an hour, but already he was scratched with dry sweat. The temperature was dropping, but the day's heat still sapped him.

His water bag was dry, and his muscles were tight with dehydration. It was a dangerous condition. Too long without water, and the kidneys and liver couldn't process the normal toxins in the body. But they had had the last of the water yesterday noon when they drank it all at once. There were myths about rationing water, but Rhom knew better even without Gamon telling him. Best to hydrate as much as possible than perpetuate the dryness.

It wasn't just Gamon and Rhom, either. The dnu—there was only one now, as they'd lost the other to a broken leg when a rock stretch collapsed beneath it—was gaunt and caked with dust. Its head seemed overlarge on its bone-thin neck, and it plodded slowly behind Gamon as Rhom took his turn riding. The older man had been following a faint trail for an hour, heading for a small seep that might give them enough water to last through the next day. If it was as low as Gamon suspected, they would have to leave even this dry track for the tenor trees that glowed in webbed lines through the desert. There was always water beneath a tenor tree—the question was how far down.

Rhom stared out at the moonlit desert. A hundred kays across the desert as the crow flies, but for them, it was more than two hundred. There were few bridges to relieve the road that wound down in and back out of canyons. With the side trips to water-holes, they were making barely twelve kays a night, not the sixteen Rhom had planned on.

They paused at the edge of another ravine while Gamon judged the best way down. Rhom's dnu took the opportunity to drag desultorily at the dead grass that clung to the cracks in the basalt, and Rhom didn't begrudge the animal its thin meal. If the next tinaja didn't have more water, they would lose this dnu too.

The rocks erupted. "Moons!" Fear jerked the word from his mouth. His dnu reared at the very edge of the precipice. He hauled back violently, yanking the beast up by sheer strength. Its forelegs scrabbled in air. Something with teeth launched itself upward along the line of the dnu's neck. Ringed teeth, round maw. Gamon shouted for him to kick clear. Instinctively, he obeyed. Hooves kicked out beside his head. He hit hard, half rolled across bone-stabbing rocks, and scrambled up, his knife in his right hand. A fury of mottled brown fur launched itself at the dnu. Rhom felt the adrenaline engulf him. He lunged and caught the reins, struck wildly, blindly at the spray of sand kicked up. There were teeth in that yellow cloud. The dnu screamed and jerked back, but there was no purchase under its feet. It started to fall. The predator's flowing claws raked Rhom. The hand holding the reins shocked open. Half blinded, he lunged forward. The beast closed around him like a cloak. Teeth ground down on his forearm. He stabbed, thrust, hammered the blade home again and again as the claws plowed his sides and back. Their legs were a tangle of boots and fur, kicking at each other. Teeth chewed down convulsively, and this time, he screamed. Then his blade cracked the casing that housed the creature's brain.

Gamon's iron grip dragged the beast back. Rhom crawled away in the sand.

"Rhom! By the moons, man, are you all right?"

Instinctively, still blinded by violence, he thrust the other man away, then staggered to his feet, leaned for a moment against a black boulder, and gasped back his breath. His arm was a mass of agony, and his sides and back burned. "Moonworms." His voice was ragged. "Moonworms. Badger?"

"Desert poolah." Gamon lifted an edge of the creature with his boot to make sure its brain casing was well cracked. "They grow smaller and flatter here, but this one is thin even for the desert. Probably been waiting for dinner for days." He glanced up. "How's your arm?"

"It's not bleeding much. The dnu?"

"Gone." Gamon looked over the edge of the cliff to make sure, keeping well back from the thin edge. He turned back to examine Rhom's wound. "It's the heat," he said with a hint of worry about the lack of blood. "You're getting badly dehydrated. You'd be bleeding like a stuck pig if we were in the mountains."

Rhom stoically bore the examination while Gamon pressed and poked at the ragged wounds. Stoically, that is, until the older man jabbed his finger into one of the gashes. "Worlag piss, Gamon, are you trying to hold it together or pull it apart?"

"Hold still," Gamon said absently. He took out his knife, squinted at the wound in the brilliant moonlight, and before Rhom realized what he meant to do, dug the point down into the gash.

The Randonnen jerked, but Gamon had his arm like a vise. "By the chin of a lepa's uncle," Rhom swore as Gamon released him. "What the hell are you doing?"

The older man turned the point of the knife to examine the strand of tissue. Silently, he held it up. Rhom, gripping his arm where the blood now flowed freely, narrowed his violet eyes. The thread writhed subtly, and it was as long as his finger. "Is that—?" he swallowed.

"Sandworm," Gamon confirmed.

"From the poolah?"

Gamon nodded. "The adult worms coil under the claws. You're lucky it was at the top of the wound. I think I got it all. Let me see your sides."

Rhom stripped off what was left of his shirt. The gashes were ragged, but already oozing instead of flowing with blood. The older man pursed his lips. "Don't see any," he said shortly. "You were lucky. A few more seconds, and it would have been tearing your gut, not your ribs."

Rhom didn't answer. Lucky? Give him the mountains any day. A worlag or poolah here and there—that was nothing. Sandworms and rockdoves and gritbugs? He caught Gamon's expression and cursed again under his breath. Then he gave a short bark of a laugh. Gamon raised his gray eyebrows, and Rhom shrugged. "If Dion didn't know I was coming before, she surely knows it now."

"She could feel this—you—at this distance?"

He nodded and dug out the bandages from Gamon's pack while Gamon got out the wound powder. "Moments of intensity," he explained. "We know when we're in danger or pain."

The gray-haired man sprinkled the powder on his gashes, then efficiently wrapped his arm. "So she feels the pain?"

Rhom's violet eyes glinted. "The danger, Gamon. Just the danger."

The older man grinned. "Right," he agreed insincerely.

Rhom grinned back. But he lost his humor as he regarded the drop into the next ravine. His heart still pounded a bit too fast. His muscles were still tense with the action. Dion had felt him—he was sure of it. But he had also felt her, and he could not help the instinctive grasp for the sword he had lost with his saddle. His voice was soft, and to himself. "There is someone hunting her through the wolves. And he is closing in."

XXII

Ember Dione maMarin

Let go the moons,
So that they may bring the night;
Let go your sons,
So that they may learn what is right;
Let go your fathers,
So that they may find life's end;
Let go the moons,
So that they may rise again.

   —From "Circles," by Wile neRaya, Kiren Songster

Dion's hand clenched on her knife. Tehena and Kiyun caught her motion and instantly thumbed off the securing straps and drew their swords. Dion backed her dnu almost blindly away for two steps before she caught herself and held up her hand to the others. "Wait," she said sharply.

The wolf pack ahead on the road paused and looked back. They caught her sudden sense of fear, the distance of the urgency, and poised as if to race back. She scanned the icy ridge to the right, the sheer drop-off on the other side. She stared at the snowy stone road. A minute passed, then another. Ahead of them, the snow stretched in a shattered expanse where a dozen wagons had left their icy ruts. There were scrubby trees in a semiprotected patch on the slope, and up ahead, where the road dipped back down and widened out, the snow lay only in patches. Nothing moved. Nothing waited. There was nothing there.

Dion stretched into the gray, tried to feel the danger. The cold wind bit at her cheeks. Finally she shook herself. The danger was not hers, she realized. It was not her threat.

"Dion?" Kiyun asked softly.

"It is nothing," she said firmly.

"Didn't look like nothing from here."

She hesitated, then explained. "It's Rhom."

Kiyun looked startled, but Tehena merely nodded to herself. The thin woman had suspected this of the wolfwalker, but it was the first time Dion had said it out loud. Kiyun did not sheath his sword. "What do you mean, it is Rhom?"

Dion shrugged, but she too was unwilling to move forward yet. The sharp edge of danger had been faint, like a hunch that struck suddenly and then disappeared, leaving one second-guessing oneself. "My brother," she said slowly. "He was in danger, in pain. I felt it clearly enough."

"Through the wolves?"

She smiled faintly. "Rhom and I don't need the wolves to know about each other. No, this was our natural bond, the bond of twins."

"But he's safe now?"

She nodded at the man. "There's still an edge to the link between us, but it's fading."

The thickset man shook his head. "I don't see how you can feel anyone as far away as Randonnen."

"He is not in Randonnen," she said softly. "He is on his way to Ariye. But I would feel him anyway."

Tehena had been content to let Kiyun question the wolfwalker, but now she raised her thin eyebrows. "Why Ariye?"

"Because I need him," she said even more softly. "I think I have been calling him to me as I've Called the wolves—through my needs."

Tehena and Kiyun exchanged a glance. Kiyun cleared his throat. "It will take him ninans to reach Ariye. We'll be halfway out of the county by the time he reaches your home."

Dion shook her head. "He's not taking the valley route."

"Surely you can't tell the route he takes—" The burly man broke off at the wolfwalker's expression. "How do you know he's not taking the valley?"

"Because he is crossing The Dry."

This time, the look between Tehena and Kiyun was almost comical. Dion caught it and actually laughed out loud. "I can feel the dry, the thirst, the heat. It's just like sensing a distant wolfwalker through the pack. Like an Ariyen wolfwalker sensing the cold here through my own link to the wolves. Don't worry. I'm not crazy, even after what happened up north."

"After what happened?" Tehena snorted. "That's about as mild an understatement as even you could make. You deliberately invaded the alien breeding grounds, and a birdman carried you off like a hare, sliced you up like a dinner goose, and dumped you on a glacier."

"I came back," Dion said mildly.

"You did," Tehena agreed. "A full day later and covered in blood."

The wolfwalker shrugged. "I was alive."

"Like poolah meat," Tehena retorted. "Something nearly tore your babe right out of your womb. You act as if you took a stroll, instead of setting yourself out to die. And just because you didn't come back completely gutted doesn't mean that it didn't happen."

Dion gave her a sideways look.

"What?" Tehena asked suspiciously.

Dion's voice was dry. "I'm just trying to parse the negatives."

"Pah." The thin woman snorted again. "So you can feel Rhom at this distance then. I thought you didn't have that kind of resolution."

Dion looked north, then back toward the wolves. "I don't know. I feel different. I am different, and it's not just from carrying this child. I hear the wolves differently now, as if there is a touch of something cold, something wrong in the packsong."

"That hunter?"

"No." She hesitated. "I think it is the Aiueven."

"The birdmen? How can you be sure?"

"I met them, spoke with them, felt their power. I channeled enough of it that I almost killed you," she added to Tehena. "I am sensitive to it now. Like being able to distinguish a touch of color where before, I thought it was just an odd part of the gray."

Kiyun said slowly, "Like an injury to your guts, and ever after you can feel your spleen?"

She nodded. "And if I can hear them, even so faintly, who knows how much I have changed in other ways? I feel urgent, drawn, pulled, hunted, and I know those things are through the wolves. But my thoughts seem sharper, my vision more acute even in the last few days. Like this child." She touched her belly. She tried to ignore the guilt that came when she thought about her children. She had adopted her eldest when he was eleven. She loved him as her first son, but had never felt him through the wolves as she had the two boys she had borne of her own body. Last spring, Olarun, her oldest blood-son, had run from her, blaming her for his younger brother's death, but she knew she had abandoned him as much as he had run from her when she rode away from Ariye. Gods, but she missed them. Cursed herself for leaving them, and cursed herself a dozen times more for still being unable to face them with the guilt for the deaths of Danton and Aranur. Yet she felt her two living sons less than she should—or rather, she realized, she felt this unborn child with more closeness than she ought to if there were only wolves in her mind. She pressed hard against her flesh. "I feel this child with a clarity I never had with my sons. I feel the edge of power in the packsong and know that I could use it as easily as you use a knife."

"To heal?"

She shrugged. She had been blinded by the legends, she realized. She had thought of Ovousibas as a tool only for fixing broken bodies. But the energies she had manipulated for years now seemed infantile compared to what was possible. The aliens used their ability to manipulate energy for everything from building tunnels to killing—as they would have killed Dion, if not for her . . . mother. She had forced a mental link between the alien and herself and her child. With the near-permanent memories of the telepathic birdmen, they had not been able to kill one of their own—as much as Dion was such. Instead, they had let her live, and she had learned as much from that brief contact as she had in the fourteen years since she first tried Ovousibas. There had always been a hint of yellow in the back of the wolfpack's song. Now she knew what it was. It was power like that of the Ancients, the power of the land, of the world, of the stars. It could be used for more than healing. She tried to hide her shiver, but she could feel the female presence of the alien like a silent, wary watcher. She had run north to escape her demons, and had bargained with the devil instead. It should have been a simple thing, a bond between mother and child, but this bond was between human and alien and was filled with power that would taint even her children's children.

She looked down at her hands, then back up at the others. "Have you ever wondered whether a wolfwalker's faster healing was because of the alien influence?" she asked. "That there might be some latent sense of Ovousibas in the wolves' memories, and that we tap into that so unconsciously we don't even realize there's something else behind it?"

Tehena studied her thoughtfully. "If that were so, then surely in eight hundred years, other wolfwalkers would have discovered that, too."

"I think the Aiueven recognize it when any wolfwalker does. We've always known they can hear the wolves, and through them, the wolfwalkers. We're like fleas in their mind, irritating the edges of their thoughts." Dion gestured with her chin to the north. "They barely tolerate humanity as it is. If a wolfwalker understood that the aliens were actually inside the packsong where their power patterns could be read— where the patterns are read by healers like me—that realization would be as distinct as a bonfire on an icefield. It would bring the aliens down on that person like lepa on a staked-out rabbit."

"If they can hear you so clearly . . ." Kiyun cleared his throat. "Dion, your wolf-bond is stronger than that of almost any other wolfwalker. And the birdmen know of you. You threw your presence in their face when you challenged them. What's keeping them from killing you?"

"We made a pact, they and I," Dion said simply.

"A pact," Tehena repeated. "Like that with the wolves?"

"Different, but just as binding." Dion's lips twisted in a humorless smile. "The Aiueven will let me live, as long as I leave them alone."

Tehena scowled. There was something more to the wolf-walker's words.

Dion fell silent and let her mind stretch out into the gray. *Graysong, thicksong, distance* . . . There was a faint sense of a crowd, as if a hundred gray voices murmured a kay away. Fur ruffed against the wind. Calloused paws broke through the crust to crush the powder beneath. Cold claws. Cold, cold dewclaws . . . Dion stretched farther, trying to reach her twin, but without the intense emotions of the moment, the sense of the hunter intruded instead, and the echo of that man's voice chilled her like the wind. The pause lengthened into minutes, and she shrugged irritably, as if she could toss off the feeling that he was tracking her through the wolves.

Kiyun said quietly. "This is the fourth time you stopped today to listen. Yesterday, it was five. Was it Rhom all these times?"

"No. Rhom could use the wolves to find me if they were willing to come to him, but he doesn't need to do that. We're too close. We can feel each other on our own."

"It's the man in the packsong," Tehena said flatly.

Dion nodded, still silent as she cocked her head to listen.

Moons, it was like pulling teeth. "Is he a wolfwalker?" Kiyun persisted.

Dion looked back at him. "No," she said finally. "I should be able to speak to a wolfwalker through the Gray Ones if that were the case. Even with the wild wolves and even at this distance, I should be able to send an impression of what I am thinking. But I cannot do that here. No, this is no wolfwalker. This man, he is something else."

Tehena studied the wolfwalker carefully. "What kind of person could hunt you through the wolves but not be a wolfwalker?"

"You don't have to be a wolfwalker to hear the Gray Ones," she said slowly. "Aranur could hear the wolves. I Called them to find him at the coast, and now, in their memories, they look for him forever to bind us together again. It is that sort of hunting, a seeking that goes beyond location to intent." Cold intent, she admitted to herself. Frighteningly focused intent. Moons, but the wolves had found a man enough like her mate that in their eyes, he was already bonded to her. Her flash of anger pierced the gray as she fought to hang on to her memories.

Kiyun glanced at Tehena. His voice was quiet. "Dion, you have to let go of Aranur. You have to move forward. He is gone. He's dead."

She gave a bitter laugh. "Then I love a ghost," she returned. She held up her hand to stop him from speaking further. Her voice was soft. "We were kum-tai, Kiyun, not kum-jan or kum-vani, not simply friendship or tenderness. We had the forever bond. Do not take even that away, or what's left of my heart will break."

"Dion . . ." He forced his voice to hide his own emotion. "Dion, your heart is already broken."

She gave him a slow, twisted smile. "Then it won't hurt to cling to the pieces."

"And the wolves?"

"The wolves . . ." Her voice trailed off. Her eyes unfocused as she stretched back into the packsong. "They don't understand. They think to direct my mating. This man . . ."

"Is hunting you," Tehena finished.

"Yes. And I am—" She broke off. She spoke more softly, as if to voice what she felt would be to call it into a more physical existence. "I am . . . afraid."

Kiyun and Tehena exchanged a glance.

Dion nodded to herself as she admitted it. She reached farther into the gray to feel that man more clearly. She had been right: he had no real voice, no real bond with the wolves. Yet she could sense his presence like a roiling cloud on the edge of the gray, cold and full of fury. It cried out with need, and it struck out in rage and vengeance as she did. It was blind will and fierce determination, and spurred on by the gray steel will of the wolves, it was hunting her down like a deer, listening to her voice in the gray, feeding on her senses. By the time they met, he would know her as well as the wolves: her strengths, her weaknesses, the ways to manipulate her skills. She would know the same about him: his pain, his goals and fears. She shook herself, but she could not rid herself of the chill that wormed its way up and down her spine. She had sacrificed her family already to the elders in Ariye. What would this man demand? If she could not say no to the elders, she could still leave that twice-damned county. Could take herself out of range of the elders and use her skills for those who would help her child to live, not use it as another tool. But this hunter was not one to stand still and wait for her to come to him or accept a quick yes or no. He projected his determination toward her like a spear. She reminded him of his family just as he reminded her of her own, and he would not let go so easily if she simply rode away.

The look she gave Kiyun was sober. "The man who hunts me, he is forced toward me either by the wolves or by his own wishes. And he is a man of fury. A man of grief and violence."

"You can tell this through the wolves?"

She laughed without humor. "Always."

"And this man, he is a danger?"

"He is strong," she whispered, unaware that she answered out loud. "He is driven. He will not give up, not to the ends of the world and beyond." She didn't realize that her violet eyes grew haunted. "Something binds them together, the hunter and the wolves. He fights it as he fights his own griefs, and he will fight me like death when we meet because I will remind him of everything he has lost." Her voice was low. "I am too close to my own griefs. I'm not yet strong enough to face his. This man, he will tear my memories, try to take over my life, make me fit his needs just as the elders did." The wolves in her head howled like drums. *Wolfwalkerwolfwalker* . . . He wanted her, wanted the strength in her bond, the power in her hands. He threw his rage at her as if he didn't know or care what it would do when she felt it through the wolves.

Tehena's pale gaze narrowed. "Then this man, he is a danger to you."

Dion opened her eyes and stared blindly at the woman. Her whisper was sharp with fear. "This man, he could destroy me." She clenched her fists on the reins, and her dnu chittered and skittered with unease. Wolves, demons, Aiueven—damn them all, she cursed to the wind. She was not ready to fight, but the wolves were pushing, shoving her toward this hunter. Until she faced him, she could not force the Gray Ones away, could not regain her own life. It was the wolves' own

Calling that she had to Answer, and she cursed them silently as they crawled inside her mind.

Kiyun frowned at her expression. "Dion?"

"We ride," she said in a hard, flat voice. She kicked her dnu to a canter. "South and west to Ariye."

XXIII

Talon Drovic neVolen

My mind is clear,
And night, stretched out before me,
Is a dark eternity;
I see no path;
My hands, still grasping sword and bow,
Find no serenity;
My eyes are black—
Their images are tainted;
What blood has done within my soul,
I do to flesh with this blued-steel knife,
And plow and plant and cultivate
The dark, the dreams, the nightmares which
Become my life.

—from "The Lost Ring"
by Aranur Bentar neDannon

Talon was heading to the barn when he felt the hot eagerness shaft through his mind. With his headache, it triggered a blinding pain. He staggered, caught himself, and stiffened as he recognized the gray tint to the emotion. He found himself sprinting toward the barn. The dogs on the back porch were barking to deafen an entire church, but it was at the wolves who streaked through the courtyard. Something was beside him, and he realized it was lupine. Gray Chenl, he recognized.

Hunt with me, the wolf projected eagerly. *Find. Protect.*

He realized suddenly that there were other wolves behind them: Ursh, Lanth, Thoi, Vrek . . . The Gray Ones' eagerness was a focused heat in Talon's limbs, and he found himself stretching his legs to race the wolves as if he could beat them to the barn. It was the hunt they had been pushing, a hunt close enough to the one they wanted that their eagerness whipped through his mind. For a moment, he ran in a tide of gray. Then the wolves left him behind, split around the barn, and swept over and through the half-patched fences to race across the fallow fields and disappear again into forest. Only moonlight was left to trace the broken line of grasses and remind him that the wolves had been beside him. His nostrils flared to catch their scent, but only fading images remained in his mind, like a dream that leaves a man panting.

Slowly, Talon came to a halt. He stared after the wolves. Then he stiffened at the curse and the cry that came from within the barn. Quickly, he moved to the doorway, keeping out of the light. With the dnu snorting and stamping and the darkness, neither Fit nor Kilaltian noticed him. Fit had the girl from the farmhouse, and he'd already stripped her, leaving torn ribbons around her ankles and wrists where the heavier seams had held. She struggled wildly in his grip, and as Talon watched, Fit struck her hard on the cheek and threw her down in the straw. Talon started forward, then realized that Kilaltian would stop Fit for him.

Fit's knife was in his hand, and Kilaltian's hands were empty, but the tall, handsome man did not flinch. "Give her back her clothes," Kilaltian said. "Or I'll dig your teeth out with a dull knife and sew up your mouth with wire so hot it'll burn your name into your gums."

Fit spat at Kilaltian's feet. The girl tried to crawl away, but Fit put his boot on her calf and ground down so that she sobbed. The move gave Kilaltian his opening, and he struck Fit like a lepa, fast and brutally accurate. The smaller man staggered back into a post. He half slid down in a cloud of dust and lost his knife in the straw. He came back up like a worlag. The two men crashed together, and the girl scrambled out of the way. Fit was a whirlwind, striking three times like lightning, but Kilaltian punched back so hard that the shorter man went down like a rock. Then Kilaltian backhanded the skinny man so that Fit fell sideways and lay like a discarded twig.

Kilaltian looked down on the other man with his hands on his hips as if Fit were an errant child. The taller man's voice was mild. "We're a venge, not a pack of raiders, and you take Drovic's orders like the rest of us. Besides, rape this girl, and even Talon might take your head for ruining this retreat. Make her want you—then it's no fault but her own."

Talon's lips tightened. Kilaltian tended to take women freely, but then to protect them from others. This girl with her frightened eyes had triggered that protective sense, and he knew Kilaltian hated himself even as the man protected what wasn't his. Talon's hand rose without volition to rub at the old gems that studded his sternum beneath his tunic. One for Promising, one for Mating. He had not protected what was his, and now the wolves were throwing that in his face.

"Besides," Kilaltian continued, as he reached down and hauled the girl up by her arm, ignoring her half scream. "It's much more satisfying when you walk away after she asks for it and leave her with her shame." The tall man shoved the girl toward the door of the barn. She fell, sobbed, then staggered to her feet. She fled in a blind, naked run.

Talon caught the girl as she spun around the barn door. She started to scream again, but he covered her mouth and hauled her up against him into the shadows. "Quiet," he breathed harshly. "Quiet."

The terror was too deep in her for her to do anything but struggle, but there was also a growing anger there now. He shook her again. In his mind, he saw eyes, dark eyes in the violet night. Eyes with no fear, but only anger, strength, and will. This girl was barely an infant echo of the strength he really sought. Wolves howled, and he closed his mind to their packsong and shook the girl again.

He dragged her quickly back into the shadows as Kilaltian left the barn. A few moments later, Fit followed the other raider, limping slightly and cursing all nine hanging moons. Talon found himself watching with narrowed eyes as the smaller man paused, rubbed a bruise on his thigh, and stared after Kilaltian. The hatred in the smaller man's stance was almost palpable, and Talon had to force himself not to move and give away his position as Fit looked over his shoulder. For a moment, the smaller man studied the yard; then the raider limped on toward the farmhouse.

The girl stood limply, half hanging in Talon's grasp. Her eyes were huge as she gulped her breath, but she no longer struggled against him. "Breathe," he said sternly, pushing her away from him to stand more on her own. "And hold your head up. Hold onto your pride."

Color began to burn in her cheeks, and she writhed to get out of his grip. He did not release her, even though he knew he bruised her further. "I will not harm you," he said sharply, though the words did nothing to calm her. "Now breathe, in and out." He captured her eyes with his cold gray gaze. "Men like us—we smell fear. We follow it like a blood trail, feed off it like badgerbear. Control your fear, and you control half a man's reaction."

The girl trembled. "What—what about the other half?" she choked out.

Talon lips twisted grimly. She wasn't so frightened that she couldn't think. "That you control with your pride," he returned. "Stand straight. Hold your head up. Only the moons should know what you're feeling. Show strength, not weakness, to men like us. And if all you have is a silent defiance, then show us that instead."

She shuddered, and slowly, he released her, keeping his gaze on her. Instinctively, she covered her breasts with her arms, but she did not run. Talon stripped off his jerkin, and she made a mewling sound and backed against the barn as the terror began to flood back. "Stop it," he said sharply. He stripped off his undertunic and held it out. "Go on; take it," he commanded. "It's not clean, but it's better than being naked."

She hesitated, then took the tunic in her small hand and struggled to put it on. Talon roughly pulled the oversized shirt over her head, automatically guiding her arms into the sleeves and her head into the neckhole. The instinctiveness of the motion made him pause, and he found that his jaw was tight as a wire. He had had sons, he thought. He'd shown them how to saddle a dnu, ride like a raider, and work a knife like a weapons master in training. Moons, but he had had sons until that twice-damned woman had left him and given his boys to Ariye. The wolves howled, and the image of the dark-eyed woman made his lips thin to bloodless lines. He knew he would take his fury out on the wolfwoman, and he found he didn't care.

He forced himself to step back. "Go," he ordered curtly. The girl stared at him as if she didn't quite believe him. Then she took him at his word and started to bolt for the house. Talon barely caught her, but he jerked her to a stop so abruptly that she stifled a half scream.

"Walk, don't run," he said harshly. "Stand straight. Hold onto your pride. Show no man fear."

She stared at him, a hare before a wolf. Finally, she gave him a tiny, jerky nod. She took a deep breath. She forced herself to walk away while her bare feet itched to flee like a mouse. He watched her, her thin shoulders tense as a bird's, as though he would grab her again from behind. His gut twisted: fear, always fear before him.

He waited till she slipped into the house past the dogs, then spat into the dust. He gathered his gear and strode across the field instead of back to sleep at the house. It was a small rebellion against his father, to sleep away from the others, but his slight smile held no humor. He would be sleeping even farther away if Drovic didn't turn east.

Three of the moons had cleared the trees. They shone across the field where the swath of grass dipped toward the forest. The farmhouse was out of sight, and only the moonlight brightened the grass. He tossed his bedroll on the flattened stalks and plumped some grass for a pillow. By the time he finished, the first of the wild wolves had arrived.

Fading out of the field, the first male circled the bedroll, then sniffed the open-sided bag. Its voice was clear as the moonlight. *The night is hot and clear for hunting, but you wish to den instead?*

Talon shrugged, but the mental sense of his answer was clear, and the wolf whuffed softly.

The sixth and eighth moons were rising close enough together that the sixth would half eclipse the other. Talon nodded toward the sky. "Howl if you've a mind to," he offered, knowing the wolf in his skull understood. "It won't bother me."

A second lupine face appeared, then a third. Lanth, the oldest male, barely bothered to sniff the sleeping bag before curling up at the end. Paksh was last as usual, her left ear so torn that it looked like two spikes. Talon reached toward the old wound, but the female snapped and shied away, and the tall man stilled. These wolves spoke with him and haunted his sleep, but they suffered his touch only lightly.

Talon shivered as his gaze met that of Lanth's, but he found himself grinning at the same time. He lay back on the bedroll, shoved Lanth aside with his feet, grimaced as the old male snapped at his boot and he felt the wolf roll back onto his leg. The old male looked longingly at his boot. "Gnaw at your peril," Talon warned.

Lanth raised his head and met his eyes. The blurred, black-and-white double vision that suddenly expanded his own sight made Talon blink in the moonlight. *One gnaws to keep one's fangs sharp and clean,* the old male returned calmly.

"Not on my boots, you don't."

Lanth whuffed and put his head on his paws, but his yellow eyes gleamed, and Talon knew he would have to watch the old wolf all night to protect his footgear. He was comfortable, he realized. This pack had been with him long enough that they almost seemed like partners.

Faren, the younger female, regarded him with tired but curious eyes as she caught the edge of his thoughts. She was barely a yearling, and after following the riders all day, she had energy only to sprawl on her back, but she tilted her head to watch him carefully. Behind Faren, Thoi—the lead female—simply sniffed his face and then rolled on her back in the grass. Faren and Vrek snarled at each other as the other male tried to take her place; then Vrek settled down with Chenl, and Faren closed her eyes.

The wolves growled softly in his skull as he dozed off, the sound becoming a wave of gray that surrounded him like a sea. He Called into it, and it Answered, surging back like a giant maw. It curled and blotted out the sky so that even the moons dimmed into a fog . . .

He woke suddenly. The wolves were slipping away with urgency, and the rustle of their passage was warning enough even without their voices. He rolled to one knee like a cat, his right hand drawing his sword, then groaned as the pain hit sharply. Instantly, the gray fog thickened along the edge of his mind. Moons! he cursed silently. Without the herbs, the pain was just as bad as the foggy memory before. Night sweat clung to his hands, and he shivered as if the breeze that dried it had come off a glacier instead of through the fields. Slowly, he straightened again.

He strained to hear what had frightened the wolves. There was a light breeze, but it was not strong enough to rustle the grasses so incessantly. Talon stiffened. Like a wave across the grains, the wash of sound swelled softly. He tensed.

The rustling became a subtle hissing, and he stood, waiting, his sword bare while the wind seemed to grow and the grasses waved with movement. A dry year, a swarm year . . . He was too far away from the farmhouse. If he ran, he'd draw the swarm after him. If he remained still, if he made no sound . . . Moons glared from the sky. The leading edge of the doglike creatures swept toward him in a rush.

They came in like a wave, the bihwadi. Slinking, rushing creatures whose fangs gleamed and whose breath stank with fetid sweetness. Talon froze. The first bihwadi sprinted toward him, breaking down the grains. His lips tightened to wire. It would kill him. He knew it. It would tear his flesh, teeth in his chest or arms, fangs in his throat. It would spatter his blood in the grass like chicken feed. It leaped forward. It would—

It leaped past. The pink-eyed beast blindly brushed his legs and raced on. Ten bihwadi followed it, sprinting through the grass. Ten, twenty, a hundred bihwadi swept at him through the fallow field. It was a putrid wash of prancing fur and half-bared claws; slitted eyes, lean-ribbed bodies, night-dirty fur, and the stench . . .

Talon's neck was rigid. His toes clenched in his boots as he willed his feet not to run. They swept around him as though he were a tree, not a man, not for eating—not *prey*. They brushed against his legs and did not care. Tiny, pink-eyed bundles clung to their mother's foreshortened backs. Yearlings ran with stiff-legged gaits and tongue-lolling, spittled exhaustion. And the males—the larger, long-backed males with their deceptive, slinking sprint . . . They panted and hissed as they sucked air into their lungs and plunged past in streaks of grayish brown, churning what was left of his bedroll and snapping the grasses like dnu.

Dust clouded above the meadow as grain sacs split and disgorged their pollenlike powder. Something burned in his lungs, and he thought it was some kind of acid from the grass until he realized he was holding his breath from the stench of the slit-eyed beasts. He stared at the sea of pink-frothing jaws. With infinite slowness, he let out his breath till he thought he would pass out. Took in another one as another two dozen passed. Let it out. And breathed, slowly and carefully as if even that tiny sound amidst the rushing and hissing and snapping would be noticed by the bihwadi.

They raced like fish to the spawning ground, all rancid fur and brutal paws, and still they did not care that he stood amidst them. A hundred males and females swept through the summer grasses, and Talon stood his ground, breathing slowly while the sweat beaded up on his skin. To his left, the stalks swayed more violently; to his right, barely ten meters separated him from the stillness of untouched field. The path of the bihwadi swarm cut through like a giant reaver.

Dust hung like fog. The thick scent of ripe grasses choked him. Three creatures brushed against his knees like greasy dogs—dogs with pink eyes, slitted eyes. Dogs that swept blindly out of the broken grasses and whispered and hissed back into the stalks behind the time-stilled Talon. The pollens clogged his throat, and he held his cough until he thought he would burst, then realized that the moonlight led another wave of beasts across the meadow.

It was a gap. It was not his imagination. Another tiny gap appeared, as if the trailing groups could not keep up. He tried not to suck in his breath as a bihwadi was shoved into his legs before careening off and going to its exhausted knees. It fell beneath the feet and claws of those that trampled it blindly, then got to its feet in the gap that followed and staggered after the flood.

The gaps grew larger until Talon realized that the main body had passed. The stillness that seemed to sweep after it was broken only by the beating breaths of three exhausted yearlings who forced themselves after the swarm. The dust shifted slightly with the breeze, and another lone beast charged past. The rush receded. Talon waited, unmoving. His tongue cringed from rancid air.

Finally, he let out his breath. He started to put his sword away, but his hand was cramped on the hilt of the blade and it took seconds to release it. He massaged his palm and stared at the trampled grass. A massive swath sliced across the corner of the field where the farmland had cut squarely into forest; then the road of fallow, broken grains disappeared again into blackness.

He became aware of something breathing nearby and moved cautiously toward the sound. It was a terrible, raspy laboring, and he knew before he finally saw the beast what it was: it was a diseased bihwadi whose mucus froth stank with the putrescence of decay, and he edged away from it as soon as he knew it was too dangerous to dispatch. Alone and away from the swarm, the predator followed him with weeping eyes, weakened from its run but still hungry for human flesh.

Talon circled and found another one, wheezing, head-down in the grass. It stood on three limbs, the white bone of its other foreleg sticking crudely out of its fur. Again, he left it standing. There would be other predators in the wake of the swarm who would not care that the beast was diseased or still vicious from its pain. Predators like the beetle-jawed worlags who would snack on these bihwadi like a starving man on an oldEarth piece of candy.

Talon made his way back to his bedroll—or rather, to what was left of the roll. He gathered up the rags—there were no diseases a man could catch from the indigenous bihwadi—and rolled them into a bundle. Then he made his way on not completely steady legs back across the fields.

When he reached the barn, he found five of the raiders sitting on bales of hay in the middle of a near-silent game of stars and moons. "Bring in the dnu," Talon ordered without preamble. "Worlags will be coming through soon."

Wakje gave him a speculative look, but none of the five hesitated at his tone. They simply tucked their stars and moons in their belt pouches—none of them trusted the others not to shift the game in one or another's favor while a back was turned—and followed him back to the fields. Ki had some trouble using his left arm, but it did not take long to gather the dnu. For all that the raiders used their dnu hard on the road, they treated their riding beasts well. They fed them grains, combed them for lice, and called them with tubers and sugarcane. They could not afford to have uneager dnu when the beasts were their livelihood.

Pen was the only one who spoke. Her nose wrinkled as she came abreast of Talon with a line of dnu, but she said merely, "Bihwadi?"

"Lower fields," he returned.

She nodded. He looked after her as she strung out her line of dnu going back into the barn courtyard. She was the same age as Talon, but she would not last much longer, he thought. Her eyes were hard and tired and old. She reminded him of someone, but the face he tried to envision was elusive, and he knew it would not be the raider's looks that reminded him of the past. He frowned after the raider woman: curly, dirty-blond hair, thin chin, strong cheekbones, and wide-set, exhausted eyes. Pen would never have been called beautiful, but each year of her life seemed to show in her face. That was what Talon was trying to remember—the unnatural aging that showed in the eyes, the stubborn clinging of a woman to the only life she had. He had known other women like that, who rubbed him against the grain with their very existence and yet who had earned his respect with the desperation of their loyalty. If he could win Pen that way . . .

He watched Pen speculatively while Ki went to the house to warn the other raiders. There was enough space for all but three of the dnu, and Wakje automatically tethered those three creatures at one end of the barn. Then the raiders resumed their game, holding Ki's place until the other man returned. Talon left them to it. He stank of sweat and musk, and he dug his other set of clothes from his gear bag and headed back into the night.

He stripped and dunked in the bathing trough, scrubbing the rancid musk from his skin before dressing again in his older clothes. Then he washed out his trousers and the dust from his jerkin before hanging them in the barn. They would have dried faster and with less of a musty smell if he left them out over the fence, but worlags would tear apart anything that smelled of humanity. Following the swarm as they should, he didn't expect them near the house, but if he was wrong, he'd have little enough to wear. He sniffed the air carefully and secured the barn on his way out.

He heard Sojourn, Dangyon, and Ki before he saw them. They were discussing fighters, sharing descriptions and styles so that each would know the others by sight and method. It was not an uncommon dialog. Raiders—and venge men, he acknowledged—who wanted to survive learned as much as they could about their potential foes.

". . . a new jack out of Randonnen—Cluss Ram neBorkt," Ki said.

"Fit ran into him a few months ago," Sojourn answered. "Gave a good description: Kilaltian's height, wavy brown hair—waist-length and always braided, heavy eyebrows, sharp chin, left dimple, flat scar on his right wrist. He'll go to jowls in a decade." Sojourn took a drink, and his voice, when he continued, was carefully enunciated. "I heard neHarn was cut up in Langdon. Three slashes to the chest, diagonal; a straight cut from left cheekbone to the corner of his mouth; and an S-cut on his left arm. They say it was an Ariyen who did him."

"For fun?"

"Of a sort. He lost a game of stars and moons and refused to pay up."

"The Ariyens always did turn out fighters," Dangyon agreed. The man's voice was slightly slurred, and Talon grinned to himself as he approached. The barrel-chested man liked his whiskey as much as Fit loved his knife. Dangyon belched quietly. "Trust them to put a sword in the hands of each babe and suckle the child on a worlag."

"Aye. The whole lot of the Lloroi's family is weapons-master graded, from the brothers to the youngest son. Drovic always—" Sojourn's voice broke off as he caught sight of Talon. "Drovic always said they were the hardest on a raid," he continued smoothly as if he had never touched the flask that now sloshed half-emptily. "And the most likely to kill for justice." He waved at Talon casually to join them on the flat-topped cutting logs.

Dangyon chuckled. "You can run a raid through the other eight counties easier than through Ariye." He noted the glint of moonlight in Talon's damp hair. "A man bathes by moonlight, he'll be frozen by midnight."

"A man who drinks till the moon goes down will be hung over the sun at dawn," Talon retorted.

"Now that's an Ancients' saying. Didn't know you had the history in you for that."

Talon shrugged. The worst part of being unwhole was that he didn't even know what kinds of things he'd forgotten. He remembered some faces without names, some years by only a single scene. He remembered martial classes with Drovic pounding the lessons into his thin, young body. But he didn't remember his father giving him the blade Talon knew he had carried for thirty years. He remembered his home with its curved lintels and arched porch, the ground pitted and dust-dry out front and the corral off to the side. But he didn't recall any of his neighbors, and although he knew he'd had formal education in town, he didn't know what he had studied. He didn't even know how many times he'd crossed Ariye or Ramaj Eilif. If there were people important to him, he wouldn't recognize them if they slapped his face. And he could only guess at some of the scars that marked his body. His was the ultimate ignorance, he thought, for most men knew the types of things they didn't know or hadn't studied, and Talon didn't even have the satisfaction of knowing whether he had explored the basics of any field other than fighting. His voice was sharper than he intended as he answered Dangyon. "I have history enough to know that if you three are out here, it's because you gave Oroan enough of your whiskey that she's wild as a wolf in there, and you couldn't find any quiet."

Ki nodded drunk-wisely, and Sojourn carefully enunciated his words as he answered, "She'll be a surly bitch tomorrow. Always is, after a few drinks."

Dangyon leaned back and stretched out his boots, then sighed in relief and wiggled his extralong toes. "Biting," he agreed. "Always biting the hands that feed her." He offered Talon the flask again.

Talon waved it away mildly. "Do you ever speak in anything but clichés?"

"No need. OldEarthers had a saying for everything—the right word at the right time."

"The right man in the right place," Sojourn put in, getting into the spirit.

Dangyon waved his flask in Talon's general direction. "A man's place is in his home."

"That's a woman's place," objected Ki.

"A woman's place isn't for speaking of in polite company."

Ki tucked his chin and let out a belch that would have done Liatuad proud. The brown-haired man followed up with a hardly less subtle set of borborygmus sounds, and Talon grinned in spite of himself. "Now there's something you won't see an oldEarth horse ever doing," he remarked dryly.

Ki frowned up at him. "What? Drink?"

"Belch."

"Everything can belch. Even a worlag belches."

Talon shook his head. "Horses—they can't do it. They'll eat themselves to death, but they just won't belch."

Ki's whiskey-narrowed eyes slitted further. "Now you're funning me."

"It's the moon's truth. Their stomach ruptures like an overblown ball. All that semidigested food goes right into the gut—"

Sojourn winced.

Talon grinned. "—and turns into a bunch of toxins. Rots

them from the inside out and kills them as dead as a badger-bear if not quite as quickly."

"That imagery is great for the digestion, Talon," Sojourn said dryly. "Anything else you want to share?"

Talon shrugged, but his gray eyes glinted with humor as he took the flask that Dangyon waved in his direction again. He swigged, handed it back, stood and picked up his bedroll, and frowned as he realized there were no other raiders nearby. "Drovic put you three out on worlag watch?"

Sojourn shook his head. "No need. They'll follow the bihwadi's path."

"Probably," Talon agreed slowly. His nostrils flared as he sniffed the air. "But they could still swerve close to the house."

Ki studied Talon's face, and Talon wondered if some sign of the wolves was now printed on his features. "How long before they hit us?" the other man asked.

"Half hour, maybe more." Talon looked off toward the fields. "Judging by the other signs, they haven't reached the ridge yet, but they're usually about an hour behind the bihwadi."

Dangyon shrugged. "An hour is as good as a dozen kays."

"Not when you're stopped in place and sitting out like masa bait," Talon returned. He stepped past them up onto the porch. "Don't stay out too late."

The barrel-chested man grinned. "Don't worry, Mother. We plan to miss the feeding frenzy—we've got ears enough to see them coming; eyes enough to run."

Sojourn took another swig and breathed out the fumes with silent pleasure. He looked sadly at the sloshing flask and confessed, "Besides, the whiskey won't last that long."

Talon rolled his eyes.

Inside the farmhouse, half the raiders were bedded down. The other half were still drinking what was left of the farm woman's store of grog or were sipping her flavored teas. The farm woman herself and her two children were huddled in the kitchen. As Talon glanced that way, he noted that the boy's face looked pinched even in sleep as he rested against his mother. The bare-legged girl still wore Talon's tunic and nothing else. He realized that the mother had been afraid to walk through the raiders to get the girl other clothes. He glanced at Drovic's snoring form, the knot of raiders playing stars and moons, then began to walk toward the farm folk.

Roc had been waiting for him and got to her feet as he turned toward the kitchen. She might have been drunk—it was never easy to tell with her—but she wanted to fight. He could see that in her eyes. He glanced at her, at the farm woman, then up toward the loft. Someone's boot was visible near the ladder, and Talon held up a hand to tell Roc to wait, then climbed up the loft ladder. It was Fit sprawled in the hay. Talon scowled and grabbed the smaller man's boot. Then he crushed the leather and the ankle within until the sleeper cursed himself awake. Fit saw Talon, grabbed for his knife, and found himself flipped over by the grip Talon now had on his leg.

"You piss-watered worlag—"

"The loft is for the farm folk," Talon said mildly. "Sleep it off somewhere else."

"Might as well be our farm now," the man muttered.

"But it isn't." Talon's voice was soft. He released the wiry man, and Fit glared at him and rubbed at his knee and ankle where they had been wrenched. Talon gave him a minute, then made as if to come all the way up to the loft, and Fit moved quickly to get to his feet and climb back down the ladder. The shorter man did not look at Talon as he threw his bedroll down between Al and Morley.

Talon glanced at Roc, who watched him with glittering eyes. Then he made his way through the room without speaking to her, gestured to the farm woman and her children to follow him. The woman barely touched her son before he jerked awake. The girl sucked in her breath as she saw Talon, but all three of the farm folk walked with seeming calm as he escorted them to the loft while the other raiders watched. He waited at the foot of the ladder until the woman and children were settled, then turned back to the room. His expression was cold. None of the others taunted him. Slowly, they turned back to their talk. Except for Roc.

The slender woman stalked toward him, her body swaying slightly so that his gaze—and half the others'—were drawn to her hips and breasts. Wakje's eyes narrowed, and Ebi's gaze lazily followed Roc's hips as the woman slipped between Kilaltian and Ilandin. Roc's lips were curved, but it was the smile of a lepa before it darts in for the kill.

Talon merely waited.

She put her hand on his arm. Her voice was a purr. "Talon, I have missed you."

It grated on his ears. Deliberately, he removed her hand. "I'm not interested tonight."

Roc's voice remained sultry. She glanced deliberately at the loft, where the girl had been bedded down, then traced her hand up his arm again. "You seem to have been interested in something tonight."

"I'd lie down with eleven lepa before I'd bed a child," he retorted coldly.

"Aye, you wouldn't bed a girl like that—" The woman started to press her body against him, and even as his loins responded, her flesh felt like that of a worlag. "Not if you valued your manhood."

He thrust her away hard and abruptly, and she hit the wall of the house before she regained her balance like a cat. Instinctively, she whipped her hand up, but he moved faster, and he both blocked and then backhanded her with his right as negligibly as if she were a child. He caught her across the cheek, and her head rocked back like a toy. He struggled to contain his instant, blinding rage. Speed, he thought. It was coming back to him.

And then another thought hit: He had struck a woman.

The thought echoed in his head in shock. For a moment, neither one moved.

Roc's voice was low and vicious. She didn't care about the blow. "The girl wears your tunic and nothing else."

He had struck a woman and not to save her life, but simply to get her away. He stared at the raider woman. "Yes." His answer was harsh.

"Did you take kum-jan with her?"

She used the term for friendship-sex, not full intimacy, and Talon's voice was curt. "No."

"Why should I believe you?"

He felt his thoughts chew down on a new idea. It did not bother him to strike Roc, only to strike the farm folk. It was respect, he realized; he had no respect for Roc. He couldn't imagine hitting the farm woman, the wolf-woman, or his aunt with her sad, blue eyes—not unless it would save their lives. But Roc had thrown her own humanity away, and she was nothing more than a killer. His voice, when he answered, was hard. "If you do not believe me, you'll cut the girl and take away her youth and doe-eyed looks, and everything else you think I want." His voice grew very soft. "And then I'd have to kill you."

She looked at him for a long moment, and her green eyes glittered like gems. "Swear you did not take kum-jan with her."

"No." He had struck Roc like a raider. And he would strike her again if he had to.

"Swear," she hissed.

His expression was icy. "If you doubt my word, then ride with—and on—someone else."

She stared at him as if she saw through him. Something changed in her eyes. It took him a moment to realize that it was a sort of desperation, as if she realized she could lose him. The gray din in his head became a howling. For an instant, he saw through to the woman within, to the need for strength, the offering of herself to compensate for the hollowness of her heart. There was grief there, as strong as his own, and rage behind it. It shocked him.

"Talon," she whispered. She half held out her hand.

Wolves surged in his skull. He felt their need like a fist. The woman, the bond. Den, home, mating . . . He reached out and grabbed her, yanking her close to his muscled chest like she needed. Like he needed. He kissed her brutally, knowing he crushed her lips against her teeth, knowing that he left bruises on her wrists. Prickles howled along his neck with the fury that fed him, and he cursed it and bent her farther back, ravaging the mouth that felt too thick to his lips, dug into the arms that were all wrong. And when he was done, and she opened her eyes, she smiled at him like a snake.

He cursed himself silently and thrust her away.

She watched him go, but she almost preened as she returned to the other raiders.

XXIV

Rhom Kheldour neKintar

To strive, to seek, to find,
  And not to yield

  —Epitaph on the marker of Captain Scott,
  Antarctic expedition, oldEarth
  (from the oldEarth poem "Ulysses" by Tennyson)

Rhom's lips were white-chapped and cracked. They didn't bleed; he was too dehydrated for the tissues to do more than split and dry again. He forced himself not to rub his burning eyes as he stared at the moonlit canyon. Desert suns, he thought of the moons. Enough light to see, but not enough to burn. It was the dark day that burned their skin. Moonworms, he muttered under his breath. His brains were getting scrambled.

Gamon squatted just back from the edge of the cliff. They weren't on the road. They had left it days ago when even the deepest well was dry. Now they followed a zigzag line from the road to springs and cave ponds that Gamon tried to find in the dark.

Rhom waited. Shifted his weight from one foot to the other. Squinted at the moonlit cracks that ran the deep ravine. It was a steep drop, overhung where the rocks had fallen away, and he could barely see the bottom. They'd be lucky to get down in one piece. His voice was hoarse from the lack of water. "Moonworms, Gamon, I'll be a mummy before we go on."

The other man did not turn.

"Gamon?"

The older man let out his breath with an almost inaudible curse. "I made a mistake."

"A mistake." Rhom glanced down at the ravine floor, then back along the print-pocked soil that now marked their path through the rocks. His voice was suddenly careful. "What kind of mistake?"

Gamon gestured with his chin. "We can't get down from here."

"Why not? We have eighty meters of rope."

"It's not the rope." Gamon pointed more clearly. "Those patches aren't shadow. They're blind lichen."

"Blind lichen," Rhom repeated.

"Touch them, and the powder gets into the air. Blinds you permanently."

"We could go down at a different spot."

"If they're in this canyon, they're likely to be all along it. Which would you rather have: a little thirst or blindness?"

"You might have mentioned these lichen before."

"Wasn't any to show you."

"What exactly does this mean, Gamon?"

Gamon stared across the bone-dry canyon. He could see the silhouettes of tenor trees kays away in the distance. "It means the water is over there, and there's no way in hell we can reach it."

"And that means?"

Gamon did not turn around. "It means we must go back."

Rhom looked at their pitted tracks in the soil. "Back to where?"

"Back to the fork in the trail."

"That was almost eight kays ago."

"Aye."

"That will take all night."

Gamon nodded.

"We'll have been two days without water by then. And it will take another day to cross the canyon and find a tenor tree."

"Aye," Gamon said simply.

Rhom looked at him through his burning eyes. Ariye was close, and the chill that ran down his spine had nothing to do with the dropping temperature. He nodded jerkily. He said nothing more as Gamon turned and trudged back along their trail.

XXV

Talon Drovic neVolen

Hammer it to a point
*   and the sharpness cannot be preserved forever*

   —*Lao Tzu, oldEarth philosopher*

Talon woke sweating and shuddering, his mind blinded by pain. His heart drummed like a running dnu. His muscles were cramped with rock-hard convulsions; his eyeballs felt like exploding. Knives cut through his temples, slashing his thoughts into incoherent screams. In the dark, with his lips curled back and his jaw nearly white from the pressure, he could not even make a sound.

An echo of gray wolves answered the binding pain he projected. Gray voices washed in, bringing with them a chaotic mixture of emotions and images he could not understand. Then the voices merged—focused into a single knot of will. A gray shield seemed to soften the blades of pain. The pressure on his eyes relaxed, then the rigid muscles of his face. Coolness, then a raging cold, fought against the burning. Fire and ice mixed into a soothing gray that swept like hands across his body, smoothing the knotted muscles of his arms and legs, his belly and his heart. He lay without moving, his limbs still shuddering, his hands clenched against the leftover rictus. His heartbeat slowed to a rolling thunder; his lips moved in a prayer. He stank of sweat.

It was a long time before he trusted himself to roll out of the sleeping bag. Then he simply crouched in place, waiting for the pain to settle. His hand clenched at his waist where his empty belt pouch would have been. If it were not for the wolves . . . His jaw tightened with icy fury. Damn the moons and murder—he would withstand this if it killed him.

"If you're up, you're awake enough to make rou," Wakje muttered from his own sleeping bag.

Talon did not answer, but he got to his feet gingerly, waiting for the blinding ax to fall across his mind. When it fell like a blunt hatchet instead, he cleared his vision and picked his way through the sleepers to the front door and the outside, moonlit porch. At the edge of the courtyard, he relieved himself against the fence. A few moments later, Liatuad and Ki joined him. Ki merely shrugged a greeting as he performed his morning duty, but Liatuad gave Talon a second glance as the skinny man caught the pinched look around Talon's gray eyes.

For a moment, they leaned companionably against the railing and watched as the second moon crossed the fourth. Neither Liatuad nor Ki was inclined to talk. Talon was grateful. It was enough to stand out in the chill air and breathe without having his head split apart by sound. With the wolves in his mind, he could smell the bihwadi musk from the night before and the acrid scent of worlag piss that had been laid down over the musk. He could smell another dusty insect scent that he could not identify, as if a third swarm had followed the worlags. He cursed colorfully under his breath. In a swarm year, it was madness to travel west of the Phye River, regardless of one's goal.

In the farmhouse, lamps were being lit in the kitchen, and the farm woman went out the back door to get an armful of firewood. The dogs greeted her with whines as they dragged their chains along the dusty ground. "Woman has some liniment," Liatuad commented, jerking his head toward the widow. "Saw it in the kitchen."

Talon abruptly quit rubbing his shoulder and shot a cold expression at the other man.

Liatuad was not intimidated. Instead, he gave Talon a faint leer. "Bet she would rub it on you willingly, seeing as how you set yourself up to protect her." From Liatuad's left, Ki watched Talon's reaction closely.

Talon felt his balance shift almost imperceptibly with instinctive grace. His hand did not move, but it was set to flash to his knife. "That so?" he returned mildly. "Thought I was protecting us."

Liatuad grinned in spite of himself. "From a farmer's widow?"

"Even a farmer's mate will bite."

"Like a stickbeast," the other man chuckled.

Talon smiled without humor, but said, "We don't need the venges on our tail when we leave."

Ki's voice was soft. "Drovic had a solution to that."

Talon glanced at the raider. "Perhaps I have a better one."

Liatuad raised his eyebrows. "With the farm woman?" Both men chuckled. "Better dead than bedded, that one. She has a mouth; she'll talk. I say give her the vertal to keep her quiet, and take her to sell in Bilocctar."

"I say we leave her be."

"Moonworms, Talon," Liatuad retorted. "You've been far too long without a woman if you turned down Roc to court an eye-tired farmer's mate. Of course," he added slyly, "you have been looking pale lately. Maybe a bony, leftover woman is all you think you can handle."

Talon kept his smile mild. "There are many ways of riding a woman. The pleasure isn't always in the padding."

Liatuad noted his ready stance with casual interest. "Aye, and it wouldn't do for you to fall out of the saddle after a night with a scrawny whip. Might want to double your medicine so you can keep up with us today."

Talon forced himself to grin. "Less might be better. Then I'd have to find a comfortable bed where I can sleep in as long as I wish, find a few women to cook for me, and laze in the sun for a ninan. Yes, that would be a tragedy. I don't know how I would withstand it."

Ki chuckled, but Liatuad gave Talon a sharp look. Talon's slate-gray gaze belied the humor of his words, and the other raider rubbed at his mustache as he studied the taller man.

Talon waited a moment more, then nodded mildly at Liatuad and returned to the house.

The raiders were rousing by the time he entered. Kilaltian nodded to Talon; ignored Ilandin, who reached for the handsome man's arm; and gave Fit a deliberate grin. Fit's expression was shuttered, and the smaller man set himself against the wall where he could repair a hole in one of the tents and watch the other raiders. If Talon had been Kilaltian, he would have backed off from taunting the shorter man. Fit was one of the best knifemen Talon had ever worked with, and the taller, handsome raider had stepped on Fit's toes hard last night. Fit would be out to carve Kilaltian's bones if Drovic would allow it. If Fit hadn't respected Drovic so much, he would never have lasted this long. Someone would have killed him for his viciousness before he turned on them all.

Talon made his way to the kitchen, took the last china mug from the shelf before someone else nabbed it, and poured himself some hot rou. He stared into the whirlpool of warmth. "To rue the day before it had started"—it was a saying of the Ancients. With abandonment and plague staring at them out of the thousands of graves they had dug, the Ancients had had good reason to name this drink. He wondered briefly how many graves he himself had dug. "Worlag piss," he cursed softly. He stalked out to the open area, waited for the rou to cool, and nodded to Drovic as his father sought him out with his gaze.

Drovic nodded in turn, but did not quite turn back to Ebi and Strapel, and Talon frowned almost imperceptibly. A thought came to him then, and as his father watched, he raised the mug, paused with his eyes still on Drovic, and then downed the rou with a grimace, as if it had been his tincture. His father nodded in satisfaction before turning away.

For a long moment, Talon stood without moving. Finally, he turned and absently tossed the empty mug toward Strapel, who lounged by the wall near the kitchen. A stream of drops trailed out like memories as it arced through the air. Strapel snagged the mug easily, tossing it on in an almost continuous motion at the startled farm woman at the sink. There was a cry, but the woman must have caught the cup; there was no sound of broken china.

Talon's face was thoughtful as he moved to his crumpled bedroll. Beside him, Wakje had just finished his packing—the man did everything in efficient patterns—and only Talon's gear was still on the floor. Talon wrinkled his nose at the sweat smell that was stronger with the wolves in his skull, ran his tongue over his sticky teeth, and packed quickly. Then he joined the raiders at the water barrel to perform his toiletries.

Mal barely nodded as Talon pulled his toothbrush from his pocket. The tall, dour man was rinsing the bandage for his forehead; the gash was an ugly wound with unhealed edges. Talon watched the way Mal leaned against the barrel to re-bandage his head and refrained from commenting. Ki must have already rebandaged his own wound; the brown-haired man merely nodded a greeting and went back to brushing his teeth. Beside him, Sojourn gave Talon a sour look around a mouthful of toothpaste, and an indistinct, "Last night, you snored like a sick worlag."

Talon's voice was mild. "How could you notice? You were near-drowned by all that whiskey."

"A few drops," the other man returned shortly.

Talon shook his head to himself. Sojourn drank like three raiders, yet never showed it the next day.

Ki grinned, spat, and started to wipe his mouth with the back of his left sleeve; he winced and switched to his other arm. "So, Talon," he said, noting with a narrowed gaze that the taller man had seen his weakness. "You never told me about the cow teeth."

Talon paused with his toothbrush halfway to his mouth. "What cow teeth?"

"Cow teeth. You know. Cows. Like livestock—chickens, sheep."

"Sheep?" He raised his eyebrows as if confused. "Our sheep or oldEarth sheep?"

"OldEarth sheep?"

"Ah," Talon answered around his brushing. "You know, they were the only creatures on oldEarth—outside of a rabbit that is—that could actually be scared to death."

Mal, who had paused to hear the answer, raised one eye-brow; Sojourn's lips twitched, but he kept silent. Ki gave him a skeptical look.

"It's true. I swear to the seventh moon." Talon's expression was carefully bland as he spat out the used paste on the ground. "Rather like the goats."

"What goats?" the man asked suspiciously.

"Well, the Ancients had these fainting goats. You could walk out into a field, clap your hands, and watch them fall down like dolls."

"Moonworms," Ki cut him off. "What do I look like, a green-backed, gullible county maid?" Talon raised his eye-brows meaningfully. Ki stalked away, muttering, "Try to get one stupid answer and end up with a dozen. Last time I ask you anything, you tamrin-ridden piece of worlag dung."

Sojourn grinned and followed the other raider. "I hear he knows a lot about women, too," Talon heard Sojourn say as the man caught up to Ki.

Mal glanced after the other two, then back to Talon. "Old-Earth goats, oldEarth sheep—you're not going to tell him about the geese, are you? I don't think he could take it."

Talon shrugged. "What's a man to do? If he is curious enough to ask . . ."

"Curious enough," Mal agreed.

But there was something in Mal's voice that gave Talon pause. He looked the question at the dour man.

"He has eyes, son of Drovic."

"As do you."

Mal did not answer. The saturnine man merely picked up his pack, steadied himself under its weight, and walked off toward the barn. Talon hid his frown. He tucked his toiletries into his pack, noted that his own hand was shaking, and quickly clenched and steadied it. He glanced after the dour man, then carefully closed the pack, slung it over his shoulder with the same forced ease, and made his way to the barn.

Within twenty minutes, the raiders were mounted. Talon led his dnu to where Drovic was saddling his beast. From the house, the farm folk watched from the living-room window. Earlier, the two children had remained in the attic loft, and

Talon was glad; Fit had been in a foul mood, and they might not have survived the morning.

Drovic caught his expression and grunted.

"Leave something." Talon's voice was low.

Drovic knew what he meant. The older man tightened the saddle cinch against the dnu's belly and did not turn around. "I leave her the lives of her boy and girl and herself."

With the pain in his temples, Talon's response was hard. "It is not enough. If we were a venge—"

"But we are not," snarled his father. "We know it; she knows it—"

"And that is not the point," Talon cut back in. "We haven't left a forkful of food in her pantry; not a pitchful of hay in the barn. We leave her children to starve—"

"It's better than they would have had after a few hours with Fit or Brentak. Let her count her blessings."

"Let her count the silver instead, so that she becomes one of us."

Morley approached Drovic, and the older man turned such a face on the raider that Morley quickly retreated. Drovic's voice to Talon was low and harsh. "Why is this so important to you? Has the fever left you soft, not just weak? Have you forgotten every goal?"

"I could hardly forget." Talon's voice was cold. "You slap your tactics in my face every time I turn around." He gestured shortly. "There is value in building a tiny loyalty where we might need it later." He rubbed savagely at his weakened wrist to relieve the tautness that was creeping back into his muscles. "A shelter, a jumping-off place—an out-of-the-way farm like this is gold set aside for the future."

"We don't need that kind of security."

"You would throw away a chance at a caching place out of what—pride? Your anger is not against this woman, Drovic, but against the Lloroi and Ariyens, and we won't reach them or the goals you have set unless we climb on the backs of others. Give the woman some silver, enough to replace what we took. If she values her home, she will never confess where it came from."

It wasn't pride or Talon's logic that angered Drovic, but the questioning of his decision. Talon had challenged his father practically from the moment of birth, and by the moons, he never would let up. He was like a mudsucker, never taking his fangs out of the prey once he thought that he was right. Drovic eyed his son narrowly, then cursed himself under his breath as he recognized a note of pride in himself that, even knowing what his response was likely to be, his son refused to back down. Love was a strange emotion, the older man thought. Even now, Talon could still both infuriate him and cadge a deeper place in his heart. He opened his mouth, then cut himself off and cursed again under his breath, this time at his own weakness. Talon merely watched him and waited, and Drovic told himself that he had to remember that Talon was no longer a little boy, but a man with a man's need to dominate. Drovic had better look to his own dnu, or he would find himself at the back of the line, riding drag, not leading. The thought brought steel to his blue-flecked eyes. He had to force himself to resist the urge to smack the sense back into his son.

Finally, he dug a small sack of coins from one of his saddlebags and stalked toward the porch. From the window, the woman had been watching, and now she went to the door.

Drovic schooled his face. "We are a rough lot," he stated curtly, without preamble. "But we would not have you think ill of us when we shelter here again." He held out the bag. "For your trouble."

The woman hesitated. Her eyes flicked to the side, where her children watched the raiders with tight faces. Slowly, she held out her hand and accepted the bag of silver. Drovic nodded just as slowly, almost imperceptibly. The woman shivered as the older man strode away; then she retreated into the house. When they trotted their dnu from the courtyard, she was still watching from the window with her children: three small faces, white in the early gloom, alone and huddled within their home, like mice while the cats are circling.

Talon felt his stomach ease, and Drovic cast him a dark look as if he could sense what his son was feeling. "Satisfied?" The older man's words were still clipped with anger.

"Aye," Talon answered shortly.

Drovic cursed under his breath in return and spurred his dnu ahead. He was no longer sure if he cursed his son or himself.

The road in front of the farmhouse was narrow until they reached the turnoff for the Circle of Fifths. Drovic eyed the fork and studied his son. North or back south to the venges? Talon could almost hear his thoughts. "We need supplies," Talon murmured.

Drovic frowned. "Western roads are still blocked."

"If I were leading," Talon said deliberately, "we would ride north and east and winter where they do not expect us."

Drovic twisted to regard him coldly. "I have led men for nearly seventy years, while you—" The older man broke off, fury clipping his voice. "I had to carry you away from Sidisport like a corpse. I had to nurse you like a babe. You—my own son—let yourself be downed like a piece of garbage, and you ride now only because I forced the healers to help you. It's not as if they were willing, not for raider spawn, not for the help you needed. And still, look at you. You ride beside me like a wounded dog. You can't even hold your own sword. Yet you'll tell me how to lead?"

Talon found his own jaw tight. He forced his words to be low. "You didn't raise me to hide and skulk. Bilocctar is just one more way of putting off the future. You have a goal. Let us reach it."

"You think you have enough strength to do that? You've been led through life on the goals of others. You've never stood on your own, boy. Never had to choose your own path, never had to rake in the consequences like black leaves. You know nothing of what you have and haven't done. You have the arrogance of ignorance." Drovic spat, and the spittle struck and killed a pocket of gnats on a leaf. Talon knew it had been deliberate.

His lips tightened. "Is there so little, Father, that was memorable about my life?" Drovic's jaw jutted stubbornly, and Talon forced the words out. "Have you never been proud of me? Did I never make a difference?"

The older man's jaw tightened until it was a white line against his weathered complexion. Drovic could not afford either pride or the approval Talon sought. The goal, Drovic told himself harshly. In the end, it was the goal, not the men, that counted. But before Talon's icy gaze, Drovic suddenly felt old, as if the goal itself had worn thin.

Talon gritted his teeth at the older man's silence. No pride in the weakling, he told himself. What had he expected? It struck him that surely there had been at least one healer willing to help a wounded man—healers had their own vows to save lives. So why had they been forced to heal him? Was it the side effects of the medicine? Was it more than a painkiller, more than a healing drug? Did Drovic hope it kept him subservient? Because the longer he had drunk that vile mix, the more he became impatient, enraged. It was only in the past few days, without the herbs, as the gray fog grew, that his thoughts had been more clear. Drovic's goal, his own goal— by all the gods, he almost didn't care which one he followed, as long as they moved, found some sense of success, not these endless backtrail circles. "The more we ride," he said harshly, "the more I chafe at this path; the more I lose respect for your goal and the way we go about reaching it. There is no honor in this path, and you of all people should know that."

Drovic kept his face expressionless. "Sometimes only dis-honorable men can act to preserve their world."

"So we raid and slaughter the innocents, and wait for some sort of perfect timing that only you will recognize? Why?" Talon snapped. "Why wait another year, or even another winter? We won't be more effective from waiting. Our men will not be stronger. Hells, but this is a swarm year, and we're still riding around instead of going to ground like any half-wit would do. We've lost two dozen men, with all their training and skills. And we won't gain anything more by holding back till next spring, or next year, or dammit, even next decade. You've been so careful that no one even knows what we want, so this terror, this fear we create, cannot pos-sibly help us reach the stars." He glared at his father. "You have waited too long for the goal. It's become unreal, something to soothe your rage without making that rage constructive."

"Watch your words, boy."

"Or what?"

Drovic's own blue-gray eyes went to ice. Liatuad trotted his dnu toward them to ask about their direction, caught a glimpse of their expressions, and reined back immediately.

"Dammit, Drovic," Talon snarled. "I'm here; you're here. Why cannot now be the time?"

Drovic spat. "Gods damn all sons to the seventh hell. It's going to take one hell of a blessing from the second moon to get these riders to the border without losing any more men. We've still got wounded who will be worthless in a fight, no supplies past tomorrow, and as you pointed out, on top of all that, it's a swarm year. But it's now that you want to fight?"

Talon's voice was cold. "Fighting is what we do." He glared right back at his father. He no longer felt icy and calm. He felt angry and mean.

The older, heavier man's lips twitched. Then he started to laugh.

"What?" Talon demanded sharply. He was in no mood to be mocked.

"I'll be kissed into next ninan by a dozen worlags. Fighting—is that what this is about?" Drovic nodded as he watched his son. "East, you keep saying, go north and east, and I'm thinking that you're still weak and want the comfort of your old home. But you've been wanting to blacken your steel. Ariye draws you, doesn't it?" The older man's voice dropped seductively. "It is in your blood, not just mine, and it beats like the drum of your heart. You say I never taught you patience. Well, you're right as a Randonnen. I never thought it would be of use, and never realized the lack of it till now." He reached across and slapped Talon's shoulder so hard that Talon had to hide his wince. "I've waited decades for Ariye, but you want that land in three months. Patience, Son. Some goals require more time."

Talon found his voice. "So we will winter then in Kiren and attack Ariye in spring."

Drovic guffawed. "With barely two dozen riders? Your opinion of your own skill has grown beyond arrogance."

"They're more than enough to take or kill the Lloroi."

Drovic sobered. "Son, you miss the point. If I wanted nothing more than the life of the Lloroi, I would have killed him decades ago. When we finally enter Ariye, it will not be as raiders, but as welcome elders ourselves."

Talon tried to control his impatience. "You treat deception like a goal in and of itself, not like the tool it should be. You wait—for what? To lay traps, to bait the Ariyens?"

Drovic's voice was cold. "To watch and judge the strength of the venges sent out by the other Lloroi. It is a measure of the Ariyen influence."

"They are not the enemy—"

"A man can learn more about his enemy from the moments between the fighting than he can from his enemy's battles. A fighting man has only four options: attack, defend, flee, or die. Once he commits himself, his tactics are predictable; his reactions can be controlled. A leader in peacetime, that is the man to watch. What does he do with his fighters? Does he keep them trained? Experienced? How ready are their weapons? What stocks of supplies are set aside to provide for them when they ride? How much do the elders support the continuous drain of resources to support those peacetime fighters?"

Talon searched his sparse memory. "Ariye once supported a wide-ranging action against Bilocctar's raiders. It was difficult for Ariye. They hadn't had to shift so many supplies or men before, or maintain camps so far from the towns. We laid out lines of scouts to watch." There were wolves in his head, wolves in his memories. "There were cliffs, a river, the waiting, the fire."

"Aye." Drovic watched Talon closely. "We lost almost everyone."

Talon's voice suddenly caught in his throat. Wolves that had torn men off the edge of the humming mountain and dropped them three hundred meters to a gridded grave that echoed with ancient energies. The woman in the wolves—she had been there. He had seen her through the smoke. The gray fog in his head tightened with his recognition, and the wolf-woman seemed to vibrate with power. Energy that flowed, healed, soothed . . . "I tasted fear," he managed. "Blood."

Drovic's voice was soft. "You lost many things in Ariye."

"As did you." Talon rubbed at his temple.

Drovic glanced back over the line. "I like this group of

riders. I don't want to lose any more." As if that decided him, he nodded to the left fork. "We still need supplies. I'll take four and go into town, do a little recon, buy what we need, see the healer for some more of your herbs. You take the rest and head north toward the Circle of Fifths. Scout the roads. Find us a way to Bilocctar that avoids the venges, and leave me a message in the cairn at Three Corners for the route. You know the codes."

Talon eyed his father. There hadn't been the slightest flicker in Drovic's eyes when his father spoke of the herbs. "Scouting is a lonely job," he said slowly. "I'd travel faster and leave fewer traces if I rode alone. I wouldn't be seen as a raider."

It might have been his imagination that Drovic's face tightened; the older man displayed nothing in his voice. "You need some swords for protection."

The words grated. "I'll not hide behind your men—"

"They're your men, not just mine." Drovic grinned fiercely as he regarded his son. "But no, you were never one to hide behind the skirts and shields of others. You may have lost your strength and your mind, but at least you have not lost that."

Obscurely, Talon was not pleased. "I'll take my ten," he conceded finally. "Mal, Dangyon, Wakje, Weed, and the rest. You keep the others."

"As if I could take a group that large into town and not cause comment. Besides, Mal, Weed, and Ki are wounded."

"They're my riders."

Drovic gave him a dark look. "Mal doesn't even look like he's healing. All three will slow you down."

"Any number of riders will slow me," Talon returned sharply. "It won't matter that some are wounded."

"Dammit, did your wounds also make you stupid as an effen? They'll be deadweight in a fight, and you're going to need every sword. I could take care of those three in two minutes or less—"

Talon cut him off with a sharp gesture and leaned close. His eyes were like chips of ice. "If you ever try to release even one of my riders, I'll draw blade on you, father or not."

Drovic's face darkened like basalt. "Go then, and ride like old women. Carry your wounded like baggage. Coddle weakness and indulge your childish sense of honor. Don't cry to me when the county folk catch you because you couldn't move quickly enough. Don't wail to me when the venge comes down on your heads, when the trial block stands gray and waiting, when you waste yourself and the future of us all in a stupid, needless death."

Talon's jaw was tight. "How many times have you saved me when I should have died? Why do less for them?"

The man's voice was harsh. "You're my *son*."

"They're *my* men."

"Chak take you," Drovic snarled. "If you won't listen to reason, I'll do what you should have done days ago." He drew his sword and spurred his dnu back toward Mal. Warned by their voices, the dour man instantly caught Drovic's intent. Mal straightened abruptly and started to draw his sword.

But Talon's blade was in his hand before he thought. His dnu shouldered Drovic's aside so that the beast reared back and nearly unseated the older man. Talon's blade was between them. His hand was steady as a badgerbear's claw. His voice was soft. "You know me well, Father. I have never made threats. Only promises. You will not kill any one of my men."

For a moment, he wasn't sure Drovic would stop. There was a rage in the older man's eyes and a blindness so sharply focused that he could not see his own son. Talon did not move. If a dnu stamped its feet, if a chunko bird cried, neither one noticed.

Slowly, Drovic lowered his blade. His dark-flecked eyes were steely, but his voice was calm. "Ride then, as you wish. You'll do so whether I want it or not. But if you're riding with wounded, you'll take the whole lot of them, not just eight or ten, and you'll stay away from the border."

Talon knew which border he meant. "And you?" he said stiffly. He did not quite withdraw his sword.

"Cheyko, neBrenton, and Slu."

"You should ride with more protection."

Drovic glared at the mimicry in his voice. "You've stood up for your riders like a leader should. But push your luck and

I'll tear that little-boy sword from your hand and feed it to you for breakfast. Those three are enough to take care of my needs and yours." Talon knew he meant the herbs.

"My needs are changing," Talon muttered.

"On that, we are agreed." Drovic's voice was dry. "We'll meet at Racton."

Talon shook his head. "Lind."

"That's too close to Ariye."

"Hardly. It's four days from the pass, the same from Ramaj Bilocctar, and offers a road to Nadugur."

Drovic's eyes narrowed. "You're pushing me more than is wise."

"As you taught me to do," Talon retorted.

His father's face was dark. "Lind, then, in two days."

"Lind," Talon agreed. "I will be there."

"Be sure you are, or I'll come hunting you again."

Talon smiled slowly. "It might be me who goes hunting."

"If it is still your fist on the reins."

Talon's grin became wolfish. He made as if to turn away, but Drovic's hand shot out. For an instant, as the older man's hand closed on his arm, Talon could not breathe. The hardness of Drovic's grip was a wave of black agony. The gray that had kept his mind from his pain could not compensate for the sudden physical vise. Wolves howled. Talon's muscles went rigid with a burning spasm. Blinded, he forced himself to remain upright.

"You have enough herbs in the meantime?"

"Enough," he managed truthfully. He would not be taking more. But he could not see his father, and his heartbeat was throbbing up in his neck. Light was fire; his colon was tight as a wire. It was all he could do to keep his eyes open and control the spasm of pain.

"I'll bring enough for the ninan." Drovic released his grip.

"Good." He bit out the word. He sensed his father turning away and said softly, "Ride safe."

Drovic hesitated but did not turn around. He merely reined his dnu off to the side so that Talon's riders could gather.

Ride safe; with the moons. Talon's mind supplied the rest of the blessing that Drovic refused to say. He forced himself to raise his arm to give the riding signal. The wolves, waiting for this, howled. *Freedom. The hunt. The woman. Find.*

Yes. It was a single word, but the packsong tightened around him like a vise. For an instant, his breath was cut off again. Then it released, and the pain began to soothe. Yes, he told himself savagely. I could leave Drovic and the raiders, but I could also take them with me. Mine, to follow me, not him. Mine to hunt with the wolves. And I want that sense of gray. I want the hunt, the feel of wind that doesn't stink of human blood. I want that woman, that wolfwalker who forces the wolves to my mind. His focus narrowed, and he felt the wolves focus with him. He felt time, the Gray Ones, the roads closing in on a point that he could not yet quite see. The forest seemed tight as he led his group away; the moons seemed to hang low in the sky. He could not tell if it was the pain from his wounds or the sense of being herded that laid the shudder over his shoulders like a spiderweb.

Drovic gestured for his three riders to hold back and watched his son move away. In minutes, each party was lost to the others, their sounds deadened by the trees. But Kilaltian had hung back, and Drovic motioned for him to come close.

"So you are letting him lead without you?" Kilaltian asked as he drew up.

Drovic's answer was curt. "I'm letting him run out his impatience."

"He'll see this as his chance for freedom."

"Let him. Better to find out his weaknesses now than lose because of them later."

Kilaltian absently fingered the hilt of his knife. "He might surprise you."

"Aye. He is stronger than he appears, and ambitious as always."

Kilaltian noted the pride that Drovic could not quite hide. "He cannot be trusted with the payroll and stashes," he warned sharply. "He'll try to use them to set himself up as leader."

If he hasn't done so already, Drovic thought dryly. "He cannot best me."

"And Aranur of Ariye?"

"Aranur is gone like a drunk's stash of whiskey. Whatever he thought to be to Ariye, Talon and I will be more." He gave the other man a hard look. "And while I'm gone, you will be there to keep him from straying—you and Ki."

Drovic had almost added something else, and Kilaltian regarded him carefully. Was there another worlag in the woodpile? And if so, what guarantees had Drovic made about Kilaltian in his own small band of riders? The core group of Kilaltian, Darity, Sojourn, and the others knew Drovic's secrets, his dreams, his fury, and like a pack of wild dogs, they fought to drink the blood of the prey he fed them. But even as a raider, Drovic was still Ariyen. There might be things about the man that even Kilaltian didn't know. He kept his voice mild. "Ki seems to have acquired other loyalties."

"Then make sure Fit knows what to do."

Kilaltian studied Drovic carefully from beneath his sculpted eyebrows. "So, you really would kill your own son if he crossed you—and after all those years of waiting for him to reach the point of usefulness." He shook his head, studying Drovic's shuttered expression. "Aye, I guess you would," he said with bald approval. "You nearly did before." He held up a hand to stop Drovic's snarl. "I'll speak to Fit tonight." He cantered after the other raiders.

Drovic watched them disappear into the forest. His goal seemed to be riding him down, whether he wanted it or not. If Talon stayed with the raiders, he would commit to the goal and become the figurehead Drovic needed. If he rode away, he would die. Drovic nodded to himself in grim satisfaction, ignoring the twinge in his chest. Either way, he would have revenge on Ariye. He didn't let himself consider that there might be another option.

XXVI

Ember Dione maMarin

Some people sink roots;
Some take their roots with them;
Some people seek knowledge;
Some gather and give it;
Some people trade the question
  For the answer;
Some people trade the answer
  For the question.

  —The Cozar

Dion's group caught up with the trade wagons by late after-noon. The wagoners couldn't help but see them coming. Their three dark shapes glittered like black jewels along the snow-white road.

As Dion and the others came within bowshot, the four rear riders lagged so that they blocked the trail. The cozar wagons did not stop—they could not and keep their momentum. On roads as steep as these, the wagons would not halt until they reached the goal of the wide, paved courtyards of the next passhouse.

Dion pulled up when she was close enough to speak without shouting. Tehena and Kiyun remained slightly be-hind her. In the cold, each rider was haunted by the ghost clouds of his own breath.

"We greet you," one of the men said.

"We greet you," Dion returned flatly.

The cozar studied the three. Dion had given the caravan greeting of equals, neither accepting nor asking for a wel-come nor extending one, and it gave the men pause. Their wariness did not surprise her. Usually only the last caravans and a few desperate travelers would take the passes so late.

She knew what they saw as they studied her group: three figures who could as easily have been raiders as venge riders or journeyers. Her silver healer's circlet was hidden beneath the war cap, which in turn was hidden beneath the layers of fur that made up her alpine cap. The wolves had been out of sight all day, hunting near the trees for the air pockets of snowbears and the winter dens of rabbits. They would not follow her much farther up the pass—they could not, unless she fed them. So there was nothing to identify her as a wolfwalker—nothing except the claw marks that wracked the left side of her face; the posture of a scout, which she could not hide; and the color of her eyes.

The four men before her were as nondescript. Each had the careful, wary strength that spoke of a lifetime of riding. Their bows were strung, their arrows ready but not nocked. The tallest one was also the youngest, but there was nothing of inexperience in his eyes. The lead drover was thicker around the middle, his nose was flattened, and one cheek was oddly sunken, as if it had been shattered and badly healed. The man beside him was as thick, but with piercing blue eyes. This man barely glanced at Dion. Instead, he kept his gaze on Kiyun. The fourth rider was oldest, with brown eyes and brown-gray hair, a long, rangy frame, and a face carved like a hatchet. The cuffs of that man's jacket had a thin band of red and brown cutting through the fur.

In the distance, the wolves became restless. *You do not greet your packmates properly.*

Dion smiled faintly at their obvious worry. *We're still sniffing noses,* she told them.

Gray Murah whuffed her disgust in the snow, and Dion resisted the urge to wrinkle her lips. The older female's message was clear: *You are stronger than them. They will accept you if you nip at their hindquarters and show them their place in your pack.*

Her mental voice was dry. *Thank you, Gray One, for the advice.* She projected an image of herself with a mouthful of trousers, and the wolfpack snorted with laughter.

The lead drover cocked his head to eye her more carefully, as if he could feel her communication, and behind Dion, Tehena's pale eyes glittered.

Finally, the lead drover said, "We welcome you."

Dion inclined her head to acknowledge his words. Her own response came automatically. "We have salt to share."

The cozar did not smile, but he lost some of his wariness. "Have you needs?"

"No."

Her answer was short but not impolite. Fourteen years ago, she had left Randonnen with a wagon train, and the language patterns she had learned with those cozar and with others since then had been set in memory along with her link to the wolves. Her terse answer was expected from someone who knew their way, and the stocky man barely hesitated with his introductions. "I am Iles; the young one is neCot: Samoska—" He indicated the man with the sharp blue eyes, then nodded toward the hatchet-faced leader. "—Berelto."

"Dion," she said with no expression. As he had done, she used a slight nod, rather than a gesture, to indicate her friends. "Kiyun, Tehena."

The young man, neCot, gave her a curious glance, but the older, hatchet-faced man simply turned with the others and left the three to fall in behind.

Dion and the others lagged behind the wagons in the center track where the snow was churned to slush.

"Friendly folk," Kiyun murmured.

"They are cozar," Dion returned absently.

Tehena pulled her scarf more closely around her chin. "At least we were accepted with the caravan. They're picky enough about their traveling companions that I was half afraid they would leave you behind," she cast at Kiyun.

"Huh." The bulky man snorted. He clenched and unclenched his hands to get the blood moving again. "We could have frozen into three-year ice caps by the time they offered that welcome."

The lanky woman raised a skinny eyebrow. "And we could offend them enough to spend another night in a snow cave. I'll take the wolfwalker's approach, terse as it is."

"No titles," Kiyun commented.

Tehena nodded. "They don't use them."

"They don't use them in greetings," Dion corrected. "They believe it is prideful and arrogant." She shrugged at Kiyun's raised eyebrow. "To introduce yourself with a title makes it seem as if you're trying to be better than the other person, or that you're trying to introduce yourself not as who you are, but as your accomplishments—which might mean nothing in their world. The cozar are judged on what they do now, not on what they accomplished before."

"A man's reputation is sometimes worth knowing," Kiyun said flatly.

"Don't think they don't know yours already," Dion returned dryly. "The cozar have an excellent network. They keep track of reputations, physical descriptions, habits, and travel patterns. They knew us the moment I said our names. Probably before. 'The cozar know a man better than he knows himself.' "

Tehena eyed the caravan ahead. "I don't think I like that."

Kiyun grinned slyly. "If I were you, I don't think I'd like that either."

"If you were me, you'd have twice the brains, and thinking would no longer be painful."

Dion hid her smile.

They rode two kays, crossed a wide bridge, then an open expanse of snow across which the wind blasted. Finally, the mountainside rose again on the right, and they could see around the next ridge. It was slow, and they had to pace themselves to remain behind the train. They could have taken up the front guard, but that would have been rude as they had joined the cozar, not the other way around. Right now, Dion preferred hanging back so that the wolves were not noticed.

Dion closed her eyes and let the sense of the Gray Ones wash through her. *Cold air cutting through the nose. Clean, wet odors. Legs breaking through the ice crusts . . .* A sense of vibration reached her, and she stiffened, automatically seeking the sound in the packsong. It was low—too low for her to distinguish, but it was there. Without thinking, she whistled the warning. Her thoughts flashed out to the wolf-pack. *Danger! The hunter in the snow—*

"What is it?" Kiyun shouted as Dion spurred her dnu into a sprint.

Dion's free hand fisted against her belly, and she fought the urge to turn her dnu and flee the other direction. *Protect.*

Ahead, the rearguard riders twisted at her whistle and waited impatiently for them to catch up. "What is it?" one of them shouted as she neared them.

"Glacier worm," she shouted tightly.

The lead rider followed her gesture. She pulled up beside them, and he frowned. "There? The snow is too shallow—"

"Not there." She pointed. "Up there, working its way along a river run, hidden under the snow. It will spook the dnu and take the wagons right off the cliff."

"It's too steep, too cold to stop. The wheels will freeze onto the road."

"Then I suggest you get ready to fight."

The cozar gave her a sharp look. He turned and whistled the signal up the line, and Dion could see tension snap through the wagons. Her small group cantered with the other cozar along the line until they passed over a third of the wagons. Other cliff-side riders met them on the snow side while the wagons rumbled slowly.

"Here," she said sharply, drawing up her dnu by a steep slope.

"I see nothing." He glanced at the men and women beside him, and they shook their heads in agreement.

"It will be here," Dion said firmly.

The cozar studied her for a moment, then nodded curtly and deployed his riders. "Heavy shafts," he directed. "We want penetration, not speed. Beren, use the autobarbs, they'll tear more when they hit. Hilian, your bow is too light. Stay back with the wagons."

Tehena and Kiyun had strung their bows at Dion's first warning, and the cozar gave them a nod as he noted the weight of their weapons. Dion herself stayed back. She ached with tension and had strung her own recurve, but she could not bring herself to stand frontline when she carried the last remnant of

Aranur as the child within her womb. As if he read her thoughts, Kiyun shifted slightly ahead of her, and Tehena stayed beside her, almost sheltering her from being able to shoot her own bow. Dion gave the woman an irritated look, but Tehena merely pointed for her to remain farther back. There was no overt sense of the glacier worm, and the wolves were far enough downslope that Dion could no longer feel its presence through the pack. She could now only wait with the others.

Her eyes scanned the slopes and tips of the rock while the wagons rumbled past. She saw nothing out of place. The snow was hard-crusted; there were no loose drifts to shiver with movement. But as she looked around, she realized that there was something else. It was the outer wall along the road, not the cliffs that the others stared at. A break in the snow that lined the wall, a break that might have been formed when some other wagon plunged off. She started to speak.

The snowbank erupted. A ringed mouth shot out toward the riders like an arrow. Even with their bows half nocked, there was an instant in which half the archers froze. Only six arrows instantly drew. One second passed as the worm elongated with its lunge—an infinite second in which someone screamed, and the arrows released, and a team of dnu spooked like rabbits. The worm thinned like a stretched sock out of the side of the mountain. Pearlized skin glistened like crusted snow. The ring of teeth was full open as it shot forward. This was no baby worm. This was a full-grown predator.

Dion held her dnu firmly with her knees and shot from the saddle, over the heads of the other archers. The maw of the worm snapped right between two archers and closed on a third as half a dozen arrows buried themselves in pearlized flesh. The man didn't scream as the worm's mouth clamped shut. Dion's ears shivered as if battered by the unnatural quiet.

Shocked archers drew belatedly, and half lost their mark as they scrambled out of the way. The wagoners were shouting at the dnu, forcing them to stay on the road. Arrows flew. The worm snapped back as pain signals worked through to its

brain. Anchored in the snowpack, it thrashed sideways across
the road, and five cozar were knocked flying. A dnu team half
reared. The glacier worm writhed. Dion could see its eyes:
tiny, glowing dots on the "face." A purplish red ichor stained
the snow. She did not think as she drew again, but the team
behind her jumped awkwardly, slamming into her dnu, and
her arrow went short, barely missing a cozar as he released.
He cursed her and drew again. The worm coiled back. It shot
out again like light, knocking aside an archer and biting at the
team of dnu.

Wolfwalker!

Dion's dnu danced to the side in terror. She rode it automatically, nocking and releasing. The second bolt sank into
the worm's pale pink maw beside another archer's. The
mouth snapped early, catching only a leg of the lead dnu.
Blood spurted. The dnu screamed. Its front leg was torn
completely off, and it reared in a twisting motion. The entire
team plunged toward the drop-off. "Back, back!" the drover
shouted.

Dion nocked, drew, released. Four others were somehow
beside her, in the relative calm of her position. Nock, draw,
hold, release . . . *The claws, tear. Heat, teeth. Protect the cub.*
Snow flattened beneath the worm. To the left, a man dragged
himself clear. A wagoner screamed, "Cut it free, cut it free!"
as two men ran beside the team and slashed at the traces of
the dying dnu, knowing that the worm could take them any
second. An older archer flung himself to the snow and braced
himself, drawing and releasing as the others worked frantically behind him.

The worm turned, slammed down, snapped, and struck a
woman so hard she was flung into a snowbank and buried
in the powder. A man sprawled unmoving in the worm's
wake. The beast recoiled to strike again, and almost in desperation, the archers pounded their bolts home. The wounded
dnu was cut free, and it bolted in panic, the upper half of its
foreleg dangling weirdly. It didn't get three meters. The worm
shot out and, drawn by the scent of blood, clamped its teeth
over the segmented spine. A spray of blood and viscera arced
out as it dragged back both halves of the beast. But the worm

did not slide back as fast as it had come out, and the arrows chased it into its hole.

Dion held her fire. Her bolt was nocked but not released, and the other archers did the same. For a long moment, the wagons rolled, and the archers held their pose. But bow arms began to ache, and two archers lowered their weapons, though they kept them at the ready. Others finally did the same. The drovers' eyes were wide as they rumbled past.

Dion put the bolt back in her quiver. It was loose, and she glanced down in faint surprise. There were only four left. Carefully, she unstrung her bow. Of the archers who had stood their ground, two were dead: the one who had become worm meat, and one who had been crushed. One woman was missing, and three of the men began to dig at the bank where she had disappeared. One man was struggling with his legs.

Dion made her way to the man, but he was cursing the others around him. "If my spine was snapped, I wouldn't be able to feel every moons-damned broken bone, now would I?" He screamed as they eased him onto a makeshift stretcher. He cursed them without pause, then bit his lip so hard the blood streamed down his chin as they lifted him and got him to the back of one of the wagons.

Dion made as if to follow, but one of the cozar stopped her. "Urowa is a healer."

She nodded.

Cozar in the wagons thrust shovels out into reaching hands. "MaShimi went in over there." The man pointed. The others were already hurrying to the bank where the woman had been flung. The air bit at their cheeks, and their hands were tense. "Hurry," the lead cozar snapped.

No one spoke. It took several minutes to unbury the woman. When they dragged her out, she was shaking. The woman gasped, cried, and did not stop shivering as they hauled her forward to the last wagon that was already passing their position. "Go, go!" the man shouted as she half tumbled and half crawled through the flaps.

The drover did not need to be encouraged. He snapped the traces, and the dnu strained from their pace into a slow trot. The rest of the riders mounted.

Dion hung back. Tehena glanced at her, reined in, and waited skittishly for the wolfwalker. One of the cozar noticed that she did not mount up. "What is it?" he called softly as he turned. Dion gestured with her chin toward the tunnel, then handed her reins to Tehena. Carefully, she worked her way around the spots of ichor to the hole. She had to stand on her toes to peer inside, and her nostrils flared as she sorted out the scents that remained.

The cozar started back. "Don't—" he said sharply as he realized what she was doing.

She held up her hand to stop him. "The tunnel has been used before. The layers of ice are old."

Gingerly, he joined her. He glanced at her, realized from her expression that she would go in if he did not, and levered himself up into the hole. He crouched for a moment to calm his breathing. He had to force himself to move deeper into the cave and run his hands over the sides. Goddamn wolfwalkers, he cursed under his breath. Always wanting people to be heroes. Getting them killed more often than not. He felt a tremble in the snow and almost bolted until he realized it was his own legs, not the glacier worm returning. He finished his examination and quickly moved back to the road.

He nodded at Dion. "Hard to say, but at least a couple of ninans."

"We should post a warning."

He shook his head to hide the shudder that wanted to cut loose across his shoulders from remaining so near the tunnel. "Worm might return," he managed almost calmly.

Dion did not notice. She was staring up the road at the wagons that had rolled on past. "It was wounded, and it has fed. It will not come back for hours."

"Banners wouldn't last long in these winds. A ninan maybe. No more."

She glanced over her shoulder. "Long enough to save one life?"

He regarded her uncomfortably. Then he nodded, mounted, and trotted after the wagons. He didn't glance back to see if Dion and Tehena remained at the site. He seemed to know that they would stay until the warnings were erected. A few moments later, he returned with another man, four poles, some line, and two squares of red cloth. By the time they were finished setting the flags, the end of the wagon train was out of sight along the cliff, and the lead wagons were crawling like largons back into view far ahead.

As they reached hailing distance of the last wagon, Dion felt the tension seep out of the two cozar. For all that they were nomadic and prided themselves on their independence, their sense of safety depended on staying close to the wagons. Those rolling platforms were their homes, their forts, their sanctuaries. They were safe, she realized, as long as they stayed together. Her voice was low, to herself, and perhaps to the gray in her mind. "My children have never been safe," she said. Only the cold wind heard her.

XXVII

Talon Drovic neVolen

Is truth, truth?
  Or is it context?

  —Question of the elders at the Test of Abis

Something was wrong. Like a blade against his throat, the threat cut into his breathing. The wolves that distantly tamped down on his convulsions also clouded his mind, and he could not focus. *Cold. Danger. Find,* whispered the gray. *Protect.*

He glanced at the riders who cantered around him, but they rode easily, their weapons slung or sheathed, their eyes constantly scanning the forest, the canopy, the ground. None of them rode with anything other than normal wariness. He studied them surreptitiously: Sojourn, Mal, Ki, and Dangyon; Oroan, Rakdi, Roc—still simmering from days before. Harare, with the vanity of his straight, blond hair bound in a long, swinging braid. Fit, with his sharp face and thoughtful eyes. Thick-shouldered Wakje, rumpled Weed . . .

Talon winced as he passed out of the shade into a patch of sunlight. He closed his eyes as he thought. Kilaltian's group of eight was west on a parallel trail; Darity's six were east and probably ahead. But the sense of danger did not seem to do with the other raiders or with a venge or a single tracker. This was a more general prickling of the hairs along the back of his neck. Worlags? There were too many riders to tempt a worlag band. The lepa had already flocked that year; the poolah would be in pairs.

Talon squinted against the sun. It was not hot; with the altitude they had gained from riding up through the foothills, the air was barely warm. Even so, the wolves seemed to set the chill into his bones, while his flesh prickled with fever. He knew the herbs would relieve the pain, soften the fever, eliminate the convulsions. He knew Drovic would meet up with him later and offer more of the tincture. Or he could ride after his father and reach him in hours to get more of those drugs. If he knew what those drugs were, he could get more himself to relieve this twice-damned pain. Unless the herbs were forbidden, he thought suddenly, and it took Drovic's "persuasion" to get them.

His fists clenched at the howling that rode his brain, and the tautness of his muscles made them ache as much as the chill. Gods damn him, but he would not turn back to Drovic. East—that was the direction he needed, and for the first time, he was riding right. The wolves were still clearing his head of pain, and he was beginning to remember the roads. " 'The wounds will heal; the strength return; the warrior ride with purpose.' " He found himself muttering, and breathed a foul oath. He was deluding himself. The pain had never lessened, and now it cramped his muscles with an intensity that made him feel like iron. He was cold, and the pit of his stomach made him taste danger with every breath.

It was late afternoon, and they were on the downside of a small valley where the trees were thick and a network of tiny streams fed down to a shrunken creek. There were no signs of forest cat; no musk scents of badgerbear. He could smell the soil faintly through the distant wolves; hear the brushing sounds as they moved through the growth. One of them leaped a blowdown, and he smelled a faint odor of hare.

The sense of danger was his alone.

"I need my mind," he muttered, trying to form and send the thought to the wolves. There was resistance in the lupine fog as he tried to clear his skull of the wolves, but Talon maintained his sense of urgency. Reluctantly, the wolves drew back. It was a mistake. For a moment, the raw pain was merely a tightening across his body. Then his guts flared bright-hot. His arms bound up with tension. He spasmed against the saddle horn. He cried out—he heard the humiliation of his own pain. Then he hit the ground with a convulsion that shot agony through his healing shoulder and wracked him into a twitching, fetal position.

"Moonworms!" Some part of his mind registered the curses as a startled dnu leaped his body.

"Boos-trimmed gelbugs—"

His vision was spotted as if the tension of his body put pressure on his eyes. His teeth were gritted together; he had not bitten his tongue, and it choked him as much as his pain.

"What the hell happened?"

"Just fell out of the saddle—"

"Talon," Sojourn snapped from beside him. The man grabbed at Talon's arm, and the taller man spasmed, his elbow catching Sojourn on the ribs. "Wakje, help hold him down."

The raider put his weight on Talon and ignored the tall man's bitten scream. "For how long?" Wakje's voice was dry.

"As long as it takes," Sojourn retorted. "Dangyon, put your weight to work. Ki, grab his legs."

Talon closed them off and screamed in his mind for the wolves. The gray voices swept close. His muscles were rock; his chest so rigid he could not breathe. His bones would snap with the spasm. Moons of mercy! Even his thoughts gasped.

The packsong swelled chaotically. *Gods,* he whimpered. *Help me.*

He shuddered horribly, the convulsion shaking the raiders.

Then the gray voices swept back in, separating his mind from the pain, soothing his jaw, then neck. He gasped and blinked.

"He's coming around."

"This one was bad." It was Oroan. She watched Talon instinctively try to straighten his limbs while they were still cramped with tautness. "Carry him?" Her voice was expressionless.

There was a pause. The question was an interesting one. Ride or die—it was basic law. But it was Oroan's day to be messenger between Kilaltian's group and theirs; if she didn't want to take the news to Kilaltian, or if Weed didn't ride to Darity . . . Weed picked at a loose thread on his sleeve as he studied Talon, and Wakje studied Weed.

It was Talon himself who spoke. "Can . . . ride," he managed. His voice was strained, but he struggled against the hands that held him now in a sitting position. It was futile. When he shuddered, his neck went into a rictus, and his lips curled back from his teeth. It was a long moment before he could breathe again.

Sojourn snorted softly. "You can ride," he agreed, "like a half-witted bollusk."

Mal motioned for the others to stand back. "I'll carry him," he stated.

Sojourn looked at Mal. "You're hardly better than he is."

The dour man shrugged.

Rakdi rubbed the side of his hook nose. "Do any of us really want to tell Drovic we left him behind?"

Talon sucked in a breath, felt his mind shelter within the gray fog, and shook off Dangyon and Ki. "I will ride," he stated harshly.

The others regarded him as if he were a child.

"Best not to let Kilaltian see him like this," Oroan murmured.

There was silent consensus.

Wakje took his arm to help him up, and fury made Talon strike aside the man's hand. He got to his hands and knees, then to one knee, then finally his feet. He swayed, but he was upright. This time, the others did not help him. When he reached for the reins of his dnu, the others remained where they were, watching silently. "Like ghouls," he muttered.

Dangyon shrugged. "It's steady work, and someone has to do it."

Talon's lips twitched, but he took the moment to rest against the saddle before trying to mount. "If you're waiting for my soul to fall out of my body, you'll have a long night."

Weed's voice was dry. "We're just wondering if we all have time to use the peetrees."

"Spit-slimed mudsuckers." But he cursed without anger.

Wakje nodded to the others, then strode to his dnu and mounted. Talon felt a measure of his strength returning and forced himself up into the saddle. The others mounted around him, and within minutes, they were cantering again down the road. Talon had to fight not to hang onto the saddle horns but, by god, he would not slow from that canter. He could still feel the danger, but he did not try again to focus on it. "Coward," he muttered angrily to himself. But he did not ask the wolves to leave his mind again.

They had lost time, and as the pain faded, Talon urged their dnu faster. Kilaltian's group did not catch up to them, but they caught a glimpse of the other raiders from the crest of one of the hills. With dusk coming and Talon's wolf-shield fading with the distance to the wolves, the pain became a grinding ache in his bones. He cursed himself, cursed the dnu, cursed the raiders until Sojourn finally tossed him a saddle rag. He caught it uncomprehendingly.

"Stuff it in your mouth," the other raider said sharply. "It will help hold in all that temper. You wouldn't want to waste such anger on us when there are so many more useful places to shoot it off."

Talon gave him a dirty look. When they finally stopped for another break he stalked to the peetree. He nearly fell when he got there, and he had to brace himself on the outer bark just to do his duty. He could barely refasten his trousers before the shakes took him again.

Sojourn was waiting for him when he returned. The other man, on the pretext of checking his saddle cinch, murmured to Talon, "The herbs are supposed to prevent the symptoms."

Talon didn't answer.

"If you need more—"

Talon cut him off. "I'll take no more herbs or tinctures."

Sojourn was silent for a moment. He kept his voice low. "Without them, the convulsions will break your ribs around you like a cage crushing in. You'll go mad from the pain."

"And from the chills, and the dizziness," Talon interrupted, "and the war bolts that keep shooting through my head. I know what I am risking."

"Do you?" Sojourn ignored his dry tone. "Talon, your wounds were extensive. The loss of blood, the parasites, the fevers—they left you worse than weak." His voice dropped even lower. "Half the time you think you can talk to the wolves. You don't even know who you are."

Talon paused and looked Sojourn in the eye. "No," he agreed, his voice suddenly soft. "But I'm beginning to remember."

Sojourn stared at him. Then he turned and walked away to hide what had suddenly flared in his nondescript, brown eyes. It was not time, the raider told himself, and Talon's challenge was not to him. He breathed once, twice, until he regained his sense of calm. Talon did not need for him to add more conflict to the group. Talon was adding enough tension himself. The thought made the slender man chuckle.

The sense of danger in Talon remained with him that evening, when all three groups converged. It haunted his fitful sleep, so that he saw more of the moons and graying clouds than he did of any dreams of a woman with violet eyes. He knew the wolves were closer at night than in the day, because the pain was more faint, but even though he bedded down at the edge of the raider circle, no wolves slept beside him. There were too many humans there, and wild as they were, the Gray Ones did not like the sense or the smell of the raiders.

Talon did not blame them. He woke beneath a scalloped sky with his mouth dry and his skin rancid from sweating. It was cool, almost cold, but he had no desire to stay in his blankets. He needed to move or run. The world was closing around him, driving him like a hare. He shifted to roll to his feet, and his right wrist buckled beneath his weight before he could catch himself. "Moons-damned, blood-sucking, piss-boy," he cursed under his breath. Angry—he was growing angrier with the kays. He snarled at the other raiders when they rose.

He had had too many mornings like this, dawns without his mate. She was—she had been—beautiful. Not like other women. Not like Roc, with her sultry body and fine-boned face; more like Oroan, with a face a man could look at forever. Lithe body, high cheekbones, dark eyes, and the temper of a moonmaid . . . She had been his life. He rubbed his sternum where two gems had been studded into the bone. The blue gem for Promising; the purple gem for the Waiting Year . . . Even the roots of the studs seemed to ache.

Talon clenched his fist, then unclenched it to test its strength. He pulled his knife from its sheath and began to move stiffly. Right step, slash left, right return, cut in, and lunge . . . Ariye, he thought bitterly. Ariye had taken his mate away. Drovic had drummed that into his head, but for once, his father was right. He cut and lunged, stepped left, and slashed. After so many years, the old patterns were as natural as instinct. Right step, stab in, circle cut, drop down, thrust up. Natural as the knowledge that Ariye had also taken his sons. The wolves began to focus with him. Right step, elbow back, reverse thrust, catch and break. *Hunt with us,* the voices came. Right step, side thrust, catch and break, reverse stab. *Blood—hot.* Right step, block up, slash down, reverse stab. Ariye had taken his strength and now it wanted him. *Scent—hot.* Right step, lunge through, back slash, back chop.

He barely acknowledged Wakje when the other raider began to move with him. Right step, block low, fist up, stab in. *Muscles—hot.* He caught a glimpse of the eyes of a wolf in the brush. Gray Ursh's voice was clear. *Heart—hot. Blood—sweet.* Ready yourself for the fight, for the blood. Right step, two-hands palm strike, left strike high, right stab low, elbow smash to the head. His mind began to focus. Pain receded as the old patterns took over. Right step, elbow smash high and circle low, femoral right grab and tear. Oroan began to echo Talon on the other side, and Dangyon, chewing on a bit of jerky, moved into the pattern beside Wakje. The other raiders silently moved back to give them a larger circle.

Abis, the martial art of Ramaj Ariye and Randonnen. Talon did not question his knowledge of it. Like Cansi and Tzua, it was in his hands, his feet, his muscles. Right step, stab in, thrust up, neck-slash down. His eyes were almost blank; his face hard and vicious with each strike. His opponent was *there*. The enemy was *here*. Right step, S-cut, femoral slash, step through, reverse kidney stab. Ebi and Strapel, then Weed and Rakdi and Mal—the group grew silently. They moved like ten images of Talon, perfectly synchronized, perfectly patterned. Ten knives with his, flashing in the gloom; ten knees that struck at the same time as his; ten elbows driving up.

Four more raiders joined in: Ki, Harare, Merek, Al. The group shifted into the left-step set of patterns. Fit snorted disparagingly, but joined in, unable to resist the movements. The smaller man's grace was that of a water cat, his shifts seamless, his thrusts like glass. Left step, elbow back, reverse thrust, catch and break. Kilaltian murmured something to Ilandin, and the woman walked stiffly into the pattern and took her place beside Weed. *Gather,* Gray Ursh whispered in Talon's mind. *Gather the pack. Join and bond. The pack, the family, the mate.* Left step, block up, slash down, reverse stab. Talon breathed almost easily, his mind blocking the pain with the anger that crystallized. Left for dead, find the dead—the images seemed twisted. Left step, lunge through, back slash, back chop.

A flock of pelan veered from the clearing as they realized there was movement below their landing site. They scattered with startled cries. Wolf eyes gleamed from the brush. Left step, block low, fist up, stab in. Darity and Mook joined in. More than half the raiders moved with Talon, their steps near-silent on the packed earth, the sounds of their movements betrayed only by the brush of cloth against leather.

The left set ended, and Fit started instinctively to take a Cansi-style pattern. The smaller man was behind Talon, but Talon saw the change through the eyes of the wolf before the man had half-shifted his balance. Talon moved deliberately; the raiders followed; and Fit grinned to himself as they moved into his favorite patterns.

Half crouch, stab in, short cut back, deep thrust and lift. Liatuad and Pen joined the Cansi-style set while Kilaltian and the others quietly built the morning fires and began to boil breakfast. Half crouch, block left, step through, double kidney stab . . . The sky blued; light began to filter into the forest. Back dance, double block, double thrust, circle cut. Side drop, reverse cut up, block back, stab in. *Gather the hunters,* Ursh whispered. Talon's nostrils flared as he caught the growing sweat scent of the raiders around him. His eyes tracked tiny movements—an unbalanced shift behind him, a pebble kicked away, the flit of a tree sprit through shadow. *Run with blood-hot veins.* The Gray One's voice was a knife prick. Left fake, drop down, right pivot, tendon cut. *Hunt,* the wolf whispered. Right slash, right reverse sweep, right lunging block, right reverse slash. *Find. Protect.* Talon's lips curled back from his teeth. Power, control—he could almost feel those things grow in that wolf-woman. Left reverse ridge-hand, right follow-up neck slash, right reverse gut slash, left claw to the guts. *Hunt.*

Talon finished the last set on a point-balance. He stilled, perfectly balanced, ready to strike. His teeth were bared; his gray eyes glinted; his breath came quickly but controlled. His hands were steady as the claws of a worlag, and the knife was simply an extension of the claws he thought were fingers. He was blinded by the voices passed on through Gray Ursh. Eerily, the other raiders froze with him in a tableau of poised, hanging violence.

Then Mal, exhausted, dropped out of the stance. The other raiders relaxed, wiped their brows, put away their knives. Weed grabbed his bota; Merek was grinning. Dangyon slapped Ki on the shoulder. Their muscles were loose; their bodies sweaty in the cool air.

"Haven't done that in years," Oroan said to Wakje. She began to stretch down to keep her muscles from tightening.

The other raider nodded. "Forgot how good it felt to work balance, not just speed."

From another side, Weed made a mock lunge at Rakdi and grinned as the ex-elder slapped him aside. "I never saw that last set before," Weed said. "Wonder where he picked it up." He attacked again, mimicking the movements Talon had shown.

Rakdi blocked, missed, and froze with Weed's blade at his

brachial artery. His voice was dry. "From a man who is dead, most likely."

Weed put his blade away. "Halo didn't join us," he observed.

"He'd rather talk than walk," Dangyon replied mildly.

"That's true enough," Rakdi agreed, rubbing the side of his beak nose. "He'll prattle on for forty minutes on whether a peach or a pear has better flavor, before he'll put his blade to use."

Dangyon shrugged. "He's handy enough, as long as his life's at stake."

"Aren't we all," Rakdi returned.

Talon stood in the midst of the mass of movement and voices and felt his heartbeat slow. His muscles were no longer as tight, but as he wiped the sweat from his forehead, the pain began to seep back. Like a balloon swelling slowly, his head filled with the pressure. He found himself holding his breath against what he knew was coming. Held it, felt the strain in his lungs, waited and finally breathed. It was not as bad as before. The wolves were still there with him.

He smiled grimly. Sojourn handed him a water bota, and he took a sip, sloshed it around his mouth, and finally swallowed. The skin was tightening over his cheekbones, and he knew the convulsion would strike soon. He was not disappointed. His arms and legs went taut; the muscles in his belly contracted—he almost doubled over with the savageness of the attack. Somehow, he remained on his feet. Yes, his fingers crushed the mouth of the bota bag; yes, his toes were cramped in his boots. But he shook his head sharply at Sojourn's silent offer of help. Instead, he took a deep breath to force his lungs to expand. Then, one by one, he unclenched his fingers and toes until he could walk. When he handed the bag back to Sojourn, his hand was steady, and if his knuckles were still white, the other man said nothing.

Talon worked his way to the breakfast fire, scooped a mug of stew, and glanced at the forest. He could no longer see Gray Ursh. The massive male had slipped away. He tried stretching in that indefinable way that the wolfwalkers had, and realized that, as the pain had softened slightly, so had the gray fog in his skull. He could still feel the edge of rictus fighting against the fog, could still feel his muscles bunch around his bones, but it was less, and his mind was more clear.

Talon's face was still pale, but his smile became wolfish. "Twenty minutes," he called out across the camp, ignoring the stab of sharpness that his voice brought to his skull. "Then we ride."

XXVIII

Rhom Kheldour neKintar

To thirst is to know how to live.
    —*Nadugur proverb*

Rhom could see the mountains. They hung just out of reach where the moons bathed them as gently as any man could wish. Glorious, Jabulisayu—call them what he would, they were a tease in the moonlit sky. He didn't speak as Gamon stumbled back from along the ravine. His lips seemed to have cemented themselves together and would bleed if he pulled them apart.

Ahead, on the other side of yet another small arroyo, was the glow of a tenor tree. There was water under the tenor trees if only they could reach it—underground streams and water tables that fed the roots. That water might be forty, fifty meters under the surface, but the tenor trees could find it. There were other tenor trees in the distance, and they whirred with the sounds of insects—an hour ago, he had watched a cloud of rockdoves swarm through one, killing everything on it. He and Gamon had been lucky. The swarm of birds had passed over a hundred meters away, and even at that distance, Rhom had heard their hunger.

He studied the ravine before them. It wasn't deep—perhaps forty meters. In the dark, it might as well be four hundred. He gestured at the rope over the older man's shoulder. Gamon nodded. There was no question as to who would go down first. Gamon had the knowledge that would say whether they would continue or if he needed to come back up. Rhom had the bulk and strength to haul the other man up if something went wrong at the bottom. Rhom looked at the black crevice and thought of sandbears and parasites. He did not envy Gamon.

They wrapped the rope twice around a boulder, letting both ends drop over the edge. Gamon put on his gloves, slung the rope through his crotch, up around his left shoulder, and back through his crotch, using his body as the pulley. He nodded at the rock, and Rhom checked the line again. "Set," Rhom said shortly. Gamon disappeared into shadow.

A few moments later, Rhom reset the rope so it could be brought down after him, then joined Gamon below. They pulled down the rope and located the rougher section where climbing up would be easier. It was a scramble, and Gamon cracked his elbow hard enough to split his leathered skin, but they made the top without mishap.

Rhom coiled the rope as Gamon approached the tenor tree. He didn't mind the older man's caution. There were enough insects, lizards, and other things living in the glowing trees that startling all that would create its own swarm, most of which would land on them. He finished with the rope and joined the older man, copying his actions when Gamon got out his treated groundcloth. Then the lean man approached the tree, moving very slowly. When he found what he was looking for, he spread his cloth on the ground and lay down. Rhom did the same, and Gamon pointed to a thin line of black that moved along the soil, appearing out of the ground. The Ariyen's voice was rough with thirst. "Bagbeetle," he said shortly. The gray-eyed man caught one and held the squirming insect over his mouth, then gently squeezed its bulbous belly. A tiny stream of water squirted out. The older man worked it around his dry tongue, let the beetle go, and picked the next in line. The released insect fluttered its vestigial wings and turned to go back down the hollowed root.

Rhom needed no more instruction. He picked a beetle, squeezed its belly, and squirted right up his nose. He cursed under his breath. His second shot hit his cheek.

Gamon grinned, caught another stream of water, and sighed. "Don't worry. There are enough beetles here for a dozen men, and there's some serious water down below. They'll bring it up all night." He watched the other man wipe his chin. "Takes a bit of skill, Rhom," he said seriously. "Like pleasing a woman—something you Randonnen men don't know half enough about." He caught another beetle. "Must come from being stuck in all those lonely mountains. You don't get the real thing to practice on often enough to—"

The third time, Rhom hit Gamon squarely in the eye.

"Worm-begotten poolah," Gamon began. He wiped his eyes with a gritty hand. "Even your twin has more respect." He grabbed another beetle, and this time aimed at Rhom.

Neither man missed after that.

XXIX

Talon Drovic neVolen

When you face a danger greater than yourself,
Do you flee like the hare,
Or stand and face and accept it?
Running soothes the fear in your feet,
But will kill when the danger courses.
Do not flee;
Stand and face yourself and your foe.
It is by facing and seeing him clearly
That you can choose the way to survival.
Run then, and you can choose your path;
Stand, and you choose your fight;
You may die in that moment,
But you die as a man.
Run first, and you are nothing.

   —Locke Berdann, Randonnen weapons master, 132 A.L.

   The forest was quiet as they rode out onto an old, over-grown road. "Too quiet," Talon muttered. He had not shaken his sense of danger, but he saw nothing that alarmed him and heard nothing from the wolves. The sky was mottled with clouds that would grow heavier as the day progressed; the air was somewhat warm; the ground dry and hard. The road led more north than any other direction, but once they were into the Circle of Fifths, they would turn west into Bilocctar or could turn due east into Kiren. They were close enough to the mountains that the peaks were hidden by their own forested foothills, and Talon felt his stomach tighten at the thought of the mountain county. In thirty years, Drovic had not been able to let go of Ariye, and Talon gnawed at the same obsession.

   His eyes narrowed as he stared at the line of slabs before him. In the dawn, beneath the fading stars, the slag stones marked the graves of Ancients' hopes; and Talon counted each section as if it hid his own hopes beneath it. Hope, time, a future . . . There were faces that never left his dreams—eyes that cried out with urgency, mouths that shrieked for vengeance. He looked down at his hands as if his bones had turned to steel. In the slanted shafts of late-summer sun, he could swear that his veins were red—not with his own blood, but with the blood of those he had killed. His jaw tightened, only half with pain. Ariye was not his future—not unless that future lay in the graves. He realized suddenly that the wolf-woman felt the same. She rode toward him, not to Ariye. Talon's lips stretched in a feral grin. She felt him, then. Felt his pain, his rage at her trap. He tried to project that fury toward her, the sense that he would take her power and turn it on her until she released him from the gray. He wondered if she shuddered like him when the chill ran down his spine.

At midmorning, they encountered a caravan, and Talon drew his riders off to the side so that the wagons could rattle by unmolested. The wagon guards paused by Talon and So-journ to look them over as the caravan passed. Two of them remained by the raiders as the wagons rolled on.

The tall one with the receding hairline studied Talon with a slight frown. "Kiaskari?" he asked cryptically. He said the name of the ramaj with a distinctive lilting accent, and Talon knew the man had been raised in the northern county.

Talon nodded. The four sat quietly for a few moments. One of the guards' dnu stamped its feet; another chirped softly. Talon shifted in his saddle, and the guards were instantly alert. Talon did not smile, but his hand remained on the reins, away from the hilt of his sword.

The other guard—the one with the gnarled wrists—offered, "Saw beetle swarm sign three kays from here."

Talon nodded. A moment later, he gestured with his chin. "Saw a bit of that to the south. It wasn't heavy. Might want to watch for bihwadi, though. Heard they went through a northern farm two nights ago. Worlags swarmed behind them."

The guards seemed to lose some of their wariness at the

openness of Talon's warning. Harare remained silent, but Talon could feel his questioning glance.

One of the caravan riders dug a piece of jerky from a pouch, then offered the pouch to Talon. "Been riding long?"

Talon accepted the jerky, popped a piece in his mouth, and tossed the bag back to the other man. "Long enough to think my ass is as hard as my saddle."

The guards chuckled. The last wagons rolled into sight. "Heard there were raiders about."

Talon nodded. "Ran into some ourselves—they killed six over near Bronton. Stirred up the venges like largons. There's so many hunters out on the road that not even a gnat can fly. Head that way, and you should find the roads clear."

The balding guard nodded. "Ride safe."

"With the moons," Talon returned.

The other men spurred to a trot to keep up with the wagons.

Harare did not speak until the last wagon was away. "How did you figure?"

Talon knew what he meant. "They were looking for danger, expected raiders, and thought they might be us. I just gave them a different threat."

"The bihwadi and worlags?" Harare shook his head. "Clever."

Talon shrugged. "Give a man what he expects, and he will rarely look hard at what is being offered."

The other man gave him a thoughtful look as Talon kicked his dnu into a canter.

An hour later, they passed a family group that watched them nervously, but Talon ignored them and let them pass unmolested. His headache had grown with the ride so that even the thought of a raid was an unbearable amount of action. With the rest of the raiders showing hard-bitten and dark expressions, the family of six rode quickly by, their faces tight with forced confidence, while the muscles of their backs twitched with the fear that arrows or swords would follow them.

At noon, the three groups of raiders met, then split up

again to pass through a chain of villages. A fine mist fell for a few minutes—not even enough to wet the dust—and Talon knew that the real rain would hold off for hours yet. By early evening, they had climbed farther into the foothills, and the temperature had fallen with a chilly breeze. It was a welcome contrast to the ninans of hotter weather.

By afternoon, they had covered nearly eight kays as the crow flies, even after the late start, and Talon was beginning to think that his sense of danger was the result of fighting off the pain. They split again into their three groups, with Darity's group cantering ahead on the road, while Talon and Kilaltian led their riders in parallel game tracks.

It was not the riding pattern that bothered Talon—the fewer men with him, the better he felt. No, it was something in the gray, an instinctive knowledge of danger and a wariness in the wolves that grew as evening deepened. He was not surprised when the gray voices sharpened, and the hair stiffened on the back of his neck. Quickly, he slowed his group. With his dnu at a half walk, he studied the forest. He saw nothing, but at his expression, the other raiders loosened their weapons. Talon sniffed the air, but the scent of wintergreen was almost overpowering. Still, distantly linked, the wild wolves wrinkled their noses and snarled deep in his mind.

He slipped the riding thong from the hilt of his knife and signaled for his group to halt. Instantly, the riders formed two loose rows, back-to-back on the rootroad while Talon trotted his dnu ahead. The riding beast sensed nothing amiss, and Talon circled the area, the other raiders watching silently. He returned to the group, dismounted with a frown, and handed the reins to Weed. He motioned for Wakje and Rakdi to join him.

The other men dismounted and automatically strung their bows. Talon still saw nothing, but the wolves had picked up the sense of danger from their link with him—that he understood. Whatever he had smelled, no matter how faint, still caught the Gray Ones' attention. He started to step off the road, but Wakje caught his arm. Talon's muscles were rockhard under the other man's fingers as Talon fought his convulsions, and Wakje raised narrowed eyes to Talon's gaze. What

Wakje saw made him step back. Talon continued into the forest.

Rakdi didn't hesitate, and Wajke shook it off and followed the hook-nosed man. But Wakje could have sworn he had seen a hint of yellow in Talon's icy eyes.

Talon did not go far. Five or six steps, and he began to get the scent of the forest instead of the scent of dnu. He closed his eyes for a moment, then looked up. Slowly, he pointed. "There," he said softly. Wakje and Rakdi, then the raiders on the road, followed his gesture. As one, several bows with nocked arrows raised.

"It's no longer present," Talon said.

Wakje put his war bolt back in his quiver. "I don't see it." He studied the direction.

"Twenty meters up, the streaks on the trunks."

"Godbeetles," Rakdi murmured, staring up. "And fresh." The raw bands of exposed wood were the work of a beetle swarm. He slung his bow over his shoulder.

Talon nodded and murmured, "An hour later, and dusk would have obscured the damage."

"There aren't so many that we should worry."

"No," Talon agreed, "but this is not the only beetle sign, either. The wagon guards saw swarm sign to the southwest." He pushed farther into the forest, ignoring the thin, sticky vines that caught on his jerkin. "Here." He ran his hands over the bark of a tree. It fell away as he touched it, leaving behind sheets of shimmering crystal.

Wakje pushed up beside him. "Stan sacs?"

"Don't touch it," Talon said sharply. "It will bind to your fingers, and you'll have to burn it off."

Wakje quickly withdrew his hand. "Stan sacs don't bind," he said flatly.

Talon leaned close and carefully sniffed the substance to be sure. "They aren't stan sacs. They're hassbug eggs protected by sugarglass."

"Sugarglass?"

His answer was returned almost absently as he examined the sacs. "It's an excretion that protects the eggs through winter. Ancients used to call them some sort of protein—a cold-shock protein. Corn sugar, to the farmers." He took a twig and poked the sac. The twig caught instantly and broke off when he tried to pull it out. "Still soft," he murmured. "In a day, these will harden and look like quartz."

Rakdi's voice was carefully casual. "You can't tell a stan sac from a hassbug sac just by sniffing at the crystals or poking a stick into the goo. And hassbugs don't leave so many sacs in one place."

Talon ignored the comment and squinted instead at the eggs. "Look at the edges. They're not uniform in depth, but the whole mass is equally dotted."

"Pressure-release pattern," Rakdi murmured.

Talon nodded slowly. He didn't have the skill in tracking that Drovic might have wished, but living with scouts, he had learned some things over the years; and, of course, he had the edge of the wolves in his mind. He knew these were hassbug eggs even if everyone else would have overlooked them as simple stan sacs. He pursed his lips as he studied the mass of eggs. "They took off all at once," he said. "If they hadn't, the pressure of each beetle left behind would have broken or smoothed out the tracks of the others."

"Hassbugs don't take off all at once."

Talon gave him a grim look. "They do when they swarm."

"When they swarm," Wakje repeated slowly. The man straightened and stared at the forest around them. "Hassbugs are followed by portons; portons are followed by rasts."

"Or skates, depending on the country," Talon agreed tersely. "We're high enough in altitude and far enough north that rasts would be fewer here."

Rakdi rubbed his hooked nose hard. "It's high enough for skates," he agreed.

Talon nodded. Skates could glide huge distances between trees, even over lakes when they unrolled and unfolded their webbed bodies. Their teeth were like bihwadi, and their claws like lepa. They were small—about the size of two of Dangyon's fists—but it only took one to draw the attention of the rest. He pushed quickly back to the road. Wakje and Rakdi were on his heels. The three men rapidly shook the mites from their war caps and did the tick dance, as Dangyon called it, stomping to dislodge anything that might have clung to their clothes.

Talon gestured for the others to put away their weapons. "Hassbugs swarmed through here an hour ago—probably just after that last group of riders. If we don't see any portons in the next hour or so . . ." He shrugged and took the reins of his dnu. The light was failing fast, and the forest was already gloomy.

"We're in the path of a swarm?" Sojourn said sharply to his back.

"Probably," he answered over his shoulder.

"Portons are followed by rasts."

"Here, it will be skates." Talon's answer was firm.

Harare shifted uncomfortably. "You're sure?"

"There was sugarglass on the tree trunks," Wakje said flatly.

Rakdi looked from the other man to Talon, who was already leading his dnu off the road. "Where are you going?"

Talon called back over his shoulder. "There's a clearing in this direction."

Wakje was already following Talon, but the others looked warily around. "We're north enough," Sojourn murmured to Rakdi.

"I'll take skates over rasts any day," Mal muttered. But the dour man's voice was worried.

"Moonworms!" Fit called after Talon, "You can't tell what will come—whether it's rasts or skates—just from a look at some bug eggs. Even when you see the beasts, you can't tell them apart till they bite. They're almost the same size, they both swarm at night, they both swarm through the trees instead of on the ground, and both swarms follow motion. Only a wolfwa—" He cut himself off at Mal's expression.

None of them had asked how Talon knew they were hassbug eggs, not stan sacs. Nor had they asked how he knew there was a clearing in that direction. As one, they stared after Talon. Then they suddenly began pushing like a group of boys to reach the clearing's safety.

It was Oroan who broke the awkward silence as they gathered in the small space. "Darity and Kilaltian?" she asked obliquely.

Talon looked back from where he examined the edges of the clearing.

"Darity's group didn't see the hassbug sign," Dangyon murmured, "or they would have stopped and started the fires here."

Harare glanced at the barrel-chested man. "Fires keep rasts away, not skates. Skates follow motion. I once saw four dozen skates throw themselves on a blaze because the flames were flickering too much. Brought the whole swarm down on us." He turned to Talon. "You're sure it will be skates?"

"Sure as a venge," Talon returned. He looked at the clouded sky, then up the road. "It will be dark soon—the moons won't clear the clouds. Darity's group always travels faster than us. They're probably just beyond Resan Junction by now, setting up the night site."

Weed's voice was flat. "Which means we're an hour behind them at a gallop. If we keep on, we could ride right into the swarm."

"Doesn't matter. They must be warned, as must Kilaltian." Talon glanced at Harare and Mal. "It's your day to ride duty."

Harare regarded Talon for a long moment. Finally, he nodded slowly. "You would do it yourself if I didn't."

"Then go." He did not hold out much hope for Harare reaching Darity in time. After a full day's ride, the man's dnu could not hold a gallop up and over each hill. If he was lucky, Harare would see the swarm coming before the skates saw him, free his dnu, and go to ground. The running dnu would draw the swarm off, and he would survive behind it. As Harare left, Talon turned to the saturnine man. "Mal?" he asked obliquely.

"I can ride."

Talon's gray gaze took in the way the man listed slightly as he leaned against his dnu. Mal had not improved over the long day's ride, and Talon nodded, then said flatly, "I will go in your place."

"No," Sojourn said sharply.

Talon glanced at the other man. "My duty—"

The other man cut him off almost before he started to speak. "Your duty is to this group—to us."

"To all of us," Talon returned sharply.

"Aye, but you know when the danger will come. You can hear—" Sojourn broke off.

"What?" Talon's gaze went to ice. He glared at the other man. "Wolves? Is that what you were going to say? You think I can hear the wolves?"

"With your background that shouldn't surprise you—" the slender man snapped.

Dangyon seemed to reach across casually, but his lightning backhand caught Sojourn on the chest and knocked him out of the saddle.

Sojourn half sprawled on the ground, stunned. Then he caught his breath and leaped to his feet. He drew his knife like a thought. The motion was slick as an eel—smooth, practiced, instinctive, blindingly fast. In an instant, Sojourn's unobtrusive patina was stripped away, and the killer inside exposed. Talon's mind catalogued the movements. Drovic was smooth; Sojourn smoother. Fit was fast; Sojourn faster.

Dangyon was already half out of his saddle to meet the other man, but Talon lunged between them. "Halt!"

Sojourn poised for a moment. He didn't seem to breathe. Then the moment shifted. Dangyon cursed softly, and Sojourn seemed to fade back into the brown-toned camouflage of his person. "You black-wormed, back-biting, son of a worlag," Sojourn returned almost mildly to Dangyon.

Talon had not mistaken the savage, hidden fury in the man, and his own voice was low and hard. "Whether or not I hear the pack, my duty is to all of us, not just to the ten of you."

"Duty among raiders. Is that like honor among thieves?" Rakdi's dry voice murmured.

"Shut up," Weed said softly.

Fit glanced from one to the other. "I'll warn them," he said. "I'm small; my dnu is fast. I'd be riding duty tomorrow anyway."

Talon, his eyes still narrowed at Dangyon, nodded sharply. "Go," he ordered.

Fit twisted his dnu in a half circle and took off back toward the road like a hare.

Road, Talon snorted to himself. It was more like a wide path. Spread out over the trails as they were, Fit should reach Kilaltian easily, since the trails were separated by only one or two small hills—unless Kilaltian had forked farther west before coming back in to meet Darity. He turned to the others. "At a guess, we have half an hour before the portons swarm. They usually follow the hassbugs closely, and usually swarm by nightfall. So we'll bed the dnu down here and take cover."

"From skates," Dangyon said softly.

Talon bit back an oath. They all suspected the wolves. It did not help that one of the Gray Ones was close by. Talon could smell the damp, musk scent even through his headache. Either the wolves had made him more sensitive overall just by being near him, or he was still linked to the packsong.

Quickly, they stripped and bedded down the dnu. To keep the beasts from moving, they hobbled the dnu's noses to their feet. "It might save a few," Talon told them. They threw the saddles and saddlebags in a circle on the treated cloths that would keep the beetles away. Then they threw down their bedding to add a layer of protection for themselves. "Four meters or more apart," Talon ordered. "Without the moons, we stand a chance of going completely unnoticed."

No one had to ask why he ordered the distance between them. If they were too close to one another when the skates descended and any one of them panicked, anything close to that one man would be torn apart alive. The death throes would draw the swarm like mudsuckers to a thrashing fish.

Rakdi glanced at the distance between his place and Weed's, then at the scattered, sloppy layout. "Well, there's one advantage to leaving a camp trace like this. Any venge following us would think twice after seeing this slop. They'll think the lot of us had the worst gas a lepa ever passed."

"That," Weed agreed, "or beetle breath." He eyed Rakdi's sleeping bag and then Dangyon's, then surreptitiously moved his closer to the brush so that some vines overhung his bedding. On the other side of the clearing, Oroan ran a stick under a log to dislodge night spiders, then threw her bedding beneath it.

"There's room for three under that log," Ki said. There was a tinge of envy in his voice.

Mal nodded. "If she trusted anyone else—or if they trusted her—to share it."

Oroan glanced around the cluttered clearing, met their challenging gazes, and finally nodded to Talon. "I'll share with him."

Weed's voice was almost dry. "Now that's thinking ahead. Choose the man who suffers from tremors when you're trying to hide from skates." There was a sharpness to his voice that Talon didn't recognize, and it took him seconds to realize that it was fear. He turned and stared at the man. It was unexpected, that fear, for Weed had ridden for years as a raider, and had seen a hundred battles. Talon didn't realize that he stretched into the faint packsong in his mind, but he suddenly smelled the sweat of the other man and knew he was right, that it was fear that charged Weed. Not fear of battle or swords or men, but fear of . . . wildlife. Of facing beasts. Of being eaten alive. It was a fear that made him impossibly fierce in the forest, while he was merely good on a raid.

Weed met his eyes, clenched his jaw, and turned silently to his bedroll.

Oroan looked from Weed to Talon. "We all take a chance with him sooner or later," she said mildly to the others. "For me, it might as well be now."

Talon turned back to the lean woman. It was trust, he realized—loyalty of a sort that she was offering. He moved toward her. "Do you realize what you are saying?" he murmured.

She studied him for a long moment, then gave a single, short, almost imperceptible nod.

Talon turned away, snagged his bedding from the ground, and tossed it to the woman. The raider caught the loose bundle and spread his sleeping bag cursorily, two meters away from hers, at the other end of the log.

Roc watched the two and cursed under her breath. She was

not gentle in arranging her sleeping bag between the roots of a massive tree. Her face was tight as she crawled, half sitting, into her sleeping bag. "They might miss us completely," she said sharply. "They might not even swarm."

"And the moons might not rise, and the dawn might not come." Dangyon glanced at the sky, then got into his blanket roll.

"Your back is exposed," Talon murmured.

"Always is," the man returned. "Comes of being twice the man that you are."

Talon smiled grimly. He looked around to make sure everyone else was down. "If they are coming, they will be coming soon."

"And if they don't?" It was Roc.

"Then we will have a cold and uncomfortable evening." Talon looked over the sloppy clearing and nodded in satisfaction. The raiders were scattered; the dnu were down between the trunks of the blackheart trees, outside the rough circle of men. If one dnu panicked, it would pull the swarm down onto it, but the feeding frenzy that would result would also break the dnu's bonds. It would bolt and take the swarm with it. The rest of the dnu might survive.

He moved quickly to his sleeping bag and burrowed in, rolling up against the log so that the ground protected his side and the log his back. He pulled up the bag until just his ears and eyes were clear. He sensed more than heard something nearby and remained still with difficulty. A moment later, a muzzle pushed toward his face.

Leader. Gray Faren whuffed against his forehead.

He shifted so that he could see her. Their gazes met. There was the shock of deep, intimate contact. His vision doubled; his arms seemed to grow fur. The packsong was suddenly real. Lupine and human voices crawled in the back of his head.

Run. Hunger . . . Do you see it? Feel the hunt. Dust. Hard dirt under the paws. Where are you?

He broke out in a sweat and shuddered. On the other side of him, Oroan heard the rustling and murmured, "Don't make me regret my decision."

He struggled to control his breathing. A soft rustling

spread through the canopy. It was faint, like a light wind, but Talon was not fooled, and he knew the others had heard it. Minutes passed, and another light rushing sound rustled through the leaves. Small shapes flitted through the sky, and tiny voles leaped from tree to tree.

Gray Faren stared into his eyes. *Leader. Danger.*

I know.

Find, protect. Wolfwalker. She pulled his own voice out of the packsong.

There was a sense of distance, and Talon shook his head imperceptibly. Through Faren, he saw through other wolf eyes. He watched with Gray Ursh as the wolves paused and looked back at the portons, which rose in a startled cloud from the far side of the lake. The narrow birds skimmed out over the waters. Their massed shadow was echoed in the lake like a claw, and Talon clenched his left fist. *They are coming,* he called urgently to the wolves.

Leader, they sent back.

Run, he shouted to them.

Gray Faren jerked, but his hand shot out and dug into her scruff. *Not you. You're too close. You must stay and be still as stone.*

She snarled, and in the clearing someone breathed, "Wolves."

In the distance, the portons reached the far side of the lake and scattered through the trees. Small sprits screamed at the sense of danger and darted into the upper canopy. Rodents flashed to their dens. A hint of movement beyond the lake caught wolf eyes. The hint became a wave, and the wave a hand of darkness. Fingers of movement spread through the trees.

Talon caught his breath. *Run,* he shouted into the gray. *Run like wind—like fire.*

The gray swelled back with urgency and fear. It was not at the birds; the wolves sensed what had started the portons swarming. "Run," he whispered.

From one side, Sojourn breathed, "What is it?"

He strengthened his voice so that the others could hear. "The portons just swarmed. One arm of the swarm is coming this way." Heartbeats pounded. A heavier rustling shook the forest. Small animals bolted through the clearing. A cloud of tree sprits fled en masse. To the north, larger animals thudded by. Vines dragged as something became caught and grunted frantically to tear free.

There was an answering rustle as the raiders instinctively burrowed down farther in their blankets. Fetal positions, genitals guarded, arms over their necks and faces.

Talon felt his limbs twitch with the urgency of the wolves. The Gray Ones were running east in front of the swarm, and behind the portons was the rustling he had heard twice before. The rustling became a subtle hissing in lupine ears, and Talon kept his gray eyes on the yellow gaze of Gray Faren. Through her, he could feel the surge of adrenaline in the other wolves as the portons flew overhead. When the flock passed the fleeing Gray Ones, Talon shouted into the packsong. *Stop! Drop to the ground.*

Half the wolves froze for an instant. The others kept on running. *Stop,* he shouted again. *The danger is in movement. Lie down. Keep still.* But his voice was like a stab at the packsong, and the wolves did not understand.

He tried to project stillness. Gray Faren growled beside him. *Danger. Death.*

In moving, he snarled back. *Keep still. The skates will pass them if they do not move. But they must, for moons' sake, keep still.*

They must breathe.

"Gods," he cursed under his breath. She was right. The wolves had been running, and a panting wolf would be a flashing beacon to the skates.

Dion clenched her fists. In the packsong, the danger was distant and faint, but it was too familiar. Lepa, which had swarmed out over Still Meadow and had torn her son from her arms. Skates, which swarmed out over the lake and chased down the pack of wolves. She tried to reach into the gray, but her memories, thickened by those of the wolves, almost blinded her. *Caves,* she cried out. *You have to reach the caves.*

* * *

Rhom stiffened. Gamon, trudging behind him, halted instantly. Both men froze, listening to the sky, peering across the bright moon streaks of sand, Rhom, because he felt the tension, Gamon because he read it in the younger man.

Something reached through the gray to Talon, a memory or a voice. Yes, he said to himself. There was a place—ten years ago he had been there. A series of caves lined the base of a ridge. They were old lepa caves, and only a few rodents would use them, but the wolves could fit inside. One kay. *One kay,* he repeated in his mind. Gray Faren snarled softly.

He forced himself to calm his thoughts. They roiled with humanness, and he knew the wild wolves would not accept it. He formed an image with difficulty and projected it into the gray. There was a hesitation; then Faren's voice joined his, and he felt the packsong agree. Their direction barely changed, but they ran with desperate purpose. The line of caves, the base of the ridge—the wolves tore through the brush.

The gray voices swelled. *Wolfwalkerwolfwalkerwolfwalker . . .* The worry in the packsong was thick. There was more than one pack running now. Talon smelled wolf musk and the raw sap of broken branches.

The rustling grew, and Talon knew suddenly that the sound was in his ears, not the wolves'.

For an instant, the forest became eerily silent.

"They are here," he breathed to the others.

XXX

Talon Drovic neVolen

Moving when you know it will kill you;
Staying still when you know you will perish;
The pain of the moment to gain the future;
Silence when you know you must shout;
Your living self given into another man;
Absolute surrender.

   —Answer to the fifth Riddle of the Ages

A hundred meters away, the forest crawled with movement. Gray Faren twitched with the instinct to run, and Talon hauled her close by her scruff. She nearly bit off his wrist. *Keep still!* he ordered sharply. He forced her head under his arm so that he protected her face, breaking the link between them. She trembled with the force of his voice. *No matter what happens, keep still.* He knew she could hear him. He curled as much as possible and ducked his head against hers, throwing his other arm around them.

Danger. Trapped. Heartbeat. Fear. Gray Faren's voice was a snarl. Her jaw pressed against his neck. Her breath was hot on his flesh. It suddenly occurred to him that having a wild wolf at his throat was not, perhaps, the best positioning.

They came with a shushing sound.

At first, it was barely a breeze. Like a cat's paw across the water, the front of the wave rippled through leaves. Gray Faren jerked with the instinct to run. Talon's fist savagely clenched her fur. *Remain still,* he snarled. *Stay with me. Stay alive.*

The gray wolf flattened in fear.

"Talon," Oroan breathed.

"Trust me," he snapped, barely audibly. "And keep quiet."

Branches whipped in the canopy. He sensed movement overhead. To his left, a dnu snorted and shifted. Instantly the air seemed charged. There was a violent sound in the trees; then the skates dove like arrows. The dnu screamed as teeth bit into its flesh. It was covered by skates in seconds. Panicked, the riding beast struggled against the hobbles. The movement incensed the skates. They swarmed over the camp, biting and clawing anything on which they landed. Dnu screamed. One broke free as the skates chewed through rope as well as flesh. It managed to lurch to its feet and bolt away, its sides covered in dark shapes that writhed and tore at its flesh. Other dnu jerked and thrashed. Blood spattered as the skates hit an artery. Talon saw it in his mind as a line of red heat.

A six-legged skate brushed over his arm, its flattened back spread out to clench its prey. Talon blocked off his mind. It clung for a second to tear at his sleeve, then leaped away. The skate that landed after it bit him. Savage little teeth tore into his flesh. He cried out in his mind. Wolves howled. A swarm flooded through his thoughts. Black skies, black ground, black blood was in his mind. Bodies and debris strewn in the grass, the heart-grinding wait while the swarm cleared the skies—the lupine memories beat at him like lepa. Some distant part of him recognized the meadow as if he had ridden through it, some other part latched onto those thoughts like an anchor.

Leader! Gray Faren howled.

Silence, he snapped viciously back. He locked his body in place and forced himself not to move.

The skate emitted a high-pitched whine and leapt away. The one after that bit down harder.

Dion froze. Pain burst in her arm. She couldn't move, couldn't throw back the sleeping bag, couldn't breathe.

Rhom stiffened midstep. His hand clutched his left arm.

Gamon's throat worked to force out the hoarse word. "Rhom?"

Rhom couldn't answer.

* * *

Talon bit back at the pack with the pain in his mind and the control it took to remain still. Around him—in his mind—wolves flattened and crawled under logs. Some made it to the caves and huddled in the back against rough stone, their noses clogged with the old odors of the lepa. The trees writhed. The skates flooded past overhead. Wolves froze with the force of his will.

Here, there—he could not see the danger. His mind was clouded with shafts of pain, with voices, with lupine gray. He clenched the wolf and stayed pinched beneath the log. A skate chewed on his leg—he could feel the claws pricking his flesh. It abandoned him so abruptly that cold air seemed to bite in its place. Another used his shoulder for a jumping-off point, while the one after it clung to his hip.

Only one dnu was still screaming, and its voice choked as the skates tore its throat.

Still. Remain still. Keep still. Still as stone. The words were a litany. He held his breath as another skate explored the wound in his leg. Held it as one landed like a slap on his head. Six legs dug into his scalp as it lunged away, and Talon took a careful, shallow breath. Cold. Like ice. No stone. No pain. A skate landed on Gray Faren, and Talon forced his mind to the wolf's.

Still, he commanded. *Like earth. Like stone.*

The skate leaped away. Then there were only the sounds of the six-legged skates feeding on the dnu: Sloppy tearing sounds, raw strips of flesh dragged through humus, a thud where a head hit the ground. Talon breathed with imperceptible breaths.

The rustling grew overhead again. Another breath, and another. Gray Faren howled without cease in his mind, and he no longer bothered to hush her. Five breaths, ten—and the forest shook with movement. Then it swept away.

He lay for long moments, listening to the receding wave. A dnu gasped as it bled out on the ground. His blood throbbed out over his arm. He did not move to stanch it. Nearby, a branch whipped with the passing of the last skate. The raiders remained still and silent.

Talon breathed. Twice, ten times, and ten times that. His ears strained through the wolves, and he knew that the other Gray Ones were on the edge of the swarm. Minutes passed, and through Faren, he felt the last of the skates. Only then did he raise his head. He glanced around counting dnu, closed his mind to the blood and meat smells, and eyed the canopy. He released Gray Faren, and she scrambled away. She glared balefully at him before fleeing.

Slowly, he eased out from beneath the log, then to a sitting position. Nothing swung back toward the clearing. "Clear," he said softly.

"Is that it?" Oroan's voice was muffled.

Talon glanced after the wolf. "There is no other movement."

Dion took a ragged breath. Her fists were still clenched, the right around the left. She could still feel the talons that had torn her back, her legs, hips, arms. Could still feel the savage bite of teeth in her right arm, and knew that that had not been memory. It was someone else's pain in the packsong, not hers from months ago. It was both familiar and strange. He'd had the strength of will to keep from moving as it happened. Her own limbs shuddered as she unfroze from the force of his Call. Then the voices faded, the gray fog subtly smoothed again.

The wolfwalker stared out at the sky and felt her eyes begin to burn. For a moment, she didn't understand. Then the tears blinded her. She rubbed at her hand and whispered the name of her mate. The packsong echoed the sound, but it didn't reach far enough to the moons to bring back what she had lost. It had been a swarm that had torn her body, killed her son. Had she been able to reach the caves, as the hunter had just directed the wolves to safety, her son would not have died. Her fault, she knew. She had not been fast enough to outrun the swarm of birdbeast lepa, had not had enough strength to hurl her child inside the cave to safety, had not had enough power to fight the lepa. She almost raged with power now. It steeled something in her to know that.

She reached for the tendrils of fear that still echoed in the pack. *He* was there behind it. She could feel his presence growing, feel it closing in. And he could feel her more clearly now, feel the power she carried. He wanted it like life. She could almost feel his hands reach out for her to assuage his agony. She clenched and unclenched her hands. They still threatened to cramp, and that too was from the hunter. He had courage, that man, to face such pain each day. The Gray Ones shielded him—she had felt the wild ones pull the knowledge of such shielding from her days ago. But even with the wolves, he felt the pain; he simply worked around it. She admitted to admiration. It was a lesson she had learned too well: feel pain, face pain, beat pain.

The gray din shivered around her in the night. She smiled faintly at it. It was no longer strong—most of the wolves would be gone by morning, and it had no subtlety. But she would give the gray wolves what they wanted. She owed them that and more. They had saved her life and the lives of others too many times to count. So she would find the hunter and face him. Release him from his pain. And then . . . She forced her hands to relax. "It will be time," she whispered to the night. "To find my heart again."

Rhom shook his head at the older man. "It is nothing," he said finally, his voice hoarse and cracked as Gamon's. "It wasn't Dion."

"You froze like a rock."

"She felt—" Rhom broke off, unable to explain the sensations that were not real sensations. He shrugged.

Gamon regarded him carefully out of red-rimmed eyes, then nodded. They trudged on in the dark.

"Report," Talon said curtly as he rose. "Sojourn."

The slender man poked his head warily out of his shredded sleeping bag. Seeing Talon standing, he gripped his right arm to slow the blood and returned, "One wound, right arm. Superficial."

"Mal." Talon stepped over the limbs of one of the dead dnu. There was no need to check for a pulse. The head and throat were missing.

Mal sat up and shivered as he saw what was left of the dnu. "Hundred percent," he said unsteadily. "The dnu?"

"Two missing, three dead, and Oroan's—over there—is dying," Talon returned. Three were untouched and alive. One of the moons gave poor light through a thin spot in the clouds, and it was just enough to see by so that he stumbled over, instead of fell on, the head of the decapitated dnu. The skull had been stripped down to bone; there were no tissues left except a jellied mass that had once been the riding beast's brain. He edged around it and went to the next creature. "Dangyon," he said.

"Two wounds, left leg, one deep."

"Mal, help him," Talon ordered. He listened to the list as the raiders gingerly disentangled themselves from their shelters and began gathering the gear. He was barely finished examining the last dead dnu when Gray Faren and Paksh crept back into his mind. He did not have to look into the shadows to see the two females. Their yellow eyes seemed to gleam. The scent of fresh meat had drawn them back—the younger wolf, Faren, was pleased that she had brought the bounty to her elders. Paksh, with her torn ear and ragged coat, seemed to reach out to Talon more clearly.

The hunt was bloody, fresh.

Aye. He could feel the hunger in her belly. He crouched as if he were looking for something so that the other raiders would not notice. When he turned his head to meet her gaze, the shock of the meeting made him stiffen. His vision was doubled, but was sharper than before. He could see his own pulse in his throat—and although he knew that was more the image of his heartbeat through the packsong than the actual sight of his pulse in the dark, the drumming made him tense up. The wild wolfsong was a primitive chaos to his senses.

He tried to focus a single thought on the image of the skates: *Are there any more to come?*

The impression the older wolf returned was without fear—of eagerness and hunger instead. He gestured toward the dnu carcass, and the two wolves crept warily forward but did not approach completely. He knew they waited for him to tear his own meal out of the flesh first. *Take what you want,* he told them flatly. *I have already eaten.* He backed quietly away.

They needed no more urging. As soon as he was a few meters back, they were on the riding beast's carcass.

"Talon?" Roc called sharply as she heard the unmistakable sound of raw meat tearing. The wild wolves stopped instantly and fled. Roc started through the brush, her bow in her hands, with Harare and Wakje beside her.

"No," Talon snapped. "Do not approach. I am fine. There is no danger."

Roc froze. Wakje and Harare peered into the dark. They could see him standing meters away from a carcass. All three had heard the sounds of eating, and the other raiders had alerted.

Talon held his hand up to stop them from approaching. He called out to the wolves in his mind. *Come back. We will not harm you. I will keep the other humans away.*

The words went nowhere. He had no bond to make himself heard. He tried again, making his thoughts more simple—a single focused image of prey down and hot and bloody.

Leader . . . The sense of the response was faint—more an image of accepting him than the word of his leadership.

He reached out with all his mental will, and his voice seemed to echo on. *Wolfwalkerwolfwalkerwolfwalker* . . . The need, over and over, for the wolves, for the gray, for the eyes in the dark . . . The wolves howled at his stretching out, as if they could match it with their own needs. *East, run, hunt, the prey, danger, cold, cold* . . . The sequence pierced his thoughts until he lost his focus and retreated to his own mind.

He was shaken. His body was taut like his mind, and he could not afford the convulsions. He took a deep breath to steady himself, then turned to the other raiders.

"Leave this area alone," he directed. "The only dnu that survived are over there. Roc, help me with that one." He pointed.

Two saddles were torn, but not so badly they could not still be used. Three saddlebags were shredded, their contents strewn. Ki ran his fingers around the teeth marks left in his metal mug. "Moons-damned skates," he muttered. He kicked at an open pack, then stooped to deal with what was left of his clothes.

Roc moved up beside Talon to study the beast in the dark. It was still hobbled into its sleeping position, but its eyes were wild, and the creature snorted unevenly with half grunts and chirps. The woman began humming, her voice a soothing four-note croon that simply played over and over again. Lilting technique, perfect tone, a beautifully slow vibrato— she could have been a ringsinger in any city she chose, but instead, she used her voice as a weapon. Beautiful face, lithe body, and that lilting, lovely voice . . . Even knowing what she had done in the past to her victims, Talon was beginning to be lulled by the sounds. He crouched beside the dnu and ran his hands over its body, checking for wounds and soothing it with his touch. "There's a small bite here, but nothing that will slow it down."

Roc added words to her croon so that they could speak while she calmed the riding beast. "I found no wounds on this side."

He stroked the dnu's head, letting it get used to the motion before he began running his hands toward the hobble ring. The dnu snorted as his hand came near its nose, but it began to calm again as he simply repeated the motion to Roc's gentle croon.

"It's been a long time since you touched me like that."

"I've had other things on my mind."

She let her hands run along the dnu's legs until she could reach the hobble. "I was on your mind before," she crooned.

He raised his eyebrows. "I've seen what you do to men who have you on their mind."

"Men, yes. But you're not some weak county rider. You're strong, hard—like Drovic. One of us." She smiled, and in the dark, the expression was not nice. "Besides, I've never done those things to you."

He glanced at her face and felt nothing inside. "Not yet," he agreed.

She nodded at him to warn him that she was slipping the hobble knot. "You know, Talon, you should think about our future—"

It was all she got out before the taut dnu, realizing it was free, grunted, jerked its head up, and struggled to its feet. Talon was thrown back; Roc was dragged up. He barely grabbed the halter again before he was dragged forward with Roc through the brush. The dnu thrashed against the small trees, crushing Talon for a moment between its ribs and the saplings. His breath went out with an *oomph*.

"Moonwormed masa bait," Roc cursed from the other side. "Dung-ridden piece of a poolah's ass—"

Talon didn't blame her language. He would have cursed, too, but he was still gasping for air as the dnu lunged, bucked, and pulled them through the growth like empty botas on a string. They were both cursing by the time they brought the beast under control.

To their left, Wakje and Weed were having the same trouble with the second dnu, and the third was not even un-hobbled. Talon dodged a kick from the dnu's middle leg, rapped the beast on its neck hump, and caught his breath only to find Roc grinning at him. He grinned back automatically.

She reached for his hand under the dnu's neck. Her flesh was hot and sticky with dnu sweat and grime. Her voice was soft. "Talon, we should talk about our future." She paused to judge his reaction. When he didn't respond, she added, "I am not unattractive, and you found pleasure with me before. We could have kum-kala, not just kum-jan." Even in the dark, she saw his face become expressionless as she mentioned sex as if they were Promised instead of sex between friends. Her voice flattened. "Drovic would not disapprove."

Talon's eyes narrowed. No, his father would not disap-prove of her—not as a raider. She was hard and effective, beautiful, pleasure-skilled, and intelligent enough to know when to push a man forward instead of holding him back. She might turn on others like a lepa in a swarm, but she would re-spect Talon because, like his father, the strength of his will could subdue her. Talon studied her without speaking. Some part of his brain analyzed her words, noting the emphasis on his father. Some other part wondered at the way she proposed the Promising between them, as if it was need, not greed, that prompted her. But this was the woman who had cut the tongue out of a singing instructor for telling her that her diction was poor, who had slaughtered her cousin's mate in front of the man after severing the man's spinal cord. Who had caught a ringsinger once and torn out his throat with her bare hands, then laughed and licked his flavor from her fingers. Talon removed his hand from under hers. Those soulful brown eyes, that creamy skin, and the voice that could drown a man—they were the crystallized shell of a woman. There was only a worlag inside.

To the side, Gray Faren began to growl low in her throat, almost inaudibly, as she echoed his rejection of Roc. Unbidden, his hand rose to his chest to press against his sternum. Like Gray Ursh and Paksh, he had once been mated. He didn't need his memories for that: he had never had the two gems removed that studded his sternum. He touched them possessively. They were his: his memory, his mate. He fought for the images. Others rose instead. A girl, a boy, a dozen others who died from blood-blackened steel. He had lost his sons, his family, his county, his mate. In the gray, with the strength of the wolf-woman's needs, with the relentless gray, with the power she seemed to control, the woman in the packsong was a taunt of what he had lost.

Like humans, few Gray Ones mated for life. Those wolves who did seemed to become one creature instead of a simple pairing that would last ten or fifteen years. In the packsong, the permanent bond would blend their voices so that they could not be separated. That was the kum-tai, the eternal bond. It was what he and his mate had achieved. Kum-jan between friends, kum-kala between Promised, kum-vani between mates; but the forever bond, that was different. It was not love—love was emotion and need and passion entwined like poison masa. Love devoured and strengthened itself, but in the end, it was not enough. The forever bond was utter trust. It balanced one love with another, one need with another, until each person was perfect and whole. He had had that once, that blend in which even anger could be perfect.

His hands clenched on the bridle so that the dnu stamped its feet. He looked across at the other woman. He felt nothing for her, and his reply to her was cold. "I am kum-tai." He turned the dnu away.

Roc stared at him for a moment, then hurried to catch up in the dark. "Kum-tai?" she scoffed. "Kum-tai is forever."

He did not answer.

She pressed. "In this world, as a raider, you think you can love someone like that? Your hands are bloodied as a sand-bear's. Your heart is cold. You don't even know who you are."

He shrugged and urged the dnu between the saplings.

Roc pushed after them through the brush. "You don't have a home, a mate, a county. You have nothing and no one, Talon—except me." But he barely glanced over his shoulder at her, and the woman's voice grew hard. "Does Drovic know—about this kum-tai?"

He paused. "No." He didn't know why he was so sure, but that gray-soothed clarity in his mind answered that even though he could not remember his mate, he remembered the depth of their bond. He regarded Roc, studying her body, the way she stood. She was a lepa, waiting to strike, violent in her love, desperate for a mate that she would as likely kill. He realized that he understood her even more than he did the shadow wolfwalker, and that he could use that—his understanding—as a weapon, just as Roc used her voice. It was a cold thought, and he felt his mind slip into old patterns of reaching a goal. This time, the goal was not Drovic's.

Roc held out her hand. "Talon . . ."

There was uncertainty in her plea, and her soulful eyes looked tragic, but he knew she was untouched by both. "We will speak about this later," he said quietly. He handed her the reins and moved away to help Sojourn with the last dnu.

Roc stayed where she was, staring after him. She was trembling. She had almost spoken the word that she had sworn never to use. What had begun as a game—to catch and use Drovic's son—had become something else to her. There was the same strength in Talon that she saw in Drovic, and it drew her like a skate to a flame. Drovic had seen that in her—her need to be around strength. The older man had used her himself. But the game had become real, and now she . . . needed Talon. She felt her guts twist hard. Drovic had been right.

Talon was still too Ariyen, and she hated Drovic for that—
and hated herself, for needing Talon.

She stared after the tall man with narrowed eyes until a soft
rustle marked the brush. Quickly, she led the dnu away. She
did not see the gold-rimmed, yellow, lupine eyes that watched
her from the dark.

Talon joined Sojourn to unhobble the last surviving dnu.
The two murmured in a half-humming tone to calm the
spooked beast. Even so, when the dnu's nose was free of its
feet, it kicked out at Sojourn and almost trampled Talon as it
tried to bolt. Talon barely kept his grip on the reins. "Easy," he
said sharply. "Down, boy."

The other man grabbed at the bridle. "This thing's skittish . . .
as a tree sprit. Sure there's . . . not more danger?" he managed
as he was dragged three meters through the vines.

"None that I can sense." Talon didn't bother to hedge his
words.

"Damn riding beast has the brain of a gelbug," Sojourn
cursed.

"Better than being gelbug dinners." He dodged a middle
hoof and kicked the joint of the leg from behind. The dnu
curled the leg up automatically against its segmented belly.
With the leg up, it was unable to buck, and Talon forced it to
stand fairly still. They finally soothed it enough to tether it
to a tree. The dnu's eyes were still half wild, but at least
it didn't tear the bridle apart to get free.

Sojourn brushed off his trousers. "Roc seems to have
things on her mind."

Talon sniffed the air but caught nothing other than the
marking smells from the swarming skates and the kill-scent
from the dnu. He glanced at the other man. "She has her
ideas," he said noncommittally.

Sojourn raised his eyebrows.

Talon shrugged. "Would you sleep with a lepa?"

The other man grinned. "Were I also a lepa and my mate
looked like that? Yes." In the faint light, his even teeth seemed
to gleam.

Talon chuckled low. But his voice was quiet when he answered, "But I am not a lepa, and I am kum-tai."

The other man paused, then finished brushing off his trousers. "You ride with Drovic, Talon. Your mate is no longer part of your life."

"But I am still kum-tai," Talon returned flatly. He reached over to untether the dnu. Sojourn's hand stopped him. He looked up sharply.

"Does Drovic know?"

"It is not Drovic's business."

"And Drovic's goal?" the other man asked softly.

"There is more than one way to reach a goal."

Sojourn looked into his gray eyes for a long moment. He started to say something, then stopped.

Talon nodded toward the clearing.

In silence, they finished untethering the beast and led it out of the saplings. It did not stop kicking, and for his trouble, Sojourn received a bone bruise on his thigh the size of Dangyon's fist.

The last dnu had been calmed by Wakje and Weed, so Talon and Sojourn helped gather what was left of the gear. Oroan lit a small lantern to help Dangyon search the edge of the clearing for other items that could be salvaged. The two raiders made their way around the perimeter of the brush, shaking the ferns and saplings to dislodge night spiders, while they picked up the shredded gear.

At ten minutes, Talon called a halt to the search. They repacked, distributing survival gear to their pockets and thigh bags and packing the rest on the remaining dnu. Talon tightened the straps on his own small pack and glanced around the clearing. His gray eyes were thoughtful.

Sojourn followed his gaze. "Do we wait for Kilaltian's group or move forward? It's a damn long hike to Darity."

"We can't stay here. There will be other hunters in the wake of the swarm, and these carcasses will draw everything from badgerbears to largons. On foot, our group is swarm bait." He did not mention the wounded men whose blood scent was in his nostrils. Mal's head wound had left the dour man weakened enough that he wasn't sure the man would make such a hike. Ki's left arm was still sore. Dangyon's legs would make the man grouchy as a badgerbear. Talon rubbed futilely at his own temple. His own arm was now bound with the last of the clean rags, but it throbbed as if his headache had relocated. He did not want to think of what would have happened had the convulsions hit with the swarm. Instead, he rubbed the stubble that had grown on his jaw. "Two or three kays," he said finally. "That ought to put enough distance between us and the clearing. If Darity was warned in time, they should ride back this way to find us when we don't show up in an hour."

Sojourn gestured back toward the south. "Kilaltian's group should be only three or four kays away if we cut across like Fit. If they lost dnu as we did, we should combine forces before riding forward."

"And if they managed to keep most of their riding beasts, we can ride double to reach Darity's camp." Talon caught a glimpse of Gray Paksh and forced himself to peer after the wolf.

You gather your pack.

He didn't bother to nod. There was a jumbled impression of wolves rejoining each other, of wet noses touching, of quiet snarls. The wild wolves did not send the clear thoughts he had been used to receiving. But he knew only Faren would trail him back toward Kilaltian's group. Her direction from Gray Ursh was clear, and the other wolves would wait and eat what they could from the dead dnu left behind.

The raiders looked at each other. It was Rakdi who, in his calm way, pointed out, "The clouds are still heavy. We can't see in the dark, and a light would draw worlags more quickly."

Talon met his gaze, then the eyes of the other raiders. "I can see well enough. I will know if there is any danger."

Harare shifted uncomfortably.

"Who rides?" It was Roc.

He barely glanced at the woman. "Dangyon, Mal, and Ki. The rest of us will run."

Weed caught the satisfied expression on Dangyon's face. He gave the heavy man a sour look. "You probably moved for the skates just so you could ride."

The barrel-chested man grinned, and Talon knew that Weed, as usual, was only half joking. Dangyon had extralong toes and fallen arches; the big raider would do almost anything to ride rather than walk.

"Count your blessings tonight," he tossed at the heavy man. "You'll be running with the rest of us tomorrow." It took almost ten minutes to load the dnu. Then they headed out of the clearing.

They rode at a slow trot that the runners could easily maintain, and they did not bother with caution. Without the moons, the forest was dark as a worlag's mouth, but the line of the rootroad glowed clearly. Talon kept to the middle, where the road was hardest. There was tension in his shoulders. He was close—close to danger, but it was not from worlags or skates, but from the decision that squatted in his mind like a toad. It was not a decision of where anymore, but only of when and who. Harare, Roc, and Fit—they were questions. Harare, with those unreadable blue eyes, he simply wasn't sure of. Roc and Fit were too vicious, too caught up in their own lust for violence. The rest would follow Talon. And with the power of that wolfwalker, he'd give his men the goal they lacked with Drovic, not the dream that was discarded among the other corpses they stacked.

XXXI

Talon Drovic neVolen

Bear the grudge to your grave.

—Ariyen saying

They found Fit barely a kay away. Gray Faren heard the man's dnu long before Talon did, and the wolf turned back toward the road. When Talon saw her, he whistled a stop to the men and an oncoming signal to Fit.

A moment later, the smaller man pulled up.

"Report," Talon ordered without preamble.

In the dark, the man's eyes gleamed. "I didn't make it to Kilaltian's group. I was close, but when I heard the skates in the trees, I hit the ground like a raw egg. They went right overhead—never knew I was there, but I heard screams farther west. I waited until the skates were gone, went to look. They were hit hard. They're dead."

Talon eyed him for a moment. "All of them?"

"Dnu, men. Saw someone's arm up in a tree. Didn't stay to burn what was left—worlags follow skates."

The other raiders muttered, but Talon was silent. He felt the cold distance of death, and his thoughts raced. "How far away were they?"

"Just over a kay from where I stopped. Hard to tell in the dark."

Talon nodded. "Let's go," he called to the others. He turned to retrace Fit's path.

The knifeman was startled. "Talon—" he urged his dnu after the tall man. "It was a bloodbath, Talon. There's nothing left but the scavengers."

Talon paused, his gaze suddenly sharp. Beside him, Rakdi rubbed his nose absently but studied the smaller man with an intensity that made Talon's gaze narrow farther. "I want to see for myself."

Fit shouldered his dnu in Talon's path. "And I tell you, they're dead. It's a swarm year, Talon, and worlags follow skates. You take us over there, and you're taking us directly into their path."

Talon eyed him silently, then signaled the forward ride. Fit stared after him, then turned angrily into the group.

Talon didn't need Gray Faren to warn him of the camp. The smell of wood smoke hit him on a lift of breeze, and the flickering light on the tree trunks showed the leftover presence of sloppy fires. From behind him, he heard Wakje swear. It was futile to breathe shallowly as he jogged, but like the others, he couldn't help trying to keep the odors out of his nose.

Talon ignored the startled rustling of small scavengers. Kilaltian must have seen some of the beetle signs, and thought the swarm would be rasts. Instead, the fires had drawn the skates like a magnet. Talon forced himself to breathe. With this stench, it was only a matter of time before the worlags found the camp, and the poolah and badgerbear followed.

"By the moons." It was Weed. The raider halted and rubbed at his bunched-up ear, then belatedly began jogging again to keep ahead of the dnu. Talon was not surprised at the sight of the camp. With the blood scent thick in Gray Faren's mind, he had already known that at least some of Fit's words were true.

The darkness closed around the clearing like a murderer. A wide pit of sticks still smoldered in the middle of the wreckage. It had been a hasty fire; most of the wood was un-burned, scattered, and now darkened with body fluids. A few coals glowed orange-black where thicker sticks had been half consumed in the heart. A human body—he thought it was mousy Ilandin—lay partly in the fire pit; Sojourn dragged what was left of the woman free of the crackling fire. Three dead skates tumbled from her body. The odor of roasting, bloodied meat was sickening in their guts.

Talon felt icily calm as he studied the clearing. Dnu and human carcasses were so torn apart that it was difficult to tell where one body ended and another began. If there was any usable gear still left in the clearing, he could not see it. It would take an hour or more of sifting and sorting to find out what could be salvaged. If there were any dnu left alive, he'd be more than surprised. He stepped forward, slipped on something, and looked down. The mud was made of blood.

Behind him, the raiders dismounted. Talon's nostrils flared; the wind clogged his lungs with odors. His hand trembled, and he clenched it.

Rakdi kicked at a shredded saddlebag. "Damn fools to build a fire."

Oroan's voice was as soft. "How would they have known? Unless Talon could have used the wolves to warn them—"

Talon turned on her savagely. He forced the words out through clenched teeth. "I . . . am . . . not . . . a . . . wolf-walker. I sent Fit to warn them—" His voice broke off. "A kay to meet Fit; a kay beyond that to the camp." He twisted to stare at the knifeman. "Twenty minutes before they hit us— there was plenty of time to reach them. At a gallop, there was time enough to warn them, settle them, and even start back before the swarm hit the camp."

In the dull light from the leftover fire, Fit's skin seemed to sweat, but the smaller man's words were steady. "I didn't gallop. Couldn't see the road well enough. You know my night sight's not good."

"The rootroads glowed well enough for us."

"Part of the way was trail."

Talon's balance shifted subtly onto the balls of his feet. Fit caught the movement and said quickly, "I'm not you, Talon, and I didn't have the wolves for a guide."

In Talon's jaw, a muscle jumped. Oroan and Rakdi saw it, and almost without volition moved subtly away from the man. Talon could feel the tendrils of gray stretching into his brain. He studied Fit and tasted the knifeman's smell. It wasn't fresh scent, but sweat scent and fear scent. "You feel no guilt, do you?"

The other man eyed him warily. "Isn't my fault they were stupid."

"No," Talon agreed. "Not your fault. Just your directions. You told them to build the fire. Told them the swarm would be rasts, not skates."

Fit did not blink. "You'd have a hard time proving that to Drovic."

"Ah." Talon took a step forward. "But it is not my father who stands here."

"You should be grateful, Talon." Fit nodded at his narrowed eyes. "You lost half your enemies here. Had he lived, Kilaltian would have cut your throat."

"In a blue moon."

"In a heartbeat," Fit snarled suddenly. "He had orders from Drovic himself. Moonworms, *I* was supposed to kill you if you tried to act against Drovic—if you tried to leave the group. I saved your life with this."

Talon swallowed his fury and turned it to ice, holding it so that it fed his strength instead of the rising wildness that echoed to him from the wolves. "You saved nothing," he snapped. "If you think I will take your word over my father's—"

"You think Drovic trusts you?" Fit shook his head, the movement designed to take attention away from the hand that crept to the knife. But Talon dropped his own hand to his blade. Fit's eyes gleamed at the obviousness of the gesture. The man's voice was oily and low. "Drovic is testing you, Talon—testing you to find out if you'll be loyal when he's out of sight. And he was right. You're going to turn. Going to take his men and ride off on your own. But you're a brain-dead gelbug if you think you'll ride away free. He has a hundred raiders in Ramaj Nadugur to draw on if you take these few with you."

"Nadugur—" Talon broke off. He took a half step forward, and Fit maneuvered subtly so that the fire played into Talon's eyes.

"You didn't know that, did you? Drovic's son—so educated, so skilled, and still blind as a babe. Your father has been collecting raiders for over thirty years. You're just his latest prize."

"His figurehead."

"For the moment, until he gets a better one. But you could take that position and make it one of power. As Dangyon would say, 'Trade up.' "

Talon's voice was soft as dust. "You killed six men and women for my . . . benefit, and you think that I should thank you."

Fit realized that the expressionlessness in Talon's eyes was not acceptance. He laughed uneasily. "I gave you the freedom you wanted. I've seen the way you chafe under Drovic. I've seen how you disagree." The smaller man grinned as he eased toward Talon's weak side. He gestured with his chin at the carnage. "Better them than you, wouldn't you say?"

"And this way, you take your revenge on Kilaltian, and pay me back as well. So for one man's grudge, half a dozen die." His voice was savagely cold.

"I've got no grudge against you—"

"That dog won't hunt, Fit. The girl at the farm—Kilaltian

pulled you off her, and I caught your expression when you saw her later in my tunic after I kicked you out of the loft."

"She was a loose little farm bitch. She wasn't worth your time."

"But you wanted her."

"I always want them. I take them when I can get them."

"And you thought I had her instead. This way, you take out Kilaltian and lay the blame on me, because we rode into swarm country under my direction."

The smaller man did not bother to deny it. "There aren't so many of us here unwounded and able that you can afford to kill me just to ease your own conscience." Dangyon murmured a soft oath, and Fit's face hardened. "I know the north part of Bilocctar and Eilif better than my own heart. Look at them—they're all from the far west counties. Not one of them knows the trails here—" The man broke off as Talon slowly shook his head. His voice took on an edge. "I did you a favor here. I'm one of your own men—"

Talon regarded him silently. "You could never be one of mine." He feinted before he finished speaking. The timing almost caught Fit unawares. The smaller man danced back, but a line of red welled out on the man's arm. Fit did not glance down, but his eyes were suddenly dangerous. "I'm better than you with a knife, county boy. This time, you've bitten a lepa."

Talon circled warily. " 'Better' doesn't mean 'winner.' "

"Always has." The smaller man feinted in. His knife glinted in the dull light. It flashed and shifted as soon as Talon could see it. This time, it was Talon who felt the heat of blood. He did not yet feel the cut—the edges were too cleanly sliced, but it stung a moment later as the sweat and grit were rubbed across it by his sleeve.

They didn't waste breath on words. Instead, the fight was eerily silent, punctuated only by the scuffing of their boots in the blood-soaked ground. Both men feinted in, danced back, measuring their movements—and both men made their targets. Talon twisted as if he slipped; Fit darted in. Talon's knife flicked; Fit warded, punched Talon in the ribs. Talon caught Fit's shoulder and threw the man in the fire. Fit rolled out without screaming, and took a brand with him. He threw it; Talon dodged, and the men behind them scattered as the coals broke free among them. The two men rushed each other in the firelight. Wolf eyes caught the balance point. Talon suddenly dropped and blocked, but it was his left hand, and it was weak. Fit caught him just above the knee and cut another line. Talon made no sound as he slashed the side of the other man's arm and cut back as Fit tried to hamstring him. They scrambled apart. Fit's knife was now in his other hand. Both men now bled freely.

Talon slowly grinned. He felt the weakness in his leg, felt the blood well out like a stream. He ignored it. Instead, he began stalking the other man, slowly, steadily, like a cat creeping toward a sprit.

Fit backed away. Even in the moonlight, there was something in Talon's eyes. The tall man wasn't a wolfwalker, but there was something not quite human in that gray, icy gaze. Fit felt his heart pound, felt the sting of his own sweat in his wounds. He backed away another step, circling the fire. "Talon," he said quickly. "Let's talk. You're bleeding like a waterfall. All I have to do is stay out of reach another couple of minutes. You know I don't carry a grudge past the payback. It's over, as far as I'm concerned. We can end it here."

Talon cut him off from the fire so that the light now flickered in Fit's eyes.

"You're already weaker—I can see it. They won't help you." Fit indicated the others.

Talon did not answer. The gash in his leg looked worse than it was, and his rage was strong enough to carry him however long it took. He smiled. His silence was unnerving.

Fit lunged suddenly as Talon went midstep. But the tall man had not truly shifted his balance. He parried out hard, caught the man's arm, stepped in, and yanked it back in a sharp bend. Fit gutted himself with his own blade. The knifeman gasped. Talon cradled the smaller man, locking the steel in Fit's body. Slowly, he laid Fit on the ground, keeping his grip tight. The other man convulsed. Gasped raggedly. Tried to curse. And died with his mouth hanging open.

Talon pulled the blade free, wiped it on the one fairly clean side of Fit's jerkin, and got to his feet. "Bandages," he said flatly to Ki.

The silky-haired man got them out, tossed them over. Talon bound his own leg. None of the other raiders moved. It was an odd silence, as if they were only now realizing that Talon had taken control. With Kilaltian's group gone, with Fit dead, almost everyone left had some sort of debt to Talon.

Rakdi rubbed the side of his hook nose. Weed picked at a loose thread on his sleeve, and Dangyon rocked absently back and forth on his heels as the barrel-chested man considered, and considering, discovered some truths.

Talon finished bandaging his leg and straightened. With all the bandages around his biceps, forearm, thigh, and calf, he looked like a beaten refugee. He shrugged back into his tunic.

Movement. Blood scent moving.

Instantly, Talon became alert. He held up his hand, and the others stiffened, their ears straining for sound as they brought up their bows. Talon half turned till he faced the sound, but he kept his head cocked to the side so that he did not look directly at it. Yes, there was movement. Something rising from the ferns. No one shot—it was too easy to shoot high in the dark, as the mind had no clear reference for size.

Man scent, blood scent. The hunter.

It was Kilaltian who moved into the light and then leaned casually on his sword. Talon's gray eyes narrowed. There was blood on Kilaltian's arms. Ki lowered his ready bow and started to speak, but Sojourn stilled him.

"Talon," Kilaltian said. The man's voice was flat, but Talon did not mistake that expressionlessness for calm. His nerves started to tingle.

Blood scent. Challenge. Lunge.

He twitched with the need to leap forward. He remained still with an icy strength. "Kilaltian," he returned softly.

The other man moved slowly toward the fire. "I didn't think you'd bother to come. Not after sending Fit." He leaned on his sword at the edge of the firelight, but Talon was not deceived. Kilaltian's stance was too casual for the rage that burned in his eyes.

"He was the duty rider," Talon said carefully.

"And he bore a grudge."

"He's never killed one of us before."

"And how long have you really known him?" Kilaltian bit the words out. "You're as ignorant of him as you are of yourself."

"He seemed to be doing his job."

"Oh, aye, and a good job it was. He reached us, all right, but he said the swarm was of rasts, not skates. Told us to build a fire, to make noise, that you had been warned by the wolves. We've all seen the signs, son of Drovic. We believed enough to obey you. So we built the fire as fast as we could—high flames, lots of twigs. But we needed wood, and you never saw a more motionless bunch of moon-licking cowards when I told them to go out and get it. So I went. Found a log that could have held us half the night. And while I was out, they hit us. Skates," the man spat. "Not rasts. Ebi, Strapel, Al— they're all dead. Nortun, Ilandin—" His voice cracked hard. "Gone," he snarled. "Every one of them torn apart while I listened to the screams."

"Once it had started, you couldn't have stopped it," Talon said softly.

"No," Kilaltian agreed. He stared at Talon. "But you could have." He lunged, his weight already shifted to the balls of his feet.

But Talon had the wolves behind his eyes, and he dodged easily around the fire. The others backed away, giving the two men room. Like dogs, they watched without moving while Kilaltian glowered and circled and Talon shifted away. The other man was fast—if his wounds slowed him down at all, it didn't show, and as Talon's rage had done before, Kilaltian's fury more than made up for any weakness.

Talon danced back as Kilaltian feinted and leaped in. "Fit is dead. We don't have to fight. He's already paid for his actions—"

"He's not dead enough until you join him, sap-blooded spawn of a gelbug—"

Talon parried another lunge, leaping lightly back. "I will kill you if I have to," he warned.

"You're confident for a man who, two months ago, couldn't hold his own sword with two hands." The man gestured with his blade, "For a man with a leg like that, you've—"

Talon's gaze almost flickered. Kilaltian took the instant to lunge again. Talon beat-parried hard to move inside the other man's reach. He palm-struck Kilaltian hard in the sternum, and Kilaltian staggered back. Talon snapped, "We don't have to do this,"

"Talk your life away, Talon. It's to my advantage."

This time, Talon didn't bother to answer. When Kilaltian lunged in, Talon closed, and realized instantly that it had been a mistake. The blood that covered Kilaltian's arms was not from the raider's own wounds. The man's knife sliced through Talon's sleeve just above the bandage. Talon parried so narrowly that the flat of the blade slid along his skin. He jumped back, stumbled, then twisted into a side roll as Kilaltian leaped forward. A flap of cloth fluttered down behind Talon, slashed from his tunic. Kilaltian caught his balance and turned as Talon lunged back. The man parried high, trying to lead Talon into an opening. Instead, Talon actually dropped his sword and grabbed the other man's wrist. There were wolves in his arms like a sea of energy waiting to tear through bone. Talon saw the shock in Kilaltian's eyes as the man felt Talon's strength. Saw the fear of comprehension. Talon headbutted the other man in the nose and pulled his knife. Bone cracked. In his grip, Kilaltian's wrist snapped like a stick. The man's face went chalk white, and in the instant that Talon felt the sound, he let go his block of the other man's knife and shoved his own through the heart.

Kilaltian's knees collapsed. His weight came down hard in Talon's arms. Talon let him fall free.

For a long moment, he stared at the raider. There were no death convulsions, no gasping, no fluttering of blood. Only a lessening of life that finally ended in night.

Talon went to one knee by the body, breathing heavily.

For a moment, there was silence. The dancing light on the trunks of the trees, the stench of cooking flesh. Finally, Sojourn stepped forward and nudged Kilaltian's body with his boot. "What will you tell your father?"

Talon ran his hand through his sweat-matted hair and straightened to his feet. He stared down at the body. "He attacked, as was his right." He looked up and met the other man's gaze. "I killed him—as was mine."

Sojourn shifted uncomfortably, but nodded his agreement.

Roc watched Talon like a wolf. "And how many others will you kill?"

Talon gave her a long, steady look. "As many as stand in my way."

Rakdi's voice was dry. "That, at least, will please your father."

XXXII

Ember Dione maMarin

Control your destiny or your fate will control you.

—Randonnen saying

Gamon glared through red-rimmed eyes. He could see it clearly, the purple-black line that marked the rise of the mountains. Two mesas and one canyon to go, and one deep-cut river they could not touch, and their dried-out bodies would drag out of the sandwormed desert.

Rhom followed Gamon's gaze with his own aching eyes. The wind was rising, chilling their day-hot skin, and he welcomed it like a lover. By dawn, they would be into Ariye. A day—no more than two—should bring them to some sort of message station or within sight of a caravan, and from there, they could take dnu again north to the Lloroi. They had angled across the desert and would arrive halfway up the county. Though Rhom appreciated the savings in distance, it had not been by choice. They had been driven north by their need for water. Rhom resisted the urge to swallow—the motion would only choke him. Instead, he lifted out his arms to catch the cold wind for a moment. By dawn, water would no longer be a consideration. And, if they didn't sleep, if they rode straight across the mountain in their way, they could reach the Lloroi's house in two days.

Rhom pressed his sand-grimy fingers under his burning eyes. The wind, the sand, the heat in the day—they combined like a hellish lotion. One touch, and he burned all the more. For all that they were in shade in the day, he felt baked as a tuber in ashes.

Gamon glanced over. Rhom nodded toward the mountains. The two men trudged ahead.

In the lamplight, Dion turned her hands over and studied the healed wounds. Her flesh was smooth again—as smooth as it could be with the old scars on the back of one hand. She wanted to clench her hand around steel, but she knew that it was not herself but the hunter who had projected that need until it became part of herself. She unbuckled her belt and laid her weapons over her pack. She had been driven by others' needs for so long. It was time to deal with her own.

"Healer?" Kiyun prompted.

She looked up. She smiled faintly in apology as she realized he had brought her a late bowl of stew from the cozar cooks. Aloof and reserved during the day, the cozar seemed to transform once the dnu stalls were assigned and the shelter was organized. Children who had remained in the wagons were let down to run and stretch their legs. Fires were started and packs moved into the passhouse.

Like the domes of the Ancients, the passhouses were built over volcanic vents. Unlike the domes, the passhouses had been no more than bored holes when the aliens brought the plague. Their walls weren't lit with the luminescent fungi that lined the domes' walls and ceilings, nor did they hum with power like the truncated, skycar mountains. The outer structure of each passhouse had been built after the plague, when technology was failing and the boring tools were breaking down. Although most of the outer walls and support pillars were smooth and beautifully arched, the inner walls were hand-built of pieced wood. Only a few stone walls were used inside. Wood was warmer, both in temperature and color. In some shelters, such as the one in Shadow Pass in Randonnen, the inner pillars placed by the Ancients were carved with stories from the county. Here, they were polished like glass.

Outside were courtyards, stone benches, and massive fire pits, the latter to allow for standing watch in summer and for providing a beacon to laggards. The deep flower boxes along the southern exposure still held the late blooms of white daisy and arcanthum. Dion could smell the scents even at night, when the flowers collapsed and exuded the sticky coating that protected them from the cold. At the other end of the passhouse was the message mirror for communicating with arriving trains. A few rare passhouses—two in Kiaskari and one in Nadugur—held a telescope like the domes; others made do with message mirrors. Out of habit, Kiyun checked the mirror, and found that his counterpart among the cozar was doing the same. They nodded silently to each other as they examined the mirror mounts and surface for damage before covering it again.

Outside the door of the room assigned to them, the cozar had chalked the symbol for "guest" on the room's message board, and Dion and the others had settled in without comment while they waited for their turn at the kitchen. The other group of three guests had bedded down in the farthest hall, which had surprised Dion at first. The three had an air about them that was cold and dangerous. She had overheard the children whispering that the three men were raiders. Dion's hand had gone to her knife, then had fallen away. It was a child's rumor, she told herself.

The windows of her room showed three of the nine moons in the half-cleared sky, and Tehena balancing her stew bowl as she entered. "You'd think the Ancients would have built more of these places before kicking off," the woman said to Kiyun's back. She set the bowl on one of the two tables and dragged over a chair. "Last night was cold as a killer's knife, and watching those cozar snuggle up in their wagons made me sweat with jealousy."

Kiyun set his own bowl down on the table and joined her. "You could always try a night in one of the Ancients' domes."

Tehena snorted. "And have plague for dinner, as well as stew? Dion would love healing that out of us." Dion's spoon paused for an instant halfway to her lips. It had been a small hesitation, but Tehena noted it. The thin woman gave Dion a thoughtful look. It had been the mention of plague that had gotten Dion's attention. "Healer?" the woman started. "You've been healing with Ovousibas for years now. Have you ever seen the plague?"

Dion calmly finished her bite of stew. She looked at Tehena for a long moment, but the thin woman didn't think the healer saw her. "Yes."

"What?" Tehena couldn't help the ejaculation. "Moons, healer, I didn't expect you to answer."

Dion shrugged and returned to her stew. Trail stew, ever-the-same stew, she thought absently. When she was home, she would do better cooking.

"You've seen plague." Kiyun turned in his chair to face her. "Was it from someone who had gone to the domes, or from using the wolves for the healing?"

Tehena cast him a sharp, angry look. "The wolves who help Dion don't die."

Dion pushed her stew aside and faced them both. "We've never known how the plague survives in the dome of the Ancients. It could be through the air, in the walls, carried by some tiny, unseen creature. We just don't know. All we know is that if you go to the domes, you die of plague; and the wolves carry plague like the domes."

Kiyun nodded. "But you still use them to do the healing; you still risk bringing back the plague."

There was an unnaturally steady tone to his voice. Just as Tehena's pale gaze showed her fear, the very neutrality of Kiyun's voice showed just how much she was frightening him. He had faced raiders and worlags and countless trail dangers, but the thought of plague gave him chills. She tried to smile. "The plague in the wolves is triggered when they use Ovousibas. That was what the aliens taught the Ancients and wolves to do. The wolves did the actual Ovousibas, and the Ancients merely guided the wolves like a sledder driving his dogs. I don't do that. With me, it's not the wolves who do the Ovousibas with me as the guide. It's the other way around. I do the Ovousibas, and the wolves guide me in the technique through their memories of the Ancients. The plague in their bodies isn't triggered. The wolves merely make a bridge between me and the patient and show me what to do. They don't do any actual healing."

"Is that what your bond with the wolves is like?"

"No." Her bond with Hishn was different—intimate, complex, and deep. "The Gray Ones were engineered to be empaths, not just to offer us communication. They can make a bridge of awareness between bodies so that I can do the healing, the manipulation of the body."

"You're not a telepath," Kiyun objected.

"No. But I am a wolfwalker, and my bond with Hishn is deep enough that I understand the added awareness they offer me of my patient."

"I don't understand."

Dion got up and began to pace the bunk room. "The wolves show me how to reach the other body, and I know enough about medicine to direct that body to heal itself. The wolves are not the active force—I am, with their direction and strength. The Gray Ones act as a shield between me and the patient, so that I don't get sucked in too far to the pain or injury. And they give me the focus to use my own energies to direct that other body to heal itself."

Tehena murmured to Kiyun, "Some of the Ancients were supposed to be telepaths—it's how they communicated with the aliens to make the original pact."

Dion nodded. "But we lost those people in the plague. And now, even if any of us have those mental abilities, we don't know how to control them or strengthen them, let alone use them. Without the wolves, we would never think of those abilities as anything but instinct."

Kiyun spread his hands. "Then you are a telepath."

She gave a short laugh. "No. Moons, I wish I were. I could have saved more than a few lives with that skill in my hands. No," she repeated. "All oldEarthers had the framework for that mental ability in their minds—it's what our hunches are based on, how a mother knows that her child is in danger. How you know it will be this instant, not that one, in which the rock will fall. They played with it, the oldEarthers. Modified their genes until they created different . . . breeds of humans who could live on different worlds. Our eyes, our sense of direction, our ability to take in toxins . . . Our Ancients weren't as mutated as some of the other colonists, and they never played much with our minds. We can't focus our thoughts like telepaths, and what we have isn't strong enough to be anything more than good luck every now and then."

"But you have it more than others, and you focus that through the wolves."

Dion shook her head and stopped pacing. "I don't think the bond with the wolves is based on telepathy. I think the bond only allows us to develop what little sensitivity we have, to become more aware of the world around us. It's the wolves who do the real talking, who open the door between us. The bond itself is based on something else."

"Love."

Dion looked at Tehena in surprise. The scrawny woman had never been one to speak of the softer emotions. She touched the other woman's arm, and Tehena shrugged it off uncomfortably. "Yes, somewhat," she agreed. "There has always been an easy dependence between men and dogs, men and wolf-dogs, and even men and wolves. But I think there is still more. The Ancients seeded this world with everything they could think of before their technology failed. Peetrees, extractors, potatoes, deer . . . They gave us every opportunity to spread out, and in eight hundred and fifty years, we have never created a new county. Why is that?" she asked thoughtfully.

Tehena's pale gaze grew sharp, but Kiyun looked uncomfortable. "There are the northern territories."

"And how many live there? Twelve thousand? Twenty?" Dion shook her head. "And why are we wolfwalkers so much less interested in history and government? Have you ever met a wolfwalker who wanted to be in politics?"

"You spend more time in the forest than the towns. Why

would you want to sit with a bunch of elders who do nothing but talk for months?"

"I wouldn't," Dion said softly, "but why don't I *care* what they talk about? Even if my life is in wilderness, I should still be involved in what happens to the future of my people— human or wolf. Look at me—how blind have I been? Aranur always thought about the future."

"Are you saying that being a wolfwalker has somehow curbed your curiosity?" Tehena said sharply. "Moonworms, Dion. I've seen you poke your head into a lepa's den just to see what was inside."

"And that was wilderness."

Tehena opened her mouth, then shut it without speaking.

Dion nodded. "I think the wolves reflect needs. Ours, theirs." And the aliens', for she knew that the yellow slitted eyes had always watched the packsong. "They talk, we listen, we think, and they pick it up. It's rare—and it's difficult—to actually project our own emotions into the pack. It's their reception and reprojection that we pick up. Almost everyone needs a home, family, some sense of the future, so the wolves project that back to us, and we explore, but return to our homes."

The home, the den, the mate . . .

Dion shook off the wolves.

"And Ovousibas?" Kiyun asked.

"That's like a strong man showing a child to hammer out a sword. The man directs the hammer and provides the skill—as if his hands were wrapped around the child's, but the child actually holds the tool and strikes. The wolves are the man; I am the child. I may hold the tool, but they show me the way. If they ever died out completely, Ovousibas would be impossible."

Tehena watched her. "So you could never do it without the Gray Ones."

"No," she agreed.

"You're very certain."

Dion shrugged. "I may be able to focus at greater distances now, but I still need their minds to form the initial link to the body, and I need their strength or yours—" She nodded at Kiyun and Tehena. "—to help me work once I have that connection. The Ancients could do more, but they had their technology to help. I have only the wolves."

"Dion, this hunter you sense in the packsong . . ." Tehena hesitated. "Can he feel you clearly enough to know you do the healing?"

Dion studied Tehena for a long moment.

"Healer?"

Dion turned and stared out the window. It was frosting up from the contrast of heat and outside cold; in the sky, the moons were now covered with clouds. She stretched into that gray as if it were the packsong, but the sense of the wolves was faint as old wood. The wagons had left the Gray Ones behind at dawn, and the mental presence of the wolves was barely carried by the life left in the snow. There was no lightening to indicate the peaks behind which the sun had gone down, no strong pull to show her the hunter, but she knew. He was there behind the peaks with that dying sun, feeling for her strength, for her presence in the packsong. He had recognized the power in her hands—she was sure of it. It would be as much a lure to him as the Call of the wolves.

She rubbed her belly protectively. He might be aware of her strength, but she knew how to use it, and she had more to protect than he did. It would be a bargaining point between them. She smiled grimly. He might try to use her to find what he had lost, but she could do the same. A flash of need blinded her for a moment, and she crushed back the grief that threatened to open the void of loneliness. She could control that, control herself. She would have to, to bargain with that hunter.

XXXIII

Talon Drovic neVolen

A man knows when his feet will falter;
When it's time to change the road or the dnu;
When it's time to change the bit to a halter;
When it's time to change his tune.
It's the blind who keep on without faith.
It's the deaf who keep singing the moons.

—From "The Shadow Wolf," by Alla maRaine

In the dark, the hard-packed dirt trail toward Darity turned into the main rootroad after two kays. Kays later, they saw Darity's site up ahead by the fire line. The swarm had missed the small group, but the worlags that followed had not. The fires that would have attracted the skates had held the worlags at bay for a while, but not long enough, and the beetle-beasts had overrun the camp.

". . . another bandage," Darity snapped to Liatuad. "And keep that fire stoked."

Talon whistled softly to announce their presence, and Darity jerked his head up, then gave the night-bird, come-ahead signal. The man barely paused in bandaging Pen's leg to peer into the dark to see them. "About time," the man said harshly as they came into the light. "We could have used your swords an hour ago. What the hell took you so long?" He frowned at their paltry number of dnu. "Worlags? Where's Kilaltian?"

"Skates." Talon said absently. "Missed the worlags." He looked over the clearing and nodded to Harare, who had just straightened up from a body. The blond man's dnu was wiped down, but still stamping its feet in exhaustion—Harare must have reached them after the skates and worlags, but not by much. Talon studied the scene and did not offer to help. Beside him, Mal shifted uneasily at his silence.

Pen winced as Darity wrapped the bandage across the gash in her leg, but her wide, dark gray eyes watched Talon, not the man tending her leg. Talon noted that, just as he noted that her curly, dirty-blond hair was matted with blood on one side, and her thin chin scraped. She had never been a woman of great physical beauty, but there was enough character in that battered face to last a dozen lifetimes. It was the kind of character that would cling to the ideal, even if she could not achieve it herself—and probably why, along with her perception, Drovic had chosen her for his core group. Of them all, Pen was the most likely besides Wakje to have discovered Talon's true link with the wolves. She would be dangerous if she realized what he was doing. And she did, he suddenly saw, for her eyes, unreadable as ever, observed him like a cat. But she said nothing, and Talon filed that note away as he studied Darity.

Liatuad handed Darity a small pack and dumped his load of branches by the fire. "You got off damn lightly for skates," the thin man said sourly. He squatted down to feed in the wood, but he favored his right arm, tucking it close to his chest.

Darity gave them a closer look as he finished. "Surprised you kept any dnu."

"We heard the skates coming. Got the dnu settled down."

"Well, you can settle the shelters now. Two were torn up before they were pitched, but the other three are still in the packs."

Talon didn't move.

Mal looked at him and rubbed at his temple. "Talon?" the man asked obliquely.

Talon held up his hand to hold him. Ten dnu—six riding and four pack beasts—were corralled in a stand of saplings, and the body of the one dnu that had been killed by the worlags had been dragged out of the hollow. The rest stamped and snorted at the scents on Talon's men. Brentak lay propped up against a boulder, but would not last out the hour—no one gutted that badly could survive long, and the man was already unconscious. Thaul and Merek were dead. Liatuad, who limped away for another load of wood, looked as if his right arm was fairly useless. Darity himself had a massive bruise on his chin, but was otherwise unharmed. Darity stared at Talon as Talon didn't move. "Well?" Darity asked shortly. "You going to help or just stand around like a stickbeast? We could use more firewood, and none of the shelters are up."

Talon cocked his head, his mind racing. They were at least a day from the village where they'd meet Drovic, and his father would have to take some time to buy supplies and scout the workshops. The older man would spend the night in town—maybe two if there was something interesting to scout—surrounded by the homes of those whom he despised. Talon felt his lips thin. His father was homeless and would be so to the grave. Drovic would never build or create, no matter what goal he claimed to follow. And men such as Drovic would never regain the stars, not while skulking in the dark. Like worlags, they were: crawling, striking, racing, and fleeing. The future would have few champions when men such as they killed hope.

Wolves howled in Talon's ears, not just in his mind, and the raiders looked warily around. Talon didn't move. There was always tomorrow, the gray whispered. Always hope in the future. Talon cried out for the wolves and the woman, and his voice echoed into the gray. No words—he could not project his words—only the burning need within him.

He had become too much a killer. He needed something, someone, who could make him believe again in humanity, in the ideal that justified the blood. Follow the wolves, and he could build those ideals again. He could take their strength and certainty, take that woman with that power, take her compassion, her justice, her will. He needed that direction and the woman behind that will. A ninan, he had promised himself, flexing his wrist. He felt the pain of the skate's bite shaft up his arm and subside, the background burn of his muscles under the gray, but his mind was clear. The chance to be free was now.

"Moonworms, Talon," Darity snapped at his silence. "Did you lose your brains in the dark?"

He felt his lips stretch in a wolfish grin. "No," he said softly. "I think that I have found them." His gray eyes were like steel. "Wakje, Ki—secure the dnu."

The two glanced at him, then at each other. But both men moved to obey. Harare raised his eyebrows, and Talon nodded at the blond man. "The packs," he directed. "Danygon—the shelters. Oroan, Rakdi—the tack."

Liatuad straightened from stoking the fire as the riders fanned out. They weren't setting up the gear, but securing it, guarding it, putting it back for riding.

Darity's face was a study. "What the hell do you think you're doing?"

Talon ignored him and instead looked a silent question at Weed.

The shorter raider pulled absently at a thread on his pocket as he studied Talon, then gave him a twisted smile. "The wolves will have their way," Weed murmured. He drew his sword and faced Liatuad, Darity, and Pen.

The heavy woman got slowly to her feet, favoring her leg. Darity and Liatuad drew their swords, but Pen did not, and Darity said her name sharply. She watched Talon like a wolf, and he recognized the look in her eyes—it was the blind hope that comes from change, any change. He kept his voice quiet, as if his very mildness would keep the men from killing. "Stand down, Darity, Liatuad."

Darity's eyes narrowed. He watched Wakje and Ki position themselves between him and the dnu. "You moonwormed son of a worlag, you're going up against Drovic." He took a half step forward. "You're breaking the brotherhood—"

Talon cut him off. "It was broken months ago."

Liatuad's lips twisted. "Kilaltian will have your head even before Drovic does."

Talon didn't take his eyes off Darity. "Kilaltian is dead."

"And the others?" Liatuad asked sharply as he realized the import of that statement. "All of them?"

"Fit and the skates killed all but one. I killed Kilaltian."

Darity's hand tightened almost imperceptibly. "You scrandon," the other man hissed. "You think you can lead anyone,

the state you're in? Without the drugs, you can't even ride."
He jerked his chin at Talon's men. "You think they're loyal to
you now? They'll follow you for two days, maybe three. Then
they'll turn on you like you turned on the rest of us."

Darity almost trembled with rage, and Talon watched him
curiously. Darity would attack—he knew it. But he felt free,
invulnerable. Even knowing that not one of his riders would
stand between him and that desperate man couldn't shake
that sense of strength. It was an old feeling, the knowledge
that he would win. It was a lesson that Drovic had taught him
after he'd been beaten up by the bigger boys just after his first
martial class. Teach him a lesson—that's what the boys had
wanted to do. He had learned, and learned a lesson hard, but
not the one they had expected. Don't quit, and you can't
lose—Drovic had pounded that in as much as had those boys.
After so many decades, it was that certainty that had kept
Talon alive. He couldn't lose, couldn't go down, if he never
let himself quit. He knew his own body trembled with barely
concealed convulsions, knew that pain washed through him
constantly under the gray, knew that his wrist was still weak
and his calves were aching from the run. And knew that
Darity couldn't beat him as long as he didn't quit.

He glanced around the clearing, and even as he noted the
positions of the men who rode with him, he acknowledged
the path he would take through their bodies and who he
would kill in what order if they turned on him to follow
Darity instead.

Darity wasn't looking at anyone else. He had seen the approval of Talon in the others' eyes and knew he himself could
not sway them.

Talon turned back to the raider. Darity wasn't known for
control of his temper. The man wanted to attack. It was an almost tangible sensation.

"Worlag droppings," Darity spat at the other raiders. He
could take Talon, and the others would follow him. "Drovic
will hunt you down through all nine counties if you betray
him." *He could take him.* "He's waited thirty years for this,
and not even you—"

He lunged.

Talon saw the attack as clear as the seventh moon. Darity flicked his hand and shifted to the right as if to attack from the side—but his balance hadn't changed. Talon saw the left hand go to the knife even as he moved. He didn't bother to draw his own blade. He simply dropped, slid forward, and kicked up with brutal clarity. He caught Darity's sword hand like a sledge. The man lost the grip on his sword, but Talon continued to roll. He smashed in Darity's right knee, heard him start to scream. He lunged like an arrow to his feet. His right hand struck the knife hand away; his left hand blocked out, jerked instinctively in, and then followed into the larynx. Darity was driven back so hard that he crashed back through the branches and hit the ground choking. No one moved to help. He died with the others watching.

Liatuad's Adam's apple stuck out of his thin neck like a fist. He began cursing under his breath.

Mal eyed Liatuad and cleared his throat. "Do we wait here?" he asked finally.

Talon shook his head. "No. We ride on."

"In the dark?"

He smiled humorlessly. "I can see the way."

"To meet Drovic?" Sojourn asked.

"No. North and east."

"To Ariye." It was not quite a statement.

"To Kiaskari," he answered, surprising them. If the wolfwalker he sought was still north of Ariye, then it was north that he must first go.

"Ariye, Kiaskari—Talon, have you lost your mind?" Liatuad finally burst out. "They'd kill us at first sight."

By the dnu, Rakdi rubbed at his chin. "I'm not lining up against you, Talon, but Liatuad has a point. We *are* raiders."

Talon merely raised one dark eyebrow, and Rakdi explained gently, as if the tall man had forgotten. "We attack and steal and rape and kill, and in the end, all we hope for is a clean death so that our path to the moons is sure. The second hell, the seventh—it doesn't matter. We know where we're headed. There's no future for us that isn't steeped in blood.

Ariye, Kiaskari—either one is sure death for all of us, especially for you."

"We're raiders," Ki added. "We're nothing now in any place that matters—"

"No." Talon's voice cut like a knife, and Ki almost stepped back at his tone. "We are what we make ourselves. You want pretty speeches to convince you? I don't have them. But I've saved your lives, and you've saved mine. You can count up those favors against me to find out if you should go on with me or not, but if you do, you're nothing but debt machines, adding and subtracting life. There is another way." Talon stared at them, as if the force of his gaze alone could give them the reason to ride with him. "Accept those debts as if they were between brothers. Do that, and we define a bond worth more than life, a bond of loyalty, of trust, not simply of movement or need. I want that bond, that ideal. I want that life for myself, for all of us."

Rakdi regarded him steadily. "We're not looking to be redeemed, Talon. We'll leave that to the healers." Others nodded, but Pen and Dangyon pursed their lips as if they would have objected.

Talon stared at the ex-elder. Redemption, the affirmation of the ideal . . . He could achieve that ideal only by facing his nemesis—the wolves, the woman who locked them to him, and the county that ordered his death. His father offered another path, but not the one he wanted. His gaze narrowed at the thought of his father. What evil had Talon committed that had put such bleakness in his father's eyes? What shame had he earned that even his own mind hid its fullness? He could live in blindness forever with Drovic, protected from himself. Or he could follow the wolves and find something more. Ariye. The wolves. The woman. Himself.

He looked around the clearing, met each man's and woman's gaze. "You're not looking for redemption," he agreed flatly. "Then what are you—we—looking for? Do we really enjoy the slaughter? Do we live for worn saddles, for mud in our morning rou, for sleeping with gelbugs and as many parasites as our dnu can carry beneath us? Have you never hungered for a home, for a place to belong again? For a mate? For a son to carry your name? Aren't you tired of ducking every time you see an elder, regardless of the county? Of cowering when you hear hoofbeats, thinking that it's a venge? Of staring down your backtrail looking for a hunter or scout who's following your tracks? How long have you ridden with Drovic, killing for some unreachable goal of fighting the birdmen instead of building something that will stand on its own? My father's goal is so distant now that it's barely even words, let alone a plan or the potential of something real." He gestured savagely. "He's never ridden north to the birdmen. He never will. He's just lingering like a woman with hairworms on the last breath of revenge."

"We do stay alive with him," Rakdi said dryly.

Talon gestured at Brentak's body. "This is living? I call it running like rasts. You want that, stay with Drovic."

"You're not worth the piss he leaves behind," Liatuad snarled.

"Perhaps not," Talon agreed. "But then again, I have better things to do than to piss away my life and the lives of those who ride with me." He looked around the clearing. "Follow me or my father. Follow the moons for all I care. I am going north. And know this: if you ride with me now, it's because you want something more than endless slaughter."

Roc eyed him for a moment, then nodded slowly, and as if that broke the resistance, the others nodded in turn. Sojourn gestured with his chin at Liatuad and Pen. "Will you kill them then, too?"

Talon regarded the skinny man for a moment, and Pen, beside Liatuad, realized that the tall man was not looking at her. "There's no need," Talon answered. "I will not leave my father without a message."

Sojourn's voice was dry. "I thought Kilaltian's group was message enough."

Talon smiled without humor. He looked meaningfully at Pen. She regarded him silently, and he could not read what was in her mind. "You still have a choice," he said softly.

Pen said nothing, and Talon simply waited. She was solid,

dependable, and took forever to make up her mind, but he would not argue with her to join him. She could see what he was, where he was going. She understood the risks. Of them all, she was the most likely to settle back into a county, and the most likely to die for her choice.

Then she stepped away from Liatuad, and the skinny man grabbed her arm. "Go with him, and you're dead, Pen."

"I was dead before," she said softly. She merely eyed Liatuad until he dropped her arm.

Talon nodded to the woman and directed his words to Liatuad. "Stay or run for Drovic—I don't care. But follow us, and I'll kill you." The skinny man gave him a hard look, then started for his dnu, but Talon stopped him. "The dnu are ours."

"My arm is useless; my calf is split like a tuber. A man by himself on a swarm night like this is blooded worlag bait."

Talon merely shrugged. "You chose. Now live with the choice." He glanced around at the others. "Mount up," he said. "We ride."

They left Liatuad with the dead.

XXXIV

Ember Dione maMarin

Whither goes your heart?
If it travels on need alone, it is lost.
Whither goes your courage?
If it runs on pride alone, it is nothing.
Whither goes your life?
If it has no goal, it has already ended;
   And you are already dead.

   —From "Jumping the Abyss,"
     by Syal Mortel, Randonnen elder, 452 A.L.

Without the constant din of the wolves in her head, Dion found herself restless. The evening had been boisterous until night's call, when the children and most of the adults went to bed. Now the night was quiet.

A group of men still stood around the courtyard fire telling stories and discussing the odd bit of philosophy. Dion paced one of the courtyards, then strode out into the snow on the moonlit slope, only to stand in an open expanse, staring at the cold moons. It was the hunter, she realized. Her thoughts revolved around him, but she could feel barely a thread of him in the near-silent packsong. He had been part of her uneasiness long enough that his absence was almost as painful as his presence.

The knot of men by the fire pit welcomed her silently. One of the others was there—one of the three men who rode separately, and he looked as dark and dangerous up close as he had on his dnu. He nodded to her, and she did not realize that her own wariness matched his—that they watched shadows like wolves and worlags together. She simply sat with the cozar until the fire died down and the brief wind grew cold enough that all but one of them turned in. Chantz dipped a mug in the pot still heating over the coals and held it out to her. Dion regarded him expressionlessly. She had heard the talk. The man might not raid against the cozar, but there was little question about what he did on his own. There was a worlag under his skin.

He watched her closely. When he spoke, she knew he had been following her thoughts. "You think we are raiders."

She raised one dark eyebrow. "Are you?"

He did not answer. He merely held out the mug and waited.

Finally, Dion took it. It was hot against her chilled flesh, and it made her shiver.

"You're cold."

She raised her violet eyes.

"Cold in the heart," he said softly. "I know you, I think."

"We have not met," she said stiffly.

"No, but I know you like myself." He paused, his voice low. "I had a mate once."

His words split the wall that she had so painstakingly built around her heart. It was unexpected, and it opened her to her grief like a flood. Her voice was barely a whisper. "As did I." She stared at him. She could not help her words. "Are we so scarred, you and I?"

The man shrugged. "They say lost souls can recognize each other."

"That saying is about the path to the moons."

"And I know you like myself," he reminded her obliquely. "Can you state with truth that you have chosen a different trail?"

Dion laughed, but the sound was a little wild. "No, though I wish I could."

He shrugged and poked at the fire. "Some of us have no hope. We long for the moons because we think we will find our love again in that coldness. Or we long for the moons because there is no real purpose in what we do. We are trapped by our past." He smiled without humor at her surprise. "You don't expect such thoughts of someone like me?"

She shrugged.

He studied her for a moment, then turned back to the fire.

"What I have—it is life, not living." He nodded at her. "You are not that far dead. You can still take a different road."

"But not you." The question was more a statement.

"No. Not now. Not for me. But if we had met when I was younger; if you had been . . ." His voice trailed off.

Dion felt the rage within her. She swallowed it with difficulty. "If I had been what? More like you? Like a—" She bit down on the words to stop them.

Chantz's eyes were suddenly cold. "Like a thief? A killer? You think men like me gravitate toward the violence? Maybe we do, but if so, it's because the moons pushed us out of the paths of accepted violence and into the ones of death. And if the choice is to die on the trial block, or continue breathing free, which would you choose, wolfwalker? It might not be much of a life, but it is life." He turned back to the fire. "Though not much of a goal for a master healer like you."

She clenched her fists around the mug.

He caught her tension. "I do not mistake the Gray Wolf of Ramaj Randonnen. I know you after all."

"You know nothing," she snarled.

He smiled slowly, but there was no humor in the expression. "I know that you ache inside like a three-month hunger. I know that you breathe only because your body can't quite stop on its own. I know that you run, from the ghosts, from grief—it doesn't matter. You run like the wolves who haunt you, and you will never face life again until you stop running and accept your guilt."

She breathed almost raggedly with the effort of holding back her fury. "And who are you to judge me? Can you claim to have stopped running?"

Chantz's voice was mild. "It's not the life I would have chosen, but yes, I no longer run. I face life. I know what it is and what it is not. I know who I am." He reached out and touched the back of her hand where new scars lay over old. "If we had lived different lives . . ."

She stared at the marks on her flesh. All the faint scars, deep scars—even the line of fingernail scars where she had not held onto her mate but let him fall to his death. All were marks of death. Her fury flared into blinding grief. If she and he had lived different lives? She caught her breath on a sob. "We did," she whispered, "and we are still the same."

They stared at each other for a long moment. He made a small gesture, and almost without volition, she went into his arms. He was tall and strong, and he wrapped her in his arms as if he could cherish her forever. He murmured words that made no sense and stroked her hair as if she were his mate, and she clung to him as if he were Aranur. There was no love between them. They were simply two souls, lost in the night, rocking in the coals of their grief.

Beside the passhouse, Kiyun's hand clamped Tehena's arm like a vise, holding the woman in place. "Let them be," he said, his voice low but sharp. "If she does not choose a mate on her own, the wolves will force her to take the one they bring her."

"The wolves chose the mate she should have—the one she needs, the one who will make her whole."

"And with their needs in her mind, she will obey them, and be a tool again, nothing more. She will never be whole. She will live for their goal and die a bit every day."

Tehena tried to wrench free. "She is not a woman who can divide her love between men, and that is not her mate. That is a worm-spawned raider."

Kiyun's grip did not relax. "Just because the wolves choose for her doesn't mean she must accept the choice. And it was raiders who took Aranur away from her. Maybe she can find some peace on her own by facing one again."

"By facing her worst nightmare? You're insane."

"You think she should give up completely to the will of the wolves?"

She shook him off violently. "And if he wants more from her than an embrace?"

Kiyun said softly. "It is Dion's life, not yours, to make such a choice."

Her life is the only life I have. Tehena did not say the words, but they all but battered the back of her gritted teeth, trying to get out. The woman clenched her bony fists, but some bleakness deep in Kiyun's eyes caught her, and she realized he felt the same.

XXXV

Talon Drovic neVolen

*Steel and blood may fill my heart,
  but Gray cuts both like butter.*

—*Ariyen proverb*

Air and noir. Sky and darkness. Moons and blackened
steel . . . Images mixed and twisted. Cold air rushed by his
roaring ears. He saw flashing steel. Heard wolves, and knew
that only their strength could save him. Cried out for the use
of their strength and speed, and felt them fill him with gray.
He grabbed for that strength. Strained toward hands, clutched
steel. Grasped the knife over another pair of thick, gnarled
hands, and the other man suddenly stopped fighting and
pulled him in instead. But it was into himself that he stabbed.
The blade went in a dozen times, cutting into other bodies,
and each time stabbing his own. The sword went through his
shoulder, and he screamed out for the strength of the wolves
even as they ripped him apart with his own weight. Then the
woman was there—soft voice, firm hands, a voice as gray as
the wolves. Hands soothed; hands reached. Dark eyes stared
into his, to the path to the moons and beyond. He felt her
let go of something dark and stretch across pain to reach
him. The convulsions eased again. She nodded and the
wolves let go, and he fell, and all that was left was the pain,
the *agony* . . .

He stared into the dawn. His jaw was like rock, his arms so
tense with a half-controlled convulsion that he jerked rather
than blinked. For a moment, gray light and gray voices still
blended. Then his mental cry reached the Gray Ones, and
they swept in, catching the agony before it could snap his

bones. He breathed raggedly. He could smell a faint musk in the undergrowth and knew the wolves had been near. Dnu piss, he thought, forcing himself to his knees. They were always near. Driving, lashing him on, and holding the only shield to the pain that lurked beneath his muscles.

He could not help the speed he set when they hit the road. The sense of urgency was stronger. The wolves remained out of sight, but the gray fog that dulled the spasms was laced with eagerness. He sucked on a piece of dried jerky for breakfast and listened to the wolves.

Every kay put distance between him and his father. Every kay was a leap north and east, loosening the chains that bound his mind. East. The wolves. The woman. Ariye. It was a litany of need.

They would have to circle the mountain that stood between him and Kiaskari, or ride back south to go north through Ramaj Ariye—a direction he resisted. Drovic could follow him, but by the time the older man caught his trail, Talon would be at least a full day ahead. Or, if Drovic guessed his intent, Drovic would cut up on the other side of the mountain to block his way back down through the pass. Either way, Talon could not avoid going north. He needed the woman first.

They wound down into a canyon and brushed through a young stand of curio trees, then back up on a wider game trail. Talon rode unerringly, choosing the paths that the wolves laid out in his mind. He could feel their eagerness, the blunt satisfaction that he was riding as they directed. It would have angered him, but there was too much gray in his mind— the pain he felt had not left him, and those wolves were the only buffer between his body and himself.

Blackheart trees turned to alpine scrub, then back to curio saplings. A redbark, twisted from box-pale fungi, marked a fork in the trail. There was a half-fallen cedar tree, the sudden scent of lemon as they brushed through hemlock grass. The forest was quiet, and no one spoke behind him. They rode swiftly, stopping only a few times for quick breaks to rest their legs and to water the dnu. They ate in the saddle and made camp only when dusk was gone. There was barely a murmur as they bedded down.

The next day began the same. Talon woke with his muscles tightening into brick. He barely caught the edge of gray that softened that rigid pain. Gods, he breathed in his mind. Should the wolves ever leave him, his body would break itself with rictus. Move forward, he told himself harshly. There were healing hands in the gray . . . There was a memory—an image, a fragment of conversation. He didn't know what, but it was of that healer. He had heard her name, had seen her before. Perhaps she had healed him in the past. Either way, she would take away the pain. There was power in her hands. Power that could reach through the gray, the power of both aliens and Ancients gripped in two slender hands. He could use that power if he held it himself, use it to reach the stars.

He rose slowly, to hide his stiff muscles. The others were doing the same. No one questioned their speed as they set out again. The threat of Drovic was enough to keep them all pushing forward.

Talon stopped them midmorning after they crossed a half-bare ridge; then he went back to scout the view. Wakje and Ki went with him, belly-crawling to a vantage point on the other side of the crest where they could see the roads. Only a few stretches were visible through the trees, and in an hour and a half of watching the distance, there were no obvious riders. Talon shrugged to himself and returned to the other raiders.

They traveled swiftly, crossing the foothills of the Illusory Mountains on an old road that was soft and mushy. Only a thin track on one side showed use—most likely by herds of eerin. The wolves did not use it; they were east, along a parallel ridge. Talon felt their presence more in the dulled sense of pain than in any distinct images or howls.

They had been following the old road for two kays when Talon suddenly held up his hand. Something had alerted him, but it was not the wolves. His own eyes had caught something different. The others halted. Quickly, Talon lay along the length of the dnu to lower his profile. The others followed suit.

They waited.

For minutes, nothing happened. Then, up ahead, to the right, something shifted in the brush. A hooved creature eased out on the road. From behind, Dangyon caught his breath. The buck looked down the road and flicked its tail up, showing its swatch of white hair. Then it moved with powerful grace out onto the open roots. It was a smooth, light brown color, with antlers branching out from the top of its head, and it had only four legs. Its body swept back in an arched line from a single set of ribs. Its shoulders were thick with muscle. Only two of Talon's people had ever seen one before, but all had heard the legends. "Deer," Sojourn breathed for them all.

As if it heard, the creature poised, midroad, and watched them for a moment. Then it moved on into the brush on the other side. Oroan held her breath; Ki didn't move; and Sojourn actually crossed himself in the ancient sign of blessing. A few seconds later, two does, a fawn, another doe, and then four others moved across and wound silently up the draw. Tawny hides and black noses, graceful movements that looked more like a languid walk than the six-legged skittering of dnu. A moment, no more, and they were gone. Talon's men were left like statues in the road, staring into the trees.

Talon slowly straightened. Behind him, the others did the same. But no one spoke, and no one moved forward until Talon finally urged his dnu into motion. It was as if they recognized that what they had witnessed was rare enough that mere words would destroy it.

They stopped briefly at a forty-home village, and the village folk seemed to gather like wary dogs as Talon and Dangyon went into the store. "Two kilos trail mix; eight kilos pan flour; two kilos of side meat, cut and wrapped in eight sections. Four kilos jerked bollusk . . ." Talon gave the store man his list in a concise, clear voice. The store man continued to hesitate, and Talon cocked his head and continued. ". . . four botas, two pairs of moccasins—these sizes here. Ten cold-weather liners—one extra long, one extra wide . . ." He set a bag of silver on the counter as he talked, and the store man's brown eyes flickered from Talon's face as he automatically judged the size of the bag. Without taking his eyes from Talon's, the store man gestured for the stock boy.

Talon didn't blame the man's wariness. He knew what they looked like. They were tough, armed, and expressionless, too ready to fight, too aware of each movement in the street as the village men watched almost nervously. All of them had the dark skin of men who had lived long enough with dirt that it colored their flesh past weathering and darkened their nails like paint. Their neck lines were grimy, their eyes narrowed with threat. Talon's own hard-planed face was tight with the pain that never left him, making him look dangerous as a lepa, and he knew that the store man would have bit off a sleeping worlag's toe before he believed they were not raiders. Talon had insisted that they ride in openly and together, but he also knew that it would take only one shift toward a sword to split this village like fire. Still, they had ridden in, and the store man was logging their order. ". . . Seal everything for rain, and wrap it for cold," he concluded.

The store man nodded but made no move toward the money. Talon merely looked at him, then used his eyes to indicate the bag.

The store man cleared his throat. "Had a good crop of learberry this year. Most of it's already dried."

Talon cocked his head to regard him.

"Two kilos?" the store man asked.

Talon nodded again.

Only then did the other man take the money bag, and Talon noted that the villager's hand was almost too steady as the man grasped the leather and turned away to count out what he needed.

Dangyon wandered to the window and idly watched the other raiders. It was a deceptive pose, as was Harare's casual leaning on his saddle horns, and Weed's joking with Roc and Mal. They were alert as badgerbear. When they finished packing the supplies and rode away, their shoulders itched like redweed. It was with a collective sigh that the curve of the road hid the village.

Harare shook his head. "Didn't think we could do it," he said to Dangyon as they cantered down the stone road.

"No threat, no fight," Dangyon returned.

"He's got the balls of a worlag," the other man said almost admiringly.

"And then some," Dangyon agreed.

They stayed on the road only a kay before Talon turned off again. The villagers had let them go, but he would not tax their generosity.

Several kays later, they began climbing toward a high, bare ridge from which they should be able to see enough to choose their next route. But Talon's eyes narrowed as they followed the trace up the steep hill. The edges of the tracks at a forked switchback were clearly defined, with little weathering. The uniform marks also made it obvious that these were domesticated, not wild dnu. Talon pursed his lips, thinking. There were no venges in this area—not with so many of the village men still in town. And these riders had been in a hurry. The pressure marks had pushed plateaus up beside the tracks, and pebbles nearby had loose shadows.

Wakje and Dangyon joined him on the ground, and together, they automatically gridded the trail in their minds to count the tracks. "Three?" Wakje murmured.

"Probably scouts," Talon agreed.

Dangyon scowled. "It's getting crowded out here like a town meeting. You can't cuss a cat without getting fur in your mouth."

Wakje grinned. "There's still room for you on the trail."

Talon rubbed his chin as he thought over the terrain, then ordered, "Wakje, Ki, Harare—with me. We'll recon the terrain from the top of the ridge. Rakdi, Weed, Roc—check the tracks where they lead down that switchback. The rest of you wait here."

Talon's group followed the tracks back up the ridge where they looked out over the valley and part of the nearby hills. "They were here," Talon murmured. He clenched a handful of soil and crumbled it to get its feel as he studied the marks in the soil. "Four hours, perhaps." He pointed to the crests in the tracks. "Left in a hurry." He straightened from squatting near one set and squinted into the distance. "Binocs," he ordered flatly.

Harare slipped them out of the pack and shaded them with his hand as he studied the distant forest. They were rarely used—the glint off the glass was as clear a giveaway to their position as waving a message flag. That and the weight was enough to make most groups leave them behind. The Ancients had had good eyesight, and they had passed that on to their children. It was rare that a man needed more than his own eyes to see where he would go.

"Can just make out a clear line of a road, north two fists past the peak snag." Harare reported. "If there was a caravan on that hill before, it would not have escaped notice. There is movement farther south—probably the wagons." He handed the glasses to Talon. "Pelan are coming up out of the canopy."

Talon took his look-see, then passed the binocs on to Wakje. He thought over the terrain. These valleys were pocked with marshes where water was trapped in summer, and the road dipped down into another one between this ridge and the next. "They'll meet the traders at the lake marsh," he decided, "where the wagons will be trapped against the mud."

Wakje, staring through the binocs, judged the distance. "In a pinch, you could make that stretch in thirty minutes. Wagons would take over an hour. That gives you twenty minutes to scout, set the flank guards, and settle in. Ten to wait for the wagons."

Talon got to his feet. "If we hurry, we can make it in time."

Wakje grinned without humor and passed the binocs back to Harare to put away. Ki, holding the dnu, handed them their reins and asked, "You want to take the same switchback?"

Talon shook his head. "The hill is fairly smooth on this side. I want to bushwhack down as soon as we gather the others. Should gain us ten minutes on the raid."

"And break a few bones on the dnu," Wakje said sourly.

"So we'll ride careful." But Talon's face was hard with focused excitement. He was eager for a fight—for anything that would let him stretch his hands with his own volition, for any way to strike out at the leash of his father and the wolves.

Harare looked downslope at the dense growth. Half-buried boulders created winding paths of soil where water ran down in spring; deep pockets of old leaves and needles could hide poolah and badgerbear. The man raised his blond eyebrows. "Bushwhacking's a dangerous sport, Talon."

Talon grinned suddenly as he mounted his dnu. "So is life." The expression crinkled the skin around his gray eyes. For the first time in months, he felt as if he believed in his direction. The wracking pain—the wolves held that at bay. His father— two days to the south. He drew in a breath and let it fill his chest like a cold gale from the mountains. It was a heady freedom. "So is life," he repeated to himself. "And I find I want to live again." He spurred his dnu and slapped the rump of Ki's riding beast as he passed it. Startled, the six-legged creature bucked. Ki half unseated before he caught his balance and streaked after Talon, with Wakje and Harare in their wake.

"You liver-lipped turkey," Ki cursed as his dnu scramble- slid down the slope.

"A turkey," Talon shouted over his shoulder. "Now there's an interesting oldEarth beast—and the only one on God's oldEarth that could drown itself on dry land." He pulled up on a flat where he regained the trail and had to cut the corner around a fallen log.

Ki glared after him. "I'm going to regret this," the man muttered to himself as he hit that part of the trail. "I'll bite," he said sourly as he came abreast. "Just how does a bird drown itself on dry land?"

"Looks right up at the sky when it rains and doesn't close its mouth. Dumbest bird on oldEarth—worse than a spotted slide."

Ki couldn't help himself. He stared at the sky, his mouth unconsciously half open as he tilted his face up with a frown. "It just looks up and stands there and drowns?"

"Just like that," Talon grinned. He spurred his dnu down the trail.

Ki called after him. "What about the cows?" He stared after the tall man. "I could follow you to the second hell, and you still wouldn't give me the answer." He kicked his dnu into a low canter and made way for Harare and Wakje.

They picked up the rest of the riders at the switchback and then followed Talon in a breakneck plunge down the hill, across a log-laden, fast-moving creek, and around another low ridge. The wolf pack was north, hunting eerin while Talon hunted men. Their hot eagerness was a match for his own, and he drew on that as he ducked the branches that threatened to slap him out of the saddle and tear the saddle from the dnu. He caught a sharp bough across his shoulders, another on the arm, and scraped a trunk with his knee as his dnu lurched over a boulder. Clouds of gnats blasted up. They charged through an ankle-deep seep, throwing water and mud up like children, then cut through a draw to avoid cresting the hills.

They came out in the patch of forest that Harare had noted before. From there, the scene was a portrait of standard strategy. The four wagons were stretched out over a curve, bordered on one side by a large grass area that was half swamp, half meadow. The other side of the road was forest. Two wagons had attempted to pull up beside each other, and the far one had tipped in the soft soil, instantly bogged down. The raiders in the forest simply shot into the wagons to drive the men into the swamp.

Talon scanned the road and let his ears listen to the distant cries and the soft sound of the gray. Heat, hunger twisted his belly. His lips curled back as he felt the flash of muscle of a dodging wolf. He had known enough violence that he understood the images without trouble, just as he understood what was happening in the wagons. "There are wounded on both sides, but the caravan is hit harder. And they're overconfident," he added of the raiders. "There's no flank guard in the forest."

Rakdi studied the scene but could not make out as many details. "You know this?" he questioned.

Talon could hear no doubt in the man's voice. A muscle jumped in his jaw. "Yes."

Oroan had her hand on her bow. Her voice was dispassionately urgent as she tensed to spur her dnu. "Talon, do we join them?"

He hesitated. "Yes," he said finally. But he held up his hand to stop the others from charging down into the scene. "We join the caravan."

"You mean we join the raiders," Oroan corrected.

"No." Talon's voice was suddenly confident. "Attack the raiders."

Sojourn raised his eyebrows. "*We're* the raiders."

"Not today, my friend. Today, we fight for the cozar."

"Why?"

Slowly, Talon grinned. "Because I like a challenge." He raised his voice to a shout. "Are you with me?"

And he charged.

Sojourn hesitated, but Rakdi kicked his dnu hard in the flanks. The beast startled and leaped forward. Ki grinned as his dnu followed Rakdi's wild leap forward, and he heard the others charge with him.

They washed through the forest like worlags. Tinder-dry sticks cracked beneath the hooves; someone behind him was whooping. Talon leaned forward as his dnu leaped a log in a two-segment movement. He let the wolves into his skull. They howled, and he howled with them. The raiders were a pack in his wake. "Shoot after my mark," he shouted. He pulled a bolt from his saddle quiver and nocked it to his bow.

The cozar had not yet panicked, but when they saw Talon's raiders sweeping out of the forest, there were fresh shouts. Talon's men hit the flat—the dnu were racing all-out. Like the others, Talon leaned to present less target, but he did not yet swing to one side. Someone in the caravan realized that half the new riders were aimed to pass between the wagons and the forest, and the other half to pass behind the attacking raiders. Talon did not hear the cheers. He was focused on the shadows, where the wolves could smell the fight through his nose and add tension to his muscles.

Something tore through the air toward his mount, but the war bolt missed by a hand's width. He released his own arrow. He missed, but one of the three bolts that cut through the brush behind him hit its mark. The Gray Ones howled with glee. *Hunt, hot blood, the prey is down!*

He shot again at a shaft of movement and this time hit the mark. The man clasped his chest and fell back with a garbled scream. Talon thundered past the first wagon. In the gap between the third and fourth, he slid from his dnu, hitting the ground in a half run. The dnu raced on, and he dove behind the wagons. He fetched up beside two men who grabbed him and dragged him behind the downplank. Dangyon, Pen, Harare, and Mal did the same, hitting the ground with bone-jarring leaps. Roc, Rakdi, Ki, and the rest passed behind the raiders, drawing fire so that the traders could pinpoint locations. Talon's riders wheeled to come back through the forest, and Talon barely glanced at the cozar—two men, a woman, three bows, only one sword—who made room for his long body. He catalogued them quickly. He simply raised to one knee and shot so smoothly that it was a single motion. His target had half risen to get the angle on Harare, and Talon skewered the man through the shoulder. Harare dropped off on another raider, and the first continued screaming.

Weed's beast went down. The dnu was hit in the chest, but it had been a weak bolt, and it cut harness more than flesh. Weed kicked free and dropped out of sight. The dnu staggered back to its feet. Talon shot almost blindly into a patch of grass—there had been a faint sense of movement. There was a choking cry, then silence.

One of the raiders broke cover and fled. A second was on that man's heels. Then all of them were scrambling through the brush behind boulders, trees, anything that gave cover. Talon whistled a command as he sprinted after the raiders. He leaped a half log, discarded his bow as he threw himself between two trees, and launched himself from a boulder toward the back of a running raider. He tackled the man like a lepa diving his prey. The man grunted as they hit ground. Steel twisted up, but rage had exploded in Talon. Rage at his father, at his life, at the woman and wolves who trapped him. Rage at the stupidity of waste. Rage at the incompetence that allowed the wagoners to be victims. He didn't bother with his knife. His fist came down and smashed the man's cheekbone. His second blow flattened the nose. The man's mouth was open— he may have been screaming, but Talon didn't hear. *Blood.* He checked a wild blow with his left and felt teeth break against his right. *Rage.* Iron bones, iron will—his fist shattered jawbone, then the orbit of the eye. *Hunger. Trapped.* There was nothing between him and the fury. Ribs snapped.

Blood pulped the man's features. But Talon's fists continued to pound; the body became limp; the gut a muscled deadness. Dead. He hit him again. The raider was dead. Hit him again. The man was dead. The thought finally caught his attention. He hesitated, his fist still raised for another blow. He was breathing like a runner with tearing gasps that were half curse, half air in his lungs. For a moment, he simply knelt on the body, letting his vision clear. He braced himself on the oddly flexible chest; then he staggered to his feet. Up the slope, the other raiders were still running. Talon's mind seemed to go into icy gear. He started after them.

A hand on his biceps stayed him.

Talon froze and looked down. The hand was unfamiliar. His narrowed eyes were like slate as he focused on the first cozar. The other two men shifted back.

The first man slowly removed his hand from Talon's arm. He forced his voice to remain steady. "Let them go. They're still dangerous. They are not worth the risk."

Talon regarded the man like a lepa. There was an ache in his shoulder, as if he had strained the muscles. His knuckles—he could feel the bruising. He did not move, but the fury seemed to pull itself back into his chest where he could control it again. Then he clenched and unclenched his fists to relieve some of the tightness. Finally, he gave the callback whistle.

The sound startled the three cozar, but they said nothing. Talon's face was still tight, his knuckles spattered with blood. The lead cozar stepped back again and gestured for Talon to return to the wagons. The tall man nodded tersely. It was like inviting a badgerbear to dine, thought the wagoner—Talon had gone through the trees with a fluid strength, never touching anything but his launching points. Had that rage been turned at them . . . The cozar pushed his way through the brush and tried to ignore the inherent grace of the man who retrieved his bow without a word and followed him back to the wagons.

Talon's riders filtered back within minutes. Only two of his men were hurt: Dangyon had caught a splinter in the face when a bolt struck a wheel near his head, and Rakdi's hip was gouged. One of the cozar came to tend the ex-elder, and Rakdi nodded his thanks as the trader finished, while another offered Rakdi unbloodied trousers.

"We thank you," the first cozar finally said to Talon. "May we offer you rest and bread?"

Talon regarded him expressionlessly. "No."

The man nodded, appreciating the terseness. "Have you needs?"

"Trail meat, if you have some to spare." His very curtness told the cozar that he understood their ways, would make no demands on their hospitality, and that the meat would cancel debt.

The man murmured to another, and within minutes, two large packs of meat were being strapped onto one of the dnu. Talon waited impatiently as Harare checked the lashings on the packs. He could feel the wolves pulling. East, and north . . . He barely waited for Harare to remount before signaling his men to ride out. He did not wave a farewell.

Rakdi studied Talon's face as they cantered away. "You're an odd man, Talon," he told him over the noise of the dnu. "You let them all live."

Talon's jaw was still tight, but his gray eyes glinted with humor. It was the irony, he realized—the position in which he had put them. "There were too many to use the vertal," he said simply.

Rakdi looked startled for a moment. They didn't carry enough of the herb for so many people, but— His thoughts broke off. That was not what Talon meant. He chuckled. "I suppose there is some logic there," he agreed.

Behind them, the cozar watched them disappear down the road. "Moonworms, but we were lucky," a woman muttered. Her voice still trembled, and she shook out her hands, as if that would fling off the dregs of adrenaline and fear.

"Lucky?" The lead man nodded slowly. "More than you could know."

"What do you mean?"

The cozar gestured with his chin after Talon. "They are as

dangerous as the raiders. Perhaps more so, for we let them inside the circle."

"They rode to help us. They fought beside us."

But the man remembered those icy eyes. They had been filled with rage and focus, and there had been desperation and hunger . . . It was like meeting the gaze of a wounded forest cat just before it killed you. "No," he said slowly. "We were a decision point, nothing more. They could as easily have turned on us as fought against the raiders." He rubbed absently at his stubbled chin. "That man—he reminded me of someone . . ." He shook his head as the memory eluded him. "Older, perhaps," he murmured, "and farther east . . ." He was still thinking as he helped his brother reset a wagon harness.

Drovic listened expressionlessly to Liatuad. The skinny man was half feverish and kept rubbing his swollen right arm. Worlag ichor had infected the wound, and the biceps were twice the size they should be. It had taken Liatuad two days to catch up to Drovic—Talon had broken away to the east, and Liatuad had missed Drovic by hours on the main road. He had stolen a dnu—which would bring a hunter-tracker in their direction, but that, Drovic forgave. It was the rest that wired him up like a mudsucker ready to strike. There had been no message cairn at Three Corners, and no sign of his son farther on. He had known instantly what had happened, and only intuition had held him in that spot for a day, hoping for some sort of word.

"Show me," he said coldly.

Liatuad's eyes were fever bright as he traced his finger over the map, locating the trails.

Drovic noted that there was an angled valley that shot like an arrow toward the 'Skarian road. He speared Liatuad with his cold, blue-gray gaze. "Northeast, not due east?"

Liatuad nodded. "He said Kiaskari, not Ariye." The man wiped at the sweat on his forehead, then ground it into the bandage on his arm as he continued rubbing it.

Drovic's voice was more to himself than to the others. "Kiaskari . . ." He shook his head. "Perhaps now, for the moment, for a few more kays. But it is Ariye that will draw him in the end." He looked up. "We'll take the Ariyen pass road," he said flatly.

"You don't want to follow?"

"No. He's going north, but only for now. Whatever he thinks he's chasing, he'll turn and come back toward Ariye. We will be there in the passes, waiting."

NeBrenton, a sturdy man with thin, curly hair, cleared his throat. "Drovic, it's almost snow season there."

"Aye, so it is," he said dryly.

"We don't have the gear."

NeBrenton and Slu were both from the western counties, not from the mountains. Even Cheyko was more from the forested lands. Liatuad, of course, was weakened already, and it would take a ninan for the swelling to go down before he could again use his arm. But Liatuad had been with Drovic for over ten years and had somehow managed to move beyond raider to the tenuous status of a friend. Where Drovic might have killed another raider rather than leave a wounded man behind, he found himself hesitating over Liatuad, and the sudden hesitation filled him with anger. His son had been tainted with the wolves, and that taint was somehow contagious. He put his hand on his hilt, found his fist clenched, and placed his hands carefully back on the map. He looked at Liatuad.

"Ride west. You should be able to make the Bilocctar border from here before being tracked for that stolen dnu. NeBrenton—arrange to pay the stable master now so we don't have to haggle at dawn. Cheyko, Slu—check the packs and make sure they're ready. I don't want to waste time in the morning. We'll pick up winter supplies in Nitenton and take the short road toward Ariye. We should make the pass in four days."

As the other men left, Drovic stared at the map. He didn't realize that his hands had begun to clench again until the paper crumpled in his fingers. Carefully, he released it. His voice was so quiet in the emptiness of walls and maps that it seemed to be a whisper. "And the wolves of Ramaj Ariye and Randonnen again steal my son away."

XXXVI

Ember Dione maMarin

"Run," said the Tiwar. His voice was sly. "Race in fear, in fury, in grief. Sprint for the goal; fly for the end of the world."

She gripped her thigh where the wound was deep. Her blood was hot on her fingers. "You cannot stop me," she managed. "I am stronger than you now."

"You trip over history and do not see it. You plunge into your past like an abyss." The Tiwar smiled, his teeth a glowing yellow. "I do not have to stop you," he said. "I merely have to watch."

—*from* Wrestling the Moons

The icy dawn was pale blue against the snow-white slopes. The wagon train was a coordinated flurry of motion. A half dozen wagons had already moved into position, stretching out onto the road. Traces were checked, the last dnu harnessed, and the final bundles repacked in the wagons. The last of the unbroken ice crunched underfoot where it had formed during the night. Then the lead riders trotted to the road, and the first wagons pulled out behind them, others sliding into place as the courtyard began to clear. One wagon was awkward with a young driver still learning to turn his team. Dion could see the young man's father, holding himself back from helping. Then the young man settled himself, and the team moved smoothly forward.

Tehena huddled into her coats and scarves, and Dion's dnu stamped its feet. Dion did not seem to notice. They should have left before the train, Tehena muttered to herself. Should have ridden out early to stay ahead of the wagons. Instead, they would spend another day trudging as slow as the slowest team before them.

But when the last wagon was rolling, and only the shattered snow was left behind, Dion turned to look north and west. For long, silent moments, she stared at the icy mountains. She could not hear the wolves. Like the day before, at this distance and altitude, with almost no life to resonate with the packsong, her mind was almost clear. Only her own thoughts filled her skull. She did not feel drawn north, or south to Ariye except by her own intentions. She felt no geas here, only the background sea of her own emotions and the hope that had begun to push tiny waves over that infinite surface as she watched the wagons roll. There were other ways to raise a child than by Ariyen methods, ways that would allow her to keep her bond with the wolves and still keep her child safe while she met her promises. They might not be the choices an Ariyen would make, but they would become her ways in time. Face the hunter, then find her life.

Find. Protect. The remembered words seemed to echo in her memory.

Chantz and the other rear riders fell in behind the last wagons, and Chantz gestured for Dion to fall in with him. She shifted as if to urge her dnu forward, then deliberately remained still. She could go with them all the way to Ariye—travel in that safety. But Chantz had his own memories to soothe, and she was done with soothing. She gave herself a twisted smile. The cozar offered her comfort, but the world did not want her safety, only for her to keep her promise. It was done with waiting, but not with taking, and so she was not done giving.

"Dion?" Kiyun asked.

She glanced at him. The very absence of snarls in her head made her promise to the Gray Ones stronger. It was as if, in their near silence, she could identify exactly what she had promised them and herself, and how she thought she could keep all those oaths. She could see the desperation and strength that had given her the arrogance to think she could succeed. She could see what it would cost to achieve those goals. Control, she told herself calmly. Control of the power she held in her hands, in her mind. Control of her fears for her child. Grief, fury, loneliness, and the endless obligations she had accepted in the past—it was control of those things that would grant her freedom. She could have gone on with the cozar to Ariye. But if she did, she would be running right back into chains. Ariye was Aranur's home, not hers. Hers was with the wolves.

Chantz looked back for a long moment. Slowly, Dion shook her head.

He raised his hand in a silent salute, then turned to folllow the wagons.

For half an hour, Dion simply sat in the cold wind, watching the wagon train wind down around the mountain. Their dnu stamped their feet to keep warm, and Tehena huddled into her coats and scarves. Kiyun tucked his hands in his armpits, and Tehena began to shiver. Dion did not seem to notice.

Finally, Dion nodded—a short motion, more to herself than to the others, then turned and reined her dnu back toward the barn.

Kicking her dnu after the wolfwalker, the lanky woman spoke. "Why?"

The wolfwalker hesitated, then glanced once more at the mountains. "Because he is coming."

Tehena's hand went automatically to her scabbard. "The one who hunts you? Dion—"

"No," she said softly, cutting the woman off. "There are no wolves here to cloud my sight. No Aiueven, no duty. I can feel myself, without any other needs. I can see what I have done and must do, and I can look at him without bias."

Kiyun stirred uncomfortably. "Rhom is riding to Ariye— to your home. He won't know you are still in the mountains."

"He will know." Kiyun quirked his eyebrow at her confidence, and she smiled faintly. "He comes because I need him. He will always know where I am, just as I know that he is already in Ariye. Whenever I didn't have the strength to stand up for myself, Rhom stood up for me. Whenever I couldn't see clearly enough to set my course, Rhom saw clearly for me. My brother will know where to find me. Hishn will show him the way."

"Your wolf is coming here? Now?"

She nodded. "I could not Call her to me before—she could not cross the mountains on her own, though she would try if I let her. But Rhom can carry enough food on an extra dnu to feed both her and Gray Yoshi."

"Her mate," Kiyun said soberly.

Dion raised her eyebrow. "They will not be separated. They are kum-tai."

"As you will be with this other man when he, too, reaches you?"

Dion gave a bitter laugh. "When he reaches me? Kiyun, the wolves are driving that man to me like raiders to the slaughter. He has as little choice as I. And if he is like Aranur, there will be kum-jan between us even if we do not Promise. Kum-jan, kum-vani . . . Neither of us will be able to help it because of the twice-damned wolves."

She had not mentioned kum-tai, and Kiyun was silent for a moment. Finally, the burly man nodded. "So we stay."

She stared out at the snow. "Aye. Without the wolves, there is nothing to smother my mind. If that man and I meet here, we will see each other as we are, and judge our future on that, not on the needs of the wolves."

"You said he was violent, driven, fierce. Can you love such a man?"

Her voice was soft. "I loved Aranur."

His voice was troubled. "You will still see Aranur when you look at *him*."

"Aye." Her hand pressed hard on her belly. The scars that ridged her left hand tightened with her fist. The deep ache of remembered burning was like tiny coals in her body. But the grief that had nearly destroyed her center was banked again within walls of control. She had been lazy, careless in her life, had let herself float through years and promises until there was nothing left but duty. She might have the power now to take up those duties again, but that was no longer enough. Control, she told herself. Her voice was still a whisper, but that near-silent sound was fierce. "By all the moons that ride the sky, I will have joy again if it kills me."

* * *

Rhom and Gamon arrived at the Lloroi's house after dark. Tyronnen—the Lloroi—and his wife were waiting for them, along with ten others.

"I apologize for the hurry," Gamon began.

His brother smiled wryly. "Always you're either running late or standing still, Gamon. There's no in-between for you."

Gamon shrugged, and the Lloroi's gaze sharpened as his brother did not respond to the old line of banter. Gamon was leaned down like a twig, hard and desiccated, his lined face weathered like bronze. Rhom was not much better, for all that he had more bulk. The blacksmith looked even harder and more dangerous, his muscles gaunt and his face grim, not welcoming.

Gamon began without preamble. "The wolfwalker is coming down out of Kiaskari—we think she's in the mountains now. But Rhom feels a sense of danger around his twin. It might be raiders, like before, or it might be something else. He says the feeling is constant, and he says its strength is growing."

The Lloroi did not question Rhom's intuition. Dione had told him that her twin had never bonded with the wolves, so this must be the link between twins, or the link sometimes between siblings, he reminded himself somewhat grimly. The man nodded at the men and women to the side who listened politely. "You have ten riders here, all of whom are climbers, all familiar with the passes, all good with bows or swords."

Gamon nodded and glanced over the ten people with sharp gray eyes. Witzen, he knew, and Bray. Ammesdo, Yale, and Bonn had been his own students when he had still been an active weapons master. The others he had not met, but the Lloroi would not have included them had they not been the best. Gamon didn't have to ask if they were volunteers. The older man knew that there must have been five times this many who were turned away. The Lloroi might have pushed Dion hard as a scout, but just as he demanded the best of her, he would give her only his best in return, and that meant that these eight men and two women were the top fighters who could climb, or the top mountain folk who could fight, who could be gathered at such short notice.

"Pack dnu?" he asked, giving the Lloroi a nod of approval.

"Ready and waiting. Although I have to ask why you're carrying so much meat."

Gamon's voice was dry. "It's for the wolves, not us."

The Lloroi looked no less startled than the others. "You're taking the wolves into the mountains?"

"I'm not. Rhom is."

Tyronnen regarded Rhom thoughtfully. "To support Dione," he answered his own question. "Hishn and Yoshi?"

Rhom nodded.

The Lloroi considered for a moment. The meat packed on the dnu should feed two wolves for nine or ten days, if they were frugal. "And if you cannot come back in a ninan?"

Rhom's voice was flat. "Then we'll kill the dnu to feed them."

Tyronnen and Gamon exchanged glances, and some of the others shifted uneasily. They didn't know Rhom, though stories of the wolfwalker's twin had certainly reached them. It was one thing to ride into the mountains, something else again to make it out again on foot. If they were delayed, it would be because of a storm, accident, or avalanche, and they would need the dnu for themselves. Killing the dnu to feed the wolves meant they would have to bear their own packs across the snow and ice and still carry weapons against the glacier worms and snowbear that would be hunting with the snow.

Gamon caught some of the doubt in their faces. "He is Randonnen," he said obliquely.

"And all Randonnens climb," the Lloroi murmured. Rhom was as good a mountain man as any—and better than most trained Ariyens. He knew the dangers. But his judgment was that of a brother, not that of an objective leader. The Lloroi's voice was soft. "You risk our men and women, not just yourself."

Rhom studied the other man. Tyronnen was slightly taller than Gamon, broad-shouldered, with peppered gray hair. There were heavy lines in his face from duty and leadership. He was more classically handsome than his nephew, Aranur; calm, steady. Rhom had never heard of him losing his temper. He wasn't sure if that was a bad thing or one to admire. But this was the man responsible for the people of Ariye. *All* the people, Rhom reminded himself coldly, feeling a touch of his own anger.

When Rhom answered, his voice was unforgiving. "When we were five," he said slowly. "My twin jumped in front of a poolah, armed with only a stick, because it was going to attack me. She was knocked flying, and my father killed the beast. I got off with a scratch on my ribs instead of a torn-out chest. When we were twelve, she dove in a white-water run because I took a cramp and couldn't make it out before I hit the rapids. She didn't think about herself—only what she had to do to keep me alive. She broke her arm on Dountuell, and begged me to leave her so that I would survive the downclimb she thought I would attempt alone. And for thirteen years, she has risked herself for your people. She has scouted for you, healed for you at the cost of her own health, fought for you and left her own blood behind, and lost her sons and her mate. Lost them in your service. Lost them because she was told there was a need and she could not decline to meet it." The rage in his voice began to break through. Driven, he thought—all Ariyens were driven to use any tool in their possession, even a wolfwalker. "But now she is in danger, and you worry about the *risk* of snow to people who have spent their lives in the mountains?" The violet eyes that flashed so in Dion's face with her anger were hard in his own face as he glared at the Ariyen Lloroi. "What kind of people are you Ariyens?" The Lloroi tried to cut him off, but he raged. "You talk of using your tools wisely—the forests, the land. Of replenishing what you take. But you don't do that with your people, do you? Not when you have someone like Dion."

"Rhom," Gamon cut in.

He ignored the older man. "There's no moderation for someone not of Ariye. Use them up before you lose them; use them all at once; use them till they drop. You can always buy another."

The Lloroi tried to speak again, but Rhom's fist clenched with his voice. "You feel no guilt at having destroyed a woman, a *wolfwalker*, a healer whose only fault was to believe enough in your leadership that she willingly gave everything you asked until there was nothing left—"

"Rhom," Gamon said sharply.

Rhom halted on an angry breath. Gamon stared at him as if he were seeing him for the first time. The older man had forgotten that the passion and strength of will he took for granted in the wolfwalker was mirrored in her twin. Rhom and Dion had been raised in the same county, by the same man, with the same morals and convictions. Like his twin, Rhom had proven his courage, loyalty, intelligence, and skill a dozen times over a decade ago and a dozen times more since then. Worlags, raiders, slavers, plague—Rhom had faced them all without flinching. Like Dion, Rhom was hard, inflexible, and judgmental when he thought his leaders had failed him, and he was not afraid to confront them on those failings or demand that his leaders change.

Rhom took a deep breath. Like that of his twin, his anger matched the reputation of those who had violet eyes. Violent violet, it was called, and with good reason. He forced himself to calm that streak of energy. It wasn't easy. He had been on edge ever since they reached Ariye, and every delay made it worse.

The Lloroi regarded him soberly. He recognized the same passion in Rhom that he had seen in the Randonnen's sister. The Lloroi chose his words carefully. A push—that was all it would take to give Rhom a reason to convince the wolfwalker to return to Randonnen. "I do not deny that we used your twin to take as much as she was willing to give. She has skills that we badly needed, that we still need. And I meant no offense to your request for supplies or men. I suppose," he admitted, "that I was testing you, or testing your conviction that you must go to meet her now when she is already in Ariye—"

Rhom cut him off, his voice still abrupt. "She is not in Ariye. She stopped somewhere in the passes, and she is waiting there, not riding down."

The Lloroi cocked his head. "Waiting for what?"

"To face the danger that hunts her."

"But you don't know what kind of danger."

Rhom began to pace. It was difficult to remain still. With so many people, he felt hemmed in already. The dnu were waiting; Hishn was nearby. "She knows that someone is hunting her, and that it is a man of violence."

Gamon shifted almost imperceptibly, his hands making a subtle gesture. The Lloroi caught the motion and nodded slowly, giving nothing away. "Wait for us outside," he said to the others. Obediently the climbers filed out. When they were gone, he turned back to Rhom. "Go on," he said.

Rhom shrugged irritably. "A man driven, a man of . . . anger and action. That's all I could get through Hishn—or rather, all Hishn could get from my twin. Dion is being hunted, Lloroi, and the man who hunts her has all the feel of a raider, but disciplined; of a killer, but far too determined to meet his goal; of a leader who doesn't lead."

"She is not alone."

"She has only Tehena and Kiyun."

The Lloroi was silent for a moment, thinking.

"There is something else," Gamon said quietly. "Someone else. Someone from long ago."

The Lloroi regarded his brother grimly, and the two men exchanged a look. Then as one, they looked at Rhom. The blacksmith raised his black eyebrows.

"This is not Randonnen business," the Lloroi said, with a nod toward the door.

Rhom's voice was mild, but his sharp violet gaze had caught Gamon's shuttered expression. "I'd say, by the way Gamon looked at you, that this something is part of what hunts my twin, and it damn well is my business."

Tyronnen regarded him for a long moment, but Rhom didn't budge. Finally, the Lloroi smiled wryly. "I should expect, from knowing your twin for so long, how stubborn you would be."

Rhom shrugged.

Still, Gamon hesitated. The Lloroi met the older man's gaze and shrugged in turn. When Tyronnen began to speak, he did not look at Rhom. Instead, the Lloroi stared out the dark window at the edge of night that threatened to encroach on the room. "It was long ago, and we were young." He hesitated, then seemed to decide. "There was an older boy named Drovic . . ."

XXXVII

Ember Dione maMarin

The wolf still hunts where angels fear to tread.
    —Randonnen saying

Dion stood, knee-deep in the snow, her body almost steaming with sweat. She took in a long, slow breath and catalogued the aches she had acquired over the past four days. Tag-sparring with Kiyun had always been a lesson in avoidance. Kiyun was fast, but not startlingly so; it was his power that made him such a danger. In tag-sparring, she didn't even have to worry about that, since they used slaps and tags to demonstrate their strikes. It was not just her pregnancy that made her slow—she had had too many injuries that year and too little rework to learn to spar around them. Her timing was off. She had better get it back on, she told herself grimly. No one who rode the trails could afford to let themselves get sloppy, and with the hunter on the way, Dion's child was in even more danger. She resisted the urge to rub the ache where she'd almost pulled a muscle in her thigh. Her only consolation was that Kiyun had a few pulled muscles of his own from that spinning leap he'd used to avoid her sweep.

She stared north along the curve of the road that led out of the courtyard. The snow was already melting; the late summer sun had turned the surfaces brilliant with mountain tears. The stubborn plants in the sheltered boxes looked scraggly, but they were still alive. The sense of the wolves, which had faded from her mind, had never quite gone away. Instead, it lurked like a thin fog on the horizon of her thoughts.

It was odd, she thought. She had crossed mountains before and had lost the sense of the wolves in the heights. It had been an awareness of emptiness, an ache, a space inside. This time, she could still hear the Gray Ones. Faint, yes, but still there. She was more sensitive now. Her contact with the aliens had given her that perception, but she had no real feel of distance. Instead, it seemed as if the life between her and the wolves was too thin to support full conversation, not that the wolves were far away.

Talon and his riders came down out of Wayward Pass in a flurry of snow. It was not a storm, only a pocket of chaos—loose snow from the drifts—that ended almost as abruptly as the road. One moment, they were rounding a steep cliff in a whirl of whiteness; the next, they were facing a drop-off as clear as the second hell. Ahead of them, the wolves barely paused. Gray Ursh raised his head and sniffed the wind; two others explored the old shattered tracks. Then they turned and trotted south along the curve of stone.

Talon, I tell you this utter truth: If you set foot in Ariye, you will die. Drovic's words echoed bleakly. Talon had ridden this road before, but it had been years ago, and he had been going home then, home to Ramaj Ariye, home to his sons, to his mate. He tilted his head and sniffed the air, unconsciously mimicking Ursh. They were too far north. The woman he hunted had moved south.

Mal huddled farther into his parka, and Oroan shivered as they spurred their dnu after Talon. Dangyon looked down over the drop-off as they turned onto the other road, and Sojourn grinned at the thick-chested man's expression. His voice carried clearly over the fresh snow. "Thinking of doing a reckon?"

Dangyon glanced at the cliff again. "Thinking of an old-Earth saying: 'Where angels fear to tread.' "

"We're no angels, Dangyon."

"Then this ice is the devil's drink, and we'll be drowning here before long."

"Sky's clear."

"Not for long. It's been days now, and we're overdue for a storm."

Sojourn twisted to look back at the cut through which they had come. The sky to the east was mostly clear, but the clouds were moving in with them. He couldn't help judging the weight of the meat packs that Talon had insisted on buying. For the wolves, Talon had said. But Sojourn's belly tightened with the thought of snow. They could make it to a passhouse—the shelters were placed throughout the mountains—but what then? He had been in a mountain storm once, trapped for two ninans, with only the food in his pack and two other men to starve with. He forced himself to look away from the meat bags, glanced at Talon's rigid back, and eyed the wolves ahead.

Dangyon followed the slender man's gaze. The nondescript man might not show much expression, but Dangyon had known him for years, and the tension in Sojourn's body was as clear as words. "Don't worry," the heavy man told him. "Talon has the wolves on his side. We won't miss a passhouse for the weather."

Sojourn nodded, but did not answer. In spite of his own fear, it wasn't the wolves or the weather that put the worry in his gut. It was Talon's push toward Ariye.

Rhom followed Gray Hishn's gaze. The wolf's yellow eyes stared north into the snow-white night. The summer moons floated between the peaks like ships. His hand gripped the gray scruff only partly to bring him closer to his twin. His touch calmed Hishn as his voice could not—it was a reminder of Hishn's wolfwalker, and of the gray wolf's own mortality. The slopes here were permanently frozen, the walls of the road ice-crusted and banked with old snow that was rock-hard with age. What trees there were were thick-barked, with a core of deep sapwood. The snowdrops poked their tiny blades through holes they made in the ice, and the only other signs of life were the faint, veinlike trails of the snoweels in some of the deeper drifts. The courtyard was wind-stripped like the road. It stretched like a beacon that begged for them to follow.

The wolf's breath made tiny clouds in the last of the evening light, and Hishn turned her head to meet Rhom's eyes. The sudden perception of lupine senses, the visceral pulse, the musky core of body heat under layers of cold-tipped fur . . . It hit him hard, and he almost clenched his fist in the thick pelt. "I know," he murmured.

She is close.

"We'll reach her in four days."

We can run ahead, reach her sooner.

The sense of speed was already in the Gray One's mind, and Rhom had to force himself to stay in place. "If something happens to us, you'll starve. Stay with us until we know where she is for sure."

The gray voice was worried. *I cannot hear her clearly.*

"It's the altitude," he explained. "There's not enough life to carry your voice through the passes."

But the gray creature surprised him. *There are other wolves,* she sent.

"Here? In the mountains?"

Coming. Hishn bared her teeth unconsciously. *Hunting.*

Hunting Dion . . . Rhom broke the link and stared out at the snow. The sky was clear and cold, and the line of moons washed out the stars over the peaks. The light brightened the snow like a reversed dawn, and the road was a clear swath through the shadows. Five days to the pass, he thought—if the weather held, maybe four. Beyond that . . .

He straightened as Gamon crunched through the snow.

The older man followed his gaze to the north. "Thought I'd find you out here." Gamon paused, then added lightly, "She won't get any closer for wishing."

"There are other wolves in the mountains."

Gamon gave him a sharp look, then glanced at Hishn.

"They're hunting." Rhom's voice was soft as he stared north. "Hunting my twin. They have her trail—I can feel it."

Gamon took off his cap and ran his hand through his hair. "Can't ride at night, Rhom. Not here."

The younger man nodded slowly, but Gamon thought that, if the Randonnen had his way, they would still be in the saddle, with their dnu chipping the ice from the road.

Drovic had stopped cursing his dnu, his men, and himself some time ago. Now he merely rode with a grim thinness to his lips. They would reach the passhouse in two days. There was weather on the horizon, but it didn't look yet like a storm. If he was lucky, it would hold off until he reached the next shelter; luckier still, and it would blow over and give them clear roads to the top.

He had no doubts that Talon was now heading south. Talon had headed straight up the mountain range. He would have had to take the northern cut through, which came out in Kiren. Talon would have to drop down again to reach Ariye. Drovic didn't expect his son to change his mind and go elsewhere. Ariye pulled his son like a mudsucker. Drovic understood it. It was the motive that drove Drovic—his need for his mate, for his family, for what he couldn't have. The need had been drummed into Drovic by his own father, and Drovic had drilled it into Talon. Neither one could turn away. But Talon thought he could regain what was gone instead of struggle for something new, and in such a fight, Drovic could lose him completely. He had one more chance to stop him, to keep Talon from the wolves. No Gray Ones could reach his son at these heights. Talon's mind would be clear and cold as logic, as Drovic had taught him from the beginning, yet he would be controlled as Drovic had arranged. Here, Talon would regain the goal. The wolves could howl all they wanted, but cut off by the peaks, they could not touch his son. Drovic's lips twisted in a bitter caricature of a smile. Wolves—they dragged men back like the aliens, away from the future, into the dirt of the world. They had made themselves part of this planet. They never strove for anything new. They simply lived, like leeches, part of a chain of blood.

He spat to the side and watched in satisfaction as the spittle froze on contact. Then he raised his head to the sky and bared his teeth, letting the cold burn in his mouth. Cold as the seventh hell, he thought. It was comforting as home.

XXXVIII

Ember Dione maMarin

Every man makes a choice.
It's not the deciding that's difficult,
It's living with the decision.

> —*Druce neRhame, Ariyen Lloroi, AL 116-194*
> *Last of the Martyrs*

Tehena was chewing the walls. The skinny woman stalked the great room, pulling a cloak irritably around her and yanking at her stringy hair. She rubbed at a window, turned to come back and speak, shut her mouth, paced again, then began to bite at her hangnails. She stared at Dion without pause.

Dion sighed. "Say it."

Tehena's voice was flat. "Healer, it's been three days. We cannot stay here forever."

"Rhom will be here soon."

"There's a storm moving in, and our food will not last through it. Without new stores . . ." The lanky woman shook her head. "We cannot take the emergency supplies from the passhouse. We don't *need* them. It's not right."

Dion shrugged, still staring toward the north. "We can hunt."

Tehena rolled her eyes. "Sure. Kiyun and I will just wander out and wrestle down a glacier worm. We can live on that for a ninan—if it doesn't kill us."

"It's food," Dion said calmly.

"For you, perhaps. You've eaten enough with the wolves that you no longer know what it is to be human. And we're on the Ariyen border. Four days, Dion, and we could have real food—not trail stew. We could have beds with more than one blanket. A ninan, and we would be home."

Dion closed her eyes.

Tehena hesitated. "Is it the wolves?"

"They are quiet here," she answered finally. "They have haunted me for so long, howling with Aranur's voice—with his memories. Here, they give me peace."

"But here, we cannot stay."

"One more day, Tehena."

"No, Dion. One more day, and we'll be caught here by the storm." The lanky woman regarded the wolfwalker steadily. "We must ride on to Ariye."

The wolfwalker stood for a long moment, staring toward the north. Tehena was right—she knew it. But *he* was getting closer. Here, she could face him on her own. In Ariye, there were always the wolves . . .

"Dion," Tehena said urgently.

Dion looked once more at the passhouse. An hour later, they rode away. Behind them, Dion felt the wolves, howling in her mind.

Talon stared at the road. Something had changed—his prey was on the move again, heading toward Ariye. He urged his dnu to a steady trot in the wake of the wolves. They turned and glanced back to make sure he followed, and he felt the leash of urgency tighten in his gut. This time, he didn't mind.

Behind him, the slim, stone walls of Melt Shelter disappeared against a horizon that thickened with subtle clouds. He had seen the promise they held, but the coming storm did not matter. One day to the passhouse that led to Ariye, one day to the wolves and the woman. After that, he could think again.

The predawn dark was as bright as the moons. The forest behind Dion was a pattern of black spiky pillars above a snow-white quilt. The air was clear; the sky a quiet, frigid blue-black. It would not last. Already the clouds were lowering over the northern peaks, and the slow fourth moon, which hung midsky, would be swallowed within the hour. Tehena and Kiyun still burrowed in their sleeping bags.

Dion patted her dnu on its neck and settled her meager saddle pack. She tried to tune out the wolves. This high in the mountains, and they still pulled like a mudsucker, but now it was not south toward Hishn and home in Ariye, but north, back toward the birdmen. The wolves couldn't want her dead. No, it was the hunter who was now out of place, somehow above her among the peaks. He had crossed the mountains behind her, and the wolves were driving her back.

She clenched her fingers into a mitted fist, then pressed them against her belly. She would show more in another month. Her child—the child she now shared with the birdmen. The child who was linked to aliens, not just humans and wolves. And the Gray Ones . . . The wolves would want her to share this child with the man they hounded to mate her. Her hand clenched again. North, and the wolves and Aiueven.

Wolfwalker, the wolves cried faintly.

"I hear you," she whispered. Automatically, she listened for Gray Hishn's voice, but the gray wolf echoed the wild ones. There was little life to carry their howls, and Hishn was farther away. But like worlags, all were relentless.

Come to us, they howled in the distance. *Run. Blood and stars, steel and ice . . .* She focused and realized that the thoughts of the wild wolves were much sharper than she expected. The distance that muted their images barely muddied their projected longing. It cut her heart, and she gasped.

You are hurting me, she cried out.

You Called. We cannot cross to you. They howled, and her name was drawn out as they reached across the ice. *Wolfwalkerwolfwalker . . .*

She glanced back at the tent. It was a form of safety, she thought, like the cozar with their wagons. It represented what she could have if she turned her back on need—friends, Ariye, the thick love of the wolves. Suddenly angry, she tightened the cinch on the hammer-headed dnu and swung onto the stolid beast. It stamped its six feet softly, but Dion did not give the signal to trot. Instead, she stared up at the three ghostly moons. "Have you ever given me a choice?" she demanded. "A choice that I could live with?" Her words left clouds in the air.

The moons did not answer. Instead, the packsong echoed. *Hunt, close, closer . . .* She stared at the dnu-shattered road of snow. Those tracks would not remain for long before they too would be swept under by the coming storm. By tomorrow, there would be only lumps and drifts across the Ariyen road. By the time the others roused from sleep, she would be kays to the north. She tightened her grip on the reins, glanced back once more at the tent, then turned and deliberately rode away.

XXXIX

Ember Dione maMarin

Don't look so hard that you miss the path;
Don't swallow whole when you can chew
*   each thought like a piece of old jerky;*
Even a simple stone can hide truth;
Even the sand holds water.

—Yegros Chu, Randonnen philosopher

Rhom urged his dnu in the wake of Ammesdo's mount. Dawn was still, with only a smattering of snowflakes to hint at stronger weather. He knew his twin was close. The wolves almost strained to leap ahead, and Gray Hishn was held by only a thread. They stayed out of survival, but their need for food would soon be crushed under their need to reach the wolfwalker.

There was another party up ahead—he had seen a tent on the slope a half day below the passhouse. *Stay,* he begged the other party silently. Stay and help him find his twin. But dawn had brought a layer of clouds, and when they had cleared, the tent was gone, and the riders had moved on to the pass.

Talon scanned the mountain. The snow was falling lightly, and he could see the ridge behind which the passhouse squatted like a stone den. They would easily make it by dusk.

There was tension in the other rai—he cut himself off from that word. Not raiders. There was tension in his *men and women*, and it was only slightly eased by the wolves. The wolf pack that bounded ahead of them had already eaten a third of their supplies, and they still had days to go to reach the Ariyen border. They would all be hungry by then. He stared at the distant ridge and bit back the eagerness that threatened to spill over to the wolves. He was close. He could *feel* her. He had to fight the strength that sang in his muscles to keep from spurring his dnu. Had to unclench the hands that threatened to crush the already flattened leather reins. But he was close enough to taste her in the gray.

One of the wolves looked back. That ragged bond between them, the chain that was no bond of love but of need—that geas that twisted his guts . . . Find her, yes. And then take back his freedom. Control his future, control his life.

Freedom, the wolves seemed to whisper.

The gray that edged his hard mind seemed satisfied.

"They are hours below us," Kiyun murmured.

Tehena nodded. She could just see the small dots of another party approaching along the pass. It was a large party—a dozen riders, perhaps—but one with pack dnu, not wagons. They seemed to be moving swiftly.

"We could wait for them."

"We could," she agreed noncommittally. "She might come back."

They both knew the chance of that. Kiyun looked north along the shattered snow. "She should make it to the passhouse before the storm hits."

"Then so can we." Tehena gave one last study of the party in the distance, then swung up on her dnu.

Kiyun didn't bother to answer. Neither of them would

allow Dion to run alone into the storm. The Gray Ones might not be beside her, but he had seen the look in her eyes last night. Even here, the wolves were strong enough to pull Ember Dione back north, and the wolfwalker was still partly feral.

"She will be all right," Tehena murmured.

"Of course," Kiyun answered firmly.

Neither one said anything about the doubt in each other's eyes.

Dion hunched in the saddle. It had been stupid to go ahead alone, no matter how the Gray Ones pulled. She had let herself listen to the howling in her skull and had not paid enough attention to the road. Now she was paying the price. A kay ago, her dnu had slipped badly on the ice, hitting one of its middle legs. Since then, it had been struggling. She had healed animals before—wolves, dnu—but never without the Gray Ones nearby. The only times she had healed herself at a distance, the wolves had been close in her mind. Here, they were growing stronger in her mind, but they were not close enough to use.

She could turn back. Neither Tehena nor Kiyun would have gone on toward Ariye without her, and both would follow her through the snow. It had been stupid to leave them behind at all. Stupid to think she could keep her daughter safe on her own. She was pregnant, for moons' sake. Whatever she had thought of her skills before, they were nothing now. She hoped it was the leftover presence of the aliens in her mind, not her own arrogance, that had skewed her judgment. Now she had no choice. She was closer to the passhouse than to her friends, and she would not risk harm to her child by turning back in this storm.

Her dnu slipped again. Unbalanced, it shifted sideways and plunged through the crust of snow. For a moment, it floundered heavily, its uninjured legs churning, while she tried to guide its hump-bucking body. There was ice under the snow, and it could not get good purchase.

"Moonwormed, chak-driven beetle-beast," she cursed. Her own anger surprised her. She forced the dnu to climb back up when it would have taken the easier slide down that it had already started. When they finally regained the road, she was breathing just as heavily as the dnu. At least she would be warm enough at the passhouse, from anger if nothing else. If she was lucky, there would be someone else at the shelter who might have better gear for treating the wounded beast. Until then, it was the dnu, the snow, and her anger. And the wolves, of course, she thought sourly.

As if her thought triggered them to affirm that she was in the pass, the Gray Ones howled louder. *Wolfwalkerwolfwalkerwolfwalker . . .*

I am coming, she returned sharply. Driven, she was always driven, but now, it was as much by her own needs as the wolves'.

Two kays, no more, and she would be up to the shelter, long before the storm. She twisted to look back and did not see the wolves who kept crawling through her thoughts. Even knowing that Rhom was closing in, the gray voices were stronger than they should possibly be, especially if there were only two wolves, Hishn and Yoshi. At this altitude, with almost no life to sustain and repeat the packsong, the sense of them still ought to be distant and faint, like half-forgotten lyrics. But when she stretched, she could hear the wolves like clear echoes.

Her attention sharpened, and it made the wolfsong shiver. In answer, out of that din rose a single gray voice. It was a snarl that caught Dion's breath.

Wolfwalker . . .

"Hishn . . ." she breathed. Faint as Hishn was, the massive wolf seemed to throw power across the distance. *Wolfwalker, we are coming . . .*

Dion bowed her head. Her hands fisted on the reins, and she struggled against a wave of emptiness that bit at her cheeks with the cold. Leaving Hishn behind had been a selfish escape, a wallowing in grief and a self-punishment for the guilt she had felt for letting her son and mate die. When she had finally begun to acknowledge that guilt and admit that she must find the heart to raise another child, she was trapped by the promises she had made: the oath sworn to other Gray Ones, the oath to the alien. She had bound herself to this world in too many ways, and the promises that bound her had, through the echoes of the wolves, bound another, as well.

She had to face that man and free him from the reflection of her own griefs. If this man heard the wolves so clearly that he was driven across three counties, his anger was justified. Like a predator wounded and driven to hunt what he had lost, he was raging against her unintentional geas while his own needs tore at her memory of Aranur's voice that still echoed in the gray. The wolfwalker and the hunter—their griefs matched, their rage and desperation blended into a single wolfsong. And if the wolves had their way, Dion and that hunter would mate in a maelstrom of need, not love, and she would lose Aranur forever. His memories would be set aside, his voice would fade, his touch would disappear from her skin as the wolves opened her mind to the hunter. She could not hold two men in her heart. This hunter would force her to face Aranur's death, then would leave her to that emptiness when she freed him from the wolves. The wolves would subside as Dion let go of her mate and raised her daughter alone. They thought the child would give her enough strength, that the cure she promised would come.

Wolfwalker, the gray voice whispered.

She closed her eyes. To face the elders in Ariye, the oath to the alien, her promise to the wolves, she knew that she must somehow hold this child apart from the promises she had made. She caught her breath. "One duty, not three, until you are grown," she told the child in her womb. "And that, only to be a child." There was a fierceness in her answer that was made not of wilderness, but of will. It was a thread to herself, one that she had thought lost. She had been will without strength, but even will could find a way to survive, could find and wield its own strength. She gathered that determination and twisted it into a stronger cord.

Wolfwalkerwolfwalker . . .

"One duty, until she is grown," she returned sharply.

There was a pause in the distant packsong. When the wolves came back, faint though they were, they came in like a claw. They cut through her determination until her promise to them was bare and bleeding, tinged with yellow and the images of plague and the alien Aiueven.

"I have not forgotten," she snarled back. "We are bound like sisters. I will neither forsake you nor let you die. But I will keep our daughter safe—"

She cut herself off. "Misbegotten moons of the north," she cursed. She could no longer tell if she was addressing the wolves. That sense of alien yellow eyes, of the bond between mother and daughter, had been pulled right out of her mind. The touch of the alien mother—a mother that was now hers—had never faded with the distance from the north as had the wolves' voices with altitude. That touch of yellow in the back of her mind had been constant. With the Gray Ones as faint as they were, the touch of alien eyes seemed stronger and more clear. It was as much a living link as the bond she had with the wolves. Fear crawled with the cold. The link she had forged with the alien had been born of desperation, not of will. All her life, she had fought death with her weapons, her hands, and finally, her mind. She wondered bitterly if that struggle had always been more a desperate fear of failure—a fear of loss, of weakness—than a determination to win.

"Or both," she whispered. She was afraid—afraid of losing the last of her mate, afraid of losing this child as she had lost her others. So she had given this child to another mother, not just to herself. Now the Aiueven mother considered Dion's child her own. Dion wondered if even the power in that alien was enough to keep this child safe from the hungry world. She flexed her fingers as if she could draw on that power from a distance, and looked down at the growing bulge. "You are bound even as I am," she whispered. "But I promise you this—and it is a third promise to bind me. You will see more than I, live more freely than your brothers ever did. Your vision, doubled with the eyes of the wolves and with a mother I never had, will be like Aranur's, greater than mine alone. You will see beyond the mountains, beyond the stars." She caught her breath. "My child, whom I promised away."

Deep in her mind, yellow slitted eyes seemed to blink, then fade back into the packsong. In her mind, the Gray Ones growled around her.

Tehena and Kiyun slogged through snow, then clattered across bare stone. The healer had left the tent gear with them, taking only emergency supplies, and breaking camp had cost Tehena and Kiyun twenty minutes after they realized her absence. They had had to stop barely an hour later when one of the leather shoes for the dnu loosened and fell off.

"Hours," Tehena muttered. They were now hours behind the wolfwalker. And Dion could leave the trail any time to reach her goal. She glanced at Kiyun and cursed his steady strength, wishing she could add it to her own and then fly to the wolfwalker's side.

Kiyun glanced back and didn't comment at her dark expression. Tehena was difficult at best, and when she looked like that, he tried to keep his distance. Tehena's expression was warranted—they would be lucky to reach the passhouse by evening, and if Dion was waiting there for them, he'd be surprised. The wolfwalker had had that look in her eyes, and wasn't one for standing still. With the wolves behind her, the healer could make it to the pass and ride on through the night to the other side of the mountain.

Talon studied the sky. He was close. She was coming to him—the wolves could feel her drawing near. She was almost close enough to feel. "Soon," he whispered to the sky. The moons barely glowed behind the clouds to shine through the growing flurries, but he saw the pass clearly. The road fell away on both sides, seeming to gather speed as it plunged down through the snow.

He barely glanced at his men. Mal was shivering, he knew, and Ki and Dangyon were feeling the chill, but he could not stop. Not now. Not as close as this. Three hours, and they would make the next passhouse. After that . . . His hands clenched in his gloves. After that, the woman, the wolves, and Ariye.

XL

Ember Dione maMarin

Fight or give up;
Fight, or you lose your choices;
Fight, or you lose your life.

   —from the Book of Abis

Dion shivered hard. The stable was not warm, but it was better than the bite of the wind. There were over a dozen dnu already there. "Pack dnu," she murmured. "Traders." She did not question her relief. It was sharp enough that the wolves must have fed her sense of danger even at their distance.

She led her riding beast to an empty stall, removed its gear and tack, and grabbed the pitchfork to toss hay into the manger. She cursed herself to keep moving while she forked fresh straw onto the flooring. Finally, she rubbed down the creature with one of the cold-stiffened lice rags. The dnu's injured leg was bruised, but not broken; it could wait while she traded for ointment. What she carried with her would do little good for the dnu. She straightened from rubbing the creature and realized as her breath came more quickly that the exertion had been needed as much to warm herself as it was to wipe the sweat from its coat.

She was trembling as she made her way to the passhouse. She had not realized how much her child was sapping her strength. She leaned for a moment against the barn wall. The cold stone clung to her gloves. When she pulled free, she left a glove print behind in the ice.

She fumbled with the door to the passhouse and closed it quietly by habit. The wood corridor glowed with light. Heat, food . . . The four traders were in the inner area. She knew there were only four; the other dnu were pack beasts.

The men had warmed a single room, and their careless voices were distorted by the walls that divided the stone building. The odor of stew—ubiquitous stew, she thought wryly—came to her nose. She was shivering uncontrollably now, but there was heat just inside that door. Her daughter would be safe. It did not occur to her that they might turn her away from their fire until she had warmed. She could see little through the heat-fogged window in the door, so she knocked quickly, then opened the door and stepped in. Heat hit her like a fist. She clenched her suddenly aching teeth and stood still, her eyes taking in the room. There was a neat stack of saddlebags along one wall, four bedrolls on the lower bunks along the walls. A broad-shouldered man stood facing the fire, talking to another; a third was stretched out in his blankets; a fourth dug through a saddlebag. They were stripped down to undertunics and trousers, and they whirled at her entrance. The sleeping man came awake, his hand reaching for his sword. The fourth straightened with his own weapon. The two by the fire whipped around. She registered their movements without shifting—she had expected the startlement. But then her gaze caught on the older man: broad shoulders, narrow waist, and blue-gray eyes like chips of ice . . .

She felt her breath freeze in her mouth. Heavy-boned eyebrows, prominent cheekbones, hair peppered like Gamon's . . .

He stared at her.

"You—" She forced it out.

The man set his mug on the mantel with exaggerated care and put his hand on the hilt of his sword. He had a powerful grace that seemed to fill the room. It was a power she had felt before. Before the seawall, before the death, on the border of Ariye. Ferns had broken beneath her as they had fought in a near-silent forest. His dnu had charged; her strike had barely made him pause. His eyes, blue and chipped with ice. And months later, the coast, the seawall, the steel stabbing in. The death of her mate . . .

Memories blinded her. She yanked at her sword, but the shivers wracked her body so that she fumbled the blade.

She jerked it free and tried to shrug, one-handed, out of her cloak. One of the raiders shifted as if to disarm her, but Drovic gestured sharply at the man to remain still. He stared at her in turn. "Dione," he said softly, wonderingly.

"Bandrovic." She choked out the name. "Lepa-spawned son of a mudsucker—"

Drovic stepped forward. His voice was mild. "Calm yourself, Dione. You will wake my other raider."

Her eyes went nearly black with rage. In the firelight, she was consumed by the blaze. She struggled to shake her cloak off her left arm. The sword shook in her other hand. She didn't notice. "You—you took me, took my mate." Her voice was tight and rising. "You've cost me everything—"

"Not everything," Drovic corrected. He gestured negligently. "The death of your son was your fault, not mine."

Dion went deathly pale. For a moment, the room seemed frozen, the flames a two-dimensional drawing, the men unmoving, Drovic's eyes like halspreth stones. The wind outside was a silent shroud that draped across the passhouse. Then the wall around her guarded heart fractured like an eggshell.

Drovic watched her color change from rage to shock to blindness. "Aye," he said softly. Slowly, he drew his sword. He was never without it, and his hand, unlike hers, was steady. "Ember Dione maMarin. You blame me, and I suppose I understand that. But you deal in death as I do," he said softly. "We are not so different, you and I. Your rage at me is a mirror."

"No," she choked. Her sword rose to attack position.

He cocked his head as if to study her. "It is fate that brought you here, Dione. Fate that gives each of us the power to destroy the other. But you are cold, Dione, and alone in the night. You have no riders with you. No other blades, no bowmen. You cannot even call the wolves because of the altitude. There is no one to stand between us now, no one to blunt the truth. It is down to you and I." Dion heard him blindly. She did not have to call the wolves—they were there in the snow already. She could feel them closing in from the heights. There was snow in their pelts, ice between their toes.

Tehena, Kiyun, Rhom, Gamon—they were in the mountain passes, and the thought of her friends, her brother, triggered a strength that did not lie in her body. It was a strength that said she was alone and would ever be so and must find her will in herself, and yet that she was not alone and would never be so again. A litany of self-judgment flashed through her mind. To seek, to fight, to heal, to grieve and flee . . . She was everything she feared, and yet she kept on moving forward. She fought to heal, then drew her sword and killed. She killed, then took up her healer's band. She reached out, but stayed remote like a wolf; she loved, but it was a love that could survive only in wilderness. Without her mate, she had no balance; without her sons, she had no hope, and without hope to protect her, she had become defenseless. It was not her world she ran from—the duties and obligations—but the fear that she could not face on her own the endless battles inside her. She knew the threads of what she lost were still there, waiting to be rewoven, and that she was afraid to touch them together. Yet the hunter was closing in, and that man would grab at the power she carried while his rage ignored what she had had with Aranur. This raider before her was the symbol of that hunter, the father of the beast. Thus, the hunter was her future; the raider before her was the step she must take to grasp the reins of her life. The hunter, Bandrovic—they were the end of a spear, the contact point, the blood point, the point at which life stopped and started again. Face them, and she found herself. The cold in her bones was a slap of realization. Her life, her world, the wolves, her child. Control, she told herself.

"So, Dione," he prompted softly.

"Bandrovic," she said, suddenly calm. "It is down to you and I," she agreed with a voice as soft as night. "But this time, I will fight."

Drovic smiled—then lunged.

She saw it before he moved. Yellow eyes—wolf eyes, alien eyes—they quickened her sight like a lepa. She beat aside the attack, ignoring the way her elbow rang with the force of his lunge. The three other raiders scrambled out of the way as they tried to get out of the door and into the relative safety of the hall. She ignored them. They would not interfere.

Deliberately, she parried high. Drovic shrugged back, struck with his fist to disarm her, and twisted back with a hiss as she flicked her blade. A tiny trickle of blood marked his ear. His smile turned grim, and he circled. The steps were from Abis, the martial art of Randonnen. She shifted instinctively into a Cansi-style stance—Aranur had taught her the moves a year after they had mated. Drovic's lunge came up short, and she smiled. She did not move in.

"Clever," Drovic said softly. Even though she was expecting it, his attack was lightning fast so that the tip of his blade pierced her tunic—another Cansi-style move, and one that Aranur had not taught her. She danced, struck wildly to make Drovic wary, and dodged around the corner of a bunk. Drovic's sword rang against her blade, then he beat-attacked and feinted. He kicked a pack under the bunk. He extended; she parried. He attacked; she leapt back. She darted inside his reach and cut back in toward his side. He wrenched unexpectedly to the left and beat her attack down, slid his blade in, and flicked it through her clothes. And chuckled.

The sound gave Dion chills. Fabric gapped across her stomach. Gray strength fed her limbs, and she darted back around the table to avoid the attack that she felt, rather than saw. She parried—and realized his move had been another feint, as smooth as Gamon's and as slick as any that Aranur had ever made. Drovic's blade snapped back and slammed across her sword. Her blade flew away.

Drovic paused. Dion watched him like a wolf. Her violet eyes were wide, not with fear, but like a wolf that protected its kill. She was edgy, poised, and the slightest move would release her. Drovic knew he could take her now, but he would have to hurt her. He had almost had this woman before. She would be even more useful now. He held himself still and made his voice soft as he eyed her. "You can continue to fight, Dione. I can't guarantee I won't break you a bit when I step in to bring you down."

Her voice was half snarl, and he knew he had been right to hold back. "Why bring me down at all? You think I'm a prize?

A trophy to brag about? The Ariyens, Randonnens will hunt you down like a rast if you think to hold onto me. Keep me, and I'll get you killed."

He chuckled. "I died thirty years ago. And with those hands—" He gestured with his chin, though his gaze never wavered. "—you're worth too much. Give up a chance to control a master healer, a wolfwalker, a scout like you? In your dreams, Dione."

Control . . . "I'll be no figurehead for you."

He nodded at that truth. He didn't need her for that.

"Why?" She could not hide the edge of frustration.

He cocked his head at her. "You represent Randonnen and Ariye. You are the way to control what I have, what I lost." He did not take his eyes off her as he nodded at Slu in the doorway. "Mix up the vertal tonic."

"Vertal in a tonic?" She stepped half forward in spite of herself. "Vertal reacts instantly with saliva. You can't sedate me like that. All you'll do is lose me my voice for a few ninans and leave me groggy for a day."

"It's not sedation I'm interested in."

"Then what?" she demanded. "You want me to lose my voice?" Her left hand pressed protectively to her belly, and she stared at him in sudden realization. "It would be that," she breathed. "Without my voice, I cannot defend myself if you take me to be sold like a slave. They will ask the question if anyone contests my sale, and I will not be able to answer."

His eyes narrowed as she understood so quickly. "Once the papers are registered, you are owned until you work yourself free. And it takes a very long time for a healer to work herself free. Add a wolfwalker on top of that, and one with your reputation . . ." He shrugged explicitly.

Her child . . . "If you do this now, this far into the mountains, you might not get to a sale in time. My voice will return. I will be able to answer the question."

"But there are other, more pressing reasons to use the vertal now."

"You think I'll kill you with screaming?"

He smiled coldly. "I think there are others with whom I wish your silence."

"I can still write."

"Not without paper and pen. And you can't carve out a message without knife and wood."

She didn't realize she had backed away until she hit the bunk behind her. "You cannot use the vertal. It will—" She cut herself off. She didn't realize that her left hand now clenched her belly. "Vertal changes when it hits the saliva. It becomes a form of enhotal and goes into the bloodstream. It affects all soft tissues. You—you can't," she repeated harshly.

He stared at her posture. Stared at the way one hand covered her abdomen.

"Dione," he breathed. It was more of a question than statement. He took half a step forward. She balanced to leap for his throat. He shook his head, holding up one hand as if to tell her to wait. It was a command gesture, one that knew it would be obeyed, and she actually hesitated. It was an instant she didn't have. Drovic's hand struck like lightning. He grabbed her collar, jerked, and ripped all three of her shirts around the rent he had already cut. Buttons flew. He stared at the belly barely covered by her undertunic. The bulge was unmistakable. "You are pregnant." He raised his gaze. "You are with child. Whose child?" His grip tightened. "*His* child?"

She stared at him, mesmerized by the expression in his blue eyes. It was amazement, wonder, hope. And it shocked her into confusion.

Drovic put his broad hand on her belly, ignoring her instinctive flinch. "Gift of the moons . . . It would be about four months now, but you carried lightly before. And you would not have taken kum-jan with another—not with the wolves in your head." He stared into her face. "It is his child."

Aranur's name rang in her head as if Drovic had shouted it. She struck him. Hard. He didn't bother to duck the blow. Instead, he simply caught her arm as she extended, rolled her elbow, and threw her to the floor. "Line," he said calmly, dropping and pinning her down with an instinctive force that was frightening in its focus. She writhed, but only bruised herself against his hands and knees and the floor.

He tied her wrists and shoved her against the wall. "This changes things," he murmured as he backed away, letting her regain her own balance. He didn't take his gaze from her face. "Throw out what is in that pot. Scrape off some randerwood bark and boil it in a cup of water," he ordered Slu as the other raiders edged back into the room. Drovic dug through Dion's belt pouches and those in her pack. After a few minutes, he found what he wanted and handed it over to Slu. "Add a pinch of this powder, and three drops of this vial."

Dion sucked in her breath as she saw the pale brown vial.

Drovic watched her eyes. "Aye, Dione. I know what it is."

"It will permanently sear my mouth before it inactivates."

"And should burn out your voice like a corpse," he agreed. "But it will be diluted by the randerwood bark. By the time it hits your throat, it should hardly burn at all, even if it does silence your vocal chords. It won't harm a hair on the child in your womb."

"You care enough about my child to keep her safe?"

"Her . . ." An odd look crossed his face. "I lost a daughter once."

"The child is mine," she snarled.

"Of course."

But he had answered her almost absently, and that frightened her worse than before. "You want me silent—I give you my word to say nothing. You don't need the vertal; you don't need that."

"Aye," he agreed again.

"I tell you I will be silent." Her voice tightened, and her tied hands pressed against her belly, clutching her shirts together. "That mixture will make an acid before it's neutralized. You can't be sure that it won't hurt my baby."

"Sure enough," he returned. "I've used it before."

Her lips curled back from her teeth. It was because of one of his raids that she had gone to do a healing, and had brought her sons back through Still Meadow when the lepa flocked. She had lost her youngest son that day, and her older son later from his guilt. She had met Bandrovic again at the coast when he tried to kidnap her. He had lost four men in the fight; Dion had lost her mate. Her voice was soft as velvet but deadly as a night spider. "You have taken enough from me."

He cocked his head, studying her. "Perhaps I will give something back."

He was mocking her, and her fury tightened into a white-hot lance. Years of touching death, dealing death, dreaming death. Years of attending the elders with their patronizing arrogance that she would simply obey, regardless of the cost. Years of drowning in guilt, or accepting duty, of sacrifice. Her life, her blood, her mate, her future, her sons, and now, this child?

She attacked blindly, without thought.

Drovic was ready, but he was not prepared for her violence. When he had first fought her, she had been lost and full of doubt. When he fought her again on the coast, she had been grieving the loss of her son. Now, there was no hesitation. No doubt, no despair, no death wish. She was simply rage and will. Even tied, her hands flashed like claws toward his throat, and only a desperate wrench protected his carotid artery. He struck her ribs, but she seemed to flow around his fist, ignoring the force of his blow as she tore for his eyes. He blocked and felt her hands tear at his ear, jerking his head forward toward her teeth. It was with desperate instinct that he threw himself back—the wolf in Dion was wild. *Blood, lust, hunt, hate.* His back hit the post of the bunkbed, her elbow caught him on the temple, and he took a blow to the inner shoulder that opened his gut to a kick. He fell back again, and she bit at his arm as he struck back, tearing cloth, not flesh. She snarled. She followed his blow, striking under his arm to the inner flesh of the biceps and then tearing again at the artery. Then his fist caught her again on the ribs and lifted her completely. She hit the wall and fell back to the floor like a rag.

Drovic watched her push herself to her elbows, then her knees. He waited until her eyes turned normal with shock and pain. Then he took the mug and dipped a small amount of liquid from the small cauldron over the fire. He held it out. "Drink, Dione."

She stared at him.

"Drink, Dione, or die."

Chantz had held out such a mug, and taking that had been

her first step toward freedom from grief. Chantz—last chance, she almost laughed. Last chance to turn back from the road she had chosen. Last chance to run from fear. The wolves had been wrong, she thought almost wildly. The danger had not been that hunter-mate, but this first step, this raider who would destroy her. She stared at the man, still gasping in her breath, until he shifted as if to force the drink down her throat. Slowly, she stretched out her hand and took it.

"Throw it away," Drovic warned mildly, "and the next mixture will be stronger."

She was not quite steady as the weight of the drink rested in her fingers. It smelled bitter, acrid, and she tried to hold back the fear of what it would do. She stretched out to the wolves in the mountains. Their strength was like a cloak. Control, she told herself. There was power in her hands if she could only use it. Wild wolves, Hishn, Yoshi—she could feel them all. Close and closing in, feeding her their strength. Her violet eyes were tinged with a ring of yellow, and her whisper was deep in her throat. "You cannot touch me now."

"I don't have to." In the firelight, Drovic watched her carefully but missed the tint in her eyes. "Once you drink that, you are mine. You'll have no voice—though it will grow back, given enough time. Not as prettily, not as clear, but it will return. Until then, I can write out whatever contract I want for your services." He nodded at her belly. "I'll have your child to help control you, and I think you will appreciate the other incentive you'll meet."

Incentive—other raiders. More humiliation, pain, death. She looked down at the mug. *Control.*

"Drink on your own, and it will sear only your tongue and throat. If you force me to administer it to you, it will be messy, Dione."

She understood. The liquid would burn her gums, lips, mouth. If it splashed on her face, she could be scarred. If it splashed in her eyes, she'd go blind. She raised it, held her breath, and gathered herself. In her mind, the wolves seemed to circle. She did not question their nearness. She needed them; they were there. She felt a touch of alien cold that shifted her focus and cut through the gray like a spear. It became a sharpness, a line of light in her mind, and she felt the wolves spread out along that line, as if they could build a shield to hold her awareness away from her body and what she knew would come. She gathered in light and gray, yellow and cold, blood and flashing steel.

Then she tossed down the acrid fluid.

Wolves screamed. Wild wolves shattered snow as they bolted ahead. Gray Hishn stiffened and could not howl, and Yoshi's scruff bristled like thorns. *Wolfwalker! Wolfwalkerrr . . .*

Dion's hand clenched convulsively. She did not notice that her fingers bent the tin of the cup before it dropped to the floor with a clatter. She choked back a scream, and the sound became raggedly hoarse as the liquid burned in her throat. Instinctively, she clutched her neck. She could not help staggering back. Her shoulders hit the wall hard, and she gagged, swallowed, choked, and shrieked a near-silent sound as the acid burned her voice. Then she dropped to her knees and retched, and the fluid was flecked with blood where it spattered the dusty floor.

Wolfwalker!

She braced herself against the floor and looked up. Drovic watched her eyes. They were dark and terrible and tinged around the violet irises. Her lips worked, and no sound came out, but a chill crawled the length of his spine as if her silent howl had a frightening substance.

He held out his hand. She couldn't help cringing back, her hands up to ward him off. Drovic did not move forward. He merely stood, holding out his hand while she eyed him like a worlag.

His voice was almost gentle. "It is done, Dione. You are mine. There is no need for further violence." She could not answer, and he cocked his head to regard her more carefully. "Someday, you might even forgive me." He saw the impotent rage in her eyes. He nodded slowly. "I understand your fury. I've held the madness of my own history in my heart for thirty years. But I'll not risk everything I've fought for on the word of a woman like you." He shook his head. "No, Dione. You believe too much in the ideal, in the heroes and good endings of the world. Your word could never be a promise when the moons went to call your name."

Dion stared at him with violent eyes that burned almost yellow in rage. Her throat convulsed. Her arms shook. Her hands, on the floor, seemed to clench.

Drovic reached down and took her arm to haul her up, and dust filtered down to the floor. He stopped and glanced down. There was a soft spot in the wood—a depression where some sort of decay had set in. Looking down on her, he paused. There was something in her eyes . . .

She tried to choke out an answer, and Drovic squatted beside her and stared into her eyes. The ring of yellow was fading back, but her breath was still horrible. He reached out and fingered the silver circlet around her forehead. "You are an interesting woman, Dione. You live your life on an edge of decision—each moment the right choice for the moment, but never quite the choice of the future. Perhaps that is why you became a master healer so young: You have to act for each moment of life, so that you cheat death again. You feel, and so you can never let logic deter you from mercy. That is your flaw, Dione. I look ahead, and I plan, and I cheat death by that planning, not by mercy or compassion. Mercy has its place, but not in my near future, and your voice at the wrong time could break the history I build." He rose to his feet, his movements light for a man of his bulk. "I am sorry," he said softly. "But you do not need your voice to heal or scout—or even to speak to the wolves. I've taken nothing from you that you value."

She snarled silently, her hands clenched against her belly.

He nodded. "We understand each other, you and I. You live, as long as you're silent." He stood and gestured for Cheyko to set out another bedroll. "Get some rest, Dione. We'll stay here till after the storm."

Hishn and Yoshi raced over the road. The familiar scents of Tehena and Kiyun were a spur to their feet, and they broke through the icy crusts without slowing. Yoshi lost one of his leather shoes, but did not stop even when the paw was cut on a line of ice and the pad began to bleed.

Wolfwalker! Hishn's voice was an unending howl.

I hear you, Dion returned faintly. Her mental voice was clear, but almost shaking, and the hunger that now gnawed in Dion's stomach twisted Hishn's guts. It was partly the hunger that followed a healing, the hunger that sapped her when she stripped power from herself. It was also the hunger of rage.

Wolfwalker we come!

Cheyko went out to check the dnu. An hour later, it was Slu's turn. The tall raider returned with curt words. "Still coming down like fleas on a sleeping dnu. Only a brain-dead 'Skarian would travel in weather like this."

Drovic nodded and finished banking the fire. He glanced at the wolfwalker, but she lay motionless in her bedroll. He knew she wasn't sleeping. In the flickering light, she looked oddly gaunt, but her violet eyes followed him like a wolf. It was beginning to be unnerving.

His voice was short. "Sleep, Dione. You'll have plenty of chances to try to escape later—if you still choose to take them."

She merely eyed him with grim intent. Her hands were still tied, but she no longer twisted them to relieve the cruel tightness. The raw flesh beneath the ropes throbbed with every heartbeat, but her throat was no longer on fire. She stretched, and could almost feel Hishn bounding over the stiffening tracks of dnu, could almost feel the heat of the wolf's body like a damp sweat on her own. Her stomach cramped with hunger, and she knew she would have to bear it. If Drovic knew . . .

Hishn, reflecting the pain, reached out. *Use my strength.*

Dion closed her eyes and let their minds mesh faintly. The Gray One must be nearly on the passhouse. Dion could not help the hope that leapt into her mind. She turned her head so Drovic could not see her expression.

The surge in her voice was answered by a dozen wild ones. She could almost see the passhouse through their eyes like a tiny contrasting block of white and black squatting up ahead.

Could almost smell the dnu in the stables. *Inside the house, to the left—*

Like an answer, the door burst open. Frigid air swept around the man in the doorway. Dion caught her breath. Her eyes were blurred. The moons themselves had come—

Steel flashed. Kiyun leapt in like a badgerbear. He caught Slu half out of his coat on the elbow and snapped the man's arm bone like a toothpick. Slu started to scream, and Kiyun stabbed home. Tehena darted into the room in Kiyun's shadow with an arrow aimed for Drovic. Cheyko caught the movement and pulled his knife. The raider lunged into the lean woman's path. Like water, Tehena dropped and loosed her bolt. Cheyko hit Tehena in the chest, but the bolt had released. The lanky woman flew back into the door frame.

Dion kicked free of the bedroll and stuck out her legs to trip neBrenton as he jumped past her to meet Kiyun's charge. Kiyun slammed the man to the floor. Cheyko tangled with them and struck the wall hard, stunned. Dion struggled to her feet, but Drovic caught her shoulder, snarled like a worlag, and threw her into the packs. She fought free with a snarl, as Tehena faced Drovic alone. Dion's throat worked, but only a tiny sound ragged its way out in a mockery of a word. Dion launched herself at Drovic's back. Tehena stabbed in, and Drovic brushed the thin woman aside. Dion's elbows caught him on the back of the head. He grunted and missed his own thrust, lost his grip on the hilt of his knife. His cross-fist punch to Tehena's jaw was a leaden hammer. Tehena took the edge of it on her jaw and fell, caught a second uppercut from neBrenton as she dropped, and stabbed up instinctively as she fell. The man took the blade in the side.

Drovic had already twisted to slam Dion. She kicked for his kidney, but he blocked, swiveled, and trapped her against the wall with a meaty arm. She took his first blow on her shoulder. He aimed high to keep from injuring her—she knew this as he avoided the obvious blow to her gut.

Her claw-hand swung up and caught Drovic in the inner thigh, and his leg jerked back. She tore muscle, not flesh, but his hand clenched her jerkin and slammed her again to the wall. Her half-hearted kick was wasted in air, but Drovic was gripping his thigh.

"Moon-spawned bitch—" he cursed.

The gray in her head swirled. There were more wolves than just Yoshi in her sight. She snarled, ripped free, and launched herself again, short range, full force. Drovic didn't bother to block. He simply punched her midair. She took the blow, but her own strength forced her forward, and her hands found the sides of his neck. He tore at her claws, roared, and threw them both against the wall, crushing her between him and the wood.

Wolfwalker!

Her ribs bowed in ominously; her grip went slack. She slipped slowly to the floor. Drovic glared down at her, but she simply lay, gasping against the wall. Then he whirled to face Kiyun.

Kiyun's steel dripped blood. Tehena swayed nearby, her sword up and determinedly steady even as her pale eyes peered dizzily at Drovic.

Dion didn't move. It wasn't pain; it wasn't fear that held her motionless. It was the howling in her mind. *Wolfwalker-wolfwalkerwolfwalker . . .*

Kiyun half turned. Drovic felt his lips stretch in a grin. Tehena yelled at Dion as a storm seemed to burst into the room. But the wolfwalker flinched back, her fists half pressed over her eyes. This was the moons—the light in her eyes, the ring of steel, the screaming of the wolves. More men shouted as they crowded the door. Her ears cringed against bone. She stared, but could see only light and steel and one man—a tall man, his image blurred by wolves. Her guts turned to ice.

Hishn howled, deafening her to the room. The Gray Ones snarled like demons as they clawed at the outer doors.

"Talon," Drovic snapped. "Kill them."

And the hunter moved to obey. His sword flicked up and he stepped into the attack, not at Drovic, but at Kiyun. Dion cried out, a wild sound that made no noise, an animal sound of silence. The wolves—her focus, her will—the wolves, they had brought her strength in steel, and that strength had betrayed her. She could not see for the gray in her eyes. She could not hear for the howling.

The Gray Ones had brought their mate for her here, and that mate—he was a raider.

XLI

Ember Dione maMarin

Who leaps to heaven in a single bound?

*—fragment from an oldEarth poem
    by Theodore Roethke, oldEarth poet*

Kiyun and Tehena went down like pebbles in a rockfall. In the confusion, Drovic grabbed Dion and hauled her fists from her temple. "Speak through the wolves," he breathed, "and I'll kill him, son or no. He'll decide this on his own, not for some wolf howl of yours."

But her eyes were on the hunter she could only glimpse around Drovic. There was something in the lupine din— something that shocked the ice and hunger from her twisted gut and shattered what was left of her control. She began to struggle wildly.

Drovic slammed her against the wall so that she could not see the hunter, the man, the *him* whom the wolves had brought. Drovic felt the tension in her like a shock. "Are they dead?" he snapped as the raiders rolled Kiyun and Tehena against the other wall and got out some line to bind them.

Wakje looked up. "No." Oroan stuffed a gag in Kiyun's slack, bloody mouth; Harare noted Tehena's bloody nose and didn't gag the woman. Wakje went back to tying their limbs. Drovic eyed them narrowly, and Dion almost wrenched free. He slammed her absently back again to the wall, and Talon jerked as if he'd been kicked. The tall man started forward.

Dion trembled violently, the air seemed to crackle, and powder sifted down from the wood where her arms touched the wall.

Drovic barely noticed the tingling along his skin, but his hands were like manacles. "Talon," he snapped. "Get back."

But Talon's head was bursting with wolf. Outside, the wild ones were circling in the snow, snapping at the stone walls. He had caught a glimpse of the woman behind his father, and the howls were tearing apart his thoughts. His eyes were blinded like hers. A stud of blue, glittering against creamy skin . . . His mate, his world, kum-tai . . . The shadow woman struggled madly, and a snarl tore through his head. For a moment, the world balanced on the back of a wolf. Then the woman screamed silently, and the sound echoed inside his skull with the gray. He dropped his sword. The steel clattered, nicking his boot. He didn't notice. He didn't realize he had fallen to his knees. Rakdi grasped his shoulder and jerked him back. Dangyon caught him like a child.

Talon's vision began to clear. He caught a glimpse of Dion's face. Black hair, silky in the firelight; high cheekbones and a slender, strong chin. Scars that raged down one side of her face—scars that he understood. They were made by claws, talons, his own fingers of grief. He met that wild gaze and froze. Then he found strength again and leaped as Drovic half turned to shove Dion down again. Like a beast, his lips twisted. He caught Drovic's arm and jerked the older man so hard that his father stumbled aside. Then Talon's hard hands dug into her shoulders. He stared into her eyes. Dark eyes, violet eyes . . .

Drovic lunged back to his feet. "Talon—"

"Mine," he snarled at his father. His teeth were bared as he half whirled, and his knife was in his right hand, guarding Dion.

Drovic stepped slowly back. He chose his words with care. "She is yours, if you want her."

"She *is* mine."

Rakdi looked from Drovic, to Talon, to Dion, to the two who were now tied. His eyes narrowed. Harare exchanged a look with Weed, and Dangyon shook his head slowly to himself. There could be only one woman with eyes like that who would be a goal of Drovic's—only one who could have drawn Talon through the wolves.

Talon ignored them and stared down at Dion. "Who are you?" he breathed.

She did not answer. Her lips worked, but she made only a rough, choked semblance of a syllable. Was it fear? he demanded silently. Was it the cringing terror of the cloaked woman in that town, the animal fear that had so disgusted him? Was that all the wolves had promised? His fingers dug in cruelly, and neither noticed that her bound hands clutched his chest just as desperately.

"Who are you?" he repeated more harshly. Her lack of response enraged him. He gripped her chin as if that would force her voice from her throat.

Her eyes blazed. Power seemed to suck from his body. She breathed something.

Wolves howled, and one voice seemed to strike out. His mate, dead in his arms. The wolves like a sea around him . . . "Who?" he shouted, enraged.

Drovic saw Dion's eyes blaze. He did not seem to move, but his hand clenched on the hilt of his sword.

Talon didn't notice. He was immobilized by those eyes, by that violet fire that reached out to his mind and consumed him. The heat of her rage was his own. Her grief, it was the fulcrum. Raw pain was a grip on his throat. The wolves that howled inside his head hammered him with sound.

She stared at him, and some part of her saw how he reflected the looks of his father. Saw that Drovic, the man who had torn her life apart, was blood of her son's blood, the father of their father. Yet Drovic was alive, as was the hunter-man before her. Alive—not on the path to the moons. She made a hoarse sound, a broken sound curled with horror and thickened with shock and wonder.

Drovic's eyes widened as he heard Dion's voice. His gaze flicked to the floor where the decay had set in, to the wall where the surface was powdered. His skin had tingled, and she had gone gaunt like a skeleton after the wall had changed. Dione, the wolfwalker. Dione, who healed her patients. Dione, the Heart of Ariye . . . The trembling, the weakness, the things his son had said in fever and at other times in passing. The woman ran with the Gray Ones, and the woman was a healer. She had come out of the north, where the aliens lived, and she had powdered the wood like flour. "Ovousibas," he breathed.

Dion stripped strength out of her starved body, out of the wolves, out of Talon himself and thrust it into her throat. Burned tissues closed, blood pounded, still draining where her throat was open. She gagged on her own blood. But she found that shred of voice again. She gasped out a single word.

"Aranur—"

Talon froze. The world seemed to crystallize.

He thrust her away like fire.

This time, when she hit the wall, she clung to it for strength. Her voice, scarred with pain, clung to his ears. He did not take his gaze from hers, but he twisted his head toward his father. "Who is she?" he choked. The older man did not answer. "Who is she?" he shouted at Drovic.

Drovic did not know how the lines suddenly deepened on his own face. He regarded his son, the woman, and felt them both slipping away. Felt his guts twist as he realized what he must do. His jaw tightened like that of his son, and his voice was curiously flat as he finally said, "She is your mate."

"My mate," he repeated dumbly.

"The Healer Dione. The Heart of Ariye. The Gray Wolf of Ramaj Randonnen." Drovic took a breath and forced his voice to steady. "She is your mate, Son, and always was—the wolfwalker, Ember Dione."

XLII

Talon Drovic neVolen

They say that Death, like God, is the reflection of a mirror
In which men become heavy with shame, guiltily cold or hollow;
They say that Death, like God, offers clarity
Of every joy and petty act in which men wallow;
They say the face of Death, like God, has two expressions,
And the judgment lips spit gritty truths to swallow;
They say that Death, like God, can offer man redemption
If he accepts the mirror and the second chance which follows.
If man accepts, Death steps
          back,
     the lungs breathe; a sporadic pulse becomes a drum,
   And man stands again—
Between the ambition of his man-made heaven and his history of hell.
First chance at life is birth and blind acquiescence of one's path;
Second is the open eyes, the mirror, and the decision to face oneself:
Birth is easy to forgive:
Initial life is shaped by many, not just one.
It is the second choice which is judged so harshly,
     And which cannot be undone.

     —From "The Face of Death,"
       by Yegros Chu, Randonnen philosopher

"My mate," Talon repeated.

Some thread of hope left over from Dion's life twisted in her like a knife. *Oh, moons of mercy, moons of light* . . . The verse ran over and over in her mind, punctuated by wolves. She tried to speak again, but the one word she had forced through the still-raw tissue had half cut off her breathing. She reached out to touch him with her hands. *Aranur,* she cried out.

Wolfwalkerwolfwalker . . . It was his voice, and she knew now that it was real. Not a stranger taunting her through the wolfsong. Not memory, not a ghost. Real.

Hishn, she cried. *Reach him. Aranur . . .*

Outside, the gray wolf snarled at the others, and the wild wolves fell back. Gray Thoi met Hishn's eyes in challenge. Both wolves' scruff was stiff. Their pelts slowly turned white as the snow dusted both in the growing storm, but Dion's need held them together. It was Gray Paksh who broke into the snarls and blended the other voices.

The Gray Ones called back. *Leader. Aranur . . .*

There was no bond between wolves and man, only through the woman. Still, some echo of that name reached him through the gray shield that still lay on his mind. A shadow of an image—tall, black-haired, with a catlike grace, a man whole and strong—it crawled on the inside of his skull.

Talon blanched, but Drovic's voice cut in before he could catch that thread and make it his own. "Talon," his father said sharply. "She might be your mate, but she killed your own son in Ariye. She took him into the meadow with the lepa and let them tear him apart. She left you for dead in Sidisport, let you fall from her own hands to the sea." The older man stepped forward. "This is the woman who took your other boy away from you, who abandoned you to the raiders. You were dying, but she didn't care. She rode away from you, straight to Randonnen, and never stopped to look back—"

Talon cut him off with a curt gesture. He cocked his head at Dion. Violet eyes, slightly unfocused, staring back at him. Dark eyes in the night. Eyes worn by grief and rage. "You . . . left me," he tried out the words. "I fell, and you left me for dead."

She shook her head, numbly. *Aranur . . .*

"I called for you—I shouted for you through the wolves, but you never answered." He felt the strength shiver in her as she gathered herself again. She seemed to pale before his eyes. He caught her before she could fall.

Her skin seemed to sparkle with energy, and his fingers tingled where they touched her. He tightened his grip as the hint of power released. She trembled and clung weakly, but he did not think it was from fear. There was too much will in her eyes. Her voice was whiskey-rough. "The moons had taken you. You were dead as the son we had lost."

"You killed him."

Despair, grief, suicide, guilt—they flashed in her violet eyes. She forced herself to speak. "The skies had been clear, the herb cutters had been there in the meadow that morning. We were halfway across the grass when the lepa flocked. We didn't make it to the caves. Olarun survived. Danton didn't, yet he left us as surely as if he had himself died. He stays now with our eldest, Tomi." Her voice was still a whisper. He didn't know, she thought, meeting his cold gaze. He didn't know about the child in her womb. She felt him withdraw, and she half moaned, unable to hold back the sound.

But he touched her cheek. His fingers traced the scars that ravaged the left side of her face. "You . . . died."

Aranur . . .

"You died in my arms." Wolves, converging like a tsunami, sweeping him along. Wolves in his mind, tearing at her soul to force it back to her body after the lepa had killed her. And wolves in her eyes, in her arms at the coast, grasping him above the wave-swept rocks when her own strength failed to hold on. She reached up, her hands still bound, to touch his wrist. "As did you. I saw you fall from the seawall. They said—" She broke off. "You were dead. You went down in the waves. You never fought the water."

He stared at her, then caught her wrists in his hands. He turned them over, his hard thumbs feeling the strength in her slender fingers, tracing the raw wounds on her wrists. "I told you to call the wolves. To take in their strength to fight."

"We were fighting the raiders," she whispered. "Fighting your father." She did not dare look at his men. Instead, she clutched his hands. "Oh moons, the wolves, they have brought you back to me."

He felt the shiver go through her as she still trembled with energy. With his gaze on hers, it was a familiar, twisting sensation that seemed to suck at his body. Abruptly, he drew his knife and worked through the lines on her wrists. He nicked the swollen flesh, but she did not flinch even when more blood welled out. Instead, her right hand went involuntarily to his chest to feel for the tiny jewels she prayed would still be there.

His hand covered hers; then he sheathed his knife and touched her sternum in turn to feel the matching studs.

Drovic stepped forward again. "Talon—"

His father broke off at the vicious look on his face. Weed removed his cap and rubbed at his twisted ear. Sojourn hesitated, but Pen merely shrugged and made herself busy picking up the scattered packs while Dangyon and two others dragged Kiyun and Tehena to another room.

"Your voice," Talon said slowly, looking down at his mate. "Vertal?"

She shook her head. "Randerwood bark. Chianshu root and cussid." At his frown, she dropped her gaze to her belly. Talon followed her gesture. His rough hands pressed against her skin, then slid inside her gapped tunic. Her swollen belly triggered memories from years ago. "Mine," he said slowly.

She nodded.

He caught her chin and stared grimly into her eyes. "You will not leave me again."

She shivered. There was something in his eyes that did not speak of the man she had mated, but the man who was Drovic's son. "We are kum-tai," she whispered.

Roc's face, hard up to this point, went blank. "Talon," the woman began.

Dion twisted her head and met the other woman's gaze. The wolfwalker said nothing, but her violet eyes blazed. It was Roc who backed down.

"Kiyun," she said to Talon. "Tehena."

He didn't turn his head. "Make them comfortable," he ordered. "Don't release them."

Dion opened her mouth, but closed it again without speaking.

Weed grunted something at Wakje and made his way to the room next door to set a fire in the grate. Oroan and Rakdi followed, but as they did, there was a rumbling outside. Talon looked up sharply, and Drovic, feeling as if he was losing control, snarled at Ki. "Have all nine moons descended on us here? First Dione, then her friends, then you? Ki, check the stables."

The brown-haired man hesitated, and Drovic's face stilled. Talon nodded, and Ki left quietly.

"So," his father said softly of Talon's men. "They are yours now, not mine."

"They are their own," he returned.

"They will never be that, not after what they have done."

"Any man can stand away from his sins and choose a different road."

"Aye. But when he does, he'll pay for those sins sooner, rather than later. Turn them now, and you give up their lives to the trial block—" He broke off at the sound of running feet.

Ki burst back in. "Moonworms, Talon, but there are over a dozen riders—"

Talon's men spilled out of the room, drawing the weapons they'd just sheathed. Talon dragged Dion with him. They reached the outer rooms just as the double doors opened and snow-dusted figures poured in. A wolf leaped in first, almost tripping the man who followed. Other men charged in their wake. The wolf seemed to fly across the room, and Dion wrenched free of Talon. "Hishn—"

Wolfwalker!

"Dion!" Rhom shouted.

Gamon took two steps in his wake and actually froze. "By the moons—" he gasped.

"Halt!" roared the Lloroi.

Both groups stiffened like stone. Men stared at each other. In spite of the years, in spite of the countless battles, in spite of every bruise of training that he'd suffered over the years, Gamon was frozen in place. His thoughts ran like lightning toward the older raider leader: the sense of familiarity at the coast, that recognition of a stance or movement, his unease at his suspicions, and Dion's description of the raider who had hunted her so many months ago. Gamon stared at Drovic, but even as he recognized the threat to his county, his men, his family, his eyes were drawn to the man beside Drovic, the man with the icy eyes. Even the frigid death of the final hell could not at that moment have reached him.

Snow dusted the threshold. The clumps of men almost vibrated with the violence of standing still. The raiders were still half dressed for the cold. The Ariyens had shed their heavy coats in the stable and wore only their fighting mail. Both sides poised in a jumble of stances, held where they had halted.

Hishn growled, low in her throat, and Dion gripped her scruff. Aranur—Talon? had grabbed her arm again to keep her from the melee, and it was a vise that crushed her biceps. She didn't care. The musk of the wolf was in her nose, and gray fur beneath her fingers. Hishn's face was jammed into the crook of her arm, and the cold, wet fur contrasted oddly with the warmth of the wolf's inner body. *Wolfwalker-wolfwalker,* Hishn simply sang. Dion held her like a lifeline and stared at her twin brother, her weight balanced against her forward lunge and Talon's hand holding her back. Her face was tight with emotion.

"Stand down," the Lloroi grated into that moment of stillness.

Wakje and Weed exchanged glances. Talon did not urge them forward. Instead, the tall man stared at the Ariyens, and Sojourn's stomach sank. Rhom, midstep like the others, held himself without moving. He was poised between the raiders and Ariyens, with only Gamon truly at his back. Twelve swords faced him. His twin was held among those blades, and the man who crushed her arm—Rhom's breath was still paralyzed—was *Aranur*.

Dion started to speak, but her throat clenched with half-healed tissue. She buried her hand in Hishn's scruff as Talon's iron grip hauled her back to her feet. The wolf bared her teeth at him, but he merely eyed her, and she subsided, leaning hard against Dion instead. Gray Yoshi remained in the doorway, a shadow in the snow.

Wolfwalker, Hishn hummed in her mind without stop.

Hishn. Dion almost sobbed the name. The bond that had been so faint was now iron-hard and howling. She could feel the wolf like herself, feel the ache of cold deep in her dew-claws, feel the heat on her tongue as the wolf panted against her hand, feel the icy needle of Yoshi's cut paw. And Hishn felt the burn of her wolfwalker's throat, the rawness of Dion's wrists, the hunger that almost blinded. None of those things mattered. It was Yoshi who reached into the two and sent the surge of unconditional energy to fill Dion's throat and bend away the burning.

I am here, Hishn answered. *We are here. We are whole.*

The Ariyen Lloroi stared at Drovic, Talon, Dion, the wolf. He stepped up beside Rhom, and Gamon belatedly went with him. The black-haired Randonnen shifted slightly to let them come abreast.

Drovic moved forward to meet them. Talon tried to move with his father, bringing Dion with him—he didn't even consider letting go of her arm, but Drovic shoved him back. Talon stiffened and stalked forward anyway. Then the five men and the wolfwalker stood in two instinctive lines, facing each other like worlags.

"Tyronnen," Drovic said flatly to the Lloroi. "Gamon." He ignored Dion's twin. Drovic knew who Rhom was—he did not mistake the looks of her brother, but as with Dion, he considered the Randonnen man only a secondary player, and this game was Ariyen chess.

"Bandrovic." The Lloroi acknowledged his older brother with a steady voice.

Gamon did not speak his brother's Shame Name. He nodded, but his gray eyes were as dangerous as Talon's.

One of Rhom's men kicked the door shut, and in the silence, both groups studied each other. The four Ariyens were like variations on a portrait. Gamon was shortest, but by barely two fingers' width. The Lloroi was next, his usually gentle face hard with a grimness Dion had not seen before. Talon, still gaunt, was taller than his uncles, but still outweighed by his father. Gamon was the most lean; Tyronnen the most handsome. Talon had that wary stillness that Dion instinctively projected; and Drovic moved with the restrained grace that spoke of immense power at bay.

Rhom started to move toward his sister, but Gamon stopped him with a hand. Gamon had seen the way that Talon tensed at the smith, and only Gamon's quick reaction stopped Talon's knife from striking. Rhom rocked back on his heels, watching the other man grimly. But then Dion met his gaze, and they seemed to exchange a message. Rhom looked down and met Hishn's yellow eyes, and he felt the reassurance flow from the wolf and his twin. He seemed to stand down. It was not a true lessening of tension, but the poise of a man who knows he cannot yet act. He recognized with chagrin what Drovic had always known: that he and Dion had never been more than bit players in the Ariyen drama. Useful in their ways, catalysts in others—it would be up to the twins to become more if they dared. He knew Dion understood. The blaze of her violet eyes matched his.

Talon watched Rhom warily. As with actions and voices, his eyes recognized the smith even when his memory did not. What he did clearly see was the threat in the men he faced. He automatically noted that the two groups were evenly matched. Rhom's group was thirteen strong—fifteen if one counted the wolves. His own was fourteen strong, and he didn't question that Dion would stand with him. The wild pack that had led him here was out beyond the Ariyens, eyeing the dnu and making the riding beasts nervous. This other wolf, Hishn—his mind picked the name from the graysong that fairly radiated from his mate—remained in the room, bristling with the hostility that pervaded the stone.

Drovic did not look at his men, but his voice was flat and his order to the men was clear as he said, "Leave us."

The raiders glanced at each other.

Lloroi Tyronnen smiled faintly as he echoed the command to his own men. "Leave us." The Lloroi motioned with his chin toward the opposite corridor.

Neither group moved.

Talon gestured sharply with his hand.

Hesitantly, the raiders fell back, one step at a time, weapons still ready. The Ariyens mirrored their movements. Neither group completely left the room. Some stood back into the corridor; others backed against the outer walls, ringing the room like spectators. They could hear, but still be separate, and Talon knew their blades, now sheathed, were still ready.

Drovic, Talon, and Dion; the Lloroi, Gamon, and Rhom remained where they were. There had been no question that Rhom would stay with Gamon. Nothing less than death could have moved him from near his twin.

As Talon watched Rhom, Gamon watched his nephew. Aranur was gaunt, and there was a look in his gray eyes that Gamon had not seen before. The older man half held out his hand toward his nephew. His voice was flinty with emotion. This was the son he had not had himself, the boy he had raised to a man when Aranur's father abandoned the county. This was the child who had become a man and then died out of Gamon's arms, where Gamon could not even burn the body. His throat tightened, and he steadied himself carefully. "You died." He barely kept his words firm. "You fell from the seawall. Kiyun saw you go down."

Drovic's voice was hard as he eyed his brother. "He was wounded—almost mortally."

"Right shoulder, ribs, lung," Dion said softly. "Right wrist. Left hand." Her voice was still rough, and Rhom's eyes narrowed as he heard her.

Drovic did not acknowledge her. "He broke his wrist when he fell. He was fevered for two full ninans."

The wolfwalker looked at Drovic then. "The saltwater should have killed him," she said. "The parasites would have been in his wounds in seconds. Even if he had survived the fall, the parasites should have killed him in days."

"It should have," the man admitted.

"But he lived." Dion's healer mind kicked automatically into gear with the question Drovic's words raised. "There are only two cures for the sea parasites, and neither can be used when the patient has open wounds—" Her voice broke off. "No." Her ragged voice roughened as she strained it. "Moons, you didn't." But Drovic had been willing to use the vertal on her, then to burn her voice out more permanently. He had been willing to risk killing his son's mate. She stared at the older man even as she stretched through the wolves toward Aranur. She could feel her mate through his hand on her arm, and the signs were unmistakable. The rictus in his muscles, the tension in the wolf pack as it held the convulsions at bay, the clarity that was missing from the thoughts he had projected. The lack of recognition—his expression was almost that of a stranger, not a lover. He looked down at her, his jaw white and his eyes tight with rage and their betrayal. *He didn't know* . . . Even if she hadn't been able to look inside him, she would have known from his face.

"Antrixi." Her voice was barely a whisper.

Gamon stiffened.

Talon nodded to himself, unsurprised. The herbs his father gave him. So now he had their name.

The Lloroi watched Drovic's face as his brother answered the wolfwalker in a flat, unyielding voice. "He would have died without it. The parasites were already in his wounds by the time I pulled him out of the bay."

She could not hide her shocked anger. "But antrixi?"

"It forced him to heal."

Dion's face tightened. "At the expense of his memories and the rest of his life. By the moons." She took a half step forward to get around Talon to Drovic. She was brought up short by her mate's hand. Her voice cracked as the rage reached her words. "No wonder he stayed with you. After two ninans of fever and antrixi, he wouldn't know his name, me, his children. And you couldn't have taken him off the drug once you started—the convulsions would have killed him." She stiffened slowly. "It's been almost four months. Didn't you know—you must have realized that it would continue to strip his memories. First the recent ones, then the later ones, and finally, even those of childhood. He would become an imbecile, unable to remember where he stabled his dnu, unable to find his own home."

"He would live long enough."

The Lloroi was nodding slowly as if he understood Drovic's rationale. Dion stared from the Ariyen to the raider as Tyronnen answered her unspoken question. "Long enough to attack Ariye."

Gray Hishn growled, and Dion's voice was unbelieving. "You were willing to destroy your own son just to strike out at your brother?"

Drovic met Talon's gaze. "You think blood should make the difference between us? I would destroy the world if I could."

Talon nodded in turn. "No." He stopped Dion as he felt her

muscles bunch. "I understand." He regarded his father thoughtfully. "You said I would die if I returned to Ariye," he commented obliquely.

"I never lied to you."

Talon raised one dark eyebrow.

"Talon—my son—is dead. You stand there now as the boy my brother stole—the man the elders raised. A man with a different name than mine. A man of Ramaj Ariye."

Talon's voice was so clipped with rage that it chopped through the room like an ax. "And I lived thirty years like that—as this other man. As Aranur of Ramaj Ariye. Three-quarters of my years a lie. My boyhood, my schooling, my sons, my mate—you blinded me to all that? By all the hells that stain your hands, the Lloroi may have taken my name from me, but you took the rest of my life."

Drovic did not even shrug. "If you were to live, there was no choice. But look at it through my eyes. It let you see the man you could have been had you stayed with me instead."

"And what man am I now?"

"You ask?" Drovic's voice was cold and bitter. "Listen to your voice, to your words. Look at your face. You are no longer my son, my Talon. No longer a neVolen. You are dead to me. Aranur. Bentar. NeDannon." He spat the names.

Talon stilled. Talon Drovic neVolen—that was his christened name. His father's name, and *his* father before him. "You took my name when you left."

"I took nothing." The older man gestured with his chin at the Lloroi. "My brother, who took my position, my mate, and my children—he is the one who stole your name."

The Lloroi started to speak, but Gamon's hand on his arm held him back.

Talon managed to hold his voice firm, but he wanted to scream, to attack, to tear the truth apart and return to the lie he had lived. "It was a name of pride, to honor my great-grandfather and his father before him."

Drovic merely looked at the Lloroi. Tyronnen's jaw was tight as he answered. "You were renamed not out of pride, Aranur, but out of shame."

Shame. Talon's rage was pure ice.

"Shame," the Lloroi repeated. "To remove the name of a man who betrayed his county. A man who took up with raiders and did not die among them, but became a killer and then a leader of that scum. He came back to our county. You did not know that, did you?" Tyronnen did not take his eyes from his older brother. "He came back when you were fourteen. You had just passed the second Cansi test, and Gamon had started you training in Abis. But Drovic wanted you with him." His voice grew hard. "With the raiders. He wanted you to learn to kill."

Talon's voice was flat as stone. "That was not a lesson you spared me, either, Uncle."

"No. But you killed to defend Ariye, not to dismantle the county. You killed for the ideal. Look at him. Look at his men. Was it easy to kill for him?"

Talon did not answer. His father did not yet know how often he had betrayed him. He turned his head to Drovic. "Why did your name not change?"

"It did." His father shrugged. "I am Drovic to you, but I am known as Bandrovic in Ariye—banned from Ariye, from my home, from my daughter and son."

Rhom's eyes narrowed. Aranur's sister was his own mate. If Aranur had been renamed in shame . . . "Shilia," he broke in. "Her name?"

Drovic barely glanced at the Randonnen. He answered to his son. "Her name descends from her mother. It was not her shame that her mother died, but mine, that I survived. It is Talon who bears part of that shame—the guilt of another name, as do his sons, now that he knows."

"And so you became a raider." Talon's voice was flat.

"It did not happen overnight," Drovic snapped.

"But it happened. How many of them knew?"

Talon didn't have to point at the raiders. Drovic met his gaze steadily. "Kilaltian, Liatuad, Darity, Sojourn, Ebi and Strapel, NeBrenton, and Roc."

Sojourn, he thought with that same strange, icy calm. Even Sojourn knew. "And the rest?" he forced himself to ask.

"I brought them in from the far counties. None of them had met you before, although I suspect that most began to realize who you were. There were enough stories about Aranur's death, and your description is distinct." Drovic shrugged. "It did not matter. Getting you through the marine parasites and fever fried most of your memory. You would have remembered your later years first had you been at home, but with me, you remembered your early years and had no reason to remember the rest. And once you had begun taking the herbs and I had given you back your name, my raiders accepted you as my son, as one of them, and didn't question your alliance."

"My shame, my brother, my enemy." It was the Lloroi, in his quiet voice, unaware that he had spoken.

Drovic's eyes iced over. "An enemy of your own making."

"And now?" Talon broke in.

"Now?" Drovic stared at his younger brothers, at Rhom, at the Ariyens who still faced them from the corridor. The Lloroi glanced at Gamon, and Gamon's gaze flickered to Rhom, and then back to Talon's people. Some part of Talon's brain noted that it would have been comical, all this glancing around, except that they all held swords.

Drovic stepped toward his son. "Talon—"

"Aranur," the Lloroi said quickly, half holding out his hand.

Gamon shifted, then held himself still. He was not part of this. Rhom hesitated, met Dion's gaze, and did the same. He found himself near one of the raiders and unconsciously moved back with them, closer to the benches. It was as if he stood in a different world, only able to watch. The raiders seemed to feel the same, for they did not interfere. Before him, as Talon regarded the man who fathered him and the uncles who had raised him, Rakdi pulled a piece of jerky from one of his belt pouches and absently offered it to Rhom. Rhom took the jerky automatically, and only belatedly realized he was sharing meat with a raider. He hesitated again, and Rakdi's sharp gaze quirked. The Randonnen nodded almost imperceptibly at the irony; then he began to chew.

Drovic did not even notice. "Come back with me," he said to his son. "Ride for a better goal. You've found your name, your mate, the truth of your existence. In four, five months, you'll have another child. Why sacrifice this daughter to the slow death of Tyronnen's leadership? Why support what holds us back? Ask him—" He jerked his head toward Ty-ronnen. "—why his world is so small. Why we still live in nine counties. Ask him if it is from fear, not courage, that we huddle in our homes. Ask yourself if you want this child to know only that, and not have the will to stand up to the future."

"The future?" Tyronnen's voice was sharp as he cut in. "You would destroy us before we could get a hundred years into the future. Allow the people to spread without bounda-ries, and we lose control of our science. Uncontrolled, they could bring about change—invention, advancement—things that we don't yet know how to hide, can't hide, as our history has shown. Things that would incite the aliens to kill us. Con-trol the people, and you control their work. Control that, and you keep the plague at bay while we find a better way to live on this world, a better path to the stars."

Drovic started to retort, but Talon cut both men off. "Do you hear yourselves?" He jerked his chin at his father. "You, Father, have fighters, but you've been a raider so long that you've forgotten how to build them into anything other than terrorists. You've forgotten your goal of the stars." He stabbed his finger at his uncle. "And you. You've been in power so long that you've forgotten how to move forward. You control the people out of fear, not because you want to touch the stars, but because you fear the aliens, the plague. Because you fear your own death."

The Lloroi shook his head. "It is not death that I fear, but annihilation. It may seem that we have lost the world to the aliens, but we Ariyens have faith in our future. We are the martyrs of the ordinary. Our county is filled with that— ordinary heroes of every kind. Not the flashy kind like Drovic wants, but the solid, steady kind in which each man's work and sacrifice lives on and furthers the world."

Talon nodded shortly. "That is your power base—the hope of the people. You use it like Drovic uses fear." He turned to his father. "And you—you've killed too long, Drovic. You forgot the dream. The stars are an excuse now, not the real goal. You live in defiance of nothing."

Drovic's voice was harsh. "Live in defiance or live in fear.

There are no other choices. You think you can have the dream with him? He would wait a thousand years before trying to reach the stars. Stay with him and you give in to fear, not courage."

"At least it is a goal. Without that, a man is nothing." Talon's jaw was tight with anger.

"Talon," Drovic said almost quietly. "Come with me. You can bring your people, your mate, your wolves, for all I care. With me, you will always have truth. The truth of the world, the truth of who you are."

Talon did not look at Dion, but he felt her sudden tension. His voice was flat. "My mate has found her will again. She'll not agree to your path."

"Then we will soften her memory so that she sees a different option. Truth can be its own strength."

Rhom stiffened. Rakdi tensed with the smith, ready to start the fight as he felt the Randonnen shift.

But Talon's eyes were for his father. "Is that truth in the context of the drugs you gave to me? You never lied to me, but every word was a falsehood. I want no part of that, and I want no puppet beside me. Touch my mate, and I'll kill you myself."

"Then leave her, or she will destroy you."

Talon's eyes were cold as he stared back at his father. "As much as the moons belong to this world, this woman belongs to me. We are kum-tai." His hand linked with Dion's, and their white-knuckled fingers gripped each other with almost desperate strength.

Drovic saw. "So you choose."

"As do you."

Father and son stared into each other's eyes. Neither moved, but it was as if they stepped irrevocably back from each other. Drovic caught his breath. "Vengeance is its own death," he said bleakly.

Tyronnen's lips tightened, but he said nothing.

Talon regarded both men for a long moment. Then he turned to his own fighters. "As I choose, do you choose with me?" Gamon stirred uneasily at his words. Talon shot his uncle a hard look and turned back to his raiders. "When I ride," he demanded of them, "do you ride with me?"

Rakdi's voice was dry. "The Ariyen trial blocks are a bit too close for comfort. Were you thinking north or south?"

Talon looked at his father, his uncles, Rhom. He looked down at Dion. He could feel the wolves in her mind. They might have relaxed their geas, but they still held the pain at bay. It was there like dread. But now he also felt Dion's mental hands strengthening the shield and softening the tension that had once bent his bones to breaking. He felt the balance of his self as he touched her mind through the wolves. It was a subtle thing, but behind it lurked the wildness he craved, the will that was built on conviction, the uncompromising direction for his strength, the calm confidence of the woman who mothered his sons. "I stay with my mate," he said slowly.

Rakdi took a breath and said, "That makes it pretty clear." But Dangyon rocked subtly back on his heels, thoughtfully. Talon had not said he chose Ariye, but that he chose the wolfwalker. The barrel-chested man kept his face expressionless, but Cheyko had an odd look on his face, and Weed rubbed his curled ear.

Talon looked over his fighters, but not one moved to stand with him. "You'll ride with Drovic, even now?"

Harare looked uncomfortable. "I'll ride with Talon, but not with Aranur of Ariye." Weed nodded slowly in agreement, and even Oroan scowled.

Talon felt his jaw tighten. "Look at him." He jerked his chin at his father. "Under him, you were nothing. With him, no one cared if you lived or died. No one cared if you were wounded. No one wanted you to be more than a body that wielded a sword. Under him, you were what you were— killers, robbers, raiders. Nothing more. If you ever want to hold something good in your hands, then stay with me, with Dione."

Rakdi regarded the three leaders askance. "Good, bad, what's the difference? He wants our steel; you want our steel; the Lloroi wants it if only to break it. We don't see a difference between you. It's all violence and blood and the pound of your heart and that edge where the steel hangs in front of your eyes before it slides into your foe. A man who stands still is dead."

"A man who stands still can sometimes see a different road than the one he runs down blindly. I give you a chance to be men again."

But Ki shook his head. "Everything you did for us was a lie, Aranur." The young fighter said his name like a curse. "You're not even a raider."

"I fought with you. I killed with you. I'm now no more than you are."

"Under the influence of antrixi." Sojourn's voice was quiet. "In all nine counties, there is no trial block that would convict you of those crimes. And there is no trial block that is not as eagerly waiting to taste our blood." He jerked his head toward Drovic. "We belong with him, not you."

Talon stepped forward, and Dion started to step with him, but he stopped her with a hard hand against her shoulder. Dion's eyes narrowed with their own dangerous glint, and she shrugged his hand off. Talon shot her a glance, but her lips drew back in a half snarl. Gray Hishn echoed the sound.

Talon almost glared at Dion, but those violet eyes were lit with their own fire. There was fear in the woman—he could almost smell it amidst all the steel, but there was also strength and stubbornness. He knew instinctively that Dione might bend, but she would fight even him with every bit of power in her if he tried to control her like that.

Slowly, he dropped his hand. This time, when the wolf-walker moved forward with him, he did not try to stop her. He came face-to-face with Sojourn. He regarded the other man for a moment, then slid his sword from his scabbard and held it out like a gift. His voice was soft when he said, "If you are no more than what you say you are, prove it to me now."

Drovic's blue-flecked gaze was suddenly sharp. He tensed in spite of himself, and Hishn growled, but the wolfwalker held the beast back. Wolf and woman poised like Drovic, their balance on edge as they watched for Sojourn's response. To the side, the Lloroi had paled, and Gamon felt his own hand clench. Rhom merely watched like a second wolf behind Dion, and Talon thought that the two Randonnens were linked by more than blood.

Sojourn looked at the gleaming steel, then up at Talon's expression. There was no flicker of fear in Talon's eyes, no tightening of the muscles along his jaw or temples. Beside him, the wolfwalker had stepped slightly back. She was poised, but not to attack. Sojourn realized suddenly that both she and Talon knew he would not do it. The realization brought with it a rush of anger. He slid his own sword from his scabbard. "If you think to push us into your old way of life, you can forget that like the second moon." Like lightning, he slapped Talon's blade down, then snapped the point of his sword to the tall man's throat.

"Do it," Talon said softly. "Prove that you are less of a man than I believe you to be."

Sojourn's muscles tensed, and a trickle of blood raced down Talon's neck.

Talon did not flinch. "Kill your future," he went on. "Make sure you believe you are nothing."

The other man's voice was low and harsh. "You did yourself no favors when you took us out of the gangs. The one thing a raider returns to is the violence that he knows."

"And the one thing some of you never forgot is the wanting of something more. You were beginning to have that with me. You touched pride again, Sojourn. You had a goal that did not depend on murder. Are you so eager to return to the man who kept your steel so bloody? That's what Drovic wants of you. He wants you so hopeless and uncaring that you will do whatever he asks because it doesn't matter even to yourself whether you live or die."

"Do you really think we care how long we live? We're alive now. That's all that matters."

Talon did not look down at the blade. He could feel the blood trickling down his neck like a worm and crawling into his tunic. His voice was soft. "If so, then slide it in."

XLIII

Talon Drovic neVolen

A grave is a simple solution;
Life carries much more risk.

   —Randonnen proverb

Sojourn's brown-gray eyes burned. His hand tensed. "Don't you care, Wolfwalker, that he will die?"

Dion's hand clenched Hishn's scruff; the other touched Talon's arm. Her voice was still rough, but her words were clear. "Faith creates its own future."

Sojourn actually took his eyes from Talon to stare at the healer. "In the fevers, he used to call out your name. You could hear him—you had the ear of the wolves—but you had no faith then that it was real, or you would not have left him."

She didn't flinch from the raider's words. They would hang around her neck forever, but Aranur was here now, and she was beside him, and even the will of the wolves could not separate them again. "I heard him," she acknowledged. "And I found nothing of him to hold. And knowing he was dead, I cursed the moons that they silenced our son and haunted me instead with *his* voice. I heard him forever," she whispered, "but grief forces many blindnesses, and I was more blind than most."

Sojourn remained silent for a long moment. There was a bleakness in the wolfwalker's words that hurt him. He started to lower his sword. But Talon's gray eyes flared with triumph, and the brown-eyed man stiffened. Without warning, he stepped in. Dion cried out. The sword stabbed into Talon's chest.

And stopped. Talon caught his cry before he breathed it

out. Felt the steel penetrate tissue, cut its tip into bone. Felt a surge of power that burned through every vein with Dion's grip on his arm even as Sojourn halted his own strike. *Power,* Talon thought exultantly. It was there in his mate like fire lancing through his body from her hand. Hishn snarled, and the graysong surged and subsided. Motion froze.

Sojourn looked down at the blade. He seemed as frozen as the others.

Talon reached up and took the steel in his hand. The remnants of fire licked through his body; Dion's hand trembled on his arm. He glanced down and saw the tightened bones of her face and *knew*. That had been the power he had sought, the thing he felt in the graysong. It was the power of the Ancients, of the aliens. The power that had drawn him, trapped him in the wolves so that his mate could be whole again. She had sent it through his body, closing the wound as it opened even though Sojourn stopped.

Talon smiled coldly. The edge of the blade cut into his palm. Blood seeped into his jerkin. He pushed the sword away from his chest, and Sojourn stepped back, dropping the point so that it stained the floor.

Sojourn could have stabbed harder, could have pushed the point home. Could have done Drovic's will or challenged Drovic and found out finally whether it was in him to lead or follow. He stared at the blood that oozed out of Talon's chest. He realized he would never know, had not yet reached deep enough in himself to know what he could do, would do, for his beliefs. He met Talon's steady gaze as his center opened like an empty grave. If it had been a challenge, if Talon had fought back, had played Sojourn's rage off against his guilt . . . But the tall man had merely waited for Sojourn to make up his mind. Sojourn looked at Dion with her hand on Talon's sleeve, then back at the man she stood with. His voice was curiously flat, almost apologetic, and his lips twisted as he heard his own tone. "I could never ride with you. My journey must be my own."

Talon nodded slowly. He looked at Drovic, then at his men and women. They did not move to join him, but except for Sojourn, neither did they move to Drovic. He nodded again, as if their very silence had been their decision. His voice was firm as he turned to the Lloroi. "What of my men and women?"

Tyronnen stepped forward. "Your chest—"

Talon cut him off. "What of my people?"

The Lloroi hesitated. Talon's face was tight, but not with fear or pain. "You want to claim them?" Tyronnen asked shrewdly. "They cannot escape the trials."

Talon's fighters tensed, and behind Gamon, the Ariyens edged slowly forward. Both groups' hands were on their hilts, but neither quite drew steel. Tyronnen, Talon, Dion, and Drovic stood in the middle. In a fight, some of each group would escape, but Drovic would make sure that Tyronnen would die, and the Lloroi did not think that Dion would leave Talon's side. It would be a bloodbath. This shelter would become a tomb for the winter, stocked with bodies, not food.

Talon did not back down, and the stain on his chest was spreading. Beside him, Dion reached for his hand, and he twined his fingers with hers. He felt the twist of vision, the shock of energy. Felt the blood clot on his ribs. Calcium spiked between the gemstones where the sword had chipped the bone, but Dion's mental voice was a layer between him and the pain. "Take them to the trial block," he said, "and I will stand beside them."

Tyronnen shook his head. "You're not one of them. You never were, no matter what kind of steel you held."

Talon frowned.

"So," Rakdi said softly, "you're giving up on us, then."

Talon did not answer. He stared at his people, but he didn't see them. Instead, he saw the face of a village boy who stared up at him through shattered wood. A face that was wide with terror, not recognition. A pair of eyes that saw only death. Talon had changed that fear into hope, and that one act had been the point at which he began to become again the man that he had been.

He hesitated, and Tyronnen's voice was uncompromising. "You cannot save them from their fate."

"Their lives are mine," Talon returned softly. "Their actions were mine, at my orders. Their journey here was my path, not theirs. And so, too, their fate is mine." With his words, the line of raiders seemed to solidify.

"Aranur, you cannot—" The Lloroi broke off. "You can't give up your life for these . . . raiders. They're not—"

"They're not worth it?" Talon's gray eyes were hard. "If you can see no value in them, then you see no value in me. Is that a truth you can live with?"

The Lloroi's voice was harsh as he countered. "Are these killers the neighbors you want us to live with? Who among us has not lost a brother or sister, daughter or son to the raiders? Who among us has not seen some kind of death at their hands?"

Words flicked through Talon's memory, but Rhom found them first. The Randonnen's voice was deceptively mild. "You sound like the Lloroi."

"I *am* the Lloroi," Tyronnen said sharply.

"I mean Lloroi Zentsis, of Bilocctar," Rhom corrected. " 'Do you want them in your county? In your city? In your home?' He was speaking of us—of Dion and me and Aranur, Gamon, Tyrel—of your own son, Tyronnen. It's what Zentsis said to his people, just before he tried to have us executed on the sands. Because we were spies, he said, uncivilized and violent. Because they had lost children and mates and parents to the Ariyen conflicts. Because we would influence the youth of his county to follow our evil ways."

Tyronnen opened his mouth, then stopped. "What would you have us do? Invite them into our homes as if they were treasured guests? Forgive a past so littered with graves that they could pave a dozen cities? And ignore blades so saturated in our blood that the very steel cries out with haunting? I have led this county for forty-four years and have seen raiders like swarms of worlags. They respond with anger to any challenge. They will break each other's arms for a harsh word."

Rhom cocked his head. "And there has been no man of the counties who has done the same?"

"If he does, he is punished."

"Then do the same to these."

Talon nodded sharply. "These men and women followed

me away from the raider pack—of their own free will. I did not threaten them or promise them riches or pardons or care-free lives. I promised them nothing, yet they did not leave me. Whether they believed in me or in themselves does not matter. That they rode away from destruction and death—that choice has meaning. They stand here, before you and your bloody trial block, not because they want to die, but because they want to live—as men and women, and no longer as murderers."

"Before, they wanted to live as raiders."

"Look more closely, Lloroi. Yes, they started out as over forty raiders. But some died, some chose to stay with Drovic, some fought me and I killed them because they wouldn't ride as I wanted, some walked away when they were given a choice of following me or my father. These are the ones who were willing to follow where I led, not where Drovic wanted to go. These are the ones who chose the ideal over the steel."

Tyronnen's gray eyes narrowed.

"On this world, what atonement is there in death?" Talon said persuasively. "Give them life, and they will prove of value. You have that power, Lloroi, to give them a chance at the life they chose when they followed me instead of Drovic, to live not as raiders, but as men and women of Ariye."

But his uncle did not waver. "For you, yes, I can give a choice. But not for them. No other elder would allow it."

"Then you deny that choice also to me."

"Listen to me—"

"Listen to *me*," he snapped back. "This is the moment, Lloroi, in which mercy tempers justice. Not because it is de-served, but because it can make a difference." He stared at his uncle. "What kind of man are you to cast that mercy down without thought? Who are you to render a judgment that you yourself won't live with?"

"Then what punishment would they have? We keep no old-Earth prisons."

"Give them four days of every ninan for themselves; the other five to work for those who need help. The elderly, the sick, the injured, the widows and the children their brethren left behind."

Tyronnen's voice had not softened. "Why not take every day of every ninan?"

"Because if there is nothing to work for for themselves, they might as well return to being raiders."

"You would treat them as if they were county men."

"They were, once upon a time."

The Lloroi was silent for a long while. Finally, he regarded the raiders with a carefully expressionless face. "Stay in Ariye, and you can no longer live as you have. You'll have jobs—boring ones, most likely. You'll have neighbors—slow perhaps, sometimes stupid. You'll go to meetings and keep your temper when you want to rage against the rules of the idiot elders. But if you don't keep your tempers—if you break a man's arm, you're responsible for his livelihood until he has healed again, not just for the five days a ninan. You take his life, and we will take yours in his place."

Rakdi rubbed his hook nose and regarded the Lloroi with a look he had once turned on other elders. "Is this the choice? A book of warnings thicker than your hatred? Do you expect your children to live perfect lives? Do *you* live a perfect life?" Tyronnen's face hardened. "What mistakes will you allow us to make before you eagerly chop off our heads? Do we live under the ax or the sky?"

"What guarantee is there that you will not kill again?"

Talon's voice was flat. "I vouch for them, Lloroi."

The older man studied his nephew. "You would vouch for them with your own life." It was not a statement.

"Yes."

"No." It was Wakje. "No man can pledge my actions for me. No man can tell me how to live—with you or against you. No man—Lloroi or not—has the right to judge me as nothing more than part of a group. You accept us—you accept *me*, Wakje, and each one of the others as they are—or you might as well kill us now."

Rakdi nodded and met the Lloroi's gaze unflinchingly. "Accept our pledge to live among you, or give us the edge of your ax."

The Lloroi studied them expressionlessly.

The raiders glared back at him.

Tyronnen's voice was dry. "I think I prefer the ax." But he did not quite state his judgment, and instead cursed his own weakness as he turned to Talon's mate. "I am not the only one with lives to risk. I will hear your words, Wolfwalker."

Dion stared at the raiders. Her eyes were violent with memories—terror, the swords biting into flesh, the blood that washed hotly across her hands, the screams that ate through her throat.

"Dione?"

Her violet eyes glittered, but she finally answered the Lloroi. "I look at these men, and feel rage in my chest like a hungry wolf. My stomach knots, my breath cuts short with the tension to grab a knife. I suck air and hear screams. I taste blood on my tongue." She steadied her voice with difficulty. She stared at each raider, pausing when she came to Roc. The other woman's eyes were vicious, carving at her like skinning knives. Dion's violet gaze narrowed. She looked at Wakje, Harare, Ki, and knew that her own violence was mirrored in their eyes. Finally she answered the Lloroi. "My hands are clean, you think, but they crawl with the shrouds of others. I have killed, and I have let others die. I am not the one to judge them."

He stared at her. "Dione, you have suffered as much at their hands as any in Ariye—"

She cut him off curtly with a gesture. Her voice was as hard as flint. "I answer you as a scout, a healer, a wolfwalker, a mother, and a woman—as all the things I have been in your county. As all the things I am. Here, now, I see my rage echoed in their hearts. My blood is on their hands, and theirs on mine. You want me to temper your need for justice, to soften your decision. You want me to accept them as neighbors and peers, or judge them like an elder to weight your decision for you. I can do neither. I can live my life and accept that they do not try to kill me today. That is all. Do not ask for more."

"Dione—"

She shook her head. "Do not ask, Lloroi. They chose for the moment to follow my mate and had no real hope of anything more. They are fury and violence, and they rage against their past. I have done the same. But they have given me back my future. I will not take their blood."

The Lloroi's jaw tightened. "Gamon?"

Gamon ran his hand through his peppered hair. He studied Dion, then glanced at Rhom. The Randonnen man waited calmly as if there were no storms of emotion, and Gamon knew suddenly that the twins had the right of it. It had been Rhom's faith in Dion that led him to his twin, and Dion's faith that Rhom would come that had allowed her to face the raiders. Faith, he thought. It was not steel or power or even hope, but faith that ruled the world. "Tyronnen," he said softly. "You believe that these men and women are raiders—murderers, robbers, an extension of Bandrovic's sword." He cocked his head. "Aranur believes that they are men who can choose to live within the law. You ask me to judge between the strength of his belief and yours." He rubbed at the stubble that had roughened his chin. "I think," he said slowly, "you have forgotten that Aranur's belief *is* yours. It is your influence and mine—the influence of Ariye—that has given him this faith in those who would follow him. Judge against him, and you judge your own self false."

Tyronnen regarded his brother for a long moment. His voice was soft. "As always, Brother, your wisdom is my own."

Dangyon regarded the four men with something akin to bemusement. "Well, I'll be a four-faced worlag," he murmured.

But the Lloroi heard him and shook his head sharply. "This is no pardon. And you'll have your reckon before the moons. But until then, we—" It was hard for him to say the word. "—welcome," he forced it out, "you among us."

Ki scowled, but Wakje simply watched Talon. Wakje had already noted that the tall man stood comfortably, seemingly unaware of the wound in his chest, and that the wolfwalker clung to his side like a burr, her violet eyes unfocused. To her right, the Gray One seemed to sense Wakje's attention. Hishn turned her massive head in his direction, and Wakje felt a shock of blurred vision, as if he saw himself from two heights. It lasted only a second; then it was gone.

You honor me. The words did not make it past his lips, but they were there in his head. The Gray One did not hear.

Drovic found his feet moving toward the outer door. Three of the Ariyens shifted to block the older man, but Tyronnen held up his hand. "Let him go. I will not spill brother blood here, two days from our border. In Ariye, if he returns again, he will die. But not here, outside our home."

Drovic's lips stretched in black humor. "It will not be me, Brother, who challenges you again. There is no more need to fear me."

Sojourn moved to the door and shoved it open to reveal the blackness outside, speckled with whirling white. Drovic hesitated at the latch and half turned to face his son. Although he had forced some of Talon back into his son, this man was still Aranur. "Conje-tai, my son," he said quietly.

Conje-tai. It was the forever good-bye, the acknowledgment of the utter break between them. Talon felt his jaw tighten. The ties of blood and intent—they had been shattered by goals and truths. "Conje-tai, my father," he said flatly.

Drovic nodded, acknowledging what Talon did not say. When he spoke, his voice was equally flat. "Comfort will kill you; pride will kill me. I see no great loss in either. But death does not change my goals. Death changes only me." He stood in the doorway for a moment while the snow whirled in around him. His voice was soft. "You won unfairly, Dione." He met her gaze and saw her understanding that he had recognized the power. Then he stepped out into the darkness.

Roc stared at the open doorway. She turned slowly to stare at Talon. "You would trade everything—us, your father—for what? For her?"

"I am kum-tai," he said simply.

"That means nothing," Roc snarled. "Look at her. She's just an old, broken-down body with a worn, scarred soul. Look at me. Look at *me*. She is not even beautiful."

He looked down at the hand that entwined with Dion's. "You're wrong," he said, almost absently. "She is the world."

Roc caught her breath in her perfect teeth. Her hand moved. It was fast—fast as a serpent strike, as a lepa dive, as light. The knife slid so easily out of the woman's hand that

Talon had only an impression of steel before he moved. Rhom, on that side, beat him to it. Dion tried to jerk away, but Talon's hand was already thrusting her aside. The smith flung out his arm. Steel sank home, and Rhom gasped.

Talon seemed to erupt. Walls in his mind seemed to rupture. The rage, the grief, the controlled frustration. He crossed the distance in a single stride and struck Roc so hard that he flung the woman over a bench into the wall. She slid down, shuddered back to her feet, swayed, and went back down to her knees. Blood dripped from her teeth. Two teeth were broken—she could feel the sharp edges against her tongue, and she spat chips and blood onto the floor. With the dizziness, the movement almost unbalanced her.

Dion clenched Rhom's arm hard around the blade. "Don't take it out," she said sharply. The smith's face was blanched. But the knife had buried itself in the lower part of his biceps, not in Dion's chest.

It was small satisfaction to Roc. Roc met Talon's gaze and knew he would kill her if she stayed. He already looked at her with an emptiness in his gray eyes, like a predator judging when to give the death blow, not one who would listen to reason. The woman pushed herself up and away from the wall and jerked her head toward the doorway through which Drovic had already gone. She had to work to clear her throat of blood before she could speak. Her voice was oddly harsh. "He is a man, and you are a man. But you are the lesser blade." She opened the door, straightened her shoulders, and walked out in the storm after Drovic.

Rhom felt Dion's hands tremble on the arm and knew that she didn't have the energy left for a healing. "Not now, Dion," he said in a low voice. "Later. I won't die before you fix me."

"A touch," she returned, "to stop the bleeding."

He nodded unwillingly, and Talon watched unsmiling as Dion eased the knife out. Energy seemed to surround her, and she paled. He reached down to grab her, glaring at Rhom as the smith pressed a bandage Gamon handed him against his wound.

The Randonnen man saw Talon's instinctive gesture toward his blade and quirked his eyebrow. "We are bound by her blood, Aranur." Rhom used the name deliberately. "We don't need our own blood between us."

Talon regarded Dion's brother for a long moment before he nodded shortly.

Rhom met Dion's eyes. The blood on their hands mixed as they clasped and worked the bandage. "Dion," he murmured. "Don't ever do this again."

She knew what he meant. "Not while the moons still ride," she agreed quietly. She finished tying on the cloths, and Rhom got to his feet. He was a powerful man, but as he met Talon's unsmiling gaze, what he saw there made him sober. There was still rage in Talon's gaze—controlled as Rhom remembered it—and a sort of despair. Dion would feel that despair—she could not help knowing what Aranur felt, and she would do anything to heal her mate. Rhom knew his twin, and knew she was not yet strong enough to define her own goals. He nodded toward Talon and said to her, "I wondered if you would be able to give him up. Looks like you forced the moons to give him back instead."

Dion caught her breath. She looked down at the blood on her hands and forced her voice to be steady. "We moonmaids have that power."

Rhom nodded. "Don't let him bully you," he said deliberately, noting the way Talon's lips tightened at his words. "He's too strong-willed for his own good. Stand up to him, twin, or you'll find yourself giving away everything you have left."

Talon took Dion's hand and drew her back against him. "You know me that well?" he demanded coldly. She went willingly, and the fit of her body against his hip stirred memories of heat.

Rhom shrugged. "You haven't changed that much. You're still Aranur—brilliant with his enemies and blind with his friends." He watched the tall man closely.

Talon's expression stiffened, and Rhom knew he had been right to use those words. He could almost feel Talon reaching into his mind for the image. "I know those words," Talon admitted, "but I cannot find the memory." His gray gaze sharpened. "I think that we were fighting."

Rhom grinned without humor. "We were. You won, as I recall."

"I usually do."

"Now there's the Ariyen arrogance I remember." Rhom reached out and touched his twin's arm.

Dion started to smile, then looked over her shoulder. "Tehena and Kiyun," she remembered with guilt. "They're in one of the back rooms, bound."

Gamon nodded. "I'll take care of it." Weed hesitated, then gestured for the older man to follow him back. The motion seemed to break the tableau that held the others, and they dispersed like sand in a wind. They began divvying up the rooms in a pattern that maintained the uneasy truce that had formed between the Ariyens and former raiders.

Talon started to pull Dion toward one of the corridors, but she slipped free with a simple twist. He halted and reached for her again.

Rhom had been right, she realized. Talon was not quite free of Drovic, and she could still be a pawn. She cocked her eyebrow at Talon's expression and shook her head. "Not like that," she said softly.

He hesitated. He had gripped her hard before—bruised her arms. She was his, but . . . Slowly, he extended his hand.

Beside her, Hishn growled. It was a low sound, deep in the throat. The wolfwalker put her hand in his, letting his fingers entwine with hers. Instinctively he found the position he knew was right—her three slender fingers against two of his. He studied their hands together, turned them over, and then met her violet gaze. She was no longer young—no woman with eyes like that could ever be young again. But she looked at him with her heart in her eyes, and he did not know that his expression was the same. This time, when they started again toward the rooms, they walked side by side.

XLIV

Ember Dione maMarin

Lost souls reach where reaching does no good;
Lost hearts love in despair.
Lost souls reach, and reaching find;
Love can break each absence.

   —*from "Lost Souls," by Jun Mak*

Rakdi assigned Dion and Talon to one of the inner rooms, not one with an outer door. Rhom, Gamon, Kiyun, and Tehena took the room to the right. Rakdi, Wakje, Harare, and Weed settled the room to the left. Neither side was taking chances that Talon and the wolfwalker would disappear like Drovic into the storm.

Gray Yoshi was outside the stables, curled in a bank of snow, but Hishn would not leave Dion, so the wolfwalker tossed a blanket on the floor for the wolf, while Talon set some wood on the fire. An uneasy silence gripped the room. Then Hishn growled at them both. Talon glanced at the wolf, then grinned slowly without humor. "Give me time," he told the Gray One.

Hishn's yellow eyes gleamed.

Dion touched Talon's forearm, and the gesture made him stiffen. He gripped her arms in return and searched her eyes. "You hounded me through three counties, and I swore that when I found you, I would take back my freedom, get you out of my mind. Now you're here, and all I can think is that you're mine. Who am I?" he demanded.

She hesitated. "You are Aranur."

"Am I?" He searched her face. "Am I a fighter or a killer? My father's son or Gamon's? And am I the man who wanted to be free of the wolves, or the man who now accepts them?"

His voice grew harsh. "By the moons, Dione, am I anything on my own, or am I defined only by others?"

"You are yourself," she whispered. "Aranur—my beloved."

He stared at her. "My youth, my life, was a lie. Even our Promising and Mating was a lie."

"No—"

"I fathered our sons with a lie, and this child—" He gestured savagely at her belly. "—is as much a lie as them. I am a mate with you, a raider with my father, a weapons master for Ramaj Ariye; and all of these things are falsehoods." He shook his head. "I am nothing without the structure of others to define me. I am no man at all."

"No," she protested. "Your heart, your goals, your beliefs never wavered. You were not corrupted by your fathe—"

"Hush!" He cut her off so harshly that she stepped back almost involuntarily. Hishn's head rose and watched him steadily. He almost snarled at the wolf. "You assume too much, Wolfwalker. You think that your words can reassemble me into some core that has not changed through time? My uncle redefined my lineage when I was eleven, and now I know it was for shame, not pride. My father rewrote me when you left me to die. And now you . . ." He stared at her. "You haunt me with your voice and your wolves as if you can drown me in eternal gray, while Ariye steeps me again in obligation." His jaw tightened to a whitened line. "I have only glimpses of my life with you, but you tell me it will return. And then who will I be?"

Her words were low. "You will be yourself, as you have always been. You have simply lived in different settings."

"Yes," he agreed sharply. "I am the same no matter where I am. A killer in one context, a killer in another—the only difference is the goal. I rode for months as that kind of man, and not the sword, the dnu, the men, or the attack felt wrong— only the incompetence of the victims who laid themselves out for slaughter. The goal was everything. The goals of Ramaj Ariye, of Drovic . . . I am a man who does not lead himself, but lets his surroundings define him."

Dion felt her own anger rise as he rejected his strengths. "A healer is no less a healer because she does not always have patients. A soldier is no less a soldier for being peaceable at home—"

"And a raider is no less a murderer for those few hours he is not killing."

Her voice sharpened. "You cannot believe that, not after what you said to the Lloroi. What about your . . . riders?" she stumbled over the term. "You said they followed you because you gave them purpose, and that purpose came from the conviction that what you did would have value. Even those . . . men and women see that. You believe in them, and they want to live to that belief. You expect, and so they deliver."

"And they ride with Talon, not Aranur."

"You are the same man."

"Am I?" He stared at her. "Look at my hands, Dione. Look at my heart."

She shook her head. "Some part of you knew, even with the pain, the drugs, your father, that what you did was not right." She laid her hand on his arm. "You are here now, and still yourself because of that strength of belief." She caught her breath as her emotion surged. "I will not lose you again."

"I will not be lost," he reassured, but his voice had a tint of bitterness. "Your wolves will see to that."

She glanced down at Hishn, and the gray wolf looked up, yellow eyes gleaming agreement. "They have bound us again."

"To each other or to them?"

"We owe them, Aranur," she said quietly.

"Aranur," he repeated softly. Not Talon. Aranur.

She nodded. "They brought you back to me."

"In exchange for what?"

She hesitated again. This admission was more painful. Finally, she said simply, "Our lives in exchange for a cure for the plague."

He stared at her.

She nodded soberly. "You do not remember, but the fever burned in you, tightened your muscles like wood, blinded you with pain. We were trapped—"

"In the snow. In the mountains."

She quelled the flash of eagerness. If he remembered anything, then he could remember it all—if she could heal him from the drugs. "Yes. The wolves helped me heal you, and I promised to find a cure for the plague that they still carry within them. It is a promise I haven't kept. It has been almost fourteen years, and still, the wolves are waiting."

"They did not wait for me."

"No," she agreed. "They drove you to me so that I could be whole to heal them."

"But they will wait another year now." He placed his hand on her belly. *Aranur.* "You carry our child, Ember Dione. We will not sacrifice her to the needs of this day or the next, not when the wolves have already waited eight hundred years."

Her voice was low. "You used to call me Dion."

"You used to call me your love."

Dion bit her lip. In the harsh light, his bones seemed sculpted from anger and grief. His jaw was tight with control, and his gray eyes bored into hers. Her voice was low as she answered. "Your father stole you from me, and I stole you back from him. Can you forgive me this?"

Aranur looked down at her hands. They were slender, tanned, scarred. They were strong hands, gentle hands, and even here in the mountains, they smelled like clean musk and forest. He looked back up to her eyes. Violet eyes, tinged with yellow, unfocused with the gray . . . His voice was hard and flat. "The wolves have kept you from me, and I will take you back from them. Can you live with that?"

She tried to speak. Her voice broke.

The last wall between them cracked. He yanked her to him and crushed her against his chest, seeking her mouth with his. His words were lost against her lips. "Gods, Dion. I need you—" She was crying, snarling, tearing at him to get closer. He roughed her, trying to hold her too close, bruised her with his hands. He didn't notice. She didn't care. Time had divided them, then thrown them back together. They simply moved together, two people, alone among the swords, while the snow beat down on the passhouse.

Epilog

Ride with me, where the white moons light our way;
Sing with me, where the gray wolves herald day;
Be with me, so our lives can now be started;
Love with me, so our hearts cannot be parted.

  —From *White Wolf and Sky,* by Alla maRaine

Over the course of two days, the storm left a meter of snow behind to clog the mountain roads. Dion's head rested on Aranur's shoulder as they watched the fire. The child moved beneath his hand. "She is strong," he murmured.

"Like you," Dion murmured back.

"Like us," he corrected. He pulled her to a sitting position and began to gather their clothes. She pulled his shirt on instead. She smelled the fabric and inhaled the scent of him. Already Aranur remembered more of his life. She had healed some of the pain, some of the memories, and had cried last night as he recalled their Promising.

He grinned as he put on his trousers and boots. "You leave me to freeze in the night air?"

"If the hells we have been through have not frozen you yet, a bit of thin air won't hurt you. Besides, I want our child to feel you around her as I am."

"There are better ways to do that." He pulled her to her feet and held her close, his arms sliding inside the shirt to circle the warmth of her body. His fingers ran along the lines left by the lepas' claws; he noted the lithe strength of the muscles that still knitted beneath the scars. On him, she felt the deep indent where scar tissue had flattened his shoulder, felt the tension that still coiled his arms. She would work more on that tension today, softening it, forcing his body to start healing away from the drugs. The gray shield against the pain and convulsions was maintained now by Hishn and Yoshi and the

419

pack of wild ones that still hovered around her mate. In time, that tension would fade, the lines on his body would fade, his memories would return, and their hearts would find the way back to kum-tai . . .

He murmured into her hair, "I could stay like this forever."

"We must ride out today. We're almost out of meat."

He was not concerned. "We can hunt down some snoweels for the wolves. The eels will be active for a few more ninans. Or are you so anxious to return to Ariye, to the duties of the elders?"

Dion pulled away and regarded him for a long moment. "We will not raise this child in Ariye."

He looked down at her soberly. "Ariye is our home."

"And our obligation."

He took her hand and rubbed her fingers between his. His gray eyes were sober. "You ask me to give up my home, my family, just when I have recovered them."

"I ask you to build a new one, and to create a life where our child can be raised without duty and burdens for toys, not be used up before her time. I have lost two children to Ramaj Ariye. I will not lose another."

"You cannot keep our daughter safe forever."

"No," Dion agreed quietly. She shrugged out of his shirt and took her own clothes from the pile on the floor. "But I can make sure she is raised as a child, not as a tool. She is not a piton or a knife or a pair of boots. She will not be forged into the sword of any elder's goal."

Aranur watched her dress, then followed Hishn with her to the great room, where Dion let the wolf out. Some of his men were already up; others were back in the kitchen—Weed was actually playing a game of chess with Gamon while they tasted the morning rou. Those in the great room nodded to him as he went to the open door. He watched the wolves with Dion.

Dion trudged into the snow and simply stood, her face raised to the dark sky, breathing in the scents. The stars still shone faintly; the moons were still bright. It would be an hour before the sun rose. Hishn nudged her impatiently and bounded out to meet Yoshi. The two wolves sniffed and then found clean spots to pee; the yellow stains were like poxes in the expanse. Dion didn't smile, but her wry attention made the wolfsong shiver. The Gray Ones were close, strong in her mind.

Icy crust, sharp scent of dnu dung, hay dust over the snow . . . They crawled on the inside of her skull.

Yoshi glanced back and growled at Dion.

I have not forgotten, Dion told him steadily.

The wolf echoed her words to the wild pack. Hishn snarled in return, and the other wolves keened into the dawn. A gray voice rose up, then fell, fell, and Yoshi tumbled Hishn. Hishn snapped playfully at his shoulder. They were both snow-dusted when they finally bounded out of sight, leaving a drag-trail where they didn't quite clear the drifts. Dion trudged back to the shelter where Aranur waited. He gave her his arm for balance as she kicked the bootstop to knock the snow from her trousers and break it off her boots.

His studied the top of her head, then finally said, "No matter what we feel for the elders, Ariye is still our home."

She looked up. "It is, but it cannot be that any longer."

"Why? We can keep our daughter away from the elders if that is what worries you. I am a weapons master. My word carries weight."

Dion straightened. Her voice was quiet. "I have discovered truths about myself, not just about you in these months. I have found that I cannot say no to the elders, to the needs and pain they offer to me to fix. I have tried to refuse them, but I see the dying, or the maimed, or I see the trail that only a wolfwalker could run well and so reduce the risk to others, and I think that if I just give a little more, work a little harder, do a bit more healing, another life can be saved."

He didn't smile. "I can say no for you."

Dion laughed softly. "You love leading too much. You love the authority, the challenge." She nodded as he did not deny it. "You've never said no to the elders yourself, Aranur. And it was you who assigned my scouting duties on top of the clinic work."

He got an odd look on his face.

"If I cannot say no to you, to the elders, and you are so eager to lead," Dion said softly, "how will our daughter learn to keep herself safe from a circle of endless duties? Every child she meets will know our names, and will want to emulate us in play. Every teacher will encourage her to be like us; every adult will imply the duties they expect her to grow into, just as your uncles groomed you to be a weapons master for the ramaj. If we don't want to give this child to the elders, we must take her away from Ariye."

"If they cannot reach you, they cannot manipulate you," he murmured with sudden understanding.

She nodded soberly. "I find myself too easily swayed by others' desperation. Away from Ariye, our daughter will not be pushed into being another pawn for the elders unless she truly desires that for herself."

Aranur was silent for a moment. "Where do you wish to go? Randonnen?"

She glanced at him, then regarded the men in the room. They were carefully not watching her, not listening. "It would be too quiet for you."

He nodded. He studied the snow trail of the wolves. "Ramaj Eilif?"

"No," she said flatly. "For you, that would be like Ariye. After riding as a raider, you cannot simply return to either county. There would be too many grudges, too many sidelong glances, too many rumors that you will turn again. You need time to prove yourself before you return to the Ariyen elders or settle in any county."

He gave her a wry glance. "You leave us few choices."

"I leave us the one that matters. But the choice means nothing if you won't be there with me."

He nodded and asked her question for her. "Can I leave Ariye behind?"

"Aye. Can you let go of the position you once held? Can you give up being weapons master of Ramaj Ariye?"

He glanced back at the raiders. "It seems I have already released that title." He looked back down at her, at her violet eyes, at the neutrality of her expression. "I do not lose my rating or skills as weapons master simply because I set foot outside of the county. And I suspect that the Lloroi would willingly hand back the title should I wish to return to Ariye."

Dion's heart clenched suddenly at the familiar wry tone. She had not heard him so since she thought he was dead; she had had only his voice in the wolf pack, crying her name for company for months. "Then there are the cozar," she managed.

"You want us to live like gypsies? Like nomads?" He couldn't help raising his eyebrows. Dion wanted to touch them, touch his face and memorize it again.

"They move often enough that any duties that find us will be of our choosing."

They would see many places, he thought. Explore much of the world they had never seen.

Dion nodded as if she read his thoughts. "There is a caravan on the western road, still close enough to catch. There was smoke in the lower passhouse yesterday."

He ran his hand through his hair. The western road was the one that Drovic had taken to reach his son. Only the moons would know if his father had made it down that road during the storm, if Drovic lived at all.

"It will take an hour to pack and ready the dnu," he said finally. "If we hurry, we can catch the cozar before they reach the last shelter."

Her voice was low. "It means leaving your home."

He brushed her cheek with the back of his hand. "Do not worry, Ember Dione maMarin. My heart is not in Ariye. It is here." He touched her sternum, where he could feel the studs set in her bone as deeply as they were in his. "Besides, we have to return the wild wolves to the coast, or they will not forgive you for binding them to this journey."

Dion felt the heat of his hand, the pressure of the gems that had grown into her sternum, and the softness of the pack-song. "What of the—your . . ." She fumbled for the right word and glanced meaningfully at the great room.

"Riders," he suggested.

She understood what he said. "They are your duty," she said slowly, more to herself than to him.

"Yes."

She was silent for a moment, accepting his words and his own obligations. "Then you will lead them, and they will come with us." She smiled with a sudden glint of humor.

"There is always a need for guards on a caravan. After all, there are raiders about." She walked away to the room where their gear was stored.

Aranur turned to his men. "Pack and get ready to ride. Harare, Ki, Cheyko—ready the panniers—" He broke off as Rakdi stopped him.

The ex-elder waved his mug of rou in the direction Dion had taken. "You talked to her about us? The wolfwalker didn't seem to say much."

He nodded, but answered, "She said enough."

"Just like that—we're in with her?" Rakdi frowned. "Either she's ignoring the fact that we're raiders, or she's blind as a winter eel. Either way, there will come a time when whatever grudges and anger she holds against us will cut loose, and someone will get hurt."

"No," he said quietly. "She understands."

Mal stirred uncomfortably. "How can you be sure?"

The dour man broke off as Dion came back through the doorway, a set of saddlebags on one shoulder and a sleeping pack in her hand. She raised one eyebrow at the man. "I know," she said simply. Then she nodded to Rakdi and made her way out to the barn.

The hook-nosed man looked after her for a long moment. "She is not what I expected," he said finally.

Aranur rubbed absently at his sternum, where the gemstones studded his bone. "She never is," he returned. He gave the other men a nod, then strode away to pack his own gear.

Dangyon and Mal looked at each other. "She's got ears like a wolf," Mal said.

"Like a badgerbear," the other said.

"Can't curse around a baby."

"Can't pee on the fence line either."

"Moonwormed rules."

"Goddamn civilization," the heavy man agreed. But Dangyon's voice was as mild as Mal's voice, and both men hid their grins.

"Might as well saddle up," Dangyon said to the rest of them. "Got to follow a man through the counties."

Rakdi regarded Aranur with a slight frown. "We follow him; we ride with Ariye."

But Dangyon shook his head. "Talon just turned his back on Ariye to follow his heart."

"Drovic's plans will not let him—or us—go so easily."

But Dangyon looked down at his burly legs. Where the skates had bitten, the flesh ached like a deep bruise, but that was all. There was no tearing, no burning in his nerves, no sudden spasms of pain. Over the last two days, the wolfwalker had tended him as she had tended the others. There had been something about her ministrations that had softened even the worst of the skate bites that had refused to heal, and Dangyon smiled half crookedly. "Even Drovic's dream must bend to the wolves. The Gray Ones own this world."

As the fourth moon rose, barely beating the sun to the peaks, the riders gathered. The Ariyens packed their own gear, since both groups would move out together although they would split at the western road. The Lloroi spoke to Aranur briefly; neither was comfortable, but there was tacit agreement about Aranur's decision. He could not simply return to Ariye, not after being a raider. And even though the Lloroi had accepted Aranur's men into the county, those men must still prove themselves. Three or four years with the cozar, and Tyronnen could better fit the fighters into Ariye. There would be friction—there was still friction over Tehena for her past, though it was as much the woman's abrasive manner that put people off as Tehena's history, the Lloroi admitted. These men had more to live down, and he regarded them soberly as he watched his nephew ready himself to leave Ariye again. He was letting his nephew go back to Drovic's world, hoping Aranur would be strong enough to hold to his convictions. He was putting a wolfwalker into the hands of raiders. And he was failing his people by letting both go, by letting their skills ride away.

Gamon noted his brother's expression. "They may be gone, but they will not let go of Ariye. The mountains are too much a part of them."

"We need them now."

"They need each other." He nodded at the wolfwalker. "They will return when they are healed. Force them, and you'll lose them completely."

The Lloroi's lips thinned, but he said nothing, letting his silence be both his disagreement and his acceptance of what he could not change.

At the other end of the courtyard, Aranur looked over his riders: eight men, two women. There were also the pack dnu, but later those would be hitched to cozar wagons. Neither Dion nor Aranur worried about arranging for that transport. At the end of the caravan season, there were always available wagons.

A low murmuring flowed through the courtyard as each rider checked his gear and reported ready. Ki tightened his cinch and murmured to Harare, "Think he'll ever tell me about the cow teeth?"

"Stay with him long enough, and he's bound to run out of other livestock to tease you with." Harare glanced at Aranur. There was something different about Aranur than Talon, and it extended to his riders. Drovic would not have given his life to save any one of them. Talon might have thought first before leaping to a rescue, but Talon would still have acted for his raiders. Aranur now, he expected them to be men, not raiders, to be more than they had allowed themselves to become. Harare found himself shrugging back toward the person he had been twenty years before. It felt awkward, like a coat too loose in the shoulders and far too tight in the waist. But it felt good in another way. He felt . . . confident, he realized. He knew that Aranur's word would stand, that the tall man would share whatever they met together, and he knew, watching the wolfwalker, that having accepted them as her mate's obligation, she would stand with them, too. Harare mounted his dnu and moved to the edge of the courtyard, where Dangyon already waited. It was enough, he told himself. And there was plenty of edge left in a blade that was used against—not for—other raiders.

Dion and Rhom worked side by side, savoring the nearness of each other as they packed the dnu. They rarely spoke; they didn't need to. Their bond was as strong as the wolves.

Aranur touched Dion often as he gravitated toward her while moving through the riders and preparing the rest of the dnu, and Rhom actually got him to smile as the smith teased him about his constant proximity.

Tehena and Kiyun stayed together on one side, their gear already packed. There was no question that they would ride with Aranur and Dion. They were not about to let the wolfwalker go unprotected among a pack of raiders.

Rhom finally moved up beside Gamon and the others. "Don't scowl so," Rhom told Tehena. "It's not Dion you should worry about."

The thin woman gave him a sharp look. "That's funny, coming from a man whose arm was nearly severed two days ago by one of that man's raiders."

Rhom shrugged, winced at the soreness left in his arm, and deliberately completed the motion. "The wolves will warn Dion if any of them plan violence, and Aranur will protect her."

"He barely protected himself."

Rhom quelled his instant response. Tehena always had rubbed him wrong, and it was only her loyalty to his twin that kept him from snapping back. "You're wrong," he said quietly. "Aranur never lost his self, only his direction, and Dion has given that back. In doing so, she has found her own focus and strength. Those men cannot frighten her. Look at them. She made their leader whole again. They don't watch her like predators. They're almost acting like guards."

Tehena's voice was dry. "As you say, it is Aranur's influence. If he leaves her alone with them . . ." Her voice trailed off ominously.

Gamon followed her gaze, but agreed with Rhom. "He's strong enough to hold them to their word."

"For now," Tehena agreed.

Gamon shook his head sharply. "I think for long enough. Forever, if he must. Look at the way they focus on him. They sit taller, have purpose. It may be self-righteous today and tomorrow, but it will become its own truth in time."

Tehena snorted. "You have the faith of the wolfwalkers, Gamon."

The older man exchanged a glance with Rhom. "I have had to. Dion forces that on those who live around her."

The thin woman's voice was dry. "She's taught you that, at least."

"That, and something else."

The blacksmith asked the question with his eyebrows.

Gamon shook his head. "Never underestimate a Randonnen. When you people want something, you go after it like a worlag after a hare. Not even the path to the moons can keep you from taking back what is yours."

Rhom grinned. "Remember that, next time you challenge me to a game of stars and moons."

Gamon chuckled. But he sobered as he regarded the busy courtyard. "The moons put them together and then tore them apart. Their wounds are still raw and uneven."

"Aye," Rhom agreed softly. "They will not fit back together again as easily as before."

"It has never been easy, for them."

"No, but she is his heart, his forever; and he is hers, like the wolves and the moons in bonding. I knew when I first saw them together. She snapped at him like a wolf at her mate, and he was sore as a badgerbear. They could no more have resisted each other than the moons could resist the night." Rhom smiled crookedly. "Look at her. She sees nothing but him. They will find their balance again."

Beside Aranur, Dion felt her brother's gaze. She turned to him from across the courtyard. Aranur turned with her. Then Dion smiled, and the light caught the slow expression until she seemed to glow.

Rhom nodded to himself. The moons had torn more than one bond, but some could never be severed. He could still feel his twin, feel her nearness, her heart, and he knew she could still sense him. He knew something else: when her child was born, it would be on Randonnen soil. Dion would want family for that. He would have to tell Shilia—they would need another nursery, even if it was only for one spring. For now, he merely sat his saddle and waited for the signal to ride. He would not be going back with Gamon, but with his twin for a while. She would need him to help face herself, her mate, and the future she was choosing. It would be a strong one, he knew. No matter what she claimed she was giving up, she could never accept less than that.

Ten minutes later, the riders left the courtyard. Aranur's ribs still felt the bone-crushing embrace that Gamon had given him. But the sky was clear, and the wind that cut across his skin was cleansing. The wolves were quiet as fog, hidden in the shadows that paced the string of riders. Aranur looked at Dion. She smiled. There was a third heart beating with them, and the sound of it was their future. Dion's right hand rested on her slightly swollen belly as they reached the western road. Then she reached out toward Aranur.

He leaned to take her hand, squeezed it hard, and asked the question with his eyes. She smiled faintly. He nodded. Then he stood in the saddle and turned to the riders behind him. "Into the dawn, into the future, like the wind and the wolves, we ride!"

In the darkness, the thunder of their hooves clipped the snow. They moved out like a long, gray shadow. A long howl rose far to the east, then ahead of them on the road. In the dawn, the wolves' eyes gleamed.

Finis

Author's Note

Wolves, wolf-dog hybrids, and exotic and wild cats might seem like romantic pets. The sleekness of the musculature, the mystique and excitement of keeping a wild animal as a companion—for many owners, wild and exotic animals symbolize freedom and wilderness. For other owners, wild animals from wolves to bobcats to snakes provide a status symbol—something that makes the owner interesting. Many owners claim they are helping keep an animal species from becoming extinct, that they care adequately for their pet's needs, and that they love wild creatures.

However, most predator and wild or exotic animals need to range over wide areas. They need to be socialized with their own species. They need to know how to survive, hunt, breed, and raise their young in their own habitat. And each species' needs are different. A solitary wolf, without the companionship of other wolves with whom it forms sophisticated relationships, can become neurotic and unpredictable. A cougar, however, stakes out its own territory and, unless it is mating or is a female raising its young, lives and hunts as a solitary predator. Both wolves and cougars can range fifty to four hundred square miles over the course of a year. Keeping a wolf or cougar as a pet is like raising a child in a closet.

Wild animals are not easily domesticated. Even when raised from birth by humans, these animals are dramatically different from domestic animals. Wild animals are dangerous and unpredictable, even though they might appear calm or trained, or seem too cute to grow dangerous with age. Wolves and exotic cats make charming, playful pups and kittens, but the adult creatures are still predators. For example, lion kittens are cute, ticklish animals that like to be handled (all kittens are). They mouth things with tiny kitten teeth. But adult cats become solitary, highly territorial, and possessive predators. Some will rebel against authority, including that of the handlers they have known since birth. They can show unexpected aggression. Virtually all wild and exotic cats, including ocelots, margay, serval, cougar, and bobcat, can turn vicious as they age.

Monkeys and other nonhuman primates also develop frustrating behavior as they age. Monkeys keep themselves clean and give each other much-needed, day-to-day social interaction and reassurance by grooming one another. A monkey kept by itself can become filthy and depressed, and can begin mutilating itself (pulling out its hair and so on). When a monkey grows up, it climbs on everything, vocalizes loudly, bites, scratches, exhibits sexual behavior toward you and your guests, and, like a wolf, marks everything in its territory with urine. It is almost impossible to housebreak or control a monkey.

Many people think they can train wolves in the same manner that they train dogs. They cannot. Even if well cared for, wolves do not act as dogs do. Wolves howl. They chew through almost anything, including tables, couches, walls, and fences. They excavate ten-foot pits in your backyard. They mark everything with urine and cannot be housetrained. (Domestic canid breeds that still have a bit of wolf in them can also have these traits.) Punishing a wolf for tearing up your recliner or urinating on the living room wall is punishing the animal for instinctive and natural behavior.

Wolf-dog hybrids have different needs than both wolves and dogs, although they are closer in behavior and needs to wolves than dogs. These hybrids are often misunderstood, missocialized, and mistreated until they become vicious or unpredictable fear-biters. Dissatisfied or frustrated owners cannot simply give their hybrids to new owners; it is almost impossible for a wolf-dog to transfer its attachment to another person. When abandoned or released into the wild by owners, hybrids may also help dilute wolf and coyote strains, creating more hybrids caught between the two disparate worlds of domestic dogs and wild canids. For wolf-dog hybrids, the signs of neurosis and aggression that arise from being isolated, mistreated, or misunderstood most often result in the wolf-dogs being euthanized.

Zoos cannot usually accept exotic or wild animals that have been kept as pets. In general, pet animals are not socialized and do not breed well or coexist with other members of their own species. Because such pets do not learn the social skills to reproduce, they are unable to contribute to the preservation of their species. They seem to be miserable in the company of their own kind, yet have become too dangerous to remain with their human owners. Especially with wolves and wolf-dog hybrids, the claim that many owners make about their pets being one-person animals usually means that those animals have been dangerously unsocialized.

Zoo workers may wish they could rescue every mistreated animal from every inappropriate owner, but the zoos simply do not have the resources to take in pets. Zoos and wildlife rehabilitation centers receive hundreds of requests each year to accept animals that can no longer be handled or afforded by owners. State agencies confiscate hundreds more that are abandoned, mistreated, or malnourished.

The dietary requirements of exotic or wild animals are very different from domesticated pets. For example, exotic and wild cats require almost twice as much protein as canids and cannot convert carotene to vitamin A—an essential nutrient in a felid's diet. A single adult cougar requires two to three pounds of prepared meat each day, plus vitamins and bones. A cougar improperly fed on a diet of chicken or turkey parts or red muscle meat can develop rickets and blindness.

The veterinary bills for exotic and wild animals are outrageously expensive—if an owner can find a vet who knows enough about exotic animals to treat the pet. And it is difficult to take out additional insurance in order to keep such an animal as a pet. Standard home owner's policies do not cover damages or injuries caused by wild or exotic animals. Some insurance companies will drop clients who keep wild animals as pets.

Wild and exotic animals do not damage property or cause

injuries because they are inherently vicious. What humans call property damage is to the animal natural territorial behavior, play, den-making or child-rearing behavior. Traumatic injuries—including amputations and death—to humans most often occur because the animal is protecting its food, territory, or young; because it does not know its own strength compared to humans; or because it is being mistreated. A high proportion of wild- and exotic-animal attacks are directed at human children.

Although traumatic injuries are common, humans are also at risk from the diseases and organisms that undomesticated or exotic animals can carry. Rabies is just one threat in the list of over 150 infectious diseases and conditions that can be transmitted between animals and humans. These diseases and conditions include intestinal parasites, *Psittacosis* (a species of *Chlamydia*), cat-scratch fever, measles, and tuberculosis. Hepatitis A (infectious hepatitis), which humans can catch through contact with minute particles in the air (aerosol transmission) or with blood (bites, scratches, and so on), has been found in its subclinical state in over 90 percent of wild chimps, and chimps are infectious for up to sixty days at a time. The *Herpesvirus simiae*, which has a 70 percent or greater mortality rate in humans, can be contracted from macaques. Pen-breeding only increases an animal's risk of disease.

Taking an exotic or wild animal from its natural habitat does not help keep the species from becoming extinct. All wolf species and all feline species (except for the domestic cat) are either threatened, endangered, or protected by national or international legislation. All nonhuman primates are in danger of extinction; and federal law prohibits the importation of nonhuman primates to be kept as pets. In some states, such as Arizona, it is illegal to own almost any kind of wild animal. The U.S. Fish and Wildlife Service advises that you conserve and protect endangered species. Do not buy wild or exotic animals as pets.

If you would like to become involved with endangered species or other wildlife, consider supporting a wolf, exotic cat, whale, or other wild animal in its own habitat or in a reputable zoo. You can contact your local reputable zoo, conservation organization, or state department of fish and wildlife for information about supporting exotic or wild animals. National and local conservation groups can also give you an opportunity to help sponsor an acre of rain forest, wetlands, temperate forest, or other parcel of land.

There are many legitimate organizations that will use your money to establish preserves in which endangered species can live in their natural habitat. The internationally recognized Nature Conservancy is such an organization. For information about programs sponsored by the Nature Conservancy, please write to:

> The Nature Conservancy
> 1815 N. Lynn Street
> Arlington, Virginia 22209

Special thanks to Janice Hixson; Dr. Jill Mellen, Ph.D.; Dr. Mitch Finnegan, D.V.M., Metro Washington Park Zoo; Karen Fishler, The Nature Conservancy; Harley Shaw, General Wildlife Services; Dr. Mary-Beth Nichols, D.V.M.; Brooks Fahy, Cascade Wildlife Rescue; and the many others who provided information, sources, and references for this project.

Return to the Beginning of
Dion's Story
An Excerpt from the Acclaimed Novel

WOLFWALKER

Ember Dione maMarin:

Dark Flight

Oh, moons of mercy, moons of light
Guide me in the darkest night
Keep me safe from evil spirit
Send your blessed light to sear it

Oh, moons of mercy, moons of might
If in shadow, dark, or night,
My body die with evil near it
Send your light to guide my spirit

It was dark, and she could not see. She could not hear for the roaring in her ears, and she could not move. *Oh, moons of mercy, moons of light* . . . She tried to spit out the panic but choked on grit and fur and dirty blood. *Guide me in the darkest night* . . . Struggling, she dragged a breath into her lungs, and then the fright that held her frozen burst and she screamed, the sound suffocating in the black death above her. *Keep me safe from evil spirit* . . . The body that pinned her to the ground was too heavy; she panicked and thrashed under it, straining back and forth to break free. Heat ate at her legs. She realized then that—oh, gods—the roaring in her ears was fire. *Send your blessed light to sear it* . . . And then the pain stabbed, rhythmically, with her pulse, throbbing, driving each second of terror deeper in her mind. Fire . . . A joint-ripping yank tore her free of the dead worlag, her ragged breathing punctuated by the fire's crackling, while sobs racked her body and the tumbling brands spread the flames and fed her panic.

The worlag's body shifted again, rolling toward her, and she jerked back in horror. Moons of mercy, were the dead rising to claim her? But the sudden movement sent a black wash of pain over her head, and she could barely see where the shadows of brush beckoned. With a silent scream against the agony, she slid into their sharp embrace like a broken doll, her teeth bared to bite back her shriek and her breath still caught in her chest from the frozen grip of fear. On the other side of the fire a worlag turned, its bulbous eyes searching. There was blood on the soil, blood on its claws. It hesitated, and then a waft of throat-choking smoke curled between them, hiding her where shadows of deep roots pressed against her back, steadying her as the burning forest swallowed her body and the blackening waves swallowed her mind. All she saw, all she heard, was the worlags tearing and snapping at the broken bodies and burning wagon, the flame-lit canvas and clothes.

Pain. Burning, crushing pain. She crawled, cringing under the brush, clinging to the gray shadow of the wolf that urged, carried, dragged her on. *This way . . . through here . . .* She could not focus her eyes, her mind anymore. *Wait . . . duck . . .* There was blood on her hands, her clothes, her face. *Hurry . . .* The roaring in her ears kept rhythm with the growls of bloated worlags feasting in the obscenely dancing light behind her, and the snap of human bones was the death drum in her ears—she did not have to look back to see the hairy forearms that dragged to their knees when they stood and the other, spindly middle arms that tore at the riding beasts like the cutters on a farmer's plow. Their beetle jaws dripped blood and tendons as they fought over a body. Ember Dione whimpered and dragged on. It was dark.

Night voices flickered in and out of her ears. But the gray shadow led her on when she cried out, and the rough tongue licked at the pain till she fell into the dark fire of her pulse, where the black heat blinded her. Blood, thin and warm, dribbled down her face and slid into her ear, and as the noise drowned, the dark again became complete.

It was dawn when she woke, her head throbbing dully, the air green with morning dusk. Her slender body was curled in the growth of a deadfall, her gashed leg stretched stiffly out to one side and her black hair tangled in the twigs. A sharp branch stuck into her cheek. Against her back, the gray wolf was warm, proof of the early chill that was seeping through the moss and the calm that greeted her wakening. No burned-out wagons met her eyes; no smoldering fires caught at her ears. Just the blood that stiffly soaked her clothes and the pain that killed her thoughts.

And she remembered . . . Her brother, Rhom, torn apart like a bird under the worlag's raging jaws. The slim woman bit back the sob, clenching her fists and closing her eyes. Oh, Rhom . . .

She forced her eyes to see again, forced her mind to admit she had seen him die. The worlags . . . She had seen him fall, slashing and cutting with his sword under the force of the beasts that tore him apart while Gray Hishn ripped at a monster's black carapace. And then the worlags closed in and the wolf jumped clear and her twin—he was gone. Just like that. Dead. Rhom, the merchant, the guards—everyone, she told herself harshly, everyone dead but her.

Her throat grew tight against the agony that racked her like a rising storm shaking a fragile house, and she pushed the thoughts away, curling closer into the wolf's thick fur. Was this the grief of death? she asked herself. The blinding ache? The Gray One's fur lay gritty against her tears, and she wondered if she was crying for the mangled bodies of those she once knew or the empty disbelief that her twin was dead. "Survive first," she whispered, gripping Gray Hishn's coat in her white-knuckled fist. "Then deal with the dead."

When she woke again, her mouth was parched into wrinkles and her tongue felt dried, stuck to the roof of her mouth. She pushed herself up on her side and rolled over, clenching her teeth against the jagged blast of pain that greeted her. Her leg felt crushed, and her head felt split. But it was the cluster of insects feeding off the filthy scabs that turned her stomach. Hurriedly she fought down the flash of nausea and scraped them off, brushing her hands on her pants while they skittered angrily back into the shelter of the moss.

Her movements awakened the wolf, whose ears had already begun to flick at her thoughts. Gray Hishn rose, and the woman felt the creature's hunger and thirst double her own. She fingered the few weapons left in her pouch, a bleak look on her face as she realized again her position. But the worlags must have been gone or Hishn would have long been alert. *Go eat,* she told the wolf, pushing a clump of long, black hair out of her eyes. *I'll be all right till you find dinner.*

Dinner for both of us, the Gray One promised, flashing her the double image of two wolves with furry rabbits hanging from their teeth. The haggard young woman managed a smile at the compliment, and the wolf melted into the woods, the gray hunter's impressions of the forest filling her head with soothing images:

cool dirt under silent footpads, soft leaves brushing against fur. Muscles tensing and shifting as trees and downfalls shaded slitted yellow eyes from the evening sun; the tangy scent of a deer herd on shadowed grass . . .

The wolfwalker's head cleared further, and she remembered again the night, the death. Her throat went tight. Rhom! she thought with despair, raising her fist to her forehead and pressing as if she could drive away the memories or hold back the tears with the pressure of her hand.

But the snap of a brittle twig brought her abruptly back, and she froze, her breath pressed against her chest from the inside. She held it without moving while the leaves rustled—it was a mottled badgerbear, slinking by not ten meters away, its brainless head swinging from side to side as it searched for a place to set its trap. With its gaping maw hidden under its flattened stomach, it tasted the ground for the trail of a careless hare or young deer. Or a wounded human. The blood on the trail—surely it would be dried and tasteless already. Or would the badgerbear sense her fear from where it paused there on the game path, its sightless eyes swinging her way . . .

Abruptly she pulled herself together. Ember Dione, she taunted herself harshly, trying to control her shattered nerves. So eager to Journey with your brother. Well, you're here now and alone because of it. Get your act together and face the world you wanted or crawl back to the village where they said you belonged.

The Journey—the test of a young man's courage and skill. Rhom's sanction to see the world outside his home. Whether he came from a village or a city or a floating town like those of the southern sea people didn't matter. Only that he explore and return to tell his story to his father at the council fires, from then on to be counted as a strong voice in the circle of judgment. But Dion had not had to go with him. Women had their own Journey of sorts: the Internship, which let them test their own skills and prove their worth to the city of their choice. Dion had already taken her own Internship—but the elders had chosen her to go with her twin on his Journey, as well. And now, only Dion would return to tell their story to their father. Dion, the wolfwalker, she thought bitterly. Dion, the healer. Who could not even save her own brother.

She lay still for a long time after the badgerbear had passed. At last, when a half hour had withered away, she hooked her finger into the rough bark of the tree, then rolled onto her left knee.

"Moons have mercy," she gasped. Her breath strangled with the waves of speckled darkness that pounded her head. Seconds—minutes?—later it cleared to dim patches, and she pulled herself up against the tree and sagged, fresh blood spreading heat down the side of her face. It felt as if the only thing that held her pounding head together was the silver band that circled her brow. Blue and silver—that was for the healer's band—and gray, the color of wolves. She snorted and looked at her hands where the dirt blackened her nails and her strong, shapely fingers were trembling and marred with blood. Healer and wolfwalker, yes, but weak and sorry as a newborn pup. With her head resting listlessly against the rough trunk of the tree, the woman stared down at the bloody gash that had laid her leg open almost to her hip. It was a filthy wound. The dirt and blood had matted together to make a muddy scab that floated on the open slash. Where the worlag's claw had reached through her guard, it had torn into her skin like a knife splitting a ripe fruit, and she wondered vaguely if the gellbugs had started a nursery in the wound already. It would be too ironic if she, a full-fledged healer, died from gellbugs after surviving a worlag attack in which the guards and fighters had been killed.

She steeled herself to touch the jagged slash. She had treated too many ragged wounds to flinch from the gash in her leg, but this was the first time she'd had to treat herself, and she was not sure she had the guts to do it without screaming or the stamina to finish it without fainting. Now, as she tried to bare her thigh to see how bad the throbbing wound was, she stifled a groan. The leather of her leggings was stuck fast, glued by clotting blood and dirt, and the herb pouches she groped for were not to be found. She must have lost them in the fight the previous night. The fight . . . *The worlag tore at her leg and she screamed, and Rhom turned and went down*—"Oh, dear moons, help him," she whispered.

She shook her head, then wished she had not when the dizzy blackness drew its veil across her eyes again. But she could not escape the images that crossed her closed eyes. Rhom's sword as it cut through the worlag's casing. His face, eyes wide and flashing, as he went down under the monsters' claws. Dion took a ragged breath. What's done is done is done, she thought, the words echoing like rocks bouncing down a canyon's steep cliff. Empty words. *Rhom!* she cried out silently. *Hishn, I need you.*

The gray wolf answered like the touch of a leaf brushing against soft skin. It eased her anguish but left the breath of her twin behind, too. Did she deny his death so much that she could not let him go? What would she tell their father? She let her head tilt back against the tree, and the shaft of pain that lanced through it brought her back to reality as abruptly as it had sent her into a pain-racked swoon a moment earlier. How could she tell her father anything if she did not heal enough to survive the journey home? She opened her eyes. As she tightened her jaw, she drew on the stubborn strength that had sustained her through the long night and regarded the open gash one more time, then braced herself against the rough tree and pulled leather from the thickening scab. Only one gasp escaped her clenched teeth. When she got enough material to dig her broken fingernails into the claw-slashed pants, she gripped the slippery leather sternly and peeled the legging back. And fainted.